Praise for

EMPRESS OF THE SEVEN HILLS

"Power and betrayal were never so addictive than in this gorgeously wrought tale of star-crossed lovers caught in the turbulent currents of Imperial Rome. Kate Quinn deftly contrasts the awesome splendor of torch-lit banquets with the thunder of the battlefield. *Empress of the Seven Hills* is a riveting plunge into an ancient world that is both utterly foreign and strikingly familiar—where you can feel the silken caress of an empress and the cold steel of a blade at your back."
—C. W. Gortner, author of *The Confessions of Catherine De Medici*

DAUGHTERS OF ROME

"A soap opera of biblical proportions . . . [Quinn] juggles protagonists with ease and nicely traces the evolution of Marcella—her most compelling character—from innocuous historian to manipulator. Readers will become thoroughly immersed in this chaotic period of Roman history."
—*Publishers Weekly*

MISTRESS OF ROME

"[Quinn] skillfully intertwines the private lives of her characters with huge and shocking events. A deeply passionate love story, tender and touching, in the heat and danger of the brutal arena that was ancient Rome . . . Quinn is a remarkable new talent."
—Kate Furnivall, author of *The White Pearl*
and *The Jewel of St. Petersburg*

BOOKS BY KATE QUINN

The Huntress
The Alice Network

The Borgia Novels
The Serpent and the Pearl
The Lion and the Rose

The Rome Novels
Mistress of Rome
Daughters of Rome
Empress of the Seven Hills
Lady of the Eternal City

EMPRESS
OF THE
SEVEN HILLS

KATE QUINN

BERKLEY

NEW YORK

BERKLEY
An imprint of Penguin Random House LLC
penguinrandomhouse.com

Library of Congress Cataloging-in-Publication Data

Quinn, Kate.
Empress of the seven hills / Kate Quinn.
p.   cm.
ISBN 978-0-425-24202-5
1. Rome—History—Trajan, 98-117—Fiction.   I. Title.
PS3617.U578E47 2012
813'.6—dc23
2011039150

First Edition: April 2012

Printed in the United States of America

Cover design by Katie Anderson
Cover photographs: woman by Alan Ayers; city by Peter Zelei Images /
Getty Images; hills by Sean O'Neill / 500px / Getty Images
Book design by Laura K. Corless

For Stephen,
who in many ways—freckles, restlessness,
short temper, loud snoring, left-handedness,
dislike of horses, speed with a sword,
impatience with superior officers,
and that one muscle under the left shoulder blade
that collects all your tension—
is quite a lot like Vix

PART I

ROME

CHAPTER I

VIX

When I was thirteen, an astrologer told me I'd lead a legion someday, a legion that would call me Vercingetorix the Red. Astrologers are usually horseshit, but that funny little man was right about everything: I got the nickname, and I even got the legion, though it took longer than it should have. But why didn't that astrologer tell me any of the important things? Why didn't he tell me that Emperors can be loved, but Empresses are only to be feared? Why didn't he tell me I'd have to kill the best friend I ever had—on the orders of the worst man I ever knew? And why the hell didn't he tell me about the girl in the blue veil I met the same day I got all these predictions?

That bitch. Not that I guessed: We were just children, me a skinny slave boy, her a pretty girl in a blue veil, all bruised up (never mind why). The first girl I ever kissed, and she had a sweet mouth. I suppose that made me soft when I met her again later, after we'd both grown up. If that astrologer was so good, couldn't he have warned me about her? "Girl in blue, beware." What would that have cost him? She cost *me* plenty over the years, I can tell you.

But that's getting ahead of things. I'm Vercingetorix: "Vix" to my friends, "the Red" to my men, and "that pleb bastard" to my enemies. I've served four Emperors: killed one, loved one, befriended one, and maybe should have killed the other. I'm Vercingetorix, and I have a story to tell.

Spring *A.D.* 102

I won't bore you with my beginnings. They weren't so illustrious anyway—my mother was a slave, and my father was a gladiator, and you can't get much lower than that. If you follow the games in the Colosseum, then I can guarantee you've heard of my father, but I won't tell you his name. The world thinks he's dead, and that's the way he likes it. He ended up on a mountaintop in the northern-most part of Britannia, torturing a patch of ground he calls a garden, and he's happy. My mother's happy too, singing at her work and producing babies to fill up the villa she got for doing an empress a favor (don't ask what), but when I hit eighteen after nearly five years in Britannia, I got bored. It was better than what we'd come from, but I'd gotten used to excitement, and a mountaintop house filled with babies isn't much excitement. Plus there was a girl in one of the neighboring houses who was starting to give me the eye, and we might have had some fun behind the barn once or twice but I didn't want to marry her, and I didn't think much of my chances if my father decided I *should* marry her. I was big at eighteen, but my father was bigger, and weapons might come easy to me but I didn't stand a chance against him. So I lit out for Rome, the center of everything, and my father was dubious but he gave me an amulet to keep me safe and a purse to keep me fed. My mother cried, but that might have been the baby she was starting.

Not much use describing the journey. It was wet, it was long, I lost my purse to a bastard of an Armenian sailor who cheated at dice, and I lost my dinner countless times over the bow. I hated boats. Still do. But I got to Rome. My parents hate Rome with all their hearts, and maybe they should after what they lived through. But I took one step off that reeking shit-hole of a boat and took in a deep breath, and I knew I was home.

Everyone describes Rome. Everyone fails. It's not like anything else on earth. I hitched my pack higher on my shoulder, turned a circle, and gawped. I'd been raised in Brundisium, back in the days when my mother was still a slave, and had come to the great city itself only later. I hadn't been able to do much exploring back then, and I'd never gotten to know the city well. Nothing to keep me from drinking it all in now: the stink, the noise, the crush; the whores in their dark robes and the sailors in their brass earrings; the vendors waving wares under my nose and the urchins trying their best to get grimy fingers into my purse. It was life, raw and noisy life as fresh as blood flowing right out of the vein.

The dock swayed under my feet. I lurched my way up the wharf, keeping one hand on the knife at my belt. Plenty of people in Rome willing to stick a knife in you first and figure out second if you had anything worth stealing. "My kind of city," I said aloud, and got a dirty look from a housewife with a basket on her arm. I kissed my fingers at her and she hurried along. I watched her hips in the rough dress—hips like barrels, but I'd been a month on that shit-hole boat without a woman in sight, and I wasn't picky. Even more than food I wanted a girl, but I didn't have enough coin in my purse even for a cheap one.

Girls would have to wait. "Where's the Capitoline Hill from here?" I asked a passing sailor in rusty Latin, and was promptly told to go screw myself. But a vendor hawking brass pans was more helpful, and I slung my pack over my shoulder and set off whistling.

Strange how much of the city I remembered. I hadn't seen it since I was thirteen, but I felt like I'd left only yesterday. The crowds thinned once I got past the Forum Romanum with its spicy smells of meat and bread, and I let my hand loosen on the knife hilt and my feet wander. I spent some time staring at the marbled expanse of palace that covered half the Palatine Hill, remembering a black-eyed madman and his games, until an irritable Praetorian guard in red and gold told me to move along. "All palace guards look as pretty as you?" I shot back. "Or have I been on a boat too long?"

"Move along," he growled, and helped me down the street with his spear haft. Praetorians: no sense of humor.

I spent a little longer staring up at the vast marble roundness of the Colosseum. Not the first time I'd seen it by any means—but I'd forgotten the sheer looming menace of it. No place on earth looms like that one, with its arches and plinths and statues in niches that stare out with blind arrogant eyes. That stretch of sand inside held all my father's nightmares, and a few of mine. I'd never told him that, but he knew. Anyone who'd ever fought for their life in that place knew.

It's many years later now, and I'm well into middle age. I've been in more fights than I can count, but none of them come back to me in my sleep like the ones that happened in the Colosseum. I'd killed my first man on those sands, back when I was just a child. A big Gaul who hadn't really wanted to kill me, and maybe it made him slow enough so I could kill him first. Not much of an initiation into manhood.

I stared up at the arena a while longer, fingering the little amulet my father had given me and wondering how men could build such fantastical places just for the purpose of mass killing—and then I shrugged and wandered on toward the Capitoline Hill. A quieter place, the streets smoothly paved, the women in silk rather than wool, the slaves wearing the badge of one illustrious family or another as they hurried about their errands. I passed the massive Capitoline Library, where a half-dozen senators in togas hurried in and out with distracted frowns, and I slowed my steps. My mother had said the house was somewhere around here . . .

"Yes?" A slave in a neat tunic looked me up and down dubiously. "Can I help you?"

"Is this the house of Senator Marcus Norbanus?"

"No beggars here—"

"I'm not a bloody beggar. Is this Senator Norbanus's house or not?"

"Yes, but—"

"Good. I'm here to see him." The slave was big but I was bigger, and I shouldered past into a narrow hall where a dozen marble busts stared down at me in censorious disapproval. "Quit your squawking," I told the slave, who had flapped after me. "The senator knows who I am."

Ten minutes of arguing got me shown to a small atrium to wait. "It may be a while," the slave sniffed. "The senator is very busy." One last dubious look, as if the slave were wondering whether it was safe to leave me alone with the valuables, and he finally backed out.

I tipped my head back and surveyed the place. Sunlight poured through the open roof, the floor had a mosaic pattern of rippling vines, and a quiet blue-tiled pool was sunk in the middle of the room. A carved nymph looked over her shoulder at me from the corner, and I'd been long enough without a girl that even her marble breasts looked tempting. I slung my pack on a marble bench and dropped to one knee, plunging my hands into the pool and splashing my face. I looked up to find a pretty little girl gazing at me, clutching a carved wooden horse and sucking her thumb.

"Hello, sprat." She looked four or five, the same age as my own little sister. "Who are you?"

She gazed at me solemnly through a fringe of blond hair.

"Don't suppose you belong to Senator Norbanus?"

She inspected her little thumb for a moment, then went back to sucking on it.

"Could you get me in to see your father?"

Sucking, sucking.

"Could you at least tell me where the *lavatorium* is? I could use a piss."

"There's one down the hall," a voice said behind me.

I turned and saw another girl, this one about my own age. Thin, brown hair, blue dress. "I'm waiting for Senator Norbanus," I said.

"There's time." She picked up the little girl, parting her gently from the thumb, and moved down the hall with that blind confidence all aristocrats seemed to have, not needing to look back to know that I would follow. I followed her to the *lavatorium*.

"There's water if you want to wash," she said, and I took the hint. Romans took a lot more baths than anyone in Britannia. I used a basinful of water and washed the shipboard grime off my face and neck.

"Better?" The patrician girl smiled as I came back into the hall.

"Much, Lady." I tried my best bow, rusty since I hadn't used it in a while. Not many baths in Britannia, but not many people to bow to either. "Thank you."

She studied me a moment longer, then smiled suddenly. She had small teeth, a little crooked but nicely so. "Ah," she said.

"What, ah?"

A sturdy blond woman in yellow silk came swooping down the hall, bearing a baby on her hip. "Sabina, have you seen—oh, there she is." She swung the little girl up onto her other hip. "Faustina, you're supposed to be with your nurse! Who's this?" The woman gave me a distracted glance, juggling the two round-eyed children.

"This is Vercingetorix," the girl in blue said tranquilly, and didn't *that* give me a jolt. "He's waiting to see Father."

"Well, don't keep him long," the woman advised me. "My husband works very hard. Faustina, Linus, it's time for your bath—" She moved off in a bright spot of yellow, the children crowing over her shoulder.

"How did you know my name?" I demanded as the girl in blue moved back into the atrium.

She glanced back over her shoulder. "You don't remember me?"

"Um . . ."

"Never mind." She brushed that away. "Why are you waiting to see my father?"

"I'm just back to Rome from Britannia. My mother said he'd likely help me—look, how did you know—"

"You were right to come here. Father helps everybody." She summoned the steward and spoke a few quiet words. "I'll jump you to the front of the line."

And just like that, I was in.

Senator Marcus Norbanus was the kind who puts you on your best behavior. My father had the same effect on people, but mostly because you knew he'd knock the head off your shoulders if you got on his bad side. Senator Norbanus didn't look like the knocking type—he was nearly seventy, and he had gray hair and a crooked shoulder and ink stains on his fingers. But he had me sitting up straight and minding my language inside the first minute.

"Vercingetorix," he mused. "I've often wondered how you and your family were faring."

"Very well, Senator."

"I'm glad to hear it. You've returned to Rome for good?"

"It's the center of everything."

"It is that." He rotated a stylus between his fingers. His study was cheerfully cluttered, pens and parchment and slates on every surface. He had more scrolls than I'd ever seen in one place in my life. "What were you planning to do here in Rome?"

"Thought about the legions." All I'd wanted once was to be a gladiator, but I got over that fast enough once I had a taste of it. Gladiating aside, there wasn't much else for a boy with a talent for weapons except the legions. Besides, even a slave-born boy could rise in the Roman army . . .

"I wonder if you're aware of the commitment one makes in joining the legions." Senator Norbanus laid his stylus aside. "How old are you?"

"Twenty," I said.

He looked at me.

"Nineteen," I amended.

He looked at me some more.

"Nineteen! In a couple of months, anyway."

"Eighteen, then. I assume you plan on advancement through the ranks?"

I snorted. "Didn't plan on being a common soldier for life!"

"Plan on being a common soldier for the next twelve years, because you cannot even be made a centurion until you reach thirty."

"*Thirty*—?"

"Even then, it's no guarantee. You will need patronage to make centurion, and I may not still be here in twelve years." The senator ran a rueful hand through his gray hair.

"Well"—I tried to regroup—"I might not stay in the legions till I'm thirty. There's other jobs."

He looked at me, exasperated. "The term of service for a legionary is twenty-five years, Vercingetorix. Sign up now, and you will be forty-three by the time you are allowed to think of other jobs."

"Twenty-five *years?*"

"Didn't you bother to learn anything about the legions before considering them as a career?"

I shrugged.

"The young," Senator Norbanus muttered. "I don't suppose you know the pay rate either? Three hundred denarii a year, if you're curious. Minus your weapons, armor, and rations, of course."

"Hell's gates," I muttered. "You Romans are cheap."

"I don't suppose you know about the laws concerning legionaries and marriage either. Soldiers cannot marry, at least until they make centurion. Even then, they cannot take their wives with them on march. Legion posts, I might add, can last many years far away from Rome."

"Don't want a wife," I said, but my enthusiasm for the legions was definitely waning.

"Think on it," said Senator Norbanus, his exasperation with me fading a trifle. "I don't mean to discourage you from army life, but at least know what you're getting into. There are other options."

I was already thinking about them. "Like what?"

"Bodyguarding, perhaps? Good guards are always in demand, and I seem to remember you had a way with a sword even as a child."

"Maybe." Not much glory in bodyguarding . . .

"Do you have a place to live, Vercingetorix?"

"Just got off the boat."

"A client of mine owns a small inn in the Subura. He'll be willing to let rent slide for a week or two, until you find some work. I'll write you a letter."

The stylus scratched busily for a moment, and I contemplated the future with gloom. Twenty-five years. Who would sign up for *that?*

"Here." The senator sealed the letter. "Stop for a meal in the kitchens before you go. And if you have further thoughts on your future, do come back. I owe your parents a debt, and it will easily encompass any help I can give to you."

"Thank you, Senator."

"And speaking of your parents—" His eyes met mine, suddenly cool. "I trust you are not stupid enough to mention their names to anyone? Or Emperor Domitian's. They are all dead, or at least officially so, and it's best they stay that way."

"Yes, sir." Damn him, I *had* been planning to do a little modest trading on my father's name. There were still some followers of the games who might remember him, maybe give me a job in his name— but the senator looked stern, and I did my best to look innocent.

"Fortuna's luck to you, then." He held out the scroll. I took it, bowed, and thumped out, wondering what in hell I was supposed to do if I didn't join the legions. The only skill I had was fighting.

SABINA

"Did you get what you wanted?" Sabina asked, looking up from her scroll when the tall boy came slouching back into the atrium. He was scowling blackly, running a rough hand through his shaggy hair.

"Not really." He scuffed to a stop by the pool, toeing one foot along the blue-tiled edge. "Thought your father might get me into the legions, but now I'm not so sure I want that."

"Why not?"

"Don't see why I should sell my soul just for a job."

"Oh, Rome always wants your soul. Didn't you know that?" Sabina marked her place in the scroll with one finger. "But most people seem to think it's a fair bargain."

"*I don't.*"

"You could always be a gladiator," she suggested.

He jumped, and looked at her again.

"You really don't remember me, do you?" She'd known him at once, even after four or five years. He looked the same: russet hair and brown arms, big feet and big shoulders and a lot of loosely bolted limbs between them that hadn't quite caught up. The same, just larger.

He was looking at her warily now. "Should I remember you?"

"Maybe not," she said. "It was a memorable day, all told."

"So who are you, Lady?"

She stood up, discarding her scroll, and stepped close against him, putting one hand on the back of his sunburned neck and standing on tiptoe. Inches away, she tilted her head and smiled. "Remember now?"

She could see the click in his eyes. "Sabina," he said slowly. "Lady Sabina—right?"

"Right."

"Didn't know you without the bruises. Otherwise you haven't changed much." He looked her over. "First girl I ever kissed."

"The Young Barbarian? I'm flattered." Sabina felt his arms begin to sneak up around her waist, and stepped back. "All the little girls loved the Young Barbarian. The year you had your bouts in the Colosseum, your name was on schoolhouse doors inside hearts all over Rome. I told my friends I'd met you, and none of them believed me."

"You tell them I kissed you?" He took another step toward her, a grin starting around the corners of his mouth.

"I think I was the one who kissed you, actually." Sabina retrieved her scroll and sat down on the marble bench again. "What's next for you, if not the legions?"

"Not a gladiator's life, that's for damned certain." He leaned up against the pillar, folding his arms across his chest and cocking his head down at her. "I suppose you're married now?"

"Gods, no." On her seventeenth birthday last year, her father had given her a pearl necklace and promised her reasonably free rein in the choice of her husband. Sabina valued the promise more highly than the pearls.

"I thought that baby might be yours."

"No, that's little Linus. He and Faustina are Calpurnia's—she's my stepmother."

Sabina went back to her book then, wanting to savor the last verses where Ulysses dealt with his wife's suitors, wishing Homer might have written just a little more about Penelope in her husband's absence. But the large sandaled feet in front of her didn't move, and Sabina glanced back up at the russet-haired visitor who looked so out of place in the quiet vine-veiled atrium. Vix's lurking grin flowered into something cheerful and lewd, and she laughed. "Fortuna be with you, Vercingetorix."

"I make my own luck," he bragged.

"Do you? That's a nice trick, if one can manage it." She wandered away, finding her place in the scroll again and reading as she walked. She didn't have to glance over her shoulder to know that Vix was looking after her.

VIX

The inn Senator Norbanus had directed me to wasn't bad. The inn-keeper wasn't happy to give me a week's free rent, but he grunted at the senator's seal. "Maybe you could help around the place," he added. "I could use a big strong lad like you. Customers, it gets late, they like having someone with a knife see them home safe."

"That pays well?"

"Not bad. Pays even better if they turn down the guard and you can hold 'em up in an alley."

I quirked an eyebrow. "I want half."

"Ten percent."

"Ten the first week, and thirty once I'm paying my own room."

"Done."

The room had lice, but at least it had a bed that didn't rock back and forth like a river. As I flopped down I saw a serving maid creak down the stairs outside. Spotty skin, but breasts like melons, and she gave me a sidelong glance as she trudged by with a basket of blankets. Maybe the day wasn't such a loss after all.

I didn't think about Sabina. Why should I? Just a patrician girl I probably wouldn't see again after she'd walked away from me in that atrium with her light brown hair swaying against her narrow back. Girls like her were off-limits, and anyway, she had small breasts. Figs, say, rather than apples. I liked apples. Or melons . . . I eyed the dank hall where the serving maid had gone.

If I'd known the trouble that small-breasted off-limits patrician girl would make for me, I might have choked her to death in the middle of that atrium rather than watch her walk away.

CHAPTER 2

PLOTINA

"Vinalia." Plotina pronounced the word disapprovingly. "A disgusting festival."

"It's harmless." Her husband's voice was muffled as he dragged a tunic over his head. "Just a little celebration of the wine harvest—"

"All Rome gets drunk! Decent women don't dare set foot outside." Plotina frowned into the polished steel mirror, remembering the tipsy shopkeeper who had pinched her on the hip during a Vinalia celebration some twenty years ago when she had been an unwed girl. *Pinched* her. *Her*, Pompeia Plotina, who could have been a Vestal Virgin had she chosen. If she had not known even then that she was destined for Greater Things.

"Will you at least attend the races after the ceremony?" Her husband's voice was coaxing. "People expect to see you."

"I will stay through the first race," Plotina allowed. "That is all. Green gown," she told the slaves, who hastened forward with the folds of deep green silk. Silk; so ostentatious, but it was expected of a woman in her position. She held her arms out—decently swathed, of course, in a long-sleeved tunic. The women of Rome might mostly bare their arms like courtesans, even the women of great birth, but Plotina would *never* be one of them.

"Gods' bones, will you leave your fussing?" Her husband swatted at his slaves as they draped the heavy purple-bordered folds of his toga. "It looks well enough!"

"Don't be a child," Plotina said without turning. A man of such power, such distinction, and he stood impatiently shifting and fidgeting like a boy of fifteen. *In many ways he is still a boy of fifteen*, she thought, tilting her head as the maid dabbed behind her ears with lavender water. Only whores wore perfume.

Does the girl wear perfume? Plotina wondered. *If so, I shall have to rethink.*

"Ready?" Her husband sounded amused. "If my wife is done primping, the priests await."

"You know I don't like jokes." Plotina cast an eye over her reflection. Dark hair tidy and coiled, covered by a veil as was only proper. Pale oval face (*no* rouge or kohl, of course) and a suitably sober expression. Deep-set eyes, a nose like a furrow with a straight mouth to match it—and could that be a thread or two of gray just starting to come in by her temples? She leaned toward the mirror, pleased. She had not liked youth, and youth hadn't liked her. A girl was nothing; a woman was powerful. A girl knew nothing; a woman knew all. As a girl Plotina had been lanky and awkward, but now at thirty-five they had begun to call her handsome. "I am ready."

She rose, taking her husband's arm. He stood tall, but she did not have to tilt her head to look into his face. Plotina could look eye to eye with all but the tallest men in Rome, and that pleased her. The goddesses of the heavens were always tall, weren't they? And Plotina liked to model herself after only the highest and greatest of examples.

Well, she wouldn't model herself after just *any* goddess. Juno, of course, queen of the heavens and always irreproachable—but some of the others were not nearly so well behaved. Plotina eyed the statue of Venus disapprovingly when they made their grand entrance into the temple. Venus: a curly-headed empty little flirt, and her statue looked it. *If I were Juno, I'd never put up with any whorish little goddess of love and her antics.* Even the gods must keep their houses in order. Plotina's house was *always* in order.

The priest raised his hands with a jug of the season's new wine, intoning a prayer for the harvest to come and thanks for the harvest past. Judging from the flush on his face, he had been appreciating the wine already for some hours. *I'll have a new priest,* Plotina decided. Not that anyone was listening to the prayers. Men stood shifting from foot to foot until they could get their hands on the wine; girls giggled behind their hands; matrons fidgeted with their festival wreaths. Plotina's own husband was trading jokes in a whisper with his slouching guards. "Set an example," she nudged him, and bowed her head pointedly low as the priest rolled into the final prayer for Venus and Jupiter. Heads lowered hastily across the temple. Including one light-brown head Plotina had spotted the moment she entered the temple.

The girl.

Oh, the agony of it. Was she the one? *Was* she? Her bloodlines, of course . . . the mother's side left a great deal to be desired, but surely Senator Norbanus's side balanced that. The face: modest and neat-featured. Beauty was not required—indeed, it could even be a deterrent. Flightiness and vanity so often came hand in hand with beauty, and the girl Plotina chose must have poise and dignity above all. Two other candidates had already been discarded on that basis. Plotina watched for some minutes while the priest droned, but the girl stood quietly, not fidgeting like the others of her age or darting looks at the dresses her friends were wearing. Quiet; that was good. She stood respectfully behind her father, eyes lowered—mindful of her elders; excellent. Plotina would be able to mold her, guide her, train her. The dress—deep red silk, and really a girl of eighteen was far too young to be wearing silk, but her father was notoriously indulgent. At least the arms were covered.

The girl looked down at her little fair-haired sister, wriggling and yawning under the drone of prayers, and put a finger to her lips in a shushing motion. Ease with children; definitely good. The girl Plotina chose would be required to bear many children. Plotina would be the one to rear the children, of course—she would see to their education and morals herself. Now, the girl's education . . . that could be a problem. Not only was Senator Norbanus too indulgent a father, but he had educated his eldest daughter far past the usual standard. *What was he thinking?* Homer and Aeschylus were of absolutely no use to a woman in the practical world. Fortunately, Senator Norbanus's third wife had reportedly taken her stepdaughter in hand as regarded the housewifely arts, so perhaps the excess education was not too great a flaw. Once the babies came, after all, the books would be forgotten.

Now—the dowry. Plotina did not count that as high as most; other things were far more important. But the girl's dowry was more than satisfactory, and there would be no denying its usefulness. The connections—those were even better than the dowry. Senator Marcus Norbanus might be aging, but his voice in the Senate was still strong. His support could be vital.

The priest finished his invocation to Venus and lifted the vessel high. Wine poured in a ruby stream. The girl watched, narrow head tilted to one side under its festival wreath of scarlet poppies. Plotina felt a flutter in her stomach, dryness in her mouth. *Is she the one? The one who will be worthy?*

No, no one was worthy. It was quite impossible.

A biddable girl who would spend her life trying, however—that was within reach.

Here. In the person of Senator Norbanus's eldest daughter, Vibia Sabina.

Yes, she'll do. She'll do very nicely.

"Thank the gods that's done with," Plotina heard her husband grumble as they left the Temple of Venus. The waiting crowd erupted at the sight of him, surging forward with lusty cheers, stretching to touch the purple edge of his toga as he passed. Praetorian guards in red and gold held back the crush, clearing a path back toward the gold-trimmed Imperial litter. He handed Plotina inside, then raised an arm in cheerful salute to the crowd. The shouting redoubled: men, women, and children screaming themselves hoarse.

"Now for the races," said Marcus Ulpius Trajan, Pontifex Maximus and thirteenth Emperor of the Roman Empire. The litter rose on the backs of six Greek slaves and went jogging toward the Circus Maximus. "Gods' bones, I hate priests and their droning."

"Yes, dear." Pompeia Plotina, Emperor's wife, first lady of Rome, Empress of the seven hills, was not listening. The races did not matter at all; nor did a grubby little celebration of the wine harvest where men and their sluts drank too much wine and defiled public morals. Nothing mattered except that the girl, the *right* girl, had finally been chosen. Plotina laughed a little—it had not occurred until now just how much the matter had been preying on her.

I shall tell him tomorrow, the Empress thought happily. *I shall tell him I've found her.*

VIX

I don't much like patricians, and it's fair to say they don't like me. *Jumped-up thug,* they tend to mutter when I'm around, just loud enough for me to hear, but I ignore them. They're a fairly useless lot, with a few exceptions—and you have to watch out for the exceptions. Senator Norbanus was an exception, a good one. As for the bad exception, he's the man I should have kept an eye on from the start. Bastard.

The day already hadn't started well. I'd gotten my lip split by what should have been an easy mark: a rich boy ducking his tutors and his father to go hunting for whores in the Subura, which was the last place anybody should ever hunt for whores. He found one, and probably a case of something nasty that would be itching him within weeks, and then he found the inn where I now lived and a good many tankards of bad wine. The innkeeper gave me a nod as the boy reeled out, and I slid out after him. Only midmorning, but it was Vinalia and everyone was getting drunk early. The boy was still reeling when I pulled a dagger on him in an alley and demanded his purse, and he was drunk enough to hit me instead of just handing it over. I got my lip split, but I got the purse too, and sent the boy home with his nose broken in two places. "Consider it a mark of manhood," I called after him as he fled wailing. "A better one than the pox that whore gave you."

There were a good many coins in that purse, and of course I skimmed a few off the top before I handed the rest over to the innkeeper to count my percentage. "Mop that lip up and keep your eyes open," he ordered. "Lot of easy marks on festival days."

"Get someone else to hit them," I said shortly. "I'm going out to celebrate like everybody else. Hail to bloody Venus and hail to the bloody wine harvest."

"Listen, boy—"

I made an obscene gesture at him and thumped out. A grimy urchin darted under my feet; I booted him out of the way and his mother screeched at me. I made an obscene gesture at her too, and slid moodily into the cheerful crowds. Truth was, this wasn't what I had planned when I'd dreamed of coming back to Rome. Oh, it was easy enough— after a month I had a room of my own, food that didn't have too many bugs in it, coins for the bathhouse or the theatre whenever I had a mind to go. It wasn't hard taking purses off wild boys and rich tradesmen, and I even had a little side business stealing goods off vendors in the Subura and reselling them to vendors in the Esquiline. An easy enough life. But it wasn't quite . . .

The Colosseum had been thrown open to the crowd for festival day, and games were planned. No doubt a thousand lions would be slaughtered by spearmen, five thousand exotic birds by archers, and a few hundred prisoners by guards, and half the unlucky bastards sentenced to the gladiatorial fights would get dragged out on hooks through the Gate of Death. I ducked the Colosseum and turned toward the Circus Maximus instead. Not that the chariot races couldn't get bloody when a team went down, but it was better than the games. Plus, at the circus the women weren't walled up in their own section of seats, so you had a decent chance of finding a girl to take home.

God, the time I spent back then trying to get girls to go home with me. Well, I was eighteen.

The tiers were already packed to the skies, families waving little colored banners and already cheering their favorite teams. The Reds, the Blues, the Greens, and the Whites—I'd never backed one faction or another, but in my red tunic I was automatically hauled along to a section of seating packed with Reds fans. "A Blues bastard do that to you?" a big gap-toothed fellow demanded, pointing at my puffy lip. "Bloody bastards, those Blues."

"Right," I agreed. Never argue with a racing fanatic.

"The Blues'll take all the heats today, you wait," a woman in blue face paint screeched down from the tier above.

"They'll be dead bloody last!" the gap-toothed man roared, and a brisk shoving match broke out. I squirmed out of my seat and went looking for another, eyeing the cooler tiers and private boxes where the patricians and *equites* seated themselves. Maybe I could sneak in . . .

"Vercingetorix?" someone said behind me.

I turned—a girl in a red dress, with a wreath of festival poppies in her light-brown hair. "Lady Sabina." I remembered to bow. "You're in the wrong section. Patricians are all up there."

"I know. My aunt Diana has a box. But I'm ducking a suitor."

"I've got a seat," I said promptly.

"How kind." She tucked her hand into my elbow. She was little, hardly up to my shoulder, but people moved out of her way. That patrician thing again.

"So, you follow the Reds?" I noted a red pennant in her other hand.

"All my family does. Aunt Diana's mad for the Reds; she'd disown us if we rooted for anyone else." Sabina took the seat I offered, tilting her head up. "There isn't room for you."

"Yes, there is. Get lost," I told the man on her other side, and added a glare. He got lost, I got the seat, and for a bonus I got a smile from the senator's daughter. Maybe my day was looking up. "Why are you ducking a suitor?" I asked, leaning back on one elbow.

"He thinks he's leading the pack, so he's trying to drive off the others."

"You have a *pack?*"

"Yes," she said calmly. "I don't have my mother's looks, but I do have her money."

"Don't know about the looks," I said, but she brushed my compliments aside.

"The Emperor's come." She pointed up at the foremost box, where a flood of royals had just entered. I didn't have to guess which one was the Emperor—the short soldier's haircut, the purple cloak, and the beaming face said it all. Emperor Marcus Ulpius Trajan raised his fist, and the crowds exploded.

The aristocrats in their languid poses, the *equites* in their self-conscious clusters, the plebeians in their masses all surged to their feet and cheered. The charioteers and stable boys paused in their darting over the arena sand, the horses waiting for entry seemed to toss their heads in salute, and I found my palms stinging and realized I was shouting and clapping with everyone else.

But Sabina wasn't. She sat looking over the crowd, thoughtful. "They always do that," she said as I took my seat again beside her. "Every time Trajan comes out. He goes all over the city without guards, and no one harms him."

I watched the Emperor fling himself down in his golden chair, raking a hand through his hair and roaring with laughter. A long ways different from the Emperor I last remembered sitting in that box. "Long as Trajan doesn't give black parties or make people call him Lord and God, I'll find him an improvement."

"Sshh, they're starting." The roars mounted through the tiered seats as the first of the chariots appeared, a quartet of blacks with green plumes dancing over their heads. Two more teams for the Greens, then a team for the Blues. Sabina hissed as they went by in a flash of blue wheels, and I laughed.

"The Blues are utterly fucking evil," she explained, bland. "Or so I've been told since a very young age."

I laughed again, eyeing her in surprise. The Reds came by last, a Gaul flourishing his red-beaded driving whip to make his team of chestnuts prance, and Sabina waved her pennant. I put two fingers to my lips and let out a piercing whistle that had all our neighbors wincing.

"How interesting," said Sabina. "Show me how to do that!"

I showed her how to double up her tongue behind her teeth. She regarded me with unblinking attention, put two fingers to her own lips, and had it on the third try. "Excellent," she said, pleased. "Thank you, Vercingetorix."

"It's just a whistle."

"It's something new. I try to learn something new from everyone."

"What about bad people?" I couldn't help wondering.

"Even villains have something worth knowing. Look at my mother."

"What did you, uh, learn from her?" I blinked away a certain memory of Sabina's mother, all airy green silks and fragrant black curls, informing me in her low sweet voice that I was a cowardly little brat destined to die in the arena. Yes, I remembered Sabina's mother quite well. Wondered how much her daughter did, though . . .

"My mother dressed beautifully," Sabina said. "Otherwise, I have to say, she was a spoiled spiteful scheming waste of life."

"That about sums her up," I agreed. "Say, if you're so interested in learning new things, I can teach you more than whistling—"

Sabina looked amused but turned back to the arena, doubling her tongue expertly behind her teeth and letting out a shriek of a whistle. "*Reds!*" she shouted, and Trajan dropped the kerchief up in the Imperial box and eight chariots surged off the line.

There was the usual jockeying against the *spina*, a team for the Whites went down promptly in a flurry of hooves and dust and screams, and then the crush thundered away toward the other end of the arena, blue plumes in front with green and red close behind. They disappeared around the hairpin turn on the far end, shouts and cries rippling to the other side of the stands, and I flopped back in my seat again. "So you've got suitors," I said idly to the senator's daughter. "Any of them leading the pack?"

"One or two." Her blue gaze came back from the arena to me, unblinking. "My father said I could choose whom I liked, within reason."

"What's within reason?"

"Well, the Emperor has to approve my choice of husband," said Sabina. "And neither he nor Father would allow me to marry a freedman in a butcher's shop, or a wastrel with a pile of dicing debts. And my father wouldn't like it if I chose a man who travels a great deal either."

"What's wrong with traveling?" The chariots thundered around the second turn, a storm of cheers going up as the Reds fought up on the outside against the Blues.

"If I marry a general or a provincial governor I'll be gone from Rome, and Father would rather I stayed close. But he's going to be disappointed on that score."

"Why? Got your eye on a general?"

"No." Her gaze transferred back to the arena. "I've got my eye on the world."

"Tall order."

"Big world."

"I've seen Britannia," I offered. "Londinium's a sinkhole, but Brigantia's pretty—that's up north."

"Tell me about it?"

"Mountains," I said. "Mountains and sea—and it's cold, but the mist wraps the tops of the mountains and makes everything funny in your ears—" I talked about Brigantia, and Sabina listened with her whole body, drinking in every word as the horses thundered through two more laps.

"I'd like to see Brigantia," she commented when I trailed off. "But I'd like to see everything."

"Where'll you start?"

"Judaea? Gaul? Egypt, maybe—their gods have animal heads, and I always thought that was interesting. Or Greece—I could visit Sparta and Athens, see which one really is better."

"Spartans have the better armies." I remembered the stories my mother had told me. "Or they did, anyway."

"Yes, but what else have they got?" Sabina looked thoughtful, and the horses whirled past again in a cloud of dust and cheers. "Might be worthwhile, finding out."

"You know how they get married?" My mother had told me the story. "They take all the girls up into the mountains at night, give 'em a head start, and send all the boys after 'em. Everybody's naked, and whoever catches who gets married."

"How fortunate we don't do that in Rome. I'm a terrible runner."

"I'm not." I looked her over. "Run you down in a heartbeat, I could."

"But would you want to? There'd be some hardy Spartan girl you'd fancy first. Much better for a legionary."

"I'm not going to be a legionary."

"Aren't you?"

"Twenty-five years' service. Not bloody likely."

"Hmm." Her eyes turned back to the arena again as the cheers redoubled—in the fifth lap, the Reds had pulled ahead of the Blues. "Oh, good. They're winning." She waved her pennant politely.

"Hey!" I stared slit-eyed at the man sitting behind Sabina, a big bearded man who had edged forward swearing at the Blues. "Keep your knees out of her back!"

"Maybe she liked it," the man jeered, looking Sabina up and down.

"Take that back!" I reared up, grabbing a handful of his tunic. I was just in the mood for a scrap.

"Are you going to fight?" Sabina said, interested.

"Not much of a fight," I said, after bloodying the fellow's nose. He slunk off swearing, and I shook out my hand. "Maybe he'll come back with some friends."

"I rather hope he does. I've never seen a fight before."

"You saw me in the arena, didn't you? My second bout, when I was thirteen and got my shoulder speared." I still had the scar.

"Yes, I saw you. You were quite good too. But you weren't fighting for *me*. I've never had anyone fight for me before. I can see why girls get all excited about it."

"You're an odd one, Lady," I couldn't help saying.

"Do you think so? I think I'm quite ordinary."

"At least we've got room to stretch now." I leaned back, extending one arm casually along the line of her shoulders. She looked amused but let it stay there.

The Reds came in tops by a length, red plumes tossing in triumph over their chestnut heads, and the red-clad portion of the circus exploded into cheers. Three more heats followed as the sun descended into the heat of afternoon. There was another victory for the Reds and two for the Greens, and I was starting to get restless. "Food?" I suggested. "There's only so many times you can watch horses run in a circle."

"It does start to look the same after a while," Sabina agreed. "Where shall we go?"

I could think of a few places to go, most with convenient flat spots and none having anything to do with food, but this was a senator's daughter. "There are vendors about." I bulled a path in the crush, and Sabina followed in my wake.

"Sausages?" she suggested, pointing to a little stand.

"Better not. More likely dog than pork."

"I wonder why we don't eat dog," she mused. "We eat geese and pigs, and they're just as domesticated. We eat eels and lampreys, and they're too vile-looking even to contemplate in their natural form. But we don't eat dog, not unless we're really desperate."

"You want to try?"

"No, I confess I don't. But I wonder why?"

"You wonder a lot of things."

"Don't you?"

"I wonder where my next meal's coming from. Or I wonder what I'll be doing a year from now."

"I already know what I'll be doing a year from now." She tucked her hand into my elbow. "Perhaps that frees me up to wonder about the odd things."

"What *will* you be doing a year from now?"

"I'll be married. What else is there?"

I got her fried bread and strips of some lean roasted meat that at least wasn't dog. We watched the fifth race from the stands, munching, and when the Blues won I taught the senator's daughter a few colorful curses to hurl down at them.

"*Die slowly, you Blue whoresons,*" she yelled down at the track where the Blue chariot wheeled in triumph, and I grinned as she added a few more choice phrases. Then, behind us, I heard a cool patrician voice.

"Lady Vibia Sabina, are you lost?"

"Not a bit." She turned, her hand still tucked into my elbow. "Are you, Tribune?"

I'd have known him for one of the well-born even without the rank Sabina gave him. Only the rich and powerful wore a toga that snowy clean, and wore it without tripping over the heavy folds like us commoners. This tribune was a tall man, perhaps twenty-six; not as tall as me but broader. Dark hair curling closely over a massive handsome head; broad calm features, deep-set eyes. Bearded, which wasn't usual for Romans. He held the folds of his toga against his chest with one large ringed hand and looked down at Sabina with calm disapproval.

"You should not be here, Lady."

"Why not?"

"Your father has a box. Far safer for a girl."

"I'm safe enough with my escort here."

His eyes shifted to me. Just one quick glance and I knew he could describe me in detail a year from now, from my worn sandals to my shaggy hair to the amulet about my neck, which, from the twitch of his heavy eyelid, he clearly thought barbaric.

"Vercingetorix," said Sabina. "Meet Publius Aelius Hadrian, *tribunus plebis*."

"What's that?" I asked, not bowing. "A legionary officer?"

"No, that's a different kind of tribune. Hadrian's kind is a sort of magistrate. The first step toward becoming a praetor."

"There are other responsibilities." Hadrian's eyes swept me again. "And who is this?" he asked Sabina.

"A client of my father's."

"Ah." Faint surprise. "Senator Norbanus always did have odd clients."

"He does," Sabina agreed. "I like them. One learns so much."

"You have strange tastes, Vibia Sabina."

"Doesn't she?" I said. "I think it's sweet."

The tribune's eyes lingered a moment on my arm, where Sabina's hand was still tucked, then dismissed me. "If you will not be escorted back to your box, Vibia Sabina, I will take my leave. I dislike the races. Too many horses die, and I hate to hear them scream."

Another bow to Sabina and he moved off in blind confidence, rippling a path in the crowd for himself. "Stiff patrician bastard," I growled.

That was the first time I met Publius Aelius Hadrian. What a lot of trouble I'd have saved if I'd just killed the bastard on sight.

SABINA

How nice, Sabina reflected, to have someone large and male on hand in a crowd. She followed easily behind Vix as he shouldered through the delirious crush of Reds fans—the Reds had taken the final race and won the day's majority. "My aunt Diana will never forgive me if

I don't come congratulate her," Sabina shouted over the roar of applause as the Reds completed their last preening victory lap, and let Vix bull a path down into the sea of red now crowding the arena.

"Hell's gates." Vix got his first close look at the racing stallions—huge and sweating, champing against the red leather reins. "I'm never getting on a horse in my life if I can help it."

"Killed your first man in the arena at thirteen," said Sabina, amused, "and you're afraid of horses?"

"Petrified," Vix said frankly. "I haven't met a one that didn't want me dead. Why would anybody want to—"

"Sabina!" Aunt Diana came up from behind, flinging her unfashionably brown arms about Sabina's waist. As usual, her red dress and white-blond hair smelled of hay. "The Reds took five of nine, did you see? I'm having the charioteers back to my villa for a party; you'll come, of course—"

"I think I'm going home, Aunt Diana."

"Gods' wheels, girl, at your age I could drink any charioteer under the table! Have it your way, I'm going to check my horses—"

Off she whirled. "That's your aunt?" Vix twisted his head after her, admiring.

"Not really. She's some sort of distant cousin on my father's side, but I call her aunt anyway." Sabina pulled a wilting poppy from her hair, twirling it between her fingers. "Don't be embarrassed gawping over her. Everyone does."

"She must have been something to see when she was young."

"Yes, men used to turn and stare whenever she walked into a room. It annoyed my mother no end—she wanted men to turn and stare only when *she* entered a room."

Sabina slipped her hand into Vix's arm again, and they made their way out of the Circus Maximus with the rest of the crowd, treading over the litter of stale fallen food and sticky spilled pools of wine, faded festival flowers, and discarded little banners. The Reds fans swaggered and the Blues fans sulked; children wailed fretfully and couples slipped off to darker places. The sky was a deep pink overhead, shading toward night. Sabina tilted her head back to see the vast oval shadow of the Colosseum in the distance and wondered how many men had died inside it today. Vix was looking at the Colosseum too—for the first time that day, she saw his lively face still.

"Do you think about it?" Sabina asked. "The Colosseum."

"No." Vix's voice was curt, and he shoved a drunk out of their path with more force than was necessary. The drunk just beamed and gave a tipsy *"Ave Vinalia!"* before lurching off into the dusk. "I dream about it sometimes," Vix added abruptly.

"I wish I dreamed," Sabina confessed. "I haven't, not since my epilepsia went."

She'd fallen into fits as a child, but she'd been cured by the usual remedy of a gladiator's blood. The closest gladiator had been Vix: thirteen, wounded, and just out of his first bout. She'd been there in the crowd to see him get the wound—a sword into the shoulder, which might not have been too bad except that Vix had forced his shoulder farther up the blade to get within arm's reach of his much bigger opponent and make the kill. *Probably why I kissed him when I finally met him face to face*, Sabina thought. *He was a sight!*

"You miss the epilepsia?" Vix asked. The sky had faded from pink to violet now.

"Mmm, not the fits. But I do miss dreams. The gods talk to us in our dreams. Does that mean they'll never talk to me?"

"Don't know if I'd want to talk to a god."

"It might be interesting. So many gods, you know."

"You might get one of the animal-headed ones. Scary."

"Oh, I'm not easily scared."

"That I believe, Lady."

Sabina let him steer her around a fat man passed out in the street. Many Vinalia revelers had taken too much of the harvest wine and now lay slumped against walls snoring up at the darkening sky. Sabina's sandals made soft echoes against the stones as they wound through a series of narrow streets, and she was just about to ask with some amusement if he wasn't taking her the long way home when someone leaped out of the shadows and bashed Vix over the head.

"You like that?" a reeking voice snarled, and Sabina recognized the Blues fan from the circus whose nose Vix had bloodied. *He must have found some friends after all*, Sabina thought, and then someone else rushed past with a rough knock to her shoulder and sent her sprawling. She raised herself on her hands, her hip stinging painfully where she'd fallen, and saw Vix get one good punch off before two men doubled his left arm up behind him. The first man in the blue tunic staggered back with a muffled grunt, bleeding all over again from the nose, but he came back with a hammer blow. Vix yelled, ringing Sabina's ears like a bell, and then another of Blue Tunic's friends came out of the shadows and got him by the other arm. Vix braced himself, swearing thickly, and Blue Tunic was just cocking a fist back when a rock descended on the back of his head.

"Goodness," Sabina said as he fell, hefting the muddy chunk of stone she'd managed to snatch up from the gutter. "That makes quite a *thunk*, doesn't it?"

"*Hit him again!*" Vix yelled, head-butting into the man on his left.

"Oh, sorry," Sabina said hastily, and knelt down with the stone. She studied Blue Tunic a moment—she didn't want to kill him, after all—and finally decided on a medium-strength blow just above the other ear. That took care of his muzzy efforts to get up, and Sabina rose to see if Vix needed any more help, but he seemed to have things well in hand. He'd dropped one thug with a cocked elbow into the throat followed by a knee up into the belly, then turned on the other two. He came at them with a snarl, teeth bared like a wolf, and suddenly they were both brushing past Sabina and stumbling up the street.

"He should have picked better friends," Sabina observed.

"You think fast on your feet," Vix panted. He cuffed blood off his lip: tall, tense, still taut with energy. "Thanks, Lady."

"Don't mention it." She rose, tossing the loose stone away and feeling quite pleased with herself. "My first fight, and I dropped one all by myself. It's been a good day."

"Yes, it has," Vix said, then crossed the cobbles in two long strides, shoved her up against a tenement wall, and began kissing her.

Well, that's different. She'd been kissed before, of course—by Vix, for one, though they'd only been children; and more recently by a few of her suitors. Sabina had encouraged them, being immensely curious about the whole experience, but none of them had ever done more than brush their lips gently against hers and keep one mindful eye on the door to make sure her father wasn't coming. Except for the one suitor whose understanding of the whole business had been to shove his tongue as far down her throat as possible, as if he were trying to find out what she'd eaten for dinner . . .

"You're too damned small," Vix growled in her ear, and lifted her up off her feet for better access. Sabina chuckled low in her throat, tipping her head back for him and winding her arms about his neck. She was half crushed between the hard wall and his hard chest, but the one was warm, so warm, as though his blood boiled a shade hotter than the ordinary. She felt his heart thudding against her breasts, and tasted the salty coppery tang from his split lip. She touched the back of his neck, tracing an unhurried circle with one fingertip, and Vix gave a muffled groan and started kissing his way down toward her shoulder. One rough hand twined through her hair, dislodging the wilted poppies.

"The idea—off my doorstep, you filthy things!" Light suddenly flooded the dark vestibule, and Sabina felt a sharp smack on the back of her head. Vix swore, and they both looked up at a housewife's broad outraged face. "Thugs and trollops, disturbing decent people with your brawling and fornicating, the idea—"

"Hadn't even got to the fornicating yet, you cow!" Vix yelled, but Sabina took his arm, shaking with giggles, and pulled him off into the night with the housewife still frothing behind them.

"Gods, how funny." Sabina put a hand over her mouth and laughed through her fingers, feeling as giddy and high-sailing as a full moon. "Another first."

"Kissing in a doorway?"

"Being shrieked at for a fornicating trollop. What fun."

"Could be more fun." Vix stepped close again, his eyes just black shadows now in the dusk, but Sabina stopped him with a hand on his chest.

"I'm afraid my father will be looking for me soon. He'll worry now that it's dark, and I don't like to worry him. Besides, the house isn't far."

Vix scowled, but stepped back. "Told you I'd teach you something better than a whistle, didn't I?"

"So you did."

His face fell visibly when they came up to the house after another block of frustrated silence, and he saw that there were household slaves waiting at the gate. "Damn."

Sabina laughed. "Hoping for a good-night kiss?"

"Or something," he muttered.

Herself, Sabina had been pondering whether it would be wise to give him one . . . but the slaves were already hurrying out into the street to greet her. "Lady Sabina, you should have been back before dark!" She started toward them, pulling a fold of her *palla* up over her head and hoping Vix hadn't left any marks on her neck that might need explaining. Behind her, she heard Vix's footsteps turn back down the street.

On impulse, she shooed the slaves ahead and then turned. "Vix!"

He turned, tall and irritated in the torchlight. "What, Lady?"

"You kiss much better now than you did at thirteen." Sabina grinned and disappeared into the house.

CHAPTER 3

PLOTINA

The Empress of Rome prided herself on laughing very seldom. Life was a solemn thing, after all, and her position in the world demanded every possible dignity. But she could not help laughing when she saw the look on Hadrian's face.

"Dear Publius, don't look so grim. It's not a sentence of death, you know. Only a marriage."

"Which is a sentence of a different kind." He hesitated. "Vibia Sabina?"

"Yes, I've chosen her. You object?"

Hadrian moved his shoulders restlessly, pacing to the end of her study. Plotina looked up from her writing tablet, reveling in the sight of him: so tall and sturdy, the picture of Roman rectitude in his spotless toga, his head handsome in the wash of spring sunshine from the window. The gods had not seen fit to grant her children, but they had granted her Publius Aelius Hadrian: her husband's ward from the age of ten, and when first she laid eyes on him she had seen his potential. Trajan had had little time to act the guardian, so his care had been hers. *Her* Publius.

"We agreed it was time you married," she pointed out as he continued to pace. "Right in this room we agreed it." A fine sunny morning; Hadrian always came to call on her before midday if his duties permitted, and she had lost no time in dismissing the slaves from her cozy study and informing him she had at last found him a bride. "It's high time you took a wife," Plotina continued, "and you asked me to find you a suitable candidate."

"Not Vibia Sabina. I don't like the girl."

"Why not? She's quiet, well mannered, decently bred. She has a fine dowry and even finer connections."

"Her mother was the greatest whore since Messalina!"

"And her father has one of the most respected voices in the Senate house. His support would carry your career far." Plotina smiled. "I do so want to see you consul someday, Dear Publius. By thirty if I can manage it, and I expect I can."

"Not with a wife like that. She may look quiet, but she has a taste for low company. I saw her at the races, rubbing elbows with plebs."

"Once you're married, she'll have to keep the company *you* choose," Plotina pointed out. "Surely you can rein in one errant little wife?"

"She's very young," Hadrian complained. "I don't like little girls."

"I wish she were younger," Plotina sighed. A ripe biddable little thing of fourteen who would do as she was told—the ideal daughter-in-law. "Sabina's father should have arranged her marriage three or four years ago instead of letting her loll about the house reading Homer. Still, if he had then she would not be available for you. The gods arrange these things for a reason." They generally arranged things to suit Plotina, she found. And what they did not arrange, she could contrive for herself.

"I don't think the girl is as biddable as you say," Hadrian was saying. "She says all the right things, but I can feel her laughing at me."

"Nonsense; who would ever laugh at you?" Plotina looked back to her wax tablet. "Just leave her to me; I will train her up to satisfaction after your marriage. Hand me that stylus?"

"Checking the household accounts again?" Hadrian shook his head, amused. "An army of stewards at your beck and call, and the Empress of Rome still does her own figures."

"My last steward tried to cheat me. I had to make an example and have his hands chopped off." Plotina scraped the tablet clean and made a fresh heading. "Besides, I have always kept my own household accounts. I see no reason to change simply because my household is larger. You will recall, Dear Publius, that when I entered the palace for the first time—"

"Yes, yes, you declared you would leave the palace the same woman as you entered it." Hadrian's eyes crinkled. "You've told me that a hundred times."

"I hope I've done more than quote it at you."

"Certainly, my lady." He bent and kissed the top of her head. "You have not changed in the slightest."

"You have, and not entirely for the better." Plotina patted his furred cheek. "I don't like that beard."

"And I don't like your choice of bride." The scowl returned, and he flung himself into the chair opposite her. "Why Vibia Sabina?"

"You require a wife of breeding and connections, with the poise to host your colleagues and rivals as you climb the ladder."

"You have always done that for me," he observed.

"And will continue to do so." Plotina began copying a list of figures out on her slate. "But a wife will give you sons, and a man should have sons."

"Trajan—"

"Is also very fond of Sabina," Plotina interrupted smoothly. "You will rise in his favor as well, marrying her."

"I should already have his favor," Hadrian grumbled.

Plotina felt a pang. "You should take more interest in Dear Publius," she had told her husband many times. "He's your ward. He should be like a son to you."

"Well, he isn't." Trajan had been short with her, very short. "I've done my duty by him, haven't I? Cold moody little bugger he was as a boy, and he's a cold moody bugger now. Enough is enough."

No, Plotina thought, *it's not nearly enough.* But she knew when to drop the matter for later. Trajan could be so stubborn.

"Marry little Sabina," she said, "and you'll get on better with my husband. He's even a distant great-uncle to her on her father's side—the marriage will make you family, not just a ward. The Emperor will see you more frequently, get to appreciate you better. You'll see."

"It'll take more than a marriage to make the Emperor like me."

If you'd kept your hands off that dancer Trajan liked so much, you'd stand better with him today, Plotina thought. What a debacle that had been! Trajan had been very cross about having his pet poached from under his nose, and in the end Plotina had had to pack that smooth-cheeked little whore off to a brothel in Ostia, just to keep the peace in her household. All young men had wild oats to sow, but couldn't they be more careful about where they scattered the seeds? It was a thought Plotina kept to herself. There were things young men fondly thought their mothers did not know. Mothers always *did* know, of course, but if they were wise they kept their own counsel. And who was wiser than Plotina, who was not just the mother Dear Publius should have had, but the Mother of Rome?

"This marriage will be a start in the right direction," she said instead. "Trajan likes Sabina, and if you marry her he'll like you. So why don't you go pay a visit on the Norbanus household this afternoon?"

"I suppose I could speak to her father." Grudgingly. "Advance my prospects."

"I'm afraid you'll have to address yourself to Sabina as well, my dear. Her father is letting her have some choice in her marriage." Plotina exhaled. "What is this world coming to? He always was far too lenient a father."

"I'll take a firmer line with his grandsons, then." Hadrian rose, kissing her hand. "You win, my lady. Senator Norbanus's daughter it is."

"Shave off that beard?" Plotina begged. "I'm sure no girl wishes to marry a hedge."

SABINA

"It's perfect." Sabina looked down at the little figure in marble. "Uncle Paris, I don't know how you do it."

He took her thanks serenely, hardly bothering to look up from the new block of marble now occupying his worktable. Sabina wandered the studio, used to his silences. Long windows letting in a flood of pale gold morning sunshine, scraps of marble and stone dust everywhere—and shelves, rank on rank of shelves crammed full of marble pieces. A bust of Emperor Trajan, looking vigorous . . . a half-finished study of a nymph, exquisite arms and shoulders rising from a rough chunk of stone . . . a granite Hercules with his lion skin and club . . . Uncle Paris might be old now, his hair gone white and his eyes cloudy, but his hands with their chisel and mallet were clearly as steady as ever. He must have been quite a scandal when he was young—Sabina could well imagine the whispers. *A boy of good family sculpting marble like a common artisan? My dear, the shame of it!* But the family had gotten used to him by now, and left him alone with his marble and his gift for shaping it.

"I wish I had a talent," Sabina confided to a suspicious-eyed bust of the old emperor Domitian. Even an awkward talent like sculpting marble, or Aunt Diana's passion for training horses—it would still make life simpler. You'd *know* what the gods intended you to be. It was just a matter of clearing any obstacles out of the way, and getting on with it.

She'd wanted to smack Vix that day at the races a few weeks ago. Anyone with eyes in their head could see what he was supposed to be, and instead he wasted his time skulking around alleys, picking fights, and kissing the wrong girls.

A deep voice sounded behind her. "Vibia Sabina."

"Publius Aelius Hadrian." She turned, aping his formal tones just a little. "Wait, hold still!"

"What?" he frowned, his broad hand twitching the folds of his toga.

"Hand out—there. Raised up, declamatory. Now, hold it." Sabina raised her voice. "Uncle Paris, come sketch him for your next statue. *Perfect Roman Senator.*"

Hadrian dropped the declamatory hand. "I see you like a joke, Vibia Sabina."

"Don't you?"

He ignored the question, looking at Uncle Paris, whose eyes were trained on a minute crack in his marble block. "Uncle, you said?"

"Another cousin, technically," Sabina said. "Father's related to half of Rome, and Calpurnia to the other half. Everyone's my cousin."

Including the Emperor—and that, Sabina knew, was the reason Publius Aelius Hadrian stood, stilted and dutiful, trying to make conversation with a silly girl who liked a joke. Soon after Vinalia, he'd decided to start courting her. Sabina couldn't decide if it was funny or exasperating. She'd never had a more reluctant suitor in her life.

"You've received the gift I sent yesterday?" he said after another pause.

"The stag from your hunt? Yes, my stepmother is very grateful. We'll have venison for days."

"I will send more. I hunt weekly, but I do not need so much game for myself."

"Then why do you hunt weekly?" Sabina eyed his immaculate hands, his toga without so much as an ink spot. "I'd have thought hunting too dirty for you."

"On the contrary."

Another silence fell.

"You've commissioned something, I suppose." Hadrian gestured around the studio, boredom suppressed in every word. "A bust of your father?"

"In a sense." Sabina indicated the little figure in rosy marble: a man dropped to one knee, tendons corded through his arms and down his neck, one shoulder twisted under the weight of a perfect sphere.

"Atlas. Bowed under the weight of the heavens." Hadrian peered at the carved face, its noble nose and broad forehead, the mouth compressed in an agony of effort. "Is that your father's face?"

"Very good," said Sabina. "It's a surprise Calpurnia commissioned for him. Her way of reminding him not to work too hard."

"She is a fine wife," Hadrian approved. "A pearl among women."

"After what my mother put him through, my father was due a pearl."

Hadrian cocked his head at that.

Sabina gave a bland blink of her lashes. "You've come for a bust?"

"Yes. A gift for the Emperor. I thought to have him carved as Aeneus."

"Better Alexander. Trajan would adore to conquer the world."

"Alexander then. The world at his feet." Hadrian bent to examine the little Atlas again, and Sabina saw the light in his eyes. "Your uncle Paris, he must have studied the Polykleitos school of thought? Action and inaction, perfectly expressed here. Have you ever seen the Polykleitos *Doryphorus?* I've seen sketches, but—" Hadrian pulled himself up. "Forgive me, Vibia Sabina. Of course this is of no interest to—"

"How do you know what interests me?" said Sabina. "You may have been showering me with flowers and dead deer for a few weeks now, but we've never had a single interesting conversation."

"Naturally a girl does not study the precepts of sculpture or—"

"You're much more interesting when you aren't patronizing me," Sabina said frankly. "You should try talking like a human being more often. So, what's so special about the Polykleitos *Doryphorus?*"

Hadrian looked down at her. For a moment Sabina thought he'd go back to boring pleasantries, but his hand reached out almost involuntarily and touched the little Atlas. "See the shift in the weight between the feet? Perfectly poised between motion and repose. The Greek sculptor Polykleitos found it was the finest way to express the beauty of the athletic form. His *Doryphorus* is the best example, but he had a very fine Hera in a temple in Argos, and a bronze Amazon in Ephesus—"

"Surely you're not a sculptor too?" Sabina looked at Hadrian's large hands. Unscarred and soft, the nails smooth and uniform, not much like Uncle Paris's chisel-roughened palms.

"No, merely a dabbler in the arts," Hadrian said with a modesty Sabina found suspect. "I make sketches, and architectural drawings—you can see the same principle in Greek architecture, you know. The Erechtheion caryatids, they don't just serve as pillars! You can see a knee raised, as if they're ready to step down off the plinth—"

He was waving his arms now.

"I'm going to build my own villa someday," he told Sabina. "The perfect blend of Greek and Roman architectural principles. The grace and beauty of Greece—Corinthian columns, we've got nothing to match them— but backed up by the solidity of our Roman domes. I've made preliminary designs, but I need more study. A tour in Greece; I want to see the Acropolis, the temples. The Greeks have the finest temples in the world."

"According to you, the Greeks have the finest everything," Sabina teased, but he was too absorbed to mind her joking now.

"Not everything." Decisive. "Rome has the finest government, the best engineering, the most perfect system of organization. But culture, that goes to Greece. Architecture, philosophy, dramatics—all we have to offer for dramatists are those dreary pantomime farces, nothing to stand against Sophocles and Euripides. And as for literature—"

"Cicero," said Sabina promptly. "Martial, Virgil—"

Hadrian snorted. "Overrated."

"Surely not Virgil," Sabina protested. "'*I see wars, horrible wars, and the Tiber foaming with much blood—*'"

"Orotund and overpolished," Hadrian snapped. "You want an accounting of Aeneas, you'd do better to study Ennius's *Annals*. Good straightforward Roman prose—"

"You will never win me away from Virgil. What about Cato?"

"Cato I will grant you. He has a textbook on public speaking, sound basis in Greek rhetorical theory—"

"Yes, I've read it."

"Have you? Extraordinary. What about his *Origines* . . ."

Eventually, Uncle Paris's voice broke into the discussion. "Go away, both of you," he said without looking up from his chisels. "You're distracting me."

Sabina realized they'd been talking loudly, enthusiastically, and for more than an hour. Hastily she bundled up the little figurine of Atlas. "We're going, Uncle Paris."

"I'd meant to commission a bust of Emperor Trajan," Hadrian recalled. "Carved as Alexander—"

"Boring," said Uncle Paris, and shut the door of his studio.

"Don't mind him," Sabina said as they came out into the street. Her litter-bearers straightened hastily, having taken advantage of her absence to flirt with a cluster of slave girls on the way to the market. "Uncle Paris carves for himself, you know, not for his living. You'd better make your commission interesting, or he won't take it."

"A true sculptor." Hadrian fingered his short beard. "I envy such men. A great talent may be a burden, but it does lighten one of destiny. The talent *is* the destiny."

"I was thinking that myself, earlier," said Sabina. "But you said it better. What's your talent?"

"I write poetry," Hadrian confessed. "Elegies in the Greek style. And I have a certain skill for drawing, and I play the flute and the lyre. But I will never number among the great artists."

"Then you'll have to find out your own destiny," said Sabina. "Most of us do, I suppose."

"I already know what my destiny is," Hadrian said matter-of-factly.

She cocked her head, interested, but he had lifted a hand and summoned his own litter.

"I fear I must leave you, Vibia Sabina—I would see you home, but I am to dine this evening with my sister and her husband Servianus."

"Lucius Julius Ursus Servianus?" Sabina asked. "I've met him."

"They say he is the most worthy man in Rome."

"I don't like him either."

Hadrian laughed aloud, taking her hand and raising it to his lips. "What an interesting little thing you are," he said, and Sabina no longer saw the sheen of boredom in his deep-set eyes.

VIX

I'll admit I was nervous when I got a summons to Senator Norbanus's house. "Hell," I swore when I got the politely worded missive, handed over by a less polite slave. But I went. When a senator snapped his fingers in Rome, unemployed ex-slaves like me hopped like frogs.

"I see you are doing well for yourself." He eyed the silver chain about my neck, leaning back in his chair. Nothing had changed in the crowded study—the desk heaped with slates and tablets, the cheerful clutter, the shelves and shelves of scrolls. "Have you found any particular work as yet?"

"Odds and ends, sir."

"I know what sort of odds and ends go on in that side of town. Not what your parents would hope for you, I'm sure."

An itch started to scratch between my shoulder blades, and I had to control the urge to twitch. Twitching looked guilty.

"Sabina tells me you ran into a spot of trouble outside the Circus Maximus a few weeks ago."

Damn it. I should have known that girl wouldn't be able to hold her tongue. "No trouble, sir," I lied. "Nothing at all."

"She said you handily saw off a pack of drunken thieves."

"She exaggerates."

"Rarely."

His dark eyes regarded me, thoughtful, and I had the feeling he was seeing clear through to the inside of my skull. A good many aristocrats could do that look, but his took the prize. He knew about the thugs, he knew about me kissing his daughter; he knew all the things I would have liked to do to his daughter given a little more time and a flat spot, and *Hell's gates, Vercingetorix, this is not the time for any of those thoughts to be invading your thick head.* I averted my eyes over the senator's ear, fastening them on a bust of somebody who might have been an emperor or maybe just a philosopher, and hoped my face wasn't reddening. Red faces looked guilty.

"I would like to offer you a place in my household guards." The offer came so abruptly, I just blinked. "This is a quiet household, but we have occasional need of a guard at the gate. You would have a room here at the villa, your meals, three new tunics a year. And a salary." He quoted it—a generous one.

I breathed easier. He'd hardly be making me any sort of offer if he knew—"Why, Senator? Must be plenty of old soldiers who'd serve you better. I've never done any bodyguarding."

"I remember a twelve-year-old boy who stabbed an emperor in defense of his mother," said Senator Norbanus. "What was that, if not bodyguarding?"

"That was a long time ago."

"Six years. Endless, indeed." His ink-stained fingers drummed the desk. "Bring a little of that verve to protecting my household, and I'll be well pleased. I have an enemy or two who might be troublesome—not to kill me perhaps, but to prevent me from reaching the Senate house on the morning of some important vote. And my eldest daughter has a habit of wandering off to odd places. A strong arm at her back might be useful."

"Did she put you up to this?" I couldn't help but ask. "Hiring me?"

"No, Sabina's gone to Baiae with her stepmother and the children."

I couldn't help a twinge of disappointment. Sabina had put me off the night I kissed her, like a good girl should, but her finger had traced those deliberate circles on the back of the neck that had raised the hair on my arms—raised more than hair, truth be told, and that was not anything to be thinking about right now either. I shifted partway behind a handy chair.

"—Sabina's idea, taking Calpurnia to the coast for a while," the senator had continued, unaware of me. "My wife is to have another child"—a smile lit his face, softening the harsh marble-carved lines out of all recognition—"and she's often queasy in the early months, so Sabina suggested sea air."

He seemed to shake himself a little, looking back at me. "My idea, in any case, to offer you this position. It occurred to me that you stand some danger of becoming a thug. Your parents, I am sure, would not want that, and I do owe them a debt."

"Hey," I said. "I'm no thug."

"You extort drunk boys in alleys for . . . what reason, then?"

Maybe he did know more than I took him for. "It's a living."

"Not much of one."

"Being a bodyguard isn't much either."

"Consider it a stepping-stone. You will encounter interesting people in this house, people who might be able to help you. A bright young household officer might find a well-placed legate willing to sponsor him as a centurion."

"In return for services rendered," I snickered. "No, thanks."

His mouth quirked. "That's a danger, true. But there are benefits outweighing the dangers. Emperor Trajan always has his eye out for bright young warriors, and his officers are beginning to look for them too."

Emperor Trajan. Rumor in the wine shops had it he was heading back up north to Germania soon, to step once and for all on a rebellious king in Dacia who wore a lion skin. I wouldn't mind seeing an emperor closer up than a box at the races. Maybe something *would* come of working here, something more than just the lodging and light work and regular pay . . . I thought of fine, flower-tangled hair flowing through my hands, but blinked that particular image back.

"All right," I said. "I'll do it."

"Excellent." The senator poured a pale stream of wine into a goblet from a decanter at his elbow and pushed it toward me. "Welcome to the Norbanus household, Vercingetorix."

"Thank you, sir. Dominus." I remembered the change just in time— I'd have to address him as master of the house, now that I'd joined the household.

Steady pay or not, I didn't really like calling anyone *Master* again.

Spring fluttered toward a damp hot summer, and I slid into the Norbanus household like an eel into a mud bank. And I had it good.

The work was light. There were only two other guards, both grizzled and graying, happy to dice in the cool garden while I headed off to escort the master to the Senate house. Senator Norbanus was a good master—he might be eagle-eyed over his scrolls, but he was absent-minded as far as his household went. In the absence of his wife and

children he was content to eat in his study, dropping crumbs uncon-
cernedly on his wax tablets, or to take a packet of bread and cheese
from the cook and limp down to the Capitoline Library, where he'd
spend half the day in research. No beatings in this house; no slaves
running away in the night or whipped for breaking a dish. I had a new
cloak, thick enough to keep the summer rainstorms off my back. I had
regular days off to go to the races or the games or the taverns or anywhere else I pleased. The hardest work I had to do was carry an armload
of scrolls for Marcus Norbanus on his way to the Senate house.

So why did I feel so bloody *sour?*

"You're so scowly, Vix," the freckled slave girl giggled at me. Gaia,
her name was, a Greek girl who'd grown up in the Norbanus household,
and soon I was counting the freckles on more than her nose. She was
buxom and giggly, a soft armful in the night, but I still lay there scowling up at the ceiling after she'd slipped out of my room with another
sleepy giggle. And I'd go get drunk on my day off, drunk as I could,
and come back with a head so sore even the senator didn't offer me his
usual absent "Good morning" on the way to the Senate house.

Sabina and her stepmother stayed up in Baiae, and that made me sore
too. I saw the letters her father wrote to them both; he might have mentioned he had a new guard in the household, mightn't he? And maybe
she'd have come home a little sooner, hearing that, but she didn't, and why
should she? Rich girls, they probably all kissed pleb boys in alleys after a
day at the races. Just a bit of spice for them, a cheap thrill before they
married and got as fat and painted and plucked as their mothers.

I wasn't the only one looking for the daughter of the house. Hardly
a day went by when some hopeful fellow in a toga didn't turn up on the
doorstep. Old or young, their faces all fell when I said she wasn't there.
"What's she got that everyone wants?" I demanded of a patrician boy
younger than me who had brought a bouquet of lilies and his brand-new
toga to the door. "There's plenty of senators' daughters in Rome. Lots
have got to be prettier than her, richer than her."

"But they don't have her connections." He was too young to be sniffy about talking to a guard. "She's great-niece to the Emperor, or maybe a distant cousin. Anyway, she's the closest unmarried woman of his family. My grandfather says if I land her, it'll be a sure boost to my career."

He dropped his armload of flowers on a nearby table. A sprat of a boy, skinny as a bean, but he had a thin pleasant face and a rueful expression. He'd given me his name at the door, some impossibly long string, but all I remembered was *Titus*. "You're young to be trying for a wife," I couldn't help observing.

"Wasn't my idea, believe me. My grandfather's ill, and he's starting to want me settled." Titus or whatever his name was fiddled with the flowers. "He said I might have a chance—Grandfather's great friends with her father, so he's already dropped a few hints for me."

"Won't do you any good," I said. "She gets to pick her own husband."

"Well, I'm sunk." He gestured down ruefully at his skinny frame. "Who'd pick me?"

"You never know. Come back when she's returned from Baiae."

"I will. Might as well practice this courtship business, even if I haven't got a chance in the world. 'No man by fearing reaches the top,' as Syrus would say." The boy picked up his armload of lilies and thrust them at me. "Give these to your girl instead."

"Violets next time," I advised. "Lady Sabina hates lilies."

I liked him, Titus whatever-his-name-was, and if I'd known then just how many times we were going to save each other's lives I'd have paid more attention when I first met him. Yount Titus aside, however, the rest of Sabina's suitors seemed like a supercilious lot. That fawning worm Tribune Hadrian came calling, and the heavy brows aligned over his nose when I told him he'd made the trip for nothing. "When will Lady Vibia Sabina return?" he deigned to ask.

"Don't know." I hooked my thumbs into my belt. "You think she keeps me informed?"

"Ah—" His eyes swept me, recognition flaring. "The boy from the races. You were rude."

"Still am," I grinned.

Hadrian regarded me with cool displeasure. "You need a good beating, boy," he said. "I'll see you get one someday."

"How will you manage that, sir?"

"I am resourceful." He swept out with a flare of purple-bordered toga, and I made a rude gesture at the stiff retreating back.

I got into a different kind of fight the following week, just after my nineteenth birthday, on a warm damp morning when I celebrated my day off by being stupid and going to the Colosseum. I didn't want to go, knew I'd hate it, but the other guards jeered at me for missing the Vestalia games, so I went. I watched spearmen die on leopard claws and leopards die on spears, and by the time the midday executions rolled around I was drunk. "Games've gone downhill since my day," I belched as a line of shackled runaway slaves were brought out for brisk beheading. "I remember when the rules weren't so damned strict. Then you'd really see the blood flow."

"What do you know?" the other guard jeered.

"I *fought* down there, I'll have you know." I waved my mug down at the bloody sand where a guard was forcing a struggling man to kneel, and spilled my beer. "I'm the Young Barbarian."

"Who?"

"The Young Barbarian," I repeated, outraged. "Youngest ever to fight in the Colosseum! Youngest to fight a bout anyway—" There were plenty of children who died in the arena, heretics or escaped slaves or prisoners, but they didn't get a sword to defend themselves. A few children huddled down there now, waiting in paralyzed terror beside their parents for the blade through the neck, and I averted my eyes. "Come on, you remember the Young Barbarian!"

They looked at each other and jeered. "Sounds to me like you're making it up. You weren't never no gladiator!"

I hit at them with the mug, and one of them hit back, and a fight broke out in our section of the stands—a free-for-all that got me thrown out before the main bouts, and I wasn't too sorry about that. I staggered out with a spectacular black eye and a bleeding ear, puked in a gutter,

then puked again as I heard the roar of the crowd rise up from the Colosseum and knew it for a signal that the gladiators had fallen on each other.
Poor bastards, I thought, and my knees gave out and I sat down on the
paved curb with my hands dangling between my knees. "No loitering,"
a housewife admonished me, pausing to adjust the basket on her arm.

"I'm the Young Barbarian," I snarled at her. "You don't want to get
too close to me!"

"Barbarian indeed," she sniffed, and bustled off. Rainwater had gathered in the hole left by a missing stone between my feet, and I restlessly
kicked at the puddle. Another roar went up from the great arena behind
me, and I wondered if I should just become a gladiator again. At least the
sentence wouldn't be twenty-five years. There weren't many gladiators who
lasted as long as *two* years, much less twenty-five. A short life, but no
questions about it—as a gladiator, you knew where you were. Fight or die.

Nothing simple about life now. Years ahead of me, and no idea what
to do with them . . . I fingered the little amulet on its leather lace about
my neck. Just a simple brass medallion of Mars, the Roman god of war;
the kind you find at any vendor's stall ten for a copper. My father had given
it to me the day I left for Rome. "You should have a proper Roman god to
look after you," he said dubiously, "if you're going back to that hellhole."

"Did Mars keep you safe?" I'd asked. "All those fights in the
Colosseum—"

"Something did," he shrugged, and looped the amulet around my
neck. The medallion had a stern, scowling, helmeted face on it—Mars
looked like a humorless bugger. I rubbed a thumb over the stern visage
and looked up at the sky. "Any hints?" I called hopefully. "Gladiator?
Legionary? Anything?"

A drop of rain fell on my neck, and the skies opened. I sat there
getting wet, trying to work out if it was an omen.

"Fighting, Vix?" The steward eyed me with disapproval when I
returned dripping to the house. "A guard with a black eye, it reflects
badly on the master. Never mind, pack your things."

"Pack?" I swayed, tired and wet and still more than a little drunk.

"Senator Norbanus is going to Baiae to join Lady Calpurnia. We leave tomorrow. You'll be needed to help with the journey—"

"What an admirable black eye," Senator Norbanus remarked mildly in the morning. "Here, take these scrolls and load them into the litter. Pliny, hmm, I'd better take him. Some Martial, some Cato—can't do without Catullus—"

A jolting journey in an ox-drawn palanquin. Baiae. I'd never been there. Pretty little town. White marble, blue water, big houses. Women in towels, trotting back and forth from the famous sulfur baths. More patricians here than anything else. Even the prostitutes on the street corners in their saffron wigs looked uppity.

"Marcus!" Lady Calpurnia came running out the front gates of the villa when the palanquin halted. She'd dressed up to greet her husband, all airy yellow silks and chunks of amber in gold settings, an elegant far cry from the cheerful housewife who wasn't too proud to bake her own bread and gossip with her slaves. Those same slaves had told me Lady Calpurnia had been one of the richest heiresses in Rome—"Oh, she brought Dominus half of Tarracina and Toscana when they married!"—and this was the first time she looked it.

"Good-looking, rich, *and* she loves you," I breathed to Senator Norbanus as he limped toward his wife. "You fell on your feet bagging that one, Dominus. Any man in Rome would take her for her bread alone!"

He gave me a familiar glance, half irritated and half amused, but didn't rebuke me for insolence. He'd never have brought down an emperor six years ago if not for me—neither of us had planned it that way, but it happened, and the bond still stuck. He let me get away with more familiarity than I should have. And his irritation faded fast enough as Lady Calpurnia flung herself into his arms. In fact, he reminded me abruptly of my rough gladiator father, who cupped my mother's face between his hands in just the same way.

It's not necessarily the beautiful girls that hook you good and tight.

It's the ones like Lady Calpurnia—the ones like my mother. One of those warm, quiet women starts loving you, and you're sunk. Be warned.

"Marcus, your eyes look squinty," Lady Calpurnia was scolding gently. "Have you been reading by bad lamplight again? Vix, take those scrolls right back to the litter; my husband will not be doing *any* work in this villa—goodness, Vix, that's quite an eye."

"I know," I growled.

"Hide the scrolls in my study," Marcus said low-voiced when his wife turned her back, and I tramped dutifully into the house as little Faustina came running out through the gates to collect her own greeting from her father. A spacious spread-out villa—pools of water sunk under open roofs, porticoed halls with slender columns, mosaics of leaping fish and twining vines on the floors. The study was already occupied when I got there.

"Hello, Vix." Sabina looked up from her book without surprise. "Is my father here already? You must have had good roads. I suppose everyone else has commented on the black eye?"

"Yes," I said. "Everyone else has commented on the damned black eye."

"It is rather spectacular." She uncurled from the couch, barefoot and bare-armed, light-brown hair hanging down her back. "Still, I won't ask how you got it."

"You should." A reluctant smile was beating its way past my irritation. "It's a thrilling tale. Robbers, thieves, dragons."

"Dragons? How interesting." Sabina rolled up her book. "I'd better go see my father. Nice to know you've joined the household, Vix."

She drifted out just as her stepmother bustled in. "Give me those scrolls, Vix—I know he told you to hide them from me—"

I surrendered my armload with a salute and went to look for the steward, feeling suddenly more cheerful. "Where do I sleep?"

"You'll share with one of the other guards. Do you realize you've got a black—"

"I know."

CHAPTER 4

SABINA

Sabina liked the terrace of the Baiae villa. On fine evenings she had the steward pull out the couches so dinner could be served outside, wrapped in warm summer breezes with the shadows lengthening across the tiles and the expanse of blue sea glittering beyond. She looked over the bowls of grapes sometimes and imagined that she was seeing all the way beyond the horizon to the great promontories at the mouth of the sea. Hadrian had been born in Hispania; he'd described those promontories to her with hands flying and eyes aglow. The Pillars of Hercules, salt spray flying about them, with the wide ocean and the wider world beyond.

"So wonderful to have a little vacation all together," Calpurnia was saying, balancing little Linus against her arm as she tried to split a pomegranate one-handed. The last baby had given her a passion for oysters, but this time around it was pomegranate seeds. "Marcus, promise me you won't go back to Rome for at least a month. You need the rest."

Sabina nibbled absently on a strip of roast goose, eyes still on the horizon. What lay beyond the Pillars of Hercules? North, of course, lay Britannia. But what lay west? What lay *all* the way west? Hadrian didn't know, and wasn't much interested. "Wild places," he'd said dismissively. "Why worry about the world's wilderness, Vibia Sabina, when the civilized world has more than you could ever explore in a dozen lifetimes?"

"I can't stay here all summer," Sabina's father was protesting. "I'm working on a new treatise." So many senators, Sabina had often noticed, looked uneasy and vulnerable out of their togas, like turtles suddenly missing their shells. But her father, even when relaxed on the dining couch in a plain tunic with little Faustina curled under his arm, looked like an emperor.

"The treatise can wait," Calpurnia was insisting. "We can all go to the sulfur pools; it'll bake that foul city air right out of your lungs." She pressed a pomegranate seed into his mouth with pink-stained fingers, stilling his protests.

"You know the rules, Father." Sabina grinned. "One month here for every pomegranate seed you've eaten. Just like Proserpina and Pluto."

"Oh, good, that's one month." Calpurnia plucked out more seeds. "Two, three, four—"

"And I thought it was a good idea to give my daughter a classical education," Marcus shook his head.

"Father, you really should stay a while. Calpurnia feels so sick in the middle months, and she's always better when you're here."

Marcus at once looked worried, taking his wife's pomegranate-sticky hand. Calpurnia squeezed his fingers with no more than a twinkle of her lashes at Sabina, who hid her own smile in her cup. Her stepmother was approximately as frail as a mountain pony, but she and Sabina had long entered into a tacit conspiracy where any method from mild misdirection to outright lying was appropriate when it came to the care of the man they mutually adored.

"We'll make a summer of it here, then," Marcus was deciding. "The five of us. I'll have time to start teaching Faustina—some Greek, some rhetoric—"

"Marcus, love, she's barely five. What are you trying to prepare her for, a career in the Senate?"

"Mix the Greek verbs in with a good bedtime story and they'll go down easy." Marcus ruffled the little fair head under his arm.

"I like stories," Faustina volunteered around a mouthful of roast goose. "Father has the *best* stories. Like the one where the king got murdered in his bath! And the one where the prince had to kill his mother—"

"Greek tragedies, Marcus?" Calpurnia gave her husband a look that made Sabina giggle. "As *bedtime stories?*"

"Sanitized," he hedged. "I leave out all the gory details . . ."

"You did not!" Sabina laughed. "At least not when you were telling them to me!"

"Did he tell you the one where the king gets ripped apart by all those lady wolves?" Faustina piped, bright-eyed. "Or the king who got boiled alive in a pot? All these dead kings, why does anybody want to be a king, anyway?"

"Wise child," said Marcus. "Maybe we should try something lighter for this summer's reading, Faustina."

"How about the one where the women of Athens refuse to sleep with their husbands anymore?" Sabina suggested.

"There's a thought." Calpurnia rubbed her heavily rounded stomach.

"We'll find a comedy to read together," Marcus said hastily. "I'll take the male parts, and Sabina can read the women's—"

"Actually," Sabina said idly, "I thought I might take my nurse for a chaperone and go back to Rome for the summer."

"Why would you want to do that?" Calpurnia rescued her bowl of fruit before Linus could knock it over. "Rome in summer—it'll be hotter than a furnace and smell worse than a sewer."

"I know." Sabina tilted a shoulder. "But if I get back to the city, I can avoid the suitors. They're all coming to Baiae now on vacation, and they'll be underfoot everywhere. Father, are there any oysters left?"

"They'd go away if you picked one," Marcus pointed out.

"I intend to pick the whole dish." Sabina scooped into the oysters.

"I meant if you picked a suitor. As you well know."

"Who *are* you going to choose, Sabina?" Calpurnia took a little silver knife to split the skin on another pomegranate.

"I wonder," Sabina said placidly.

"You are leaving it rather late, you know. Eighteen years old—there's plenty who have a baby already by your age."

"Trying to get rid of me?"

"Nonsense," her father protested. "I've never been in favor of these young marriages. Eighteen is young enough."

"Not too much longer before I choose." Sabina cracked another oyster. "But I would like another month or two of peace. Tribune Hadrian has been very persistent."

"I thought you liked Hadrian now. You talk for hours every time he visits."

"He talks for hours, anyway," Marcus shook his head, amused. "He does love the sound of his own voice."

"I don't mind," Sabina said. "He's quite interesting if I can get him talking about his travels. He's been all over Hispania and Gaul—Father, can't you just accept the next provincial governorship you get offered, so I could go somewhere interesting like Hispania or Gaul? Or Egypt—"

"I don't know about Hadrian," Calpurnia said doubtfully. "He's very charming, to be sure—"

"Of course he's charming to you," Sabina said. "He thinks you're the pearl of Roman womanhood."

"Yes, and very nice of him to say so. I like a man who has a way with pretty compliments—"

"Do I sense a reproof?" Marcus wondered.

"—and Hadrian's distinguished as well as charming, so he's sure to have a fine career ahead of him. *But*—" Calpurnia held up a pink-stained finger, just like her husband when he pounced in the Senate with a legal loophole. "Hadrian comes with a mother-in-law."

"His mother's dead," Sabina objected.

"But the Empress isn't," Calpurnia said ominously. "And she had the raising of him, more than his own mother did. Believe me, you do *not* want Empress Plotina for a mother-in-law."

"So that's why you married me?" Marcus laughed. "Not for pretty compliments, but because my mother was safely in her grave?"

"Oh, be serious, both of you." Calpurnia captured little Linus's plump fist and waved it for attention. "The last thing any young wife needs, Vibia Sabina, is her mother-in-law's nose poked over her shoulder criticizing her housekeeping, her character, and her children." Shuddering. "And Empress Plotina has a very long nose."

"So, an interfering mother-in-law," Sabina agreed. "Any other objections to Hadrian?"

"He has a far from spotless reputation. He's keeping a singer in very luxurious lodgings on the Aventine, and—well, not in front of the children." Calpurnia raised her eyebrows. "Not to mention that he's eight years older than you."

"You're one to talk!" Sabina laughed. "How old was Father when you married him, Calpurnia? Sixty-three?"

"That's different. Your father was settled, steady, and ready to marry; a man of twenty-six is not. And I was madly in love with your father, and you aren't in love with Hadrian or anyone else as far as I can tell—"

"I'm too old for this bantering," Marcus protested, and as Sabina had hoped, the discussion descended into lighthearted family teasing, and by the following afternoon she was loading her books and gowns into a palanquin for the journey back to Rome.

"Oh, dear," she whispered to her father as one of the older heavyset guards tramped out with his spear to act as escort. "Do you suppose I could have Vix instead, Father? I want to go on a great many long walks this summer, and I always worry that Celsus will throw his back out if he has to do anything harder than lifting a wine cup . . . yes, that would be nice, thank you—" She hadn't really decided what to do about Vix, but it would be good to have him on hand.

Just in case.

"Bliss," Sabina said as she came into the quiet summer-dusked house on the Capitoline Hill, shaking the travel dust out of her dress. "No visitors, no family. All alone at last." As much as she loved her father and Calpurnia and the children . . . well, all she seemed to crave lately was quiet. Space. Time—to herself, to think, to decide. So many things to decide, it seemed lately.

"Fruit on the terrace, Quintus," Sabina told her father's steward. "After that, you may please yourself. Go to the races, go to the games, go to the taverns; we're all free now."

TITUS

Titus Aurelius Fulvus Boionius Arrius Antoninus took a deep breath and looked his father in the eye. "Any advice?"

His father stared back, kindly but silent.

"I haven't really done this before, you know," Titus said. "Gone courting a girl, I mean. I called on her once before, but she wasn't there. She's back now, so I don't really have any more excuses to dodge this. I could use a few tips."

His father looked encouraging, but stayed silent. That was the problem when your father was dead, and all you had was a marble bust of him mounted on a plinth in the atrium.

Titus straightened his thin shoulders. "Well, wish me luck."

He checked his toga for stains, rearranged the folds over his arm, tried vainly to smooth down the tuft of hair that kicked up on the back of his head no matter how short he told the barber to razor it. The last time he'd gone calling on Senator Norbanus's daughter, he'd tried desperately to flatten his hair down with goose grease, and his grandfather had told him he looked like a Bithynian bum-boy. "No need to trick yourself out, lad! Your name will do the trick; her father and I are like brothers. I've already spoken to him; now all you have to do is charm the girl a bit."

Titus sighed. His friends at school complained about tight-fisted fathers, unsympathetic uncles, demanding grandfathers. But Titus had a grandfather who thought he was perfect and a father who had *been* perfect and was now dead, and that was far harder to live up to. It was absolutely no use telling his grandfather that an heiress related to the Emperor and courted by half of Rome was not going to be impressed by a boy of sixteen with nothing to boast but an armload of violets and six unpronounceable names. She'd probably laugh him right off her doorstep.

"You're in luck today," the broad-shouldered young guard told him. "She's in the library. I'll show you back."

"Thank you for the advice about the violets," Titus said, lengthening his stride to keep up with the guard's long swaggering steps. He dearly wished for a little swagger himself.

"She likes sort of ordinary flowers instead of stiff fancy ones," the guard answered. "I told that bugger Tribune Hadrian she goes mad for lilies, the big expensive ones, and now he sends so many she feeds them to the horses." A chuckle. "She can't stand the smell."

"Tribune Hadrian?" Titus's grandfather really thought he could win out over men like Tribune Hadrian with his distinguished voice and rising career and oceans of poise? *I'm sunk.*

The guard clapped him on the shoulder. "Good luck."

"Thank you," Titus gulped, and marched into the library before his courage failed him.

Well. Vibia Sabina didn't *look* like the kind of girl being courted by half of Rome. He'd met her before, even been introduced, but she'd been dressed up and quiet at her father's side; a senator's daughter just like any other. Now she was lying on the floor of the library on her stomach, hair hanging over one shoulder, crunching on an apple. She had maps spread out all around her, and she was apparently drawing a line across them with a stylus. She looked up at Titus, and he saw she had blue eyes.

"Oh no." Her voice was mild. "Not another one."

"Sorry?"

"I take it you're a suitor? I'm sorry, I don't mean to be rude. But I'm not really in the mood to be proposed to today."

"I'm not in the mood to do any proposing," Titus surprised himself by saying just as frankly. "Why don't you just turn me down now so I can go away?"

A dimple appeared by the corner of her mouth. "Shouldn't I know whom I'm turning down first?"

He bowed. "Titus Aurelius Fulvus Boionius Arrius Antoninus."

"Vibia Sabina." She held out her hand; he took it and she scrambled up. "Pardon the mess. I'm planning a trip across the Empire, and I'm trying to work out whether to go east to west or west to east."

"'They change the sky, not their soul, who run across the sea,'" Titus said before he could stop himself.

"What?"

"Sorry. Just quoting Horace; it's a bad habit."

"So where would you start?" she pressed. "In the west, with Britannia? Or in the east, with Syria?"

"I'm afraid I can't help you. I don't much want to go to either one."

"Oh dear, I really will have to turn you down. I must have a husband who travels." She disposed of the half-eaten apple and waved him to a seat. "I suppose your father sent you to court me?"

"My grandfather." Titus perched on the edge of a couch, noticing how easily Sabina curled up in the chair opposite. She had a fragile silver chain about one ankle, and her feet were bare. "My father is dead."

"Yes—come to think of it, I've heard of him."

"Everyone has," Titus sighed. "He was a great man."

"Hard to live up to, isn't it?" Sabina smiled. "I think my brother will find it hard, when he grows up. Girls have it easier. I don't have to follow in my father's footsteps, just adore him." She clapped her hands. "Well, let's hear that marriage proposal."

"I thought you were going to turn it down."

"Well, I am. Sorry about that. But I've gotten to be a bit of a connoisseur of proposals lately, so perhaps I can help you with yours. Then you won't be so nervous the next time you have to do this."

Titus felt the tension ebb in his stomach as he started to get the flow of this odd conversation. "How do we start?"

"Well, normally you won't be proposing to the girl herself," Sabina instructed. "I'm an odd case, since my father is letting me vet my own suitors. In future you'll more likely go to the girl's father. So just pretend I'm an old man scowling at you censoriously over a desk"—she straightened, furrowing her brows into a glower—"and give me a list of all your good qualities."

"Is that how it's done?" Titus rested his bony elbows on his knees, thoughtful. "If it were my daughter, and I were the one vetting her suitors, I think I'd want to hear about their *bad* qualities."

"Points for originality." Sabina pushed her hair behind her ears. "So? Let's hear about your flaws."

"Well, to start, I'm just sixteen years old," he said. "Just finished my education, so obviously I have no career yet. And no money except an allowance from my grandfather, so I can't offer you a house of your own."

"Go on."

"I'm a dreadful stick," he confessed. "I'm not witty. I'm not brilliant. I'm certainly not handsome. I never have anything original to say, so I just quote other people. Like Horace. Cato too; I'm terribly boring about Cato."

"You're doing very well at this," Sabina approved. "Keep going."

"I expect I'll have the usual sort of career—tribune, quaestor, praetor, and so forth. But I'm a thoroughgoing plodder, so I doubt I'll ever bring much luster to the family name."

"Does that worry you?" Her smile was gone; she looked serious.

"Not really," he found himself saying quite honestly. "The Empire runs because of plodders. I'll do my work, and I'll do it well. But I won't rise high—I'll just serve. No wife of mine is going to end up an empress, that's certain." He spread his hands. "That's all, I suppose. There isn't much to say about someone as insignificant as me."

Sabina tilted her head to one side. "I give up," she said at last. "You need no help from me in learning how to propose marriage. Just give that same speech to the right girl, and she'll fall headlong into your lap."

He grinned and looked down, smoothing a hand back over his cow-lick. "You're sure you won't marry me?" he asked, looking up. "I may not be very keen on going to Syria, but I think we'd have a good time together anyway."

"I'm tempted." Sabina rose. "But you'd find me a very unsatisfactory wife in the long run. I hate parties, I love adventures, and I'm very fond of getting my own way. If you gave me all your faults, it's only fair you know mine."

"I like your faults." He rose too, holding out the armload of violets. "I suppose we never like the people with the right faults to match our own, do we? It's always the unsuitable person we want instead."

"Yes, it is." She looked thoughtful at that. "Sometimes a *very* unsuit-able person."

"Have you got your eye on one?" he said a little wistfully.

"Thank you for the flowers." She buried her nose in the bouquet. "I love violets."

"Your guard said you did."

"Vix?" She chuckled. "How nice of him. I shall have to find some way of saying thank you."

VIX

"Vix?"

I halted abruptly in my hazy stumble across the gardens. Night had fallen, and there was no moon telling me who had called my name. My hand slipped to the short sword I still carried by habit at my belt, even when I just went out for a quick drink. "Who's there?"

"Just me." The vague shape of an arm waved over the blackness of the grass.

"Lady Sabina?" I took a step forward.

"Don't stab me." Another movement in the dark and I made her out: stretched full length in the grass, waving a lazy hand overhead.

My hand loosened on the sword hilt. "What are you doing out here?"

"It's the first night in a week it hasn't rained."

True, it had been a hot, wet string of days. Warm air had wrapped the city like a damp wool cloak ever since we'd returned from Baiae, and almost every night it had rained in a hot restless flood that ran fitfully over the rooftop gutters without relieving the heat. No wonder the rich preferred their seaside villas. I had a fleeting yearning for Baiae with its uppity whores and cool sea breezes, but I took another step into the dry grass of the garden. "What are you doing here, Lady?"

For the past week she'd been holed up with her books and maps in her father's study, while her nurse fussed at her with fans and cold drinks and the few remaining suitors still in the city drifted off to cooler breezes and less elusive targets. But my eyes had grown accustomed to the dark now, and I saw the senator's daughter stretched out flat on her back on the grass, ankles crossed and arms folded under her head. "I'm stargazing." She tilted her chin at me. "Is that wine you've got?"

"Um. Yes, I brought a jug from the tavern." Hoping I could get the freckled maid named Gaia to drink with me and maybe let me under her blankets again. "It's my night off, I wasn't coming on duty drunk—"

"I'm not the steward, Vix. I'm not going to scold you. Not if you let me have some."

"It's unwatered."

"Really? My father won't let me drink wine, much less unwatered wine."

"He shouldn't. It's very strong."

She sat up in the grass. "Give it over, then."

I sat down in the grass, handing over my jug. The garden had turned to shadows all around—jasmine bushes in fragrant shadows, something silvery and night-blooming in paler shadows, columns framing everything in tall shadows—but there were no torches. The rest of the household had long since gone to bed. "No cups," I warned.

She took a swallow straight from the jug, and shuddered. "Ugh. I can see why civilized people water it."

"Give it back, then. Unwatered wine is for barbarians like me."

She took another optimistic swallow and handed back the jug. I took a long drink myself, tilting my head back. No moon, but no clouds either—just stars, thousands of them, and I wondered if Romans in their legions had as many men as there were stars in the sky.

"Vercingetorix, if I asked you something, would you tell me?"

I sat up straighter, a little self-conscious. "Of course, Lady."

"Good. Tell me what happened the day I kissed you, six years back."

"What does it matter?" I plucked a blade of grass by my foot, plucked another. "We were just children. What were you, twelve?"

"Vix. We met by chance, and I kissed you, and I went home. While I waited at home, my brother died, and my mother died, and the Emperor of Rome died. And my father came home looking like death, and told me there was a new Emperor."

"What makes you think I'd know anything about it?"

"Everyone knew the Young Barbarian was Emperor Domitian's pet. And the Young Barbarian vanished as soon as Domitian was dead."

I made a movement to get up from the grass, but her cool small hand caught my wrist. I tugged away. "Ask your father what happened, Lady."

"He says the Emperor was murdered by a slave with a grievance. He says my brother died a hero. He says my mother died in the chaos."

"Your father's a good man. He wouldn't lie."

"Yes, but he does omit a truth now and then. It's the best way to lie without actually lying." She was a dim shape in the darkness, just a shadow of an oval face and plaited hair and bare arms. "Please, Vix."

I took a swig of wine out of the jug, and then another. "I locked your mother in a closet," I began slowly, and that whole strange day spilled out when an emperor had died, my parents killed him, and I'd been witness to it all. There were gaps in places—gaps where I had to reconstruct what happened from things my mother said, gaps where I just didn't want to go on because all in all it had been a hellish day and one I wished I could forget. But the senator's daughter waited in the dark, wordless until I was done, and her first question surprised me.

"Your parents got away?"

I hesitated, thinking of the rambling villa on the mist-wrapped mountaintop where my mother raised babies and my father tortured his garden, both dead to Rome and happy to be that way. I hesitated, but Sabina's smile came through the dark.

"Good."

She took the jug from my hand and took a healthy swig. "Gods, that's vile. Did my brother really die a hero?"

"Yes." I'd liked her older brother, a black-haired officer in the Praetorians who had tried to do his best by everybody. It never worked, doing that, but he'd tried anyway. "He *was* a hero."

"I miss him." Sabina drew up her knees, resting her folded arms on top. "A girl likes having a brother."

"You have Linus."

"Yes, but he's my *little* brother. As long as he lives, I'll be the one watching out for him. A big brother, now—a girl always knows she's safe."

"He threatened to take my head off for kissing you," I remembered. "Told me to keep my grubby hands off."

"See, there you go."

"Sorry about your mother." I swigged from the jug. "The closet, and all."

"I'm not," Sabina said. "She wasn't much of a mother. Wasn't much of a human being, truth be told."

"Well, no." Her mother had been a bitch of the first order, and I was glad Sabina didn't look like her even though she'd been a beauty, because I couldn't have kissed any girl who looked like *that* she-viper. "I don't know who killed her in that closet, though," I added. "Wasn't me."

"She had a lot of enemies. In all the chaos, someone saw a chance." Sabina tugged the jug out of my hand. "This disgusting wine is growing on me."

"It does that."

She took a swallow and lay back in the grass. "Thank you for telling me, Vix."

"Glad I could." I slid down on one elbow, cocking my head back at the dark sky. "You like stargazing?"

"Yes. Makes everything down here very small."

"An astrologer read my stars once." The same day Emperor Domitian had died, actually. "He said I'd have a legion someday, and that I'd be called Vercingetorix the Red."

"Did you believe him?"

"Don't know. He was a funny little man—tubby and cheerful, not like you picture an astrologer. But the things he said had a habit of coming true."

Sabina was still gazing up into the sky. "I don't think I believe in reading the stars. Why would the gods bother laying out our lives for us? I think they'd rather keep us in suspense."

"I believe in *my* stars. I'll make them go where I want."

She regarded me thoughtfully. "I think you actually could."

I tilted my head up. "Good stars tonight."

"Vix."

"What?"

"Are you going to kiss me now? Or do we have to talk about stars some more?"

I thought about how to answer that, yes or no, and neither one seemed right. So I just leaned down and kissed her, tasting wine but smelling dry grass and summer. Her breast filled my hand, and her cool fingers were tracing their unhurried circles again on the back of my neck, and this time there was no indignant Roman housewife to bang me on the head and stop me from pulling the dress off Sabina's shoulder. I buried my mouth in her neck, tugging her fine hair out of its careless plait so it spread on the grass, and that was when her hand moved to my chest, pushing me firmly back.

"So that's it for tonight?" I flopped on my back, not resigned but not exactly surprised either. Still, if I'd gotten a kiss last time and a kiss plus a breast this time, then maybe next time . . . "Where are you going? We can talk about stars, have some more of this awful wine—"

"Shut up, Vix. You want to wake the whole house?" She got to her feet, brushing bits of grass off her skirt, and offered me her hand.

I squinted up at her. "What are you doing, Lady?"

She grabbed my hand. "Come with me."

"Where are we going?" I asked as she tugged me through the atrium and then down a darkened passage.

"Your room. Fewer questions if there's blood. This way?"

"Blood?" I felt like a squawking parrot, always a step behind and echoing everything she said. We were tiptoeing past the darkened kitchens now, toward my little chamber.

"It's my understanding there's blood sometimes after this sort of thing," she explained in a whisper. "The first time, anyway. Now, no one will ask any questions if there's blood in your bed, since you're always stumbling in with cuts and scrapes after getting into fights. But my bed? That's just the kind of thing nosy slave girls are always looking for."

My head was spinning and not from the wine. "You've been— thinking this out, haven't you?"

"Of course I have. For quite a while, actually. Is this it?" She pointed at a narrow door.

"Yes." I'd left the shutter open inside my chamber, and light flickered on the wall from the guttering torch at the back gate outside as I drew her in. She laid her hands on my shoulders and walked me backward until the bed's edge at my knees made me sit, and in a flash of torchlight I saw her smile, a slow delighted smile that crinkled her blue eyes. Amid the shock I'd been thinking sudden cautious thoughts about this good job I had, about Senator Norbanus and the penalties that would await me for touching his daughter, but everything fled after that smile. I pulled her into my lap and began kissing her again and her mouth opened sweetly under mine. "Why?" I muttered. "Why me?" Because this was more than I ever thought I'd get, more than I should get because girls like her just didn't *do* this. "Why?"

"Vix, can we talk later?" Her lips moved to my ear. "I'm a little nervous about this, after all, and I'd rather we got on with it."

I got on with it, because when you're nineteen and you've got a girl pulling your head down and her skirts up, you stop asking questions. I gave up and laid her back on the narrow bed.

"Be gentle," I'd been told once. By my mother, of all people, after I'd gotten caught two years ago in a compromising position with a neighboring farmer's daughter. My father growled and said he'd thrash me if I got anyone pregnant, but my mother gave me a little sound advice, and some of it was, "Be gentle with girls, especially if they're new to it." Not advice I'd ever had a chance to use, since the girl who'd yanked me headlong into the pleasures of the flesh had been a cheerful big-boned Brigantian three years my senior who had been dragging boys off to her favorite haystack for years, and the girls I'd had afterward were all in the same general mold. But somewhere in the soft dark with the flickering torchlight shadows, I remembered the part about being gentle, and I tried my best. Don't know how well I did, because at one point Sabina took a deep sudden breath and gripped her lip in her teeth.

I froze. "Did I hurt you?"

"A bit," she said, her voice beneath me incongruous in the dark. "But don't stop, please." She twined her arms about my neck, drawing me closer, and I kissed her again as I tried to remember to be slow, to be gentle, until the point when I forgot everything including her name and probably my own.

Afterward we lay in a sweaty silence that might have been awkward, except that Sabina was never awkward. "Goodness," she said, lacing her fingers comfortably through mine. "I think I can see what all the fuss is about."

"Sorry if you hurt. I didn't mean—"

"No, I'm just a bit sore. No blood, I think." She sounded pleased. "And now I've got the hang of it, I'm sure I'll be better next time."

"Next time?" I picked my head off the pillow.

"Yes, please." She snuggled her head against my shoulder. "If you don't mind?"

"No," I laughed up into the dark, bemused. "Most girls don't put it that way, though. You're an odd one, Lady."

"I think you can call me Sabina now."

"Sabina." I felt strange suddenly, despite the comfort of her body pressed against mine in the dark. "You didn't answer my question."

"What question?"

"Why me? Why at all? Girls like you don't go giving it up to a bodyguard."

She gave that chuckle low in her throat, the one I already knew I liked. "You'd be surprised."

"Don't think so. Most well-born girls, they save everything for their husbands, or at least they're supposed to. What's your reason?"

"Maybe it's just you." She twined herself over my chest in the dark to kiss me again. "You are rather lovable, Vix." Her fine hair curtained my face, and I slid my hands over her smooth waist and forgot the question.

Stupid boy. Vibia Sabina never did anything without a reason.

CHAPTER 5

SABINA

What a pity, Sabina reflected, that Vix couldn't lie.

Oh, he *could* lie, but he was useless at it. His face flamed up till it looked as russet as his head, and after that he started hooking his thumbs into his belt and stammering. She'd nearly groaned aloud when she last saw him talking to her father.

"Fine day, isn't it?" Marcus had said absently as Vix came dashing up to the litter still tugging his sword belt into place. "Not so hot."

"No, Dominus."

Sabina had been loitering beside the litter after getting her own good-bye kiss and could clearly see the flush start to rise from Vix's collar.

"I understand you've had a wet summer? Pity for you my daughter was so insistent about staying in the city. Baiae was much more agreeable."

"We've kept busy," Sabina had said, bland, and Vix threw her an appalled glance over Marcus's head that nearly had her laughing aloud.

"Good, good. Lend a limping old man a pair of strong arms, would you?"

They had handed her father up into the litter, and Sabina hoped he would be too preoccupied with the upcoming business of the Senate to give a thought to his bodyguard's apple-colored face.

"Are you mad?" Vix hissed as the litter retreated down the street. "We'll never get away with this, not now that they're back from Baiae!"

"Yes, we will." She gave a blink of her lashes instead of a kiss. "I'll be down tonight."

"A houseful of slaves, that suspicious old bag of a nurse who chaperones you—your stepmother sees everything—the senator, he *knows* everything!" Vix raked a hand through his hair, leaving it standing on end. "Someone'll see, and then all hell will break loose."

"I don't think so," Sabina mused. "My father would be very disappointed in me, of course, but I doubt he'd flog me or exile me from the family."

"And what about me? I'm off to the galleys for deflowering a senator's daughter—"

"No, because we won't get caught." Vix might be a terrible liar, but that didn't mean Sabina was. Hadn't she grown up seeing her father work on his fellow senators in pursuit of some new law or edict, so expertly they didn't even know they were being strummed like harps? Hadn't she seen the effort that went into all that expert strumming, the preparation and care that backed all her father's plays in the Senate?

By comparison, a clandestine love affair was child's play.

"Well, not child's play," she explained that night as Vix let her through his door. She tossed herself down on the moonlit bed, crossing her arms behind her head to look up at him. "It just takes a certain amount of groundwork, that's all. Like taking a few weeks to establish myself among the slaves as a bad sleeper—one regularly to be found slipping out of her room on a hot night to read in her father's study."

"Have you been slipping out seeing someone else?" Vix scowled down at her, arms folded. "Like that skinny boy Titus you're so taken with? Not that I understand why—"

"Don't be silly, Vix, I really *was* reading in my father's study. You have to be caught a few times in innocent pastimes," Sabina explained, "before you can move on to the guilty ones. Next, I made a habit of slipping down to the kitchens after these midnight reads to grab a snack before going back to bed. The kitchens that are just a dozen feet or so from your door."

A grin was starting to tug at Vix's mouth, but he refused to give in to it yet. "So?"

"So, there is not one slave in this house who will blink at finding me out of my own bed at night, sneaking through the slave quarters toward the kitchens."

"It's no guarantee," Vix warned. "The wrong person at the wrong time—"

"I've made an offering to Fortuna, to give us luck," Sabina said. "And sacrificed a rather nice pearl bracelet for hard coin, in case we need to bribe a nosy slave."

"You've thought of everything, haven't you?" Vix gave in to the grin, unbuckling his sword and tossing it into one corner.

"Why do you think it took me so long to come back from Baiae?" Sabina sat up and began taking the pins out of her hair. "You wouldn't believe how much groundwork I had to lay. In the first place it took quite a few days planting clues so my father would offer you the body-guard job—"

"I thought that might be your idea."

"Of course it was, but he had to think it was *his* idea, and he's quite clever so I had to take my time about it." She shook her hair down around her shoulders. "Then I had to find out what I could do to pre-vent babies—"

Vix coughed. "*What?*"

"Babies, Vix. This is what causes them, or so I'm told. You wouldn't believe how long it took me to find out what worked. Calpurnia wants a dozen children so she doesn't use anything, and she doesn't have any of the more loose-moraled friends who might be informative. My mother must have known a useful trick or two . . . anyway, I finally had to consult some helpful whores. They recommended a sort of pessary from Egypt, supposed to be infallible—"

Vix dived onto the bed, pinning her down. Sabina obliged him by struggling, and he forced her arms apart effortlessly. He kissed the space between her collarbones, his favorite spot, then followed his way up to her ear. "You're a born schemer, aren't you?"

"Oh, yes." Sabina kissed him back for a while and then started to tell him about the rest of her scheming—she really felt quite smug when she thought how handily she'd managed everything, and wouldn't have minded a little applause. That trip to the brothel for advice about babies had been hair-raising in some parts, though the whores themselves couldn't have been more helpful once they realized she was there for information and not some exotic perversion. Nice girls, really, and after giving her a jar of that Egyptian pessary they'd added all kinds of helpful tips for her upcoming seduction, including one demonstration on a wooden flute that had been quite eye-opening. But Vix started to look uneasy when she talked about her scheming.

"Do you realize what kind of trouble you could have landed yourself in?" He shifted his weight over her. "And how long *have* you been planning this, anyway?"

Since the day you kissed me after the races. Though she hadn't really made up her mind to take the final plunge until the day Titus had proposed to her. That sweet awkward boy with his unexpectedly steady eyes, saying something about wanting the one with all the wrong faults . . . it had resonated, somehow. And he complained that he could never think of anything original to say!

But Sabina decided to keep that particular thought to herself and ducked back to Vix's first question. "A very wise man once told me something about trouble." She took his hand and plaited her narrow fingers with his big rough ones. "You get in trouble no matter what you do, so you might as well do everything you can."

"Who said that?" Vix cocked his head down at her.

"Not Plato, that's for sure."

"Sounds like something I'd say."

"You *did* say it, Vercingetorix. Years ago, when we met the first time." She twined her arms about his neck. "I've never forgotten."

He shouted laughter then and grabbed her up so tight she could hardly breathe. "At least you know wisdom when you hear it."

"Blow out the lamp," Sabina giggled when she got her breath back. "And let me try something—bear in mind, I've only seen this done on a flute . . ."

VIX

Sabina. Vibia Sabina.

A pretty name. But I still had trouble using it, no matter how many times she slipped through my door, no matter how many times I held her warm and naked against me. *Sabina.* Even in the darkness of the night it still rolled awkwardly off my tongue.

And Hell's gates, there were a lot of nights.

There's nothing like being young and obsessed. There were prettier girls in the world than Sabina—overall I usually liked girls with more breast and fewer questions. But no other girl had ever dragged *me* to bed before and had her way with me. That was usually my line. But Sabina couldn't get enough of me. Me, Vercingetorix, son of a slave and a gladiator, and soon I couldn't get enough of her either. There were long hot damp days where I fidgeted at the gate through my guard duties, fidgeted through a dinner too hot and sticky for eating, fidgeted in my bed till the moon went up, and by the time the shadow slipped in and barred the door, half the blood in my veins would be smoking and I'd lunge across the room and pin her up against the wall. Afterward we'd stretch out and talk for hours, and that was something else new for me. I'd never done much talking to girls. Mostly under the blankets it was just giggling, and me trying to get out without being spotted by fathers or brothers. And it wasn't like I had much to talk about. "You're sweet, Vix," the Brigantian girl who had broken me in once said. "But you're not the brightest, are you?" I couldn't say she was wrong, but Sabina had me talking anyway.

"Brundisium," she'd say, propping her chin up on her hand in the dark. "You grew up there, didn't you? Tell me about it."

"Don't you ever get sleepy?" I yawned.

"Not when there's things to be learned. You grew up so differently from me—tell me something that happened to you when you were a child. Something funny."

I thought about that for a moment. "When I was seven years old in Brundisium, a bald man in a toga collared me on the street and offered me oysters for dinner. I knew what he really wanted, but I wasn't about to pass up free oysters."

"What happened?"

"I went back to his house with him, and as soon as I was done stuffing myself he started edging his hand up my thigh. I took his first two fingers"—demonstrating—"and yanked in opposite directions. While he was screaming and leaping around in agony, I climbed out the window."

"This is a *funny* story?"

"The way he rolled around on the floor cursing at me was funny. Served him right. I stole a very expensive vase on my way out the window too."

"You're a savage." Sabina's eyes sparkled. "Tell me more."

"I stole anything that wasn't nailed down from everybody I could find—sips of beer from the mugs in taverns, sweets from my master's kitchens, coins from beggars. And when I was eight and my mother got sold to Rome, I ran away from my master to join her. I got all the way from Brundisium to Rome on my own, hitching rides on wagons and thieving food from vendors."

"Brundisium," Sabina said, thoughtful. "I'd like to go there. Could take a ship to Greece after that. Hadrian's always talking about Greece."

"Hadrian?" I turned on one side, tugging her into the crook of my chest. "Who cares what that gorbellied bootlicker thinks?"

"He's not a bootlicker," Sabina laughed.

"He laps at your heels hard enough," I grumbled. "Why do you always take so many walks with him?"

"Because if I start turning suitors away, people are going to look for a reason why. When you're living a lie, Vix," she instructed, "you have to give people something to look at so they don't start looking anywhere else."

"Don't have to make such a good show of it, though, do you?" I demanded. "Walking arm in arm, always putting your heads together over a book—"

"Jealous?" she teased.

"No!"

Maybe a little. Sabina didn't seem to care a fig about any of her suitors except two: that shy patrician boy named Titus, who made her wrinkle her nose affectionately, and Tribune Hadrian. The skinny prat with the violets didn't worry me—he was only sixteen, and he hardly had the courage on his visits to thrust some flowers at her and stammer a few shy compliments. Hadrian, now . . . he came to call at least twice a week, and he and Sabina would walk the gardens, his big head bent down toward hers. Talking, always talking, and Sabina's little chin had the same attentive angle it did when she cocked it at me over the pillow at night.

"I don't see what there is to be jealous of," Sabina pointed out, bumping her nose gently against mine. "You think Hadrian's pouring pretty compliments into my ears? Last time we talked about architecture, and the time before that it was Greek philosophers, and before that it was the Eleusinian Mysteries."

"Exactly." All things I didn't know anything about.

"Mostly he goes on about Greece," Sabina continued, unruffled. "He keeps telling me Athens is the center of civilization, not Rome. He can go on quite a while about that. Behind his back, they call him *the Greekling.*"

"I call him *that boil-brained lout,* and I'll do it to his face."

She laughed softly in the dark. "I would like to see Athens. And Brundisium. A hundred other places."

"Rome's big enough to keep you occupied."

"And why did you come back to Rome, Vix?" She cocked her head up against my shoulder, her blue eyes just dark pools in the night. "Your parents hated it."

"I didn't."

"Rome made you a slave. Rome put you in an arena to fight for your life. Rome nearly killed you."

"That was all a madman's fault. The madman's gone now, so there's no reason for me not to come back. My father didn't want me to, but—"

"Ah."

I scowled. "What, *ah?*"

"Your father hated Rome, so you like it."

I shrugged. "A mountaintop in Brigantia might get a little small for us both. He's a big man."

"I remember. I saw him just once, up close—he was all tied up and bleeding and cold-eyed. He looked like a big wounded dog, all bound and determined that if he was going to die, his enemies were going down with him. You look like him, you know."

"I know, I know." My little brother had my mother's dark hair and eyes, but I was my father's spitting image and tired of being told about it. We had the same russet-colored hair and gray eyes, I was a finger's breadth away from his height and growing into his heavy shoulders, I was left-handed like him and had his knack with weapons, and so what? "I'm not my father."

"No, you're not," said Sabina. "You'll be a bigger man than he is someday."

"You mean taller? I'd like to be—"

"No, not taller. *Bigger.* Too big for Britannia, much less a mountaintop. Rome might not even be able to hold you."

"Thanks. I think?" I snugged her in against my shoulder, yawning, and soon drifted off to sleep.

"Dream, Vix," she whispered, or I thought she whispered. "Dream about those stars of yours, the ones that are going to lead you to glory. For all your crashing and shouting, I think you're a bigger dreamer than me."

* * *

Senator Norbanus and his family dined at the Domus Augustana once a week with the Emperor and Empress, but I never took duty those nights. There might still be slaves or guards who remembered me from the old days at Emperor Domitian's side. But as Saturnalia approached I realized I'd get my chance to see Emperor Trajan up close after all: when he and his entourage honored the Norbanus house by coming to dinner.

"I don't see what all this fuss is," Senator Norbanus said mildly, looking up from his scrolls at his madly rushing wife. "He's a soldier; he's easy to entertain. Put a slab of meat on his plate and enough beer in his mug, and he's happy."

"But Empress Plotina notices everything," Lady Calpurnia groaned, "and I won't have her wrinkling her long nose at *my* housekeeping." Very heavy now, Calpurnia went lumbering about the house trailing lists and menus and worried slaves. Even the daughter of the house was pressed into service, and I saw Sabina down in the kitchens with her hair tied up in a rag and a smudge of flour on her chin, wrestling gamely with a lump of bread dough. "Show me," she said, watching the cook's expert hands pummeling and punching. "How interesting." I hid a grin because she'd said the same thing to me last week, in exactly the same tone, when I showed her something under the blankets (never mind what).

"Gods, it's cold," she shivered, diving into my bed that night. "Warm me up."

"As my lady commands." I wrapped my arms around her. "You're late tonight."

"I was busy with Calpurnia, picking menus for the Emperor's dinner."

"I'll be glad when this bloody dinner's over."

"Don't you want to see the Emperor?"

"I've seen emperors before. Don't want to see any more."

"Liar."

She could always catch my lies. I *was* curious to see this Emperor. A soldier, they said, but the Senate doted on him as they usually didn't dote on soldiers. Popular. Intelligent. But what else was he?

Sabina poked my chest. "Can't you warm me up any more than this?"

"Doing my best, Lady . . ." I ran a hand down her bare back and lower, and as usual we'd finish all the talk by making love a few more times—nothing like nineteen for stamina—and do it all over again the night after.

"Sabina, you're looking tired these days," Calpurnia exclaimed the following morning. "Rings under your eyes! Am I working you too hard for this ridiculous Imperial dinner?"

"I just haven't been sleeping much," Sabina said, placid, and I thought I saw a sharp look from Lady Calpurnia to her stepdaughter. But if she watched Sabina, there was nothing to see. No bright glances in my direction, no attempts to brush my hand as she went by in the halls, no more than the friendly interest she gave all the slaves and freedmen. The same friendly interest she gave me when we'd met in her father's atrium that first time, and at the races afterward . . . not much changed from the interest I got now, really, in between the rest of it.

And a good thing, really. I'd had one or two girls get moony over me before, and it just made things uncomfortable. Moony girls always started pressing to see how you felt back, and usually the result was floods of tears for her and a slapped face for me. Nothing moony about Sabina, and that was good. I might not be able to get enough of her, but I certainly wasn't moony about her myself. To be honest, I didn't know what I felt about Sabina. So, good thing she was sensible.

Very good thing.

CHAPTER 6

PLOTINA

Sometimes Plotina despaired, she truly did. Nearly five years now her husband had been Emperor of Rome, and would he ever learn to act like it?

"So pleased to see you," Plotina murmured to Senator Norbanus and his wife as they entered the atrium, but Trajan's shout of greeting drowned her out.

"Marcus! You limping brilliant bastard, happy Saturnalia!"

Plotina cast her eyes to the heavens as her husband enveloped Senator Norbanus in a bear hug. The senator just looked amused as the Emperor of Rome set him back on his feet.

"Gods' bones, Calpurnia, you look ready to drop that foal any minute." Trajan kissed his hostess's cheeks soundly. "If it's a boy, name it after me and I'll do something nice for it. Better yet, name it after his big brother—Paulinus was the best man I ever knew, far better than I—"

Plotina lifted a hand to signal their entourage. Quite a crowd had joined them at Senator Norbanus's dinner party that evening: senators and their coiffed wives, giggling girls and laughing young men, sleek pretty page boys, red-and-gold Praetorians, and Trajan's ever-present tail of blunt-spoken legates and legionary officers. "You cannot always travel in a cloud of soldiers," Plotina had protested many times.

"Why not? Ensures I never get bored."

And of course so many of his retinue of soldiers were *handsome* men. Really, her husband's private arrangements were none of her business, but why couldn't he just bed pliant little slave boys as most men of his tastes did? Then she wouldn't have all these hulking figures with their armor and their rough accents cluttering up her parties.

"Empress Plotina," Lady Calpurnia was exclaiming. "How lovely you look. You'd put Juno to shame in those emeralds."

"I care nothing for jewels." Plotina bent her head to brush cheeks with Marcus's little wife in her blue silks. "I had none at all until I entered the palace. I never saw how a truly thrifty wife could stomach the ostentation."

"Well, I find jewelry very comforting during these late months." Calpurnia rubbed her rounded stomach, sapphires at her ears and throat winking like blue eyes in the lamplight. "None of my gowns fit anymore, but at least my necklaces still do."

Pregnant *again*—Marcus certainly hadn't wasted any time. Such a levelheaded man, really the backbone of the Senate, but everyone knew what a fool he was for his wife (and at his age too!). Though Calpurnia was a nice little thing, if prone to levity. Not to mention the occasional display of *bosom*. "Lady Calpurnia, I do hope you will forgive my husband looking like a peasant? I simply could not stuff him into a proper synthesis for dinner."

"I'm strangled half the day in a damned toga," Trajan complained good-naturedly. "I knew Marcus wouldn't mind if an old soldier abandoned custom for once and made himself comfortable."

"Men." Plotina lifted pointed eyebrows to Calpurnia. The atrium was filled with guests now, drifting and chattering, the women tinkling laughter over the lower rumble of male voices, backed by the trickle of water in the central fountain and the plucking of lutes from an alcove. Trajan was already laughing loudest of all, making jokes, clapping backs hard enough to flatten them. "He's such a child," Plotina said to Calpurnia. "Most men are, I find, but some more than others. Perhaps I might steal you a moment for a real discussion? I've a matter of great importance—"

"Of course, Empress. Wine?"

"Barley water. I never touch wine." Didn't everyone know that?

The two women fell into promenade along the colonnaded end of the atrium. Calpurnia paused here and there to direct a slave, drop a quiet word in her steward's ear, greet a guest, give a murmur of instruction—"go rescue Marcus from that crushing old bore Servianus, will you?"—and Plotina gave a regal nod to the curtsies that followed her in a ripple across the room. "It's about your stepdaughter."

"I knew you'd notice Sabina's lateness," Calpurnia said ruefully. "I'm sure she's still primping. You know how girls are."

Certainly not. Plotina had never primped before a mirror in her life, girl or not. But she brushed that aside. The matter had to be settled, and it might as well be settled tonight. "Vibia Sabina's marriage. Surely it's been put off long enough."

"I'm afraid she hasn't made up her mind. Marcus means to let her have her own way—within reason, of course."

"Senator Norbanus is far too lax with her. It is not for a green girl to make such an important decision."

"Sabina has a good head on her shoulders." Calpurnia smiled. "Far wiser than I was at her age."

Plotina felt the beginnings of a headache at her temples, right where the coiled bands of her hair had been anchored down with long pins. When the headaches really came, the pins felt like they were boring all the way through her skull. "I will speak frankly, Calpurnia. Dear Publius is besotted with her."

"Is he?" Calpurnia sounded noncommittal. "Really."

"He is." Plotina forced herself to take a sip of barley water. "And I do not like to see him thwarted. Clearly he is the best possible husband for your stepdaughter." For any girl, anywhere on earth.

"He's certainly a fine young man, Empress."

He is a perfect young man, Plotina wanted to snap. *Your stepdaughter should be on her knees thanking the gods for such a husband.* "Perhaps you could drop a word in her ear. A line from you would surely stop all this dithering."

"Oh, Sabina never dithers." Calpurnia paused to speak to two slave girls; they curtsied and began circulating with fresh cups and trays of fruit.

"A word to your husband, then." Plotina tightened her arm through Calpurnia's, woman to woman. "It won't take much, I'm sure. All Rome knows you can twist him around your little finger."

"I'm sure I don't know what you mean." Calpurnia's voice cooled.

"It's quite simple. You have only to make him take his daughter in hand."

"I wouldn't know how to *make* Marcus do anything, Empress. And I don't wish to learn."

It was not good manners to roll one's eyes, but Plotina was tempted. Didn't the woman know how the game was played? Men bellowed laughter at parties like this one, talking so importantly in the middle of the room, thinking they were making their laws. The women walked the edges of the room, letting them have the glory. Silent and respectful, of course, as was a wife's duty. But it was also a wife's duty to make sure the right decisions trickled down from all that masculine furor. Did such a thing need explaining?

Apparently to *some.*

"I'm sorry if Sabina is taking too long with her decision to suit either Hadrian or you, Empress." Calpurnia's voice was no more than polite now. "But her father is not inclined to rush her, and neither am I. If you will excuse me, I think I see my cook hopping about trying to get my attention. I do hope he hasn't burned the snails."

She threaded swiftly away through her guests, and Plotina stood gripping her cup of barley water beside a vine-veiled statue of Pan. She never should have trusted Marcus Norbanus's wife to help Dear Publius—the woman was clearly nothing but a simple-minded little breeder.

Plotina raised a hand to her head and massaged her temple. A headache was definitely coming on, one of the bad ones that pressed in whenever people *thwarted* her. If people knew how much it hurt, they simply wouldn't do it.

"Sabina!" Trajan gave a shout of welcome as a figure in silver drifted into the atrium. "Little Sabina, you're late."

"I hope you'll forgive me, Caesar?" The girl bowed, then stood on tiptoe to kiss his cheek.

"Of course not; I missed you." He gave her a hug too, then stood back approvingly. "You're a pretty thing, Vibia Sabina. I can see why half my officers want to marry you."

They can't have her, Plotina wanted to spit. *She is for my Publius, does no one see that? For my Publius.*

Publius's voice at her shoulder soothed her, so deep and cultured and authoritative. "I am hard-pressed to decide whether my Empress or my future wife looks the more beautiful this evening."

"Flatterer." Plotina offered her cheek to be kissed. That beard: He still hadn't gotten rid of it, but he did look very distinguished in his fine linen synthesis, calm and handsome with a chased silver goblet in one hand and a seal ring glinting on one finger. He nodded to some acquaintance hailing him across the room but lingered at Plotina's side.

"I must thank you, you know. You were right about Vibia Sabina— I see now she will be the perfect wife for me." A smile gleamed in the close-cropped beard. "I should never have doubted your judgment."

"Sometimes I doubt it myself." Only to Dear Publius would she ever admit such a thing. The Mother of Rome must never have doubts. "I understand the girl is still stringing you along—I'd hoped to see it settled by now."

"On the contrary. The delay gives me a chance to know her." Hadrian looked across the room at Sabina, cornered between two tribunes and looking politely bored. "And I like what I see."

"I don't." The girl would not get one word of approval out of Plotina until she became Dear Publius's wife. Then she would be as a daughter, but now she was a nuisance. "I don't like the dress." There wasn't really anything to fault in the narrow silvery gray gown with its high neck, but somehow it looked . . .

"The word you want is *glamorous*." Hadrian swirled the wine in his cup, thoughtful. "The other girls here tonight aimed merely for *pretty*. And in ten years or so they will look like their mothers—fat and over-painted. Not my Sabina."

"How nice you've come to like her," Plotina said tightly.

"I remember meeting that monstrous mother of hers once or twice," Hadrian continued. "The woman was appalling, but one couldn't deny she had style. She had a very effective way of gliding into a room . . . Vibia Sabina seems unlike her in most respects, but she does have style. Even better, she has a mind. Given a few years"—Hadrian lifted his cup in an appreciative toast—"she might be quite a collector's item."

"Hmph." Plotina closed her eyes. Her temples were pounding now—the room was loud—and the guests were streaming into the triclinium to eat. "Take me in to dine," she told Dear Publius, who at once offered his arm. "I must do my duty, even if I can't eat a bite. I have *such* a headache."

TITUS

Some discreet elbowing went on, Titus noticed, as the guests took their places on the dining couches to eat. Everyone wanted to be at the Emperor's side on the couch of honor, heaped with silk pillows and draped with ivy. No one, on the other hand, seemed quite so eager to share cushions with the Empress. And a whole cluster of young men were jostling to eat beside Vibia Sabina. Tribune Hadrian claimed the place on her left, but Titus (by stepping firmly on a young aedile's foot) managed to stake out the couch on her right. "Hello," he said to her. "You look quite wonderful." The girl he saw on his periodic shy visits, usually flopped in the library in a careless braid and a plain tunic, had given way to a very sophisticated creature indeed: a gleaming nymph reclining on a silk-cushioned couch, her dress narrow and silvery and short enough to show her ankles, her hair brushed up very high and sleek. No jewels, not like the other girls decked out to glitter for the suitors—just one earring like the Egyptians wore, an elaborate silver earring that reached her shoulder and winked garnets. "I'm glad you didn't look like this when I proposed to you," Titus told her frankly. "I'd never have gotten the words out."

Sabina laughed, but Tribune Hadrian on her other side just frowned. The first stream of slaves were entering with silver dishes, and the smells of roast pork and smoked oysters uncoiled in tantalizing whiffs. "Who are you, young man?"

"Titus Aurelius Fulvus Boionius—"

"Yes, I've heard of you. Of your father, rather. Shouldn't you still be in school?" Tribune Hadrian turned his attention on Sabina, dismissing Titus altogether. "I'd hoped to continue our discussion on the architectural studies of Apollodorus, Vibia Sabina. I don't care for his domes at all—"

Titus never got another word in after that. Hadrian claimed Sabina with an ease Titus envied. *Oh, to be twenty-six instead of sixteen. To be charming instead of shy.* To be a man of the world reclining easily at Sabina's side like this; speaking with just the right blend of intelligence and humor; offering her the choice bites from each dish with just the right air of insouciance; knowing exactly how often to touch her wrist with one finger to draw a bubble of intimacy around their conversation. *Oh, to be Tribune Hadrian instead of Titus who should still be in school.*

Titus shrugged ruefully and applied himself to his food. Until the day finally came when he was no longer inevitably the youngest fellow at the party, he supposed he was bound for a good deal of silent nodding while other men held forth. He ate his smoked oysters and spiced sea urchins and listened to the conversation flowing easily between the couches. It was Trajan responsible for that, Titus thought—he might be Emperor, but he clearly felt no need to monopolize the talk. He urged others to speak as often as he did himself, and listened raptly to what they had to say. He even cast a kind eye over at Titus once and said, "Well, boy, you're a quiet one. I knew your father; we were tribunes together a hundred years or so ago. You planning on a stint in the legions too, young Titus?"

Titus couldn't imagine anything more horrifying. Mud? Marching? Fighting? *I'd rather be eaten by wolves.* But he couldn't say that to his tall, well-built Emperor, vigorous and sun-browned in his plain tunic and short military haircut, the laugh lines radiating out from his eyes as he looked down so kindly at his least important guest. His Emperor, who at forty-nine could have been ten years younger and looked ready to leap off his couch at a moment's notice and charge right into any fight that presented itself. "Caesar," Titus said brightly, and Trajan laughed and addressed some question to Senator Norbanus. Titus had observed before that you could get through most conversations with powerful men simply by repeating their names (in varying inflections) and looking respectful. Thank the gods, no one else spoke to him in the course of the meal. Titus ate his oysters and sipped his wine, content to be ignored, and it wasn't until the fruit and nuts had been cleared away that the fight broke out.

Titus had already left his couch, gone to watch the moon rise in the open roof of the atrium, but he heard the chorus of shouts and followed the noise out into the shadowed garden, where lamps had been lit along the pillars. One of the Norbanus household guards brushed past him, sword leaping halfway out of its scabbard, and Titus put a hand on his arm. "I think it's just guests," he said, eyeing the dark figures lurching and grappling across the raked paths. "Not thieves."

Two of the Emperor's young tribunes had quarreled over Sabina, it seemed, each claiming her silver earring as a favor, and in the process knocked over a vase full of orchids, and Emperor Trajan had taken them by the scruff of their necks like puppies and tossed them outside. "Settle it like soldiers," he yelled after them. "Take it out on each other, not your hostess's house! Lady Calpurnia, I apologize for my men—"

But Lady Calpurnia was laughing, and more guests were spilling out of the triclinium into the fresh-scented darkness of the garden to watch the two tribunes, who had drawn swords and sworn a good-natured bout to first blood. "And it had better just be a scratch," the Emperor shouted at them, flinging himself down on a marble bench with his elbows on his knees. "I'll need both you young sods when I go back to Dacia next year, so I won't have you killing each other."

Dacia? Titus wondered. *Dear gods, I hope Grandfather doesn't decide to send me to war.* He could hear the words now: "A stint of military service is most useful in toughening the young." No use at all to protest if you were the young person in question who didn't particularly want to be toughened.

More of the guests had gathered now. Titus could see Marcus Norbanus standing beside his daughter, amused, and Sabina rolling her eyes at her suitors, her single earring glinting. The tribunes fell on each other with loud shouts, but even to Titus's eyes they were too drunk to make it much of a contest. Some noisy clacking back and forth, an awkward stumble or two, and then one managed more by luck than skill to knock his opponent's blade to the ground. "I win," he proclaimed, waving his sword unsteadily up at the night sky. "Lady Sabina, I claim my prize—your earring, a token of—*hic*—token of love—"

"Not for a display like that," she teased. "I like my tokens going for some show of genuine skill, please. I've got a household guard here who could mince you up like tripe within half a minute."

"Do not!" the tribune bristled. "I could—*hic*—take any common bodyguard—"

"Let's see, shall we?" she said, and Titus wondered if he'd seen a gleam of satisfaction in her eyes as they scanned the crowd. And then she was saying, "Care to show these professional soldiers how it's done, Vix?"

The young guard who had told Titus to bring violets instead of lilies never hesitated. He tossed off his cloak, swung his arms in a quick

limbering stretch, and was already unsheathing his sword as he shouldered his way through the drunken hoots of the crowd. "Don't mind
if I do, Lady."

The tribune whooped and put up his sword. His friends applauded
mockingly. Titus bent to pick up the guard's fallen cloak, and by the
time he straightened the tribune had been disarmed.

Titus blinked, brows shooting up.

"That wasn't fair," the tribune protested.

The guard—Vix, Sabina had called him—crooked a finger in invitation, and his smile gleamed like a knife's edge. "Come again, then."

"This is not a proper display for a dinner party," Empress Plotina
was complaining. No one listened to her.

Titus managed to follow the fight that time, what there was of it.
Pass, counterpass, feint—and the blade was on the ground again.

"Who else?" The guard named Vix turned a circle, spreading his
arms. "I'm just getting warm." He was tall, confident, swaggering, barely
breathing hard; the lamplight cut shadows over his bare muscled arms.
"'I sing of arms and a man at war,'" Titus quoted Virgil to himself, and
looked down at his scrawny unimpressive self. No one was ever going
to sing of *his* feats, that was for certain.

Three more tribunes came clamoring forward to try Vix. The first
had a sword stroke or two Titus vaguely remembered from the advanced
class of swordsmanship but still found himself disarmed on a backhand
pass; the second was drunk and stood empty-handed in under a minute;
the third made a duel of it. Guests clapped across the circle, calling
encouragement as the two battled back and forth across a section of
raked garden path. Titus thought he saw a place or two where Vix could
have ended the fight, but the russet-haired guard didn't bother. He
moved loose and lazy across the ground, the sword an extension of his
arm, and he was grinning ear to ear as he finally whipped the *gladius*
about and clipped the blade from his opponent's hand.

The tribunes and their friends were all grumbling, not too pleased
to be humiliated by a household guard, but Titus burst into applause

and the rest of the guests followed suit, ready to be entertained by anything. Vix gave a grand flourish of a bow, and Titus saw him drop a wink at Sabina. Titus wondered how many years of his life he'd give to be able to swagger and preen for a girl like that. Ten seemed excessive, but five . . .

"Didn't I tell you, Caesar?" Sabina's amused voice. "He's good, isn't he?"

"Very." The Emperor's eyes rested on Vix, friendly and speculative. "You're gladiator trained, I'll wager."

"How'd you know, Caesar?"

"All that *slash-slash-slash*, boy! You look like you're making hay. Legion-trained, you'd be keeping your arms in close behind the shield and jabbing in short strokes." Trajan demonstrated. "Keep in close formation behind the shields and use the point. The point always beats the edge."

"Fine if you're in formation, Caesar." Vix rested the tip of his blade against the gravel. "What if the formation breaks?"

The Emperor's arrogance was quite unconscious. "My formations don't break."

Empress Plotina cast her eyes to the heavens, but Titus couldn't help smiling. Vix smiled too and spread his arms wide, sword still in hand. "That's because I haven't tried to break them, Caesar."

"Care to try, boy? My way against yours?" Trajan cocked an eyebrow at Vix.

He won't, Titus thought. *He won't take him up on it, not the Emperor of Rome.*

But Vix just bowed acknowledgment, and Emperor Trajan vaulted off his bench laughing like a boy. "Somebody lend me a sword."

Open whispers now. "Caesar, it is not fitting to your dignity," his wife reproved, but he shouted her down.

"Gods' bones, Plotina, it's been weeks since I've had a good fight. No one's got a shield, do they? No? Then someone just lend me a sword and we'll settle this."

To Titus the first cuts looked lazy, exploratory. The grin had fallen away from Vix's face now, replaced by taut focus. Trajan held himself closer together than his opponent, feet planted, head hunched to present as little a target as possible—yes, that was how it was done, as Titus remembered from his boyhood tutors. It was the way the legions were all trained, the way they won their battles across the world against armies of howling savages. Every Roman knew that. Vix moved very differently, spreading himself wide, a tempting target begging to be struck. Trajan's short sword began to flicker out like a snake's tongue, darting for a neck, a knee, an elbow. Vix beat the point of the *gladius* aside and slashed at him, but Trajan retreated in solid order. Vix came after him, swinging, and found himself rebounded off the Emperor's nearly fifty-year-old but still rock-hard shoulder. They fell back and began to circle again.

Dear gods, Titus thought. *He really means to* fight *the Emperor of Rome. Fight him properly.*

And the Emperor of Rome was clearly having the time of his life.

"All this hopping around," Trajan complained as they circled each other. "You think you have the advantage, making me chase you?"

"Don't I, Caesar?" Vix looped another cut at his shoulder.

Trajan deflected it. "Maybe if you've got a whole ring of sand to move around in, but battles aren't roomy." He chopped at Vix's knee, and the guard dodged. "Battles are tight! Tight as a virgin boy."

Vix didn't bother answering, just began to rain blows on him. None at his face, Titus saw—even a boy as rash as this one clearly was didn't want to be responsible for blinding the Emperor of Rome. But the cuts came fast and hard at shoulders and ribs, and it was all the Emperor could do to keep up. Vix looped a quick cut at Trajan's outer shoulder, and he brought his shield up to counter—only he wasn't carrying a shield. The blade opened his arm instead, and the breath froze in Titus's throat. Blood spilled, glossy in the lamplight, and the guests drew a shocked breath. The Emperor examined his arm, blood trickling between his fingers. Vix fell back a step, gray-faced, and the Emperor's guards closed suddenly in a taut unsmiling circle.

Trajan threw back his head and laughed. "Victory to you, boy."

"Not really, Caesar." Regrouping. "If you'd had a shield—"

"But I didn't, and I forgot. Bad habit. Victory to you, and welcome." He waved the guards away, clapping a hand on Vix's shoulder. "Maybe there's something to that haymaking style of yours after all. What's your name?"

"Vercingetorix, Caesar."

People began to descend fussing at the Emperor's arm, but he waved them off. "A scratch, that's all, I've cut myself worse shaving." His eyes were on the young guard again, friendly as if they'd just been two friends sparring in a gymnasium. "I take my legions north next year, Vercingetorix. There's a Dacian king up there who wants a good drubbing. I need good men—always do. You'd be an advantage in my legions. Want to help me make war?"

"Maybe, Caesar." Titus could see him wavering. *With that hand on my shoulder and those eyes on mine, I'd probably be signing up for the legions myself—me, the boy who would rather be eaten by wolves than be a soldier.*

"*Maybe* nothing, Vercingetorix," the Emperor was saying. "I'll make a Roman legionary of you yet. The point beats the edge, just remember that." He clapped the sturdy shoulder again and turned. "Anyone else want a crack at this young warrior here? Legate? Young Titus? Maybe you, Tribune Hadrian?"

"Not him." Vix's voice was loud and scornful. "When's the last time anyone saw *him* get dirty?"

Trajan laughed, and the rest of the party laughed with him. "The boy's got you there, Hadrian," the Emperor said, sheathing his sword. "Be a man for a change, take a sword in hand!"

"Thank you, Caesar." Hadrian, among all the laughers, did not even smile. "I can do more damage with a pen."

"My sword, your pen." Vix raised the blade again. "Let's see who wins."

More laughter and Hadrian opened his mouth, but Titus to his own astonishment felt himself speak first.

"Maybe you could show me a few strokes," he offered to Vix. "I don't mind admitting I'm hopeless with a sword."

"That's the spirit," Trajan laughed, and flung one arm around Senator Norbanus and the other arm around Sabina as he strode back into the triclinium. Hadrian attempted to move with the Emperor, but was somehow shunted aside . . . Titus couldn't help a chuckle at that.

The gardens were emptying now, the guests exclaiming over the cold now that they no longer had excitement to warm them and moving back inside toward cups of hot wine. Vix had found his cloak, slinging it over one arm as he sheathed his sword, and Titus approached him.

"You don't really have to teach me how to use that thing," he said, nodding at Vix's *gladius*. "I'll always be hopeless. I was just trying to get Tribune Hadrian distracted. He looked ready to cut your heart out and fry it for making them all laugh at him."

"Don't care if that prissy bastard—"

"You should not have wounded the Emperor, young man." A female voice sounded behind them, measured and rather deep.

Titus turned, bowing very low as he saw the Empress. It was the first time he'd ever seen her up close—a statuesque column of a woman in a great many emeralds, almost as tall as Titus, which made her very tall indeed. Her deep-set eyes flicked past Titus who was glad to be invisible as she turned the Imperial frown on Vix. "You should not have presumed to fight him in the first place. My husband may have thought it funny. I do not."

She rotated in place like a statue being wheeled out of a temple and glided off.

"Empresses," Vix said in disgust. "They're always trouble, the tricky bitches. Emperors might forgive you if you cross them, but *never* empresses."

"And how many empresses have you known?"

"You'd be surprised," said the guard who had just sent the Emperor of Rome away with a bloody arm, and loped off whistling.

VIX

"I saw you fight the Emperor," Gaia greeted me when I ducked into the kitchens. "I don't see how you dared—the *Emperor*, isn't he splendid—"

Yes. *Splendid* was the word. The friendly growl of his voice, the strength behind the blows we'd traded, the muscles of his left arm broader than his right because that was one old soldier who still practiced with a heavy shield, Emperor or no. That hand with its Imperial seal ring had rested on my shoulder like I was a friend. And it was a rare Emperor who laughed off a wound as a joke.

Hell's gates, it had been good to feel a sword in hand again. The easy flow of feet back and forth, the comfort of muscles working warm and smooth, the flash of the swords and the whisper of steel as blades crossed and touched and crossed again. I'd missed that: the pleasure in a good fight. I'd been having too much fun to lose; not to those patrician boys, not even to Trajan. He might be good, but even the Emperor of Rome hadn't been lucky enough to be trained since the age of eight by Rome's greatest gladiator.

The old restlessness stirred in my chest again. Sabina had stilled it for a while—nothing like the pleasures of the flesh to distract you at nineteen—but it was still there. My eyes fell on the other two guards, grousing amiably at each other over dice in the far corner of the kitchens. Would that be me in thirty years, getting fat and ogling the slave girls and telling the same old story about how I'd once crossed swords with an Emperor?

"Let me have some wine," I said abruptly to Gaia.

"Oh, now you want a favor?" She raised her eyebrows. "I thought you were too good to mingle with the slaves these days, Vix. Certainly haven't seen you hanging around my door lately."

I got free of her, stole a dish of honeyed cakes and a flagon of wine, and thumped back to my own chamber. I could still hear the guests in the atrium, chattering in their long patrician drawls, but I had no more desire to watch the festivities.

Tribune Hadrian's distinctive deep voice came clearly to my ears as he droned on about something, showing off for Sabina and anyone else who would listen. He'd been at the other guards earlier, pressing coins into their hands and asking if Sabina favored any suitors over him; if her father disapproved of him and was that why she hadn't accepted his suit yet. "Her father thinks you're a long-winded bore," I'd volunteered unasked. "Here's some advice, Tribune—give up on Lady Sabina. She'll never have you."

I'd hoped he would flush or clench his fists, but he just gave me a superior glance. "What do you know, bodyguard?"

It was on the tip of my tongue to list a few of the things I *did* know about the girl he was courting—how she arched her back when I kissed the hollow of her neck, how she closed her eyes and gasped when I kissed something else—but I didn't. I just gave an insolent smile and watched him and his gold goblet and his supercilious gaze move off.

He looked ready to cut your heart out and fry it, that skinny boy Titus had told me, *for making them all laugh at him.*

Hell with him. I wasn't sorry.

I munched on the cakes, lying back on my bed and getting honey in my blankets, and watched the moon rise in the window slit. I saw the litters come one by one to take the noble guests away, saw the other guards go through the gardens dousing the lamps, heard the cook grumbling about her blisters as she swabbed down the kitchens for the night. I heard Lady Calpurnia fuming good-naturedly in the atrium, "You would not *believe* what the Empress said to me!" and Marcus

Norbanus's soft laughter as he led her upstairs. Slowly, the house went to bed. *She won't come tonight,* I thought, but an hour or so later a shadow slipped into my room, carrying a pair of silver sandals in hand.

"My feet hurt," said Sabina. "I hate these shoes."

"Don't wear 'em."

"But they're pretty, aren't they?"

I sat up. "Did you arrange that?"

"What?"

"You know what. The fight."

"Maybe I did."

"Why?"

"I thought the Emperor might like you."

I thought of Empress Plotina and her barbed warnings. "His wife doesn't like me."

"Plotina?" Sabina chuckled. "I expect not. She doesn't seem to like anybody. Especially if they're having a good time."

"How'd Emperor Trajan end up with a wife like *that?*" I couldn't help asking. "It'd be like bedding a marble statue."

"Where do beds come into it?" Sabina looked surprised. "She manages his household and gives him sensible advice; he runs the Empire and sleeps with strapping young soldiers. They get along very well." She swung her silver sandals. "There aren't many marriages like Calpurnia and my father, Vix. But there are a lot like Trajan and Plotina."

"He likes soldiers?" I raised my eyebrows. "Is that why you thought Trajan would like me? Because I don't—"

"No, you oaf! I thought he'd like you because except for the preferring-soldiers-in-bed part, you're just like him."

"I'm an oaf, am I?" I lunged out and caught her around the waist, yanking her toward me. She still wore her elegant silver-gray dress, the one silver-and-garnet earring sparkling beside her throat.

"You're an oaf who fought a marvelous bout against an emperor, so you get the prize." She tugged her earring loose and dropped it into my hand. "Those tribunes were fighting over it, though I'm not sure why. You beat them, so it's yours."

"And what about you?"

"Oh, I'm already yours," she said lightly. "I do love you, Vix. Quite a lot, actually."

Unease squirmed in my stomach as I tried to think of a way out of that one. She'd never acted moony around me before, that was certain, but she did *talk* to me, and that made me suddenly cautious, considering the fact that my parents were always talking, back and forth about anything and everything, and they were linked up for life and probably death beyond. Sabina's father and Lady Calpurnia were always talking too, come to think of it . . . Was it the talking that made what went on under the blankets more than just a giggle and a good time? Was that what pulled a man in too deep to get out?

I didn't know what to say; didn't know what I thought or felt or wanted. Didn't know much of anything, really, and I wondered again how I was going to get out of this, but then Sabina laughed a little and climbed on top of me for a kiss. I buried my hands in her smooth, piled hair and brought it tumbling down, and the moment disappeared.

CHAPTER 7

SABINA

"Not too many more of these this year." Sabina took a pomegranate from the old fruit-seller's wrinkled hand, passing over a coin in return. "Thank you for saving me one, Xanthe."

"Of course, Lady," the old woman beamed, bobbing a curtsy. Sabina moved on, holding the pomegranate to her nose. A little withered but still sweet.

"You knew the woman's name," Hadrian observed at her elbow, offering her a little silver knife to split the skin as they walked.

"Xanthe? Of course, I always buy fruit from her. It's good to remember people's names."

"Even commoners?"

"Especially commoners." Sabina levered the first seed out of the pomegranate and popped it into her mouth. "My father knows every one of his clients by name, and they'd do anything for him. And look at Emperor Trajan—he knows all his Praetorians and their families. He remembers the names the centurions give their horses."

"Yes." Hadrian sounded thoughtful. "It does seem to work for him, doesn't it?"

The morning was cold and blustery, the sky gray and scowling above. Awnings and curtains flapped briskly all over the Forum Romanum, and harried shopkeepers swore as they battened down some unruly corner of cloth or chased a cap that the wind had tossed across the flagstones. Sabina led the way idly between the stalls and booths, well wrapped in a rose wool *palla*. Hadrian paced beside her, tall and calm in his snowy toga as he steered her around the wind-skimmed puddles, and a Norbanus household guard tramped dutifully behind. Not Vix—Sabina had been quite careful to ask for one of the other guards when Hadrian came calling and asked her if she wouldn't enjoy a walk in the city. She didn't want Vix's eavesdropping ears straining to pick up every word this morning, or his black scowl boring into her every time Hadrian touched her elbow.

"Wait, I'm going to buy this." Sabina paused by a stuffed leather ball from another vendor's display of goods, tossing it up and catching it. "Soft enough for Calpurnia's baby to play with, once it's born."

"A fine choice, Lady," the shopkeeper said. "And perhaps a ring, to aid in cutting teeth?"

"Yes, Linus had terrible trouble with his teeth . . ." Sabina scooped out another handful of pomegranate seeds, inquiring after the shopkeeper's own children. She listened to a long story about the shopkeeper's favorite daughter, who had begun to walk a full month earlier than expected, traded a recipe for easing sore gums—"my little brother would never have got through all his teething without oil of cloves"—and fished out more coins.

"You do that very well," Hadrian observed as they moved on and left the shopkeeper bowing and waving behind.

"It's not so difficult. Just act interested in people."

"People don't interest me," Hadrian confessed. "Unless they're clever."

"I know that. I didn't interest you either, until I proved I had a brain." Sabina gave the package with the ball and teething ring to her guard to carry. "But you can *pretend* people are interesting, and they'll like you for it."

"I don't have your gift for that, Vibia Sabina." Hadrian's bearded lips curved. "For being—easy. With people of all stations."

"Start with learning their names," Sabina advised. "Smiling when they greet you. Talking to them—you remember that amendment to the *Lex Cornelia* that my father proposed, the one about the corruption of public officials? He got the notion after talking to one of our freedmen who knew more about bribing officials than anyone alive. Slaves, freedmen, commoners—you underestimate them, and you shouldn't. You can learn a great deal."

"Perhaps." Hadrian's close-cropped beard was a shade darker than his hair, but she could see little wiry glints of gold in it up close. "Or I could marry you, and you can charm the slaves and freedmen and commoners for me."

"And how high does that rank on my list of assets?"

"Higher than your dowry, to be sure. Sesterces are common. Charm, less so."

Sabina sucked another pomegranate seed off her fingertip, tilting her head to admire the Temple of Concord's streaked African marble. A harried-looking woman hastened past, trying to tether her *palla*, her shopping basket, and her two children in the restless wind. "Empress Plotina invited me to come to the palace yesterday. To help her with the household weaving."

"She's very fond of you."

"She seemed rather put out with me, actually. I didn't have a tight enough hand at the loom, my warp was uneven, and my dress was indecent because it had no sleeves. You were praised to the skies, however. Any conversation we had came round to you. Is it true you organized her garden into provinces when you were a child, and took turns being governor of each one? She says your filing system was impressive for an eleven-year-old. And there was the story about the wolf you killed on a hunt at fourteen, and how you slept under the pelt until it was bald—"

Hadrian coughed embarrassment. "Did you hear the Empress is to be honored with the title of Augusta?" Hastily. "Such a great honor.

Trajan tried to give her the title before, but she refused it. She said she would not be named Mother of Rome and honored by the Senate until she had earned it."

"I'm sure she did earn it." Sabina tossed a pomegranate seed into the air, catching it neatly between her teeth. "I doubt I'd have been such a model empress if I'd married Trajan."

"You?" Hadrian halted. "Was there talk of a match when you were younger?"

"Not precisely. But when Emperor Domitian died, the Empire was offered to my father—"

"*What?*" Hadrian's eyes flicked around them with appalled furtiveness. "Where did you get that idea?"

"I spent a lot of my childhood listening at doors," Sabina explained, digging out a few more jewel-like seeds. "Nobody ever told me anything, so I eavesdropped. You'd be surprised the things I heard . . . anyway, if my father had become Emperor, he'd have adopted Trajan as heir and married him to me to solidify the alliance. So, Trajan could have been my husband instead of my favorite relative. But my father didn't want to take the purple, so now Trajan's naming Plotina as Augusta of Rome and you're paying me court instead."

"Dear gods," said Hadrian faintly. "I hope you don't go around talking like this all the time."

"Not at all. I know how to keep my mouth shut. Anyway, I'm rather glad I didn't end up empress. I used to dream of it now and then—most girls do—and I suppose in some ways it would be quite interesting. But it does tend to be a job one holds for life. And I wouldn't want to be stuck in a palace under a diadem for *all* the rest of my days. Though Trajan would have made a good enough husband. I do adore him."

"These simple soldiers are easy to like." Hadrian sounded grudging.

"He's more than that!" Sabina argued. "He's so good at keeping the Senate in one hand and the legions in the other . . . he may look like a simple soldier, but a bluff legionary couldn't do the balancing act he does."

"He should concern himself with the Empire's administration rather than its expansion." Hadrian's voice took on the teacherish tone he often used when telling Sabina about Greek philosophers, whether or not she'd already read them. "He should begin a building program—temples, aqueducts, a new forum. I've told him a hundred times, but he ignores me." A scowl. "He doesn't care for my advice. Or for me. You saw that, the night of your family's dinner party. When your bodyguard made me look a fool." Hadrian's face hardened briefly.

"I don't think Trajan dislikes you, exactly." Sabina thought it best to keep the conversation well away from Vix. "He's just warm-blooded. You're cooler. Hot and cold don't mix." *Like Vix and Hadrian . . . but I'm cool-blooded too, and Vix and I mix just fine.*

Better not to think of that, at the moment.

"Anyway," Sabina continued. "Even if Trajan doesn't favor you, Empress Plotina does. And he listens to her. You may get your building program yet."

"And be too busy making this city beautiful ever to think about leaving it." The words burst out of Hadrian like a flood of water from a broken dam. "Half my life I'll spend debating in the Senate house, making speeches and overseeing officials and reviewing lists, and there's so much in the world to *see!* The Nile in flood, and the Sibyl at Delphi, and those mist-covered mountains you told me about in Brigantia—" He was waving his arms again, the way he always did when enthusiasm ran away with him. "The temple of Artemis in Ephesus—the great forests in Dacia—"

"Will you ever see them?" Sabina asked. "Plotina has so very many plans for your future . . ."

"Yes, she does." Hadrian worried at the corner of his thumbnail.

They walked along in silence for a moment.

"The Empress has high hopes for me." Hadrian sounded guarded, and the wind tugged at the snowy folds of his toga. "I do try to oblige her. She had the raising of me, after all. I owe her a great deal."

"You owe her a great deal," Sabina acknowledged. "Not everything."

They fell silent again. A Numidian slave girl swayed past with a basket balanced up on one shoulder, brushing off a sailor who leered at her from a wine shop. An astrologer with a frayed display of star charts gestured invitingly, crying out to the crowds, and Sabina paused. "Perhaps we should have your stars read. That would settle the question for you—if you put much faith in astrologers, that is."

"Oh, I do."

"And you call yourself a man of reason," she teased.

"I had my stars read by Emperor Domitian's astrologer Nessus, when I first put on the toga of a grown man." Hadrian sounded thoughtful. "He gave me such a strange prediction, I hardly knew what to think . . . so I taught myself to read the stars, just to check him, and I kept getting the same prediction. Every time."

"Really?" Sabina cocked her head. "That's what you meant in Uncle Paris's studio that time, when you told me you already knew what your destiny was. What was your prediction?"

"That no man would see more of the world than I. So I think Plotina is destined to be disappointed in her plans for my future." Hadrian looked down at Sabina—not condescending, not teacherish, just a straight serious gaze with a core that burned. "You could come see the world with me."

Sabina held his gaze a moment, then looked down at her pomegranate. She should have counted the seeds as she ate . . . her fingers were stained as pink as a new dawn. "How many seeds do you think there are in a pomegranate?"

"About six hundred," Hadrian said promptly. It was the kind of thing he always knew.

"And I ate more than two thirds," she said. "So if we take Proserpina's scale from the myth—one month of marriage with Pluto for every pomegranate seed she ate . . . I think that gives you and me more than thirty-five years to see the world together. Do you think that's long enough?"

VIX

I couldn't find Sabina in her room, or the library, or the atrium. I finally ran her down in the farthest part of the gardens, sitting on a marble bench before a fountain stilled for the winter, a pale-blue *palla* around her shoulders and a scroll half unrolled across her lap. I'd worked up a fairly good rage by that point, so I just stamped toward her and bellowed, "*Hadrian?*"

"Hello, Vix." She marked her place in the scroll with one finger, looking up. "You might have come sooner, you know. It's cold down here, but I wanted to give you a place where you could shout all you liked."

I refused to be derailed. "You're marrying Tribune *Hadrian?*" A goggle-eyed slave girl had given me the news when I returned from an errand to the Capitoline Library. "Hadrian. That prim fish-faced arse—"

"He's not really fish-faced," Sabina mused. "The beard will take some getting used to, though."

"*Why?*" I shouted.

"Well, I'm used to kissing you and you don't have a beard, so I imagine it will feel strange at first—"

I grabbed the scroll out of her hands, and heaved it into the fountain. The fountain was frozen, so it just bounced and unrolled. Not as dramatic as I would have liked.

"I'm sorry, Vix." Sabina rose, penitent. "I'm teasing you, and I shouldn't. Yes, I'm going to marry Senator Hadrian. Why shouldn't I?"

"Why shouldn't—" Words failed me.

"I have to marry somebody." She was such a little thing, standing there in the cold winter sunshine with her hair hanging down her back like the first time I'd seen her. "What else am I going to do? Stay in my father's house forever, reading and playing with Linus and Faustina?

Be a Vestal Virgin? A bit late for either of those options. It's time I married, and Hadrian will do as well as anyone. Better, even."

I found myself pacing back and forth in short steps along the length of the fountain, unable to keep still. "Why is that?"

"He wants to travel, Vix. He says he'll take me to Athens after the wedding, and Thebes, and maybe Egypt. Everywhere." She looked around the garden as if she were already seeing the pyramids and the Greek temples, and the sleek-lined ships that would take her to see them. "Much better than some dull praetor who just wants children and dinner parties. We'll leave Rome to the politicians and travel the world together."

"Not if that bitch of an empress has her way," I threw back. "Empress Plotina, she'll keep her thumb on you, all right. Checking up ten times a day, making sure you're good enough for the boy she raised. You want to travel the world, you don't go marrying some mother-ridden bastard who has to get permission from his mummy every time he leaves the city."

"I can handle Plotina," Sabina said. "She isn't half as clever as Domitian's Empress, after all."

"And what about me?" I snarled. "What was I? Just a bit of fun?"

"No, not just fun." Sabina pulled the pale-blue *palla* closer around herself. "But what did you think would happen, Vix? Were you going to marry me? It's not even legal, patricians and plebeians. Even if it were, if I'd said I wanted to marry you, you'd get that shifty look you always get when you feel cornered, and you'd probably be gone by morning with your cloak under your arm. That's why you left Britannia, isn't it? Some girl wanted to marry you?"

I ducked that one and shifted onto firmer ground. "You *used* me."

"For my enjoyment—just like you used me for yours." Her voice was maddeningly calm. "Do you regret it?"

"It's the last enjoyment you'll ever have." I yanked her against me, one hand digging deep into her hair and the other roughly claiming her breasts. "You think you'll get anything like this from Hadrian? It might shock you to know, Lady, but the only way you'll ever interest him is from the back." I spat it out at her, the conclusion I'd drawn the day I met Hadrian. "I've seen the bastard eyeing the slaves when he comes to call on you, and it isn't the girls he likes to look at. I even got a glance or two myself, when I had my tunic off. Your Hadrian likes *boys*."

Sabina snorted. "I know that."

My hands dropped from her as I did my best not to look like a fish.

"Of course I knew, Vix. Calpurnia told me early on that Hadrian keeps a lover: a boy singer, to be exact; twenty years old and much prettier than me." Sabina seated herself on the marble bench again. "Why do you think she and my father were dubious about Hadrian as a suitor in the first place? They wanted me to find a husband who'd love me, give me children. But I don't want children, and I don't need love from a husband. Hadrian will take me traveling by day and leave me alone at night. We'll be good friends, and that suits me well enough."

It dropped like a stone into my stomach, the answer to the question I'd been pondering on and off ever since the night a senator's daughter had first dragged me into her bed. "That's why it was me, wasn't it? You *picked* me. Hadrian for a husband and me for a stud—"

"Hadrian for a husband," Sabina corrected, "and you to love."

"Don't even bother trying that on me." I started my pacing again, hands wrapped through my belt so I couldn't reach out and throttle her.

"I knew Hadrian wouldn't be any use to me in bed," Sabina said calmly. "So I thought you might show me the ropes. You certainly seemed like you'd know what to do . . . and I had a suspicion I might love you too, which was a bonus."

"You have a funny way of showing it," I snarled.

"Not really." Her blue eyes were clear and guileless as she watched me pace back and forth. "I want to be in love as much as any girl, Vix. I just don't want to be *obligated* by it. Hadrian as a husband won't obligate me to anything, and you as a lover won't either. Not since you're going to the legions."

Somehow that enraged more than anything she'd said yet. "*I am not going to the bloody legions!*"

"Yes, you are. It's plain as the nose on your face. You're what the legions are made of." She rose, slipping her arms about my neck. "You'll probably conquer us some new province, and the whole city will shout your name and shower you with rose petals."

I reached up and gripped her wrists before she could come closer. "Stop that."

"I'm not competing with that, Vix. I don't even want to."

"Shut up!"

"I don't see why you're so upset," she pointed out. "I should be the one upset with you. Here I've just told you I love you, and you haven't even been nice enough to say it back."

"After you *used* me?" I growled.

"Who used who, Vix? I came to your room every night, bedded you, loved you, asked absolutely nothing in return. You seemed happy to get all you could."

I ducked that one. "If you think I'm letting you set one foot in my room again—"

"I won't come if you want," she sighed. "Though I hope you'll change your mind? It's a month till my wedding, and I'd like to make the most of it."

I wrenched away, pointing at her. "Sabina," I yelled, using her name for once without feeling the least bit awkward, "I wouldn't touch you now with a bloody *pole!*"

"I wonder where that saying comes from," she mused. "Why a pole? What kind of pole? Why not a rod or a spar or a beam? I'll have to look that up . . ."

She fished her scroll out of the frozen fountain and wandered away. I stared at her, fists clenching and unclenching at my sides, and I remembered something I'd overheard Hadrian say to the Empress. Sabina didn't look anything like her beautiful snake of a mother, but she *did* have exactly the same way of gliding out of a room. Or in this case, a garden. She was welcome to glide right out of my life, the bitch. She and Hadrian deserved each other.

But when she tapped at my door that night, I went wordlessly and lifted the bar I'd sworn I wouldn't lift even if she begged, and she slipped into my arms as if nothing had happened.

"I'm sorry if I hurt you, Vix." Her voice came quiet in the dark. "I've never been in love before, you know—I suppose I mishandled it. I'll go if you like."

My voice sounded like a rusty scrape. "No."

I used her hard that night, twisting my hand painfully tight into her hair, kissing her until her lips were swollen, marking her neck deliberately with my mouth. "Explain that to your betrothed," I said in a savage whisper, but her arms just tightened wordlessly around me.

"Now you can get out," I said when I'd finished. "Now that you got what you came for."

It came through the dark, that low chuckle of hers I'd always liked so much. "Vix," she said, gathering her clothes, "I do love you."

PLOTINA

"So you see it all turned out well," Plotina said contentedly. "I knew it would. Dear Publius has his bride, and his foot on the path. We both know where it will lead, don't we?"

The massive statue of Juno gazed benignly over Plotina's head. Rome had a great many statues of the queen of the heavens, but Plotina preferred this one in the Capitoline Hill's great Temple of Jupiter Optimus Maximus. This was not Juno as patron of women and marriage, overseeing her worshippers like a good housewife as they prayed for husbands and babies. This was Juno seated on a massive throne at Jupiter's side, sternly beautiful in her diadem and goatskin cloak. Juno, empress of gods, just as Plotina was empress of mortals.

Plotina had come to the temple immediately after hearing the news, and the priest had shooed away the other worshippers so she could pray in private. But she did not pray, merely sat on the cold marble of the dais and allowed herself to slouch for once, leaning against the side of Juno's oversized marble throne as she looked up at the massive statue and told the news. They understood each other very well, Juno and Plotina.

"Little Sabina will be a daughter to me," Plotina told her sister queen. "I sent her a pearl necklace as soon as I heard the news, to welcome her to the family. I will take her in hand myself, train her for Publius. She will know how to mix his wine as he likes it, what dishes are his favorites, how he prefers his slaves disciplined and his house arranged. She seems most eager to take my advice . . ."

Plotina's thoughts flitted momentarily to the moment Hadrian had brought his new betrothed to the palace with their news. "My dear girl," Plotina had cried, kissing Sabina on both cheeks. "I cannot tell you how happy you have made me. You will be the daughter I never had— of course I will see to the wedding arrangements, and afterward you must both come live in the palace until a suitable villa can be readied. Dear Publius's house is entirely unsuited for a new wife—"

"We won't be needing a new villa just yet," Sabina said, and tilted her head up at Hadrian, who put a fond arm about her shoulders. "We're going to Greece. And after that, who knows?"

"He says he's taking her to Greece after the wedding," Plotina told Juno. "To spend a year as magistrate in Athens. But that's absurd. He must be here in Rome if his career is to proceed as I've planned. I want him consul as soon as he is of age—how is he to manage that gallivanting about Athens?"

Juno looked sympathetic.

"You have sons," Plotina conceded. "So you know what a trouble young men can be. Dear Publius has always had these useless dreams about traveling the world. What good will that do his career? He can think about leaving Rome after he's consul, when he has a province to govern. Egypt, I think. Trajan won't mind giving him that now that he's a member of the family."

Plotina frowned. The only blot on her happiness was her husband, who had most decidedly not been pleased by news of the impending marriage. "Little Sabina could do better," he said shortly.

"She could *not*—" Plotina began in outrage, but Trajan had cut her off with rare rudeness.

"No more of your prating, Plotina! The boy's capable enough, I grant you, so I'll allow the match, but that doesn't mean I like him any better. And don't expect me to start treating him like he's family just because he was cunning enough to marry into it!"

Trajan had stalked away in a bad temper, and Plotina had allowed him his huffy exit. "Husbands," she said to Juno. "So troublesome."

Juno understood.

"At least my husband has never humiliated me as yours does you." Plotina rested an elbow on the dais, tilting her head so she could see the massive marble Jupiter in the center of the temple. "Mortal women and bastard children—really, my dear, I would not put up with it for a moment. But with Trajan it's all strapping young men, and they are no trouble to me."

She had not always been so sanguine. The early days of her marriage had been most disappointing. Men had certain tastes as bachelors, she had known that, but it was nothing to prevent them from doing their duty by their wives. Eventually they might grow out of such things altogether. So Plotina had waited, tolerant. Waited longer, less tolerant. Waited still longer. Until the day Trajan had said Those Things to her, quite gently over his morning plate of pears. As if being gentle would take the sting out of such words! "If you think I would ever take a lover," she had told him stonily, "you are quite mistaken in my character. And I am grieved to hear you propose such a thing! Grieved!"

"Gods' bones, Plotina—"

"As if it matters that you 'don't mind at all!'"

"I just want to see you happy," he placated. "There are plenty who do the same and are happy all around." But he had never referred to the matter again. Instead, chastened, he had offered to make her Augusta as soon as he became Emperor. Plotina had made a swift and icy refusal to *that*. "If you think I am the sort of wife to break her marriage vows," she said in her coldest tones, "then I am obviously not worthy of the title of Augusta."

He let the matter drop, though he proposed it every year after. This year Plotina had a mind to accept. Why not? *I am already the Mother of Rome.* This would just make it official.

"Dear Publius is so proud of me," she told Juno. "My achievements are his, and his are mine . . . A pity he takes after Trajan in *those* ways, but perhaps a blessing. He'll do his duty by little Sabina, I've made it clear to him that it's necessary, but I'll remain first in his heart. As a mother should."

Juno agreed.

"Sabina will come to understand. The babies will console her—at least three sons. Dear Publius must have heirs. An emperor needs heirs, and he's going to be Emperor of Rome."

Juno approved.

Plotina rose, dusting off her skirts. "I fear I must go now, my dear." She gave an affectionate pat to Juno's marble foot, nearly on a level with her eyes. "I have a wedding to plan, and then I must see if I can't get this journey to Greece stopped. Really, *what* an idea."

Plotina raised her veil over her hair, lifting her skirts a modest inch as she descended the outer steps of the Temple of Jupiter. When Dear Publius was Emperor, perhaps she could have the statue of Jupiter recarved with her dear boy's face? Her own face for Juno's statue, of course. Sabina could take some minor goddess. Vesta, maybe. A little domestic goddess who troubled nobody.

Plotina knew every step of the path ahead of Dear Publius. Legate during Trajan's upcoming war in Dacia, then governor of somewhere (Gaul, perhaps?), then consul, then Prefect of Egypt . . . and eventually,

Emperor. Emperor Publius Aelius Hadrian. She was perfectly certain. So was Juno.

And really, was there any difference between the two of them?

VIX

"We'll be sorry to lose you, Vix." Lady Calpurnia set down the little robe she was embroidering for the coming baby. "Can I persuade you to stay on?"

"No, I'm grateful for everything—you'll thank the senator for me?" I shifted from foot to foot. "But guarding's not for me."

"Send us word how you get on, then." Lady Calpurnia gave me a purse. "And take this for all your service to us. You won't wait an hour? My husband just left to take Sabina to the Capitoline Library."

"No, I'll be going now." I'd been very sure to pick an hour when both Sabina and her father were out. "Thank you, Lady."

The day was cold and blustery as I left the Norbanus gates. So much for a job. So much for the year to come—the city looked gray and list-less after the previous night's Agonalia festivities: forgotten pennants lying in the gutters, the occasional wreath of festival flowers lying brown and crushed underfoot. Men winced as they plodded along, nursing headaches from the night's drinking, and housewives looked harassed and cross from the day's cleaning they were doubtless facing. Hooray for a new year.

Last year in my father's house in Brigantia, the year's-end festival had been a cheerful thing. My mother had been born a Jew but wasn't too strictly devout anymore after her upbringing in Rome; my father had had most of his belief in any kind of divine power drubbed out of him during his years in the Colosseum—but there had been a celebra-tion anyway, meat and mead and games, my father and I fighting a friendly bout on the grass with wooden swords while my mother and sister cheered, my baby brother choosing that day to take his first steps, a neighboring family coming over to join us for a long and friendly firelight dinner.

The turn of this year had been far less pleasant.

I pulled my cloak about me and trudged along to the Subura, arguing with my old landlord to give me my room back. Half of Lady Calpurnia's purse did the trick, and I promptly set out to dispose of the rest.

I got roaring drunk that night. Had a girl, had two, hoped Sabina was eating her faithless heart out. "Here's to patrician bitches!" I shouted, raising my cup, and the rest of the tavern drank with me. I drank the rest of Lady Calpurnia's purse away and was digging at my pouch for more coins when I found something and tinkling—an elaborate silver earring set with tiny garnets. I looked at it a while and was tempted to toss it to the table to pay my bill, but it was worth more than I'd drunk, and only the rich can afford grand gestures. I might as well have full value out of that earring. "First full value I got out of her," I growled, and tucked it away again.

It was midnight by the time I staggered out, and I must have gotten used to living in a nicer part of the city because I forgot the cardinal rule of the Subura: Don't travel alone.

"This is from Tribune Hadrian." A snarl came from behind me, and a massive blow on my skull drove me to my knees.

I fought, but there were at least five of them and I was reeling drunk. Three of them held me while the other two alternated hitting me. By the time they were done I had a broken nose, a handful of broken ribs, and a face so bruised even my mother wouldn't have known me. They dropped me and kicked me around for a while, and once I curled up in a ball trying to protect my innards, the leader leaned down and yanked my head back by the hair. "Next time you want to make a man look ridiculous in front of the Emperor," he recited in the tones of a memorized message, "don't choose Tribune Hadrian."

"Tell the tribune his bride's a whore," I mumbled. "Tell him I had her three times a night for months." But my mouth was full of blood and the thugs had already swaggered off. I lay there spitting out blood for a while. Some urchins came along and stole my sandals and cloak.

It really hadn't been a very good week.

TITUS

Titus blinked, looking down. "Hello there," he said. "What are you doing here?"

"Lift me up," the little girl said imperiously, tugging again at his sleeve. "I want to see."

Titus reached down and lifted up the little fair-haired girl in her embroidered blue dress. "I don't think you're supposed to be here."

"Yes, I am. I'm Antonia, my mother came to the wedding—"

"No, you little liar, you're Faustina. You're Sabina's little sister, and after the wedding feast I distinctly heard your mother say that you were too little to walk along with the wedding procession."

Faustina scowled, caught. "But I want to *see*!"

"So did I, at your age." He shifted her to his right arm, her five-year-old weight warm and sweet-smelling, and joined the back of the wedding procession that had just formed at the Norbanus house. Senator Norbanus looked proud and a little rueful, reaching up to hold hands with his wife, who rode in a litter because she declared she could not walk one more step on her swollen feet, much less the mile to the house of her new son-in-law. Beaming slaves had come out with torches to light the way, casting shadows over the chattering crowd of guests. Tribune Hadrian stood triumphant, his massive handsome head thrown back against a darkening twilight sky as he spoke with a beaming Empress Plotina. And on Hadrian's other arm stood a small figure in a saffron cloak: the bride, smiling serenely under her scarlet bridal veil. In the torchlight, the veil looked like a sheet of flame.

"I like the red veil," Faustina said critically in Titus's arms. "'Bina's pretty in red."

"Yes," he said. "She is."

The procession flowed down the street in a wave of music and well-wishes. Slaves sang wedding songs, the bawdier verses causing the Empress to exhale threateningly. Hadrian paced along, tossing walnuts out at the guests who called congratulations—a symbol of the prosperity to come. Sabina was led along by a trio of pages, one at each hand and one lighting the way with a torch. Evening passersby pointed and waved, calling out good-luck wishes. Titus paced slowly at the back, Faustina craning in his arms.

"There's the house," she said breathlessly. "Now he carries her over the doorstep, Mama told me. Mama said she didn't want Father to carry her when they were married; she thought he'd hurt his bad shoulder. But he said he'd manage it somehow; he didn't even try with the first two wives and look how they turned out. An' he did, he carried Mama right over—"

Titus watched as the threshold of Sabina's new home was sanctified, the prayer uttered. Then Hadrian handed aside the basket of walnuts and came toward his bride, and she smiled at him and held her arms up. He lifted her easily, tossing her up as the crowd cheered, and carried her over the threshold. The guests followed in a bright stream.

"I think that's all we can see," Titus told little Faustina. "Your mother will catch us if we go in. I'll take you back, and you'll be safe in your bed with no one the wiser by the time they all get home."

Faustina gave a reluctant nod. Titus shifted her to his other arm and summoned one of the torchbearers to light their way back to the Norbanus house. It was nearly dark, just a streak of red and purple remaining in the west where the sun had vanished.

"You're sad," Faustina said suddenly as they rounded the corner of the street and Hadrian's house disappeared from sight.

"I am?" Titus tried to smile.

"Yes." The little girl's frown was implacable. She was pretty even when she frowned—a little blond thing with a snub nose. Nothing like Sabina.

"Well, I am a little sad, Faustina."

"Why?"

"Because I am in love with your big sister." *The first time I've said it,* he thought with a twist. Even to himself. "Quite wildly in love with her, actually, and I have just watched her marry someone else."

Faustina frowned again. "She could marry you."

"I'd have liked that. But she wouldn't. And she was right—we're not suited, you see. Hadrian, he's clever and handsome and he's going to give her the world. I couldn't give anybody the world. Just a dull little life here in Rome, married to a dull little plodder like me."

"I'll marry you," Faustina offered.

He mussed her hair until she scowled. "You'll marry a prince, Faustina. Or an emperor. Someone far better than me."

She fell asleep on his shoulder shortly after that, and he carried her in the deepening darkness back to the Norbanus house. "See she gets put to bed," he told the slave with the torch. "She wasn't out at all, you understand."

"Don't worry, sir." The slave smoothed Faustina's fair head affectionately. "I won't get the little mistress in trouble."

"Little mistress no more." Titus gave a lopsided twist of his mouth. "She's the only daughter of the house now."

"Right you are, sir. Gods, I remember when Mistress Sabina was this little."

The slave vanished, Faustina waking enough to give Titus a sleepy little wave over his shoulder. Titus waved back, then turned slowly and ambled away. He felt like crying, but he felt like smiling too when he thought of Sabina lying on the library floor with her chin propped on her hand. Looking up at him and saying, "Oh, no, not another one."

"You don't love him," he told her through the shadows. "And he doesn't love you." But what did that matter? Most marriages weren't about love at all. They were about money, or family, or advancement, or need. In Hadrian and Sabina's case—adventure. *You would do it differently, Sabina,* Titus thought. *You're always different.*

So was Hadrian. Hadrian didn't look at the Nile and think *croco-diles*, as Titus would have. Hadrian thought *adventure*. Hadrian wouldn't blink twice at walking the wild northern hills of Britannia, or scrambling up the rocky paths of Delphi to see the Sibyl. At the wedding feast he'd spoken eagerly of doing exactly that on their arrival in Greece, and Sabina had brought out a coin and bet him she'd be first to the top. Hadrian had grinned at her and taken the bet, and Sabina had leaned over and and kissed him on the cheek. Titus would have given twenty years off his life to be the one getting that kiss.

But he got it. Even though he doesn't love her.

Never mind. Only dull little plodders like Titus were so stupid as to think a man should love his wife.

He looked up at the night sky. Full dark now, with stars pricking dimly through the haze of the city. Titus searched his memory for a quote, something by Virgil or Cato or Homer, some elegant string of words put together by a genius who could make heartache beautiful instead of pathetic. His memory failed him. His mind for once was empty of quotes; full of Sabina. Sabina crunching on an apple, Sabina drawing a stylus over a map, Sabina with a single earring glinting by her naked throat. One painful perfect image after another, and no words by any great poet were going to help.

All Titus could offer up to the uncaring gods was a matter-of-fact "This is really going to hurt, isn't it?"

VIX

"You're two weeks overdue on your rent," the landlord snarled at me. "Pay up!"

"Later," I hedged.

A month gone in the new year. The bruises on my face had faded, but my nose and ribs were still knitting from the beating Hadrian had paid for. I was doing sword exercises in the inn's cramped yard and cursing my aches and pains when the innkeeper's two spotty-skinned maids came back from shopping. "Glad we didn't have to go to the forum last night," one of them was saying. "That wedding procession had the street blocked for miles."

"A senator's daughter! Did you see her dress?"

Sabina and Hadrian's wedding? Maybe. I'd been careful not to learn the date, but weeks had passed. Surely they were wedded by now. Wedded and bedded. I wondered how much Sabina had enjoyed *that*.

I drank again that night, but not much. Just sat sipping, watching the raddled whores trudge past outside, watching the footpads skulking in the shadows, watching the drunks go reeling past.

Then I rose, and skipped out on my bill, and went to join the legions.

PART II

DACIA

CHAPTER 8

Autumn A.D. 108

SABINA

Faustina put her little fists on her little hips and looked around the new atrium critically. "I don't like it."

Sabina laughed at her little sister. "When did you get so opinionated?"

Faustina assessed the snowy marble walls, topped with the frieze of laurel leaves and stern-faced goddesses. "It's cold."

"Hadrian will be crushed; he designed that frieze himself. I think he was aiming for 'classic.'"

"It's stiff," Faustina decreed, her eleven-year-old face looking just like Calpurnia's. "Everything's stiff. No one could ever get dirty in a house like this."

Sabina mussed her little sister's hair. "Do you want to get dirty?"

"No, I want to try on all your dresses! You have the *best* clothes . . ."

Hand in hand they wandered across the atrium to the stairs, decorated with mosaics in swirling blues and greens, also designed by Hadrian. This house wasn't the architectural wonder he had sketched for himself with its never-ending improvements—"That will have to wait," he told Sabina wistfully, doodling domes and columns in the margins of his official documents—but he had taken an interest in every detail of decoration in the new house on the Palatine Hill that Empress Plotina had finally persuaded him to acquire, from the pristine lines of each column in the triclinium to the matched perfection of the slaves who stood in silent symmetrical rows as Sabina ushered her little sister upstairs.

"Why do they just stand there?" Faustina whispered.

"Because Hadrian likes silence in his household."

"I like slaves who talk. This is like living in a statue garden!"

Sabina laughed again. Calpurnia had produced three more bouncing boys after Linus, all healthy and handsome, but little blond Faustina with her out-thrust chin was still Sabina's favorite of the whole brood. "Come on, little bossy. I've got a new green dress you can try on."

"I look like an asparagus in green," Faustina said decidedly. "Have you got anything blue?"

"I think I can offer you a fine selection, madam."

Sabina settled herself cross-legged on the long couch in her own bedroom, watching with amusement as her sister picked through the pile of gowns. "I can't wait to wear a proper *stola*," Faustina said, voice muffled as she swam headfirst into a swath of blue silk. "When can I get married?"

"Not until you're at least sixteen." Sabina held up two belts. "Pearl or silver?"

"Pearl," Faustina pointed. "Antonia Lucilla says she'll be getting married at fourteen—"

"Over our father's dead body will you do the same." Sabina tucked up the blue silk skirts for her sister's shorter limbs. "But at least you'll get to pick your own husband."

"I already picked him," said Faustina. "Earrings?"

"The rosewood box on the table. Who did you pick?"

"Gaius Rupilius! His father brought him to Father's last dinner party; he's very handsome *and* he's fourteen—"

"I see you inherited your mother's taste for older men."

"Well, Gaius won't make me live in a statue garden." Faustina selected a pair of pearl drops, looking around the room approvingly. "At least you've got some clutter in here."

"I like it," Sabina confessed. Her own bedchamber was scattered comfortably with books half unrolled, cushions on the floor for flopping down and reading, a vast map of the Empire nailed to one wall, and a bust of Emperor Trajan over which Sabina usually tossed her shawls. Hadrian liked neatness and order, but he hardly ever entered Sabina's quarters. His own bedchamber lay in the other wing of the house, and traffic between the two was . . . infrequent. "I hope Gaius Rupilius makes you very happy, Faustina."

"My nurse says that isn't the point of getting married. Being happy, I mean."

"No, but it's nice when it happens. Hadrian makes me happy."

"But he's boring. He droned about Eckian cary—cary-something—"

"Erechtheion caryatids."

"Those. Are they bugs?"

"No, they're a kind of column."

"Well, he droned about them all through Father's last dinner party."

"He does do that sometimes," Sabina agreed.

"Mother says he's a crashing bore."

"He's that sometimes too."

Faustina looked down at herself: pearls in her ears, blue silk dress looped up through the pearl girdle to fit her own height. "Too long," she clicked her tongue. "Oh, why don't I *grow?*"

"You will. Hopefully taller than me. Here, try the red dress and slide my gold bracelets up over the elbow; you'll look *very* exotic—"

"Domina?" A slave girl curtsied in the doorway. "You have a visitor. Tribune Titus Aurelius—"

"Tribune?" Sabina uncurled her legs from the couch. "Oh, no. Faustina, try on the Indian silk, it feels like water on your skin—I have to see something . . ."

Titus bowed as Sabina bounded downstairs and back into the atrium. "Vibia Sabina," he said. Her onetime suitor had gone from a shy boy of sixteen to a tall young man of twenty-two, but he still had the same endless skinny limbs and peculiarly sweet smile. " 'Hail, beauteous nymph with eyes cerulean bright.' "

"But my eyes aren't cerulean," Sabina objected. "You've been reading Homeric hymns again, haven't you?"

"I'm afraid so. I tend to reach for poetry when I'm stumped for words." He gave an elaborate bow. "The sight of you usually does that to me."

"Today I'm the one who's stumped." Sabina eyed his uniform: brand-new breastplate and red tunic, greaves and cloak and a helmet tucked under his arm with a stiff crest of plumes. "Your family finally made you do it, didn't they?"

"I'm afraid so." He saluted. "You see before you a tribune of the illustrious legions of Rome."

Sabina sighed. "I told your grandfather you'd rather be eaten by wolves than join the legions! At Father's last party—"

"Yes, well, other members of my family told him all about the benefits of military service in seasoning the young. Mostly those members who have not served in the legions themselves. 'War is sweet for those who have not experienced it,' as Pindaros would say." Titus looked down at himself ruefully.

"My father was a tribune when he was your age," Sabina consoled. "He said he got through it by keeping his mouth shut and his boots dry. Where are you stationed?"

"The Tenth Fidelis, in Germania. Some ghastly frontier town with a name I can't even pronounce. I leave tomorrow, unfortunately."

"Germania," Sabina said enviously. "And you don't even want to travel! I'd love to see Germania."

"At least you saw Greece."

"Not enough of it." Sabina dreamed of Greece sometimes; the rocky cliffs, the blue seas, the sunlight with its peculiar brilliance. She and Hadrian had spent a year in Athens, where he had been appointed magistrate, and it had been everything he promised. Athens had clung like a white jewel to the dry cliffs, and she'd scrambled sunburned and happy among the temples in the sky while Hadrian hunted massively tusked Greek boar and joined fierce philosophical debates with bearded men who looked far more like him than his fellow politicians in Rome. "You really are a Greekling," she'd teased him, and he'd released a rare rueful laugh.

They'd planned to go on to Sparta, Corinth, Thessaly . . . but Plotina had written with news of some crisis back in Rome that required Dear Publius's *immediate* attention, and that had been that.

Sabina banished the thought, waving Titus to a couch. "Sit down; tell me everything. We'll have ourselves a good chat, if it's the last one before you leave. How long does your stint in Germania last?"

"A year." He managed to sit, his stiff new armor creaking.

"A year?" Sabina made a face. "Who's going to take me to the theatre now when Hadrian's busy working?"

"I think you'll be able to find another escort."

"Nobody who tells me my eyes are cerulean when they're plain ordinary blue. You have to write me from Germania, tell me if the tribesmen really cook Romans over a bonfire they way they did in Emperor Augustus's day—"

"I think I'm going back to the blue dress." Faustina's voice came from the door. "Red is not my color at *all*."

Sabina took care not to laugh as her little sister paraded in for their inspection. The hitched-up red *stola* was already slipping down around Faustina's feet, gold bracelets hung like shackles on her wrists, and she'd clearly gotten into Sabina's rouge pots.

"I think you look very fine indeed," Titus said gravely.

"I look all washed out and diseased," Faustina said, but gave him a grin that wrinkled her little nose. "Hello, Titus."

"Faustina's going to marry Gaius Rupilius," Sabina explained. "I thought I'd let her try on my dresses, since she's going to be needing grown-up gowns very soon."

"He won't marry me if I don't look pretty in red." Faustina plucked at her skirt. "All brides wear red."

"Try a rosier red." Titus rested his still-bony elbows on his still-bony knees. "With those pink cheeks, you'll be prettier than any bride alive."

"As pretty as Sabina?"

"Now, I don't know about that." Titus rose, his new boots squeaking, and crossed the tiles to Faustina. He took her hand and raised it high, twirling her in a circle and giving her his most thoughtful frown. He had become a great favorite, not just with Sabina but with all her family—Sabina could hardly visit home anymore without finding Titus there: unashamedly begging Calpurnia for a taste of her fresh-baked bread, arguing books with Sabina's father, romping with the boys in the garden . . . "You really should have married him," Calpurnia had scolded Sabina.

"I'll stick with the husband I've got, thank you."

Titus was still twirling Faustina under his arm. "It's true your big sister is very pretty, Annia Galeria Faustina," he said, judicious. "I don't think you're going to be pretty when you grow up, though."

Faustina stopped twirling. "I'm not?"

"No. You are going to be a true, genuine, undoubted, and undisputed beauty." Titus bowed, kissing the plump little hand. "Helen of Troy had forty suitors, but you should beat her easily. Young Gaius Rupilius will have to fight off the other men lining up for your hand."

Faustina danced over to the still pool of water in the center of the atrium, bending over to survey her own reflection. "You know," she said as she straightened, "I think you're right!"

"She'll miss you when you go north to Germania," Sabina told Titus as her little sister dashed upstairs; a little blond whirlwind leaving a trail of gilded sandals, silver belts, and the occasional pearl earring in her wake. "All of us will miss you. My father thinks very highly of you."

"Goodness, why? I'm such a dullard." Titus picked up his helmet. "I should be going."

"You can't stay? I want to tell you lots of horror stories about my father's time as a tribune. Like the night when the centurions froze his only toga into a solid block of ice—"

"Tempting," said Titus. "But I've still got to creak over to the Forum and see about my travel arrangements."

"Or the time a hawk swooped down and stripped the feather crest off his helmet," Sabina added brightly. "That's a good story."

"You are not being encouraging."

"Or my older brother Paulinus; he had some stories from his tribune days. Like the time he got the maps mixed up and marched a whole cohort sixteen miles in the wrong direction . . ."

"I'm leaving now!"

"Cheer up." Sabina stood on tiptoe to kiss his cheek. "I'm sure it won't be that bad."

TITUS

It was.

"Any advice?" Titus asked his father.

His father stared back. Sympathetic, Titus thought. But unfortunately still just marble. A small hand-sized bust his grandfather had pressed into his pack the day he left to join the Tenth Fidelis. "To keep you on the right path, boy. You'll do well as long as you remember your father and obey your legate."

"Anything else?" Titus had asked hopefully.

"Try not to pick up the pox from any German whores."

Titus rested his chin on his folded arms. Tribunes had their own quarters, as barren or as luxurious as their private allowances would supply, but he wouldn't have minded sharing. At least it would have given him someone to talk to besides a bust. "'Obey my legate,'" he told his father. "Not very useful advice. The legate doesn't even know my name. I haven't done a thing since I got here but watch clerks file records, and scrape the mud off my boots."

The trouble, Titus decided, was that tribunes as a whole were utterly useless. The legionaries, now, those stamping swearing creatures with their swagger and their scars and their rough stubbled faces, they were frankly intimidating but undoubtedly useful. There didn't seem to be anything they couldn't do, from fighting endless drills to marching end-less miles to building endless additions on their crude German fort. Then there were the bustling clerks and quartermasters who apparently found it no strain at all to maintain, in the middle of a dank German forest, a camp large enough to hold three legions at once—useful fellows, no doubt about that. And then there were the centurions, mostly ex-legionaries risen from the ranks, even tougher and more terrifying than the men they commanded, and the prefect of the camp, who was built like a mountain and seemed to know all five thousand or more men in the legion by name, and then there was the legate who did a great deal of frowning and stamping and ordering about. But the tribunes?

"We're nothing," he told his father. "A handful of layabouts who are here only because our families bought us our posts. So we're second to the legate, but everyone hops over us down to the camp prefect and the centurions. What are we good for? Sitting around playing dice and talking about the rain and waiting till we can go home with a stint of service on our records so we can get elected quaestor."

Rain was dripping outside even now. Nothing stayed dry in the fort; the camp was a sea of mud half the time, and so were the half-paved streets of the town that had sprung up between the camp and the river. "Moguntiacum, it's called." Titus rolled the word off. "At least I can finally say it now—only took me a month. Mostly everyone calls it Mog. Not much of a place. Mostly it's here to keep the legionaries in taverns and whores and all the other things that keep the men from mutiny during the cold months."

Precious little for entertainment. No arena, no libraries, just taverns with never-ending dice games and a few wet and forlorn-looking shrines. "I don't think Grandfather has to worry about the whores," he told his father. "They all look so sullen, I wouldn't dare make any of them an offer." The only other women were legionary wives—the sol-diers weren't supposed to marry, but wives and mistresses found their way into the fort anyway: tough and terrifying creatures in hobnailed sandals who could have snapped Titus over one knee.

A year he would be stationed here, and just one month of it gone. A year in a wet dark place that sounded like a cough full of bile, without a good book or a pretty woman or a decent conversation to be had for five hundred miles. "'The same night awaits us all,'" he quoted, but Horace wasn't much comfort tonight.

A brisk tap sounded on the door. "Tribune!"

One of the legate's aides greeted him, frowning over a wax tablet. "You're the one who quotes, aren't you?"

That should make you proud, Father, Titus thought. *A whole month in the Tenth Fidelis, and I've already made a name for myself. I'm universally known as 'the one who quotes.'* "That's me," he sighed.

"The legate wants a thorough report on the Dacian garrisons," the aide went on. "A tribune, a centurion and *optio*, and double guards. You're to go."

"Me? The Dacian garrisons—you mean all the way across Pannonia?"

"That's how you get to Dacia, yes," the aide said irritably. "Tribune Celsus was supposed to lead the party, but he came down ill this morning."

More like he doesn't want to spend the next two weeks riding through the mud and getting shot at by Dacian bowmen. "I've never been on a route march," Titus hedged. "I've just come last month, I haven't even left Mog yet—"

"Legate said it would be good for you. Suit up! They leave in an hour."

"I'm supposed to *lead* them?"

"Just do what the centurion tells you." The aide smirked. "You might make it back alive."

"That's what I love about the Tenth Fidelis," Titus said. "Such humor and wit, such encouragement and support. So comforting to a newcomer like me."

The aide was already hurrying away, shuffling another armload of wax tablets. "Enjoy the rain, Tribune!"

* * *

"Dacia's a bad place," Titus heard one of the legionaries whisper to another, the first week on the road. "Bad, and getting badder. That king of theirs, he wears a lion skin and he's eight foot tall!"

"Ten," another legionary disagreed. "Counting the horns."

"You know what he does to Romans when he catches 'em? I heard the last scouting party came back without their heads!"

A hoot from behind Titus. "If they lost their heads, then they wouldn't be coming back from anywhere, would they?"

"Just sayin' . . ."

Titus turned to look over one shoulder at the legionaries. Six of them, hulking and identical in their armor and muffling cloaks, faces so wrapped against the cold in scarves and helmets that he couldn't tell them apart. A double guard, because Germania had been restless lately with Dacia looking troublesome again. Trajan had drubbed the Dacians into submission a few years back, but Titus knew the submission hadn't lasted long. Already there were rumors of scouts picked off in Dacia, supply lines harassed, messengers shot at from the trees . . . but the six legionaries guarding Titus and the centurion on their expedition to the Dacian garrisons didn't look worried. They laughed and they joked, they cursed and they sang filthy songs, and Titus envied them. At least they had someone to talk to. Whenever the scouting party stopped for the night at a way station, the legionaries put up their booted feet and passed around wineskins and dirty stories. Titus watched wistfully from his own table—alone, of course, because officers and legionaries didn't mix on the road any more than they did in the fort. He couldn't even take his father's little bust out of his pack and talk to that. The men already despised him enough for his brand-new plumes and his soft hands and his utter uselessness; he wasn't going to give them something else to jeer at by talking to a statue.

Soon enough the firm roads and traveler way stations of Germania gave way to the muddy tracks and forested hills of the Dacian border.

The centurion had the tents pitched close every night and began posting sentries on watch. "No one's going to catch us napping," the centurion said shortly, and Titus wondered if he'd heard the rumor too about the heads.

"I can take a shift," Titus volunteered.

They all looked at him blankly. "Why, sir?"

Titus couldn't think of a reason either. *Gods, I want to go home.*

Weeks on the road, and it never stopped raining until the day they crossed into Dacia. "We'll raise the first garrison tomorrow," the centurion announced, "so get some sleep." But Titus wandered out of his tent that night instead, away from the guttering campfire, feeling the mud squelch under his boots. He raised a hand in greeting to the shadowy shape of the legionary standing the dawn watch, getting a salute in return, and wandered farther down the muddy track that passed for a road. *Are there stars in Dacia?* If only the clouds would roll back for once . . .

The attack came silent, black, and sudden.

Stars exploded, not in the sky but in Titus's head as something clubbed him behind the ear with shattering force. He was facedown in the mud before he even knew he was falling, and booted feet were buffeting his side. He let out a yell and choked on mud. Someone hissed a warning in words he didn't know, and he felt a blaze of pain as a spear haft thumped into his belly. He fought to breathe, his mouth full of muddy water; he tried to curl around his belly but a knee pressed into his back. He felt fingers in his hair, yanking his head up, and then there was the touch of steel at his throat.

There was a sudden yell, and a clatter of blades.

The knee disappeared from Titus's back. He heard a shout, more rushed words in a language he didn't recognize. Two shapes were lurching across the muddy road, hardly more than shadows in the moonless night. A grunted curse; they both went down, and one shape got its hands into the other's hair and banged his head into the ground. Titus's breath froze as one of the men staggered upright, but then he saw the outline of a Roman legionary helmet. Another shadowy figure lunged, and the sentry who had been on duty drove his *gladius* up under the man's sword arm. There was a crack of thunder overhead, drowning the scream, and suddenly the rain began to drench down again. The sentry lifted his sword, but the two black shapes were disappearing into the rain, dragging their wounded friend between them. Titus blinked water out of his eyes, and they were already gone.

"Damn," muttered the sentry, and turned to Titus. "You alive, Tribune?"

"Hopefully not." Titus prodded cautiously at the lump he could already feel throbbing behind one ear. "But I believe I hurt too much to be dead."

"Try standing up," the legionary suggested.

Titus tried to gather his legs under him, froze, and sank back down. "Oh, gods. That was a bad idea."

"It's a very good idea, unless you want to lie here as bait for more Dacian savages." The legionary put a hand out, found an elbow, and gave a haul. "Up you go, Tribune."

Hammers banged briskly around the inside of Titus's skull, but he found himself on his feet. *Don't be sick,* he told himself, swaying. *You're already the tribune who got himself beaten up by thugs and rescued by a sentry because he was too stupid to take his sword along stargazing. Don't throw up too.* He swallowed hard, and the hammers redoubled.

"What were you doing wandering around the Dacian border in the middle of the night?"

Titus wished the man wouldn't speak so loud. "The rain stopped for once. I thought I'd go outside and look at the stars."

"You're in Germania now." The legionary sounded more amused than contemptuous. "No stars. Just rain. You should have taken a guard with you. It's my head on a plate if something kills you on my watch, you know."

"I'm sorry," Titus said, before he remembered an officer should never apologize to his own men. "Was it footpads?"

"Maybe not." The soldier found the shield one of Titus's attackers had dropped, cursed the lack of light, felt over it instead. "Plenty of footpads in these woods, deserted legionaries and robbers and the like. They don't usually carry round shields, though."

"Dacian rebels carry round shields," Titus said. "Not that I've ever seen a Dacian rebel, but reports say—"

"Better come back with me, Tribune." The soldier rose, hardly more than a dark bundled shape in the shifting rain. "We reach the first of the Dacian garrisons tomorrow; you can stargaze safely there."

"Agreed," Titus said, and fell into step beside his rescuer. The road was black and quiet—in the driving rain, clearly no one had heard the shout of alarm and armed themselves for a rescue.

"You probably saved my life, legionary," Titus said after a moment's silence. "What's your name?"

"Vercingetorix of the Tenth Fidelis. Most call me Vix."

Titus paused. "Do I know you?"

"Took you long enough." Definite amusement in the soldier's voice now. "Five years back I was a guard in Senator Norbanus's house. You were a sprat with an armload of violets come courting his daughter."

Titus raked his memory. "That was you? The one who fought a mock bout with Emperor Trajan at a party?"

"You nobles never remember pleb faces." Vix pointed out a pothole in the road before Titus stumbled in it.

"I remember the name, anyway," Titus said. "Anybody would remember a name like yours."

"What's wrong with it?"

"Well—it's not a name, really." In Latin, *vix* was just a nebulous adverb, something along the lines of *slightly* or *hardly* or *barely*. "I don't meet too many people named Slightly." The hammers in Titus's head were starting to subside, but the lump behind his ear was already the size of a plum.

"Vercingetorix is a *Gallic* name," Vix snapped. "Not Latin. Means 'great warrior king,' I'll have you know. There was a famous warrior king in Gaul named Vercingetorix—"

"Who got himself by defeated by Julius Caesar, spent years wallowing in prison, and was finally strangled to death," Titus pointed out. "How well-omened of a name is it?"

"Well, it still doesn't mean *slightly*." Vix sounded defensive. "Nobody's ever called me *slightly* anything unless they wanted a fight."

"At least it's a short name," Titus offered in apology. "Better than Titus Aurelius Fulvus Boionius Arrius Antoninus."

Vix grinned through the dark; Titus barely caught the gleam of his teeth. "How did you get saddled with all that, Tribune?"

"Titus after my father." Titus supposed this wasn't a proper conversation to be having—*A certain distance must be maintained between legionaries and their officers*, the tribunes were instructed often enough by the legate—but on a rainy night in Germania with blood trickling down the back of his head and mud sticking to both of them head to toe, legion etiquette didn't seem to matter much. "Aurelius because it's the family name—the Aurelii. Fulvus because it's my father's second name, and why not be as confusing as possible by having two of us. Boionius, that was after a rich uncle my mother was hoping might leave me some money. Antoninus, another family name. Arrius, that's supposed to be from my mother's side of the family, but I think it really came from the fact that my father loved the gladiatorial games. I don't know if you've ever heard of him, but there was a famous gladiator years back named Arius the Barbarian—"

Vix let out a shout of laughter.

"What?" Titus looked at him quizzically as they rounded the curve in the rough road and came back to the camp.

"Nothing, Tribune," Vix chortled. "Maybe I'll tell you someday. I need to make a report to the centurion now, but you'd better go back to your tent. In case you haven't noticed, it's wet out."

CHAPTER 9

VIX

The following morning dawned sunny and rain-washed when we mounted up. Tribune Six-Names rode ahead with the centurion and the *optio*, very grand again in his plumes and red cloak, and I assumed that our odd informality of the previous night had been banished by daylight and the proper order of things. But just a half mile down the road, he twisted in his saddle and beckoned me to ride up on his right side. He was still scrawny for his height, and his armor positively creaked with newness, but his face was friendly.

"I found our conversation of last night most interesting," he said a trifle pompously. "'As long as we are among humans, let us be humane,' as Seneca would say, and good conversation is truly the most humane of all arts. Particularly necessary in barbaric settings like these."

I stifled a grin as I nudged my horse up beside his. So the young bugger was lonely. Tribunes did tend to keep to each other for company, since no one else particularly needed them, and Tribune Six-Names here had been on the road several weeks without a friend. He ignored the reproving scowl of the centurion on his other side and pressed for a little of my history, riding along sniffing the rain-washed air with as much pleasure as any legionary on a pleasant march. The horses' hooves clopped cleanly on the road, and everywhere was the smell of wet earth and leaves that hadn't yet been deadened by the approaching winter.

"So you came all the way from Britannia just to join the legions?"

he said after hearing my (carefully edited) life story. With all the interesting parts left out, like the Emperors I'd helped to kill and the bouts
in the arena that I'd fought, it made short telling. "I don't mean to be
rude—but in the name of all the gods, why?"

"I've asked myself that a time or two." Particularly in the first year,
when I was getting poked and weighed and measured by critical recruit-
ers, or slogging through sword drills I'd mastered at eight years old, or
gritting my teeth as centurions shouted at me about the point beating
the edge, *you gladiator-trained scum*—and let me tell you, they were not
nearly as kind about that last point as Emperor Trajan had been.

Why had I joined the legions? I was twenty-five now, and I still
didn't know. But I'd finally broadened into my height; I had scars on
my back from the odd caning and was hoping to get a few scars on my
front from battle wounds; I had friends in the ranks who were like
brothers, and a place in the world. Like it or not, I was a soldier of
Rome, Vercingetorix of the Tenth Fidelis, and even now I had to grit
my teeth when I thought how right Sabina had been—that it had been
the place for me all along.

"Have to do something with this life," I said finally, and it was all
the answer I could give.

"Pity to get stuck in Germania, though," he sympathized. "I was
hoping for Africa. Some place very hot and thoroughly uneventful."

"Or Egypt," I agreed. "I hear it's all sunshine there, and sparkling
rivers and big temples and women with painted eyes." Though they
couldn't be as pretty as the girl I had waiting for me back in Mog—*she*
was a beauty and no mistake. And besides, what use was dreaming
about Africa or Egypt or the world's hot places? I was stationed in the
cold north, and likely to stay there the next twenty years.

Anyway, Germania was where the heat was, in battles if not in
weather. Anyone with eyes in their head could see that. I wasn't planning on being a legionary forever, but you didn't climb the ladder in the
Roman army without either family backing or glory in battle. I couldn't
do anything about the family backing, but the glory . . .

My bad-tempered horse took a sideways leap away from a puddle and nearly unseated me. I clung to the saddle, swearing.

"He's being a bastard, isn't he?" the patrician boy said tactfully. "Try tucking your foot into the girth on each side; that should keep you steadier."

"All horses hate me," I grunted, hauling myself upright. "What's the point of a horse, anyway? One end bites, the other end shits, and all four corners kick."

"You can't ride to save your life," the *optio* jeered. "Vix here could get bucked off the wooden horse of Troy!"

I glared. There wasn't an *optio* in the Tenth who wasn't universally hated. Every centurion had one, a second-in-command, and for the most part they were bullying tattling toadying prigs. I was still trying to figure a way to climb the ladder to centurion without becoming *optio* first. And after more than five years in the Tenth, neither option was exactly presenting itself.

"We can't all ride like you, *optio*. To each his gifts." The tribune smiled. Under the plumed helmet he had one of those profiles that all patricians like to think they have, but so rarely do; the kind that shouts at least fifteen generations of distinguished ancestors. He lifted that aquiline nose and sniffed the clean air appreciatively. "I suppose we'll all be marching this way again if there's war with Dacia?"

"Hope so," I said, wistful.

He grimaced. "I'll never be a soldier."

"Then why are you?" I asked boldly. The centurion glowered at my impertinence, but I ignored him again. "Don't you want a career in the legions?"

I couldn't help but be envious. Tribune at twenty-two—with his connections, he could be vaulted straight on up to legate in a few years if he showed any aptitude at all. What I'd give for backing like that . . .

"Wet," the tribune said. "Cold. Blood. No thank you. My dearest wish is to go home and become a thoroughly dull little public servant.

The kind who never gets out from behind his desk and is always home in time for a good supper."

"At least you won't be cold and wet," the centurion conceded. "Plenty of that in the legions, sir, sure enough."

"And how did you come to the legions, Centurion? A Greek, I can hear that in your voice—"

With the two of them nattering, I saw the smoke first. It should have been the centurion—he prided himself on his eagle eyes—but he was too smug at being flattered by a tribune to see the wisps of black rising suddenly beyond the next bend in the road.

"Wait!" My voice cut sharply across the cheerful chatter at my side.

"I thought you said the garrison was just ahead," the tribune said, but the centurion was already barking orders and I dug spurs into my horse and cantered down the road. Black smoke, never a good sign, but I was expecting a granary fire, perhaps at the worst an attack on the outer walls from some Dacian skirmishers.

The entire garrison was aflame.

I pulled up swearing, my sword leaping out of its scabbard along with six others as the legionaries and the officers caught up with me, but it was no good. A quartet of sentries lay dead in the road, and not newly killed either. Their bodies had already been rifled and stripped, and the roof of the *principia* smoldered fitfully, its tiles still damp from the night's rain. Even from a mile distant I could hear the howls, the sounds of smashing tiles and smashing statues.

"The round shield," I snarled. "I should have known, I should have bloody *known*—" There were shaggy men with round shields darting through the broken gate now, holding sacks of loot.

"What is it?" the tribune shouted from where the centurion had bluntly ordered him to stay back.

"Dacians," I yelled back. They'd likely attacked the fort under cover of the rain last night—the three who jumped the tribune would have been advance scouts up the road.

"What can we do?" the boy called.

"Prayer might work."

One of the other soldiers was swearing helplessly, hand at his sword hilt, but he didn't attack. None of us did. The granary would have been looted by now, the records room put to the flame, the barracks emptied, and the men slaughtered. The statue of Emperor Trajan would have been toppled from its plinth and smashed into shards of marble. All done last night, while the rain whipped down. Now that the skies had cleared this morning, the rest of the garrison was being put to the torch.

Too late.

"Back to Moguntiacum," the centurion rapped out. "Now."

But a yell went up before we could turn our horses. A small advance party of scouts on horseback—for all I knew, the same ones the tribune and I had tangled with last night. Distantly I saw a spear pointed in our direction, heard a long shout—and the horses began to move.

Ten of them.

I dragged my horse's head about, back toward the bend in the road. "Back!" the centurion shouted, "back, back!" but no one needed his orders. We were all fleeing.

The patrician boy whitened, but he wheeled his mount too. I thumped my horse in the ribs, but the hell-beast just squealed and veered violently into another horse. That legionary went over his mare's head, and by the time I clutched mane and hauled myself upright in the saddle, a bubbling war scream reached my ears and I saw that the first of the Dacians was catching up to us. "To me!" I shouted to the man I'd spilled in the road, spurring toward him as his own mare dashed away in panic, but he gave a shriek and ran away from me, straight up the road with his arms flailing.

I yanked my horse at the first Dacian as he spurred toward that stupid fleeing soldier, and I had a bare impression of greasy beard, meaty mail-clad arms, a gap-toothed snarl as he turned his eyes to me instead. I barely had time to touch the lump under my breastplate that was my father's amulet, and then the Dacian was on me. His spear went through my shoulder, or it would have if his horse hadn't stumbled, and

I took the opportunity to lop the head off the spear and leave him with a haft of wood. I reversed the thrust and bashed most of his teeth in with the *gladius*'s heavy hilt, and as he shrieked I turned. The other Dacians were catching up fast, and the man I'd unhorsed was still keening fear as he sprinted up the road. The centurion on his good horse was drawing away at a flat gallop, not caring how many of us were killed in the rear as long as he could get back to Mog with the news, and the other soldiers galloped after him without a rearward glance. It was Tribune Six-Names who turned his horse, putting a hand down to give the man an arm up. The legionary gave such a panicked yank that he tumbled the tall boy out of the saddle and into the road.

Another war cry sounded behind me, and I saw two spears leveling.

"Hell's gates," I swore, kicking my horse ahead again. The legionary had hauled himself onto the tribune's horse and was fleeing up the road. The boy was on his knees in the mud, dazed, and in another moment I'd be past him. *Leave him*, the thought went through my head; *how far do you think you'll get with your horse carrying double?* But I put my arm down as I went past, and somehow he got hold of it and came flying up behind me.

"Thank you," he gasped.

"Keep my sword arm free," I snapped, and there was no more talking for a while. The Dacians came after us, and when my horse began to labor we had to stop and fight. I killed one, knocked another out of his saddle with a backhand blow of my free arm, and then the others weren't so keen on catching me. They finally retreated back to the ruined garrison with derisive whoops, but I pressed my horse back into a flat gallop and kept him there till he was white and lathered under the double weight, till we finally caught up with the rest of our party.

"I'm sorry," mumbled the shame-faced soldier on the tribune's horse, but I hit him with the boss of my shield and knocked him out of the saddle into the mud.

"We ought to leave you here to die," I snarled. "Like you left your tribune!"

"Never mind," the centurion barked. "He'll get the lash when we're back in Mog, and no mistake. For now, we ride. Sextus, give the tribune his horse back. You can double up with whoever can stand to have a coward like you at his back."

"No, he can ride with me." The tribune slid off my horse, offering a hand to help up the man on the ground, who seemed near tears. "Don't worry, I'll speak on your behalf to the legate. You won't be flogged."

"He should be," I grumbled, ramming my *gladius* back into its scabbard. "You're letting him off easy, Tribune."

"Maybe." He looked around at the centurion, the *optio*, the other men. "But let's not discuss it now. I'd like to be as far away from here as possible, frankly, so why don't we get back to the Tenth as fast we can and tell them we're being invaded?"

PLOTINA

The Empress of Rome was annoyed. An hour's work, and the two looms working side by side still refused to get into a rhythm. Her own shuttle passed smoothly back and forth with a rhythmic *swish-swish-swish*. The other shuttle went *swish*—pause—*swish*—pause—*swish*.

"Rhythm, Sabina," she said for the fourth time. "You must get your weaving into a rhythm. You are far too easily distracted."

"Mmm." Dear Publius's wife passed the shuttle along through the threads, yawning. "Perhaps we could go outside for a walk instead. Such a beautiful afternoon, it's a shame to be cooped up inside." Sabina glanced up at the long windows, which Plotina had ordered shuttered tight as soon as she arrived.

"Unhealthful," Plotina said. "This wind will tan your skin, and then what will people think?"

"I don't know if anyone spends much time thinking about my skin."

Plotina cast a glance at the girl who should have been all but a daughter to her by now but was somehow not. Sabina's face was smooth.

Surely she could not be laughing at the Empress of Rome? Such a thing was impossible.

But Vibia Sabina had not proved as satisfactory a wife for Dear Publius as Plotina had hoped; there was no doubt about that. Look at her now, barefoot and careless with her hair hanging down her back like a girl's, her hands far too casual as she flung her shuttle back and forth. Any cloth she wove was loose-warped. And after Plotina had helped her to begin that new piece—a cloak for Dear Publius—and admonished that only an hour's daily work at least would see it done, the girl still had left it untouched until this morning! Most vexing. And it was not only the weaving . . .

"I've finally managed to track down a copy of that new Greek poet everyone's talking about," Sabina was saying. "Hadrian will be so pleased. With any luck the poet will be terrible. We'll spend an hour over dinner tonight tearing the verses apart, and he'll have some new material for his standard rant about Rome's declining intellectual tastes."

Plotina frowned. Poetry again. The dear boy had always had a weakness for verse. Poets had their uses, at least for the idle, but the future Emperor of Rome should not waste his time on such things. "Steer him to rhetoric, my dear, instead of Greek poets. They already call him the Greekling in the Senate; it won't do to give them any more fodder."

"When does anyone steer Hadrian to anything?" Sabina pointed out.

"A clever wife can always manage her husband."

"Well, we both know I'm not very clever."

But she was, when she chose to be. Plotina knew that perfectly well. At the last Imperial banquet, Sabina had spent an hour deep in the kind of serious well-informed discourse that was just the sort of thing to advance Dear Publius's career . . . if she hadn't wasted it on some doddering intellectual friend of her father's. A nobody! Ignoring all the provincial governors, the senators, the *useful* people Plotina had taken such trouble to cultivate. "He was interesting," Sabina had shrugged. "They weren't."

Juno grant me patience. It was enough to drive even a goddess to distraction.

Never mind. Plotina had certainly not dropped in uninvited on her almost-daughter-in-law to get distracted by her loose-warped weaving and odd views on guests. Plotina had News, and such News it was. "When is Dear Publius returning this morning? I have a surprise that I believe will please him more than any amount of Greek verse."

"Oh, I never track his comings and goings. Wine?"

"I do not drink wine, you should know that by now. Barley water, if you please. And let me see that slave girl's hands—just as I thought." Plotina gave the slave a frosty look. "Clean your nails before you come back with those cups, girl. Vibia Sabina, I don't know where you find your maids! Such clumsy untrained creatures—"

"That one came out of a whorehouse on the Aventine." Sabina nodded after the girl who had just filed out. "I offered her a change of job. So far she's settling in just fine, though she does get the cups mixed up."

Plotina blinked. "You aren't serious?"

"Aren't you always telling me about a Roman matron's duty to aid the unfortunate?"

"The *clean* unfortunate. The *moral* unfortunate. Not dirty whores."

"Well, she's not a dirty whore anymore. She's learning to weave—eventually I'll free her and get her a job in a shop. Shouldn't take long; she already weaves better than I do. You mentioned a surprise?"

Plotina debated a continuation of the lecture but couldn't hold back any longer with the news she had been storing up all day. "Dear Publius has been appointed legate of his own legion!"

That made the girl sit up. "Legate?"

"Of his own legion," Plotina repeated with relish. Oh, how much work it had been, so many headaches pressing in at her temples, so many people determined to thwart her, but she had done it. She had done it: his next step upon the ever-upward path.

"Which legion?" Sabina gave her shuttle another yank.

"The appointment has not yet been finalized." Plotina's shuttle passed back and forth without thought on her part, an unthinking rhythm as if it had been magicked into perpetual motion. "My husband was not at all eager to appoint him, you know—it took a great deal of persuasion on my part. Dear Publius's last stint in the legions . . ." A troubling time. He had run up a great many debts in his idle months as a twenty-three-year-old tribune of the Twelfth Primigenia, and Trajan had *not* been pleased. "The dear boy could be rather wild," Plotina temporized.

"Let me guess," Sabina smiled. "Hunting dogs and handsome young men."

"That is an indelicate speculation." The shuttle snapped across with a little more force.

"I know my husband." Sabina put her hands to her back for a moment, stretching like a sleek and sleepy young cat. "What is there to do in these frontier towns except hunt or make love? And he's devoted to both."

"Dear Publius is far more settled now." Plotina's lips pressed tight. "And of course you will accompany him on his appointment to legate, wherever he will be stationed."

"At last we agree," Sabina said sweetly.

So the girl wasn't putting up a fuss about *that*. Good. "You will find the provinces quite different from anything you are used to in Rome," Plotina said, mollified. "Rougher accommodations, rougher company— and of course it is quite impossible to get decent bread, even for a legate's table. But one must endure."

"Coarse bread? Goodness, how shall I ever survive?"

"Even in rough circumstances, certain standards must be maintained. Especially by a legate's wife. Never less than three courses at dinner, even if they must be simple ones, and a proper *stola* worn at all times regardless of the weather." Plotina patted the severe, elegant folds of her own gray silk. "None of this dabbling in local customs. One hears of wives who go to Britannia and come back all over blue paint and native jewelry!"

"Perhaps Hadrian will end up in Britannia. I think I'd look rather well in woad."

"Well may you joke." Plotina raised significant eyebrows. "Now, some mixing with the wives of lower officers is inevitable, but you should keep it to a minimum. The wives of the magistrates and governors make better company. Naturally they will look to you to set the standard of behavior."

"I wonder if he might get a legion in Egypt?" Sabina mused. "I long to take a barge down the Nile like Cleopatra . . ."

"You will be far too busy for riverboat cruises, my dear. Dear Publius will be relying on you to further his career. The right kind of friendships with the provincial governors, the correspondence with useful people here in Rome, the proper parties hosted for the proper guests." Sabina was a rather good hostess, Plotina would grant her that, though she invited far too many of what she called *interesting* people. And there did seem to be a tendency for her dinners to lapse into loose laughing affairs with a great deal of wine and banter, rather than serious functions with serious discussion. Plotina shuddered to think of that one dinner where everyone had ended the night wading in the fountain and passing a jug back and forth like carefree plebs on holiday. Why Trajan and his friends had been so charmed, she really could not understand.

"Most importantly," Plotina concluded, remembering her lecture, "you must not allow Dear Publius's relationships with important people in the city to lapse simply because of a few hundred miles. Men are so forgetful when it comes to writing letters, so I shall rely on you for regular reports—"

"Really?" Sabina's eyes snapped up. "So you won't be coming to the provinces as well?"

"Naturally not. My husband relies on me here. Though of course there are visits." Plotina cleared her throat pointedly. "For example,

Vibia Sabina—if you should find yourself with child while in the provinces, then of course I would come to assist with the confinement."

"Oh, look," Sabina said. "Your barley water."

"Don't change the subject." The Empress laid her shuttle aside altogether, fixing Sabina with a stern gaze. "I had hoped you would have provided Dear Publius with an heir by now, Vibia Sabina. A child of three or four could not accompany you to the provinces, of course—so unhealthful—but I would have been pleased to rear the child in your absence."

"So kind."

"To give birth in the provinces is not ideal. There are difficulties finding a decent physician, and as for a wet nurse—! But the problems are not insurmountable. Complete bed rest, retirement from public entertainments, a diet of barley and fish to avoid stimulation of the blood—"

"Calpurnia says it's silly to shut yourself up like an invalid when pregnant. She goes rolling about the house like a great ball up till the minute the baby starts coming."

"Your stepmother has very *advanced* ideas, but I cannot recommend them."

"My stepmother has given birth to five healthy children." Sabina blinked, innocent. "How many have you had?"

Plotina looked at her coldly. "Children are not granted to us all."

"I have a feeling they won't be granted to me either," Sabina murmured. "Not unless Dear Publius's tastes shift in fairly dramatic fashion."

"Dear Publius will do his duty, and so will you," Plotina snapped. "A man needs a son."

"Trajan doesn't."

"I assure you, he has felt the lack keenly."

Well. Perhaps that was not *quite* the truth. Years ago, Plotina had been certain that once Trajan became Emperor, he'd change his mind about the importance of begetting a son. She had been only thirty-one when he took the purple; it had not been too late. An Emperor needed heirs! But when she said as much, the words just rolled off him. "I'll appoint an heir when the time comes. Best way to do it anyhow. Who knows what kind of son the Fates would send us? This way I can pick the best to follow me, not just pin all my hopes on blood ties."

Plotina had let the subject drop from conversation but certainly not from mind. Trajan didn't know everything, after all. Emperor of Rome or no.

"Dear Publius has become the son my husband always wanted," she said instead. Perhaps that was not strictly true either, but all in good time. "I would not see Dear Publius as deprived as the Emperor. He will require sons, and sooner rather than later. You must—"

A familiar deep voice in the doorway interrupted her. "How domestic you both look. 'Juno and her daughter-in-law Venus, busy at their looms.'"

"Flatterer!" Sabina laughed up at Hadrian. "That's the first time anyone's ever compared me to Venus."

You give me just as many headaches as Venus gives Juno, I'm sure. But Plotina looked at Dear Publius, noble as a column in his crisp toga, and held up her cheek for his kiss. "My dear, I was hoping to catch you."

"Don't tell me. The legate's post?"

"How well informed you are." Plotina sighed. "I should have known you'd charm it out of some freedman."

"So? What legion did you get?" Sabina gave a crisp little military salute as Hadrian bent to greet the trio of hunting dogs who had loped in from the gardens at his footsteps and were now winding eagerly around his feet. "Where is it stationed? Egypt, Syria, Britannia—"

Hadrian tousled the ears of his favorite coursing hound, glancing over at Plotina. "What, our dear Empress didn't tell you?"

"Our dear Empress knows everything," Sabina said sweetly. "How to raise children, raise public morals, and raise cultural standards in the provinces all at the same time! But her omnipotence must have failed her this time around."

Hadrian frowned at the same time Plotina did, but he didn't reprove his wife. *He never does.* Sabina took entirely too teasing a tone with Dear Publius, at least for Plotina's taste, but he didn't seem to mind. He almost seemed to enjoy it!

"So?" Sabina abandoned her loom and danced up to him, looking like a child waiting for a gift. "Where are we going, Legate?"

He straightened from the dogs, tweaking Sabina's cheek in what Plotina could only call affection. *You weren't supposed to be fond of her,* the Empress wanted to snap. *She was merely supposed to be useful.*

But she *wasn't* useful, and he *was* fond, and none of it had quite worked out like Plotina had planned.

"I believe a toast is called for." Hadrian held out a hand, and a well-trained slave instantly filled it with a cup. "To our coming days in . . ."

"*Well?*" Sabina bounced on her toes. Plotina lifted her eyebrows.

"Germania," he relented. "To be specific, Moguntiacum."

TITUS

The journey back west toward Moguntiacum took far less time, Titus noticed, than the journey east. He was content to let the centurion set the pace, signing his name wherever the man pointed so they could commandeer fresh horses from each way station. "With a different horse every day," Vix complained, "you'd think I'd get a good one at least once. But no. They all hate me." Titus got used to leaning over and hauling Vix back into his saddle by the neck of the tunic whenever he started sliding down the horse's shoulder. Even with the grueling pace, Titus didn't mind the return journey so much. Maybe it was just the difference of having someone to share dinner with at the way stations now. "I'm sure Cicero or Juvenal had something clever to say about exhaustion and dirt grinding away the barriers of birth," he told Vix one night, head tipped back in his chair, their boots propped identically before the common-room fire. "But I am for once too tired to come up with a single quote."

"God be thanked," said Vix, his eyes closed. "Pass the bread."

Titus stared into the fire in the crude little way station's common room. His boots were steaming. "I suppose you'll think me a dreadful coward if I tell you I was terrified," he found himself saying. "When I saw those Dacians coming at me . . ." His feet had felt like they were bedded in stone; all he could do was stare frozenly as they grew closer, closer—until Vix's arm found his, jerking him up onto the horse so violently he could hardly move his arm in its socket the next day. "*Terrified* is putting it mildly," Titus concluded.

"I pissed myself the first time I was in the arena and I saw a man coming at me with a sword." Vix tore off a mouthful of bread, reaching up unconsciously to touch the little amulet hanging at his neck. "Everyone's terrified, when the moment comes at you."

"What did you do?"

"Pushed the fear down and killed him first. All you can do, if you don't want to die."

"I *would* have died, if you hadn't picked me up out of that road." Titus felt awkward. The words *Thank you* seemed hopelessly inadequate.

"Don't mention it," Vix said, eyes still closed. "And don't mention what I said either, about pissing myself, or I'll have to kill you."

"Done." Titus tore off a chunk of bread for himself. "What's that token around your neck you keep playing with?"

"Nothing much."

"You made sure to touch it before you jumped into that fight with the Dacians," Titus noted. "Good-luck charm?"

"My father gave it to me," Vix admitted. "Mars—he said the god of war would keep me alive in a fight. Truth is, it's my father's face I see every time I touch it. He was a gladiator too; survived eight years in the Colosseum. I'd rather have his luck than any spear-toting Roman god's." Vix tucked the little disk back under the neck of his tunic. "So far it's kept me safe."

"Father and son gladiators?" Titus wondered.

"Well, there was an emperor who hated both of us . . ."

They made it back to Mog at dusk after a full day's gallop, barely squeezing through the gates before they closed for the night. The centurion was already striding away toward the legate's quarters. "Come along, Tribune, he'll want a report."

"What do you need me for?" Titus wondered. "I don't have anything to contribute. All I did was get yanked off my horse."

"Come along!"

By the time the legate was through with them, it was full dark. Titus trudged into the *principia*, wondering tiredly about dinner. Messengers ran back and forth across the hall, slaves were trotting to and from the records room, legionaries paused to scan the wall for new announcements. New barracks were to be raised, Titus read; a detachment was to be welcomed from Thrace on temporary assignment; a stern reminder had been posted that local women were to be visited off-duty and outside fort walls only . . . no sign here that anyone knew what Titus had seen in Dacia. No sign they were all soon to be at war.

Titus felt a tingle in his belly, like the first tendril of smoke to creep up from a pile of kindling. *Why did I complain about a year of boot polishing and boredom?* he wondered. *Better boot polishing and boredom than battles and blood.*

"Well?" Vix lounged against one wall beside the bust of the Emperor that presided over the *principia* of every fort in Rome. Even in stone repose, Trajan looked friendly. "What news? What did the legate say?"

"To me, nothing." Titus took off his helmet, raking a hand over his hair. "All I did was stand there nodding while the legate grilled the centurion on the details. Then he told me to get out and go eat, and started dictating dispatches."

"I knew it." Vix socked one fist into the other. "War for sure—Trajan won't stand for assaults on his garrisons. That Dacian king will be sorry he was ever born."

"Not as sorry as I am that we missed dinner." Titus winced. "Not that dinner from those hacks the legion calls cooks is much to miss."

"Burned barley and boiled pork," Vix agreed. "Not much like roast dormice and minced flamingo from Rome, is it, Tribune?"

"You saved my life at least twice on this journey, Slight." Titus repressed a shiver. He had a feeling those screaming Dacians were going to be bearing down on him in his dreams for some time yet. "I think you can call me Titus now."

Vix laughed. "Centurion'll have the skin off my back."

"Out of his earshot, then. Perhaps that's best. As Ovid would say, 'One who lives well, lives unnoticed.'"

"Ovid must have known a few centurions." Vix took his proffered hand, a little self-consciously. "Titus, then."

"Good night to you, Vix." Titus staved off a bone-cracking yawn. "I think I'll go see if I can scrape up some of that burned barley and boiled pork. I could eat a dead horse raw."

Vix hesitated a moment. "Tribune—Titus. I've got a girl in town, and she's a better cook than any of those legion butchers. If you want—"

Titus interrupted. "Lead the way."

The lamb stew smelled tantalizing, but Titus was still trying not to stare at the girl who eyed him nervously as she put the bowls down on the table. Full lips in a lovely oval face; skin as clear as new cream and dark-honey hair roped into a thick braid that lapped the back of her knees . . . Vix's girl should have been wearing silk and jewels in a golden palace, not a flour-dusted smock in a one-room tenement over a bakery.

Then Titus took a bite of the stew.

"Oh, gods." He closed his eyes as the first swallow went down. "Marry me, lovely lady?"

"Told you my Demetra could cook." Vix threw a careless arm around the girl's waist. She smiled but cast a nervous glance at Titus. She had gone quite white when he introduced himself.

"*Tribune?*" Demetra squeaked. "What's Vix done? I swear he doesn't visit me often, sir, only when he's off-duty, and I never come into the fort! I know the rules—" It had taken all Titus's reassurances to convince her he wasn't here to haul Vix off for a flogging. Even now she was eyeing Titus as if a dragon had come to roost in her kitchen, despite the ecstatic noises he couldn't help making as he bolted down her stew.

"You're a lucky man," he told Vix in a low voice as the girl retreated to the stove. "Emperors would beg for that girl's favor, Vix—for the stew alone, not to mention the beauty. How did she end up cooking *your* supper?"

"I found a few auxiliaries pestering her at the market one day last year and ran them off." Smugly. "It's easy to get a girl when you've got that rescuer glow."

Titus filed that bit of advice away for future reference. On the other hand, what was he ever going to rescue a girl from? A misattributed quotation?

He was scraping the bowl before he knew it, and Demetra scurried to bring another. He thanked her with a bow, looking around the cozy little room. Not a large room, and it served as kitchen and bedchamber both, but it glowed warm and cheery—a far cry from the sweaty masculine ugliness of the fort. The bed had a bright covering pieced together from colorful scraps of cloth, the rickety table had a cluster of the last autumn asters crammed into an old jug, and there was still a lingering smell of fresh bread drifting up from the bakeshop downstairs.

Vix had already plunged into his own second bowl. "What are you staring at?"

"All this." Titus cast another envious glance around. "Domestic bliss. I never knew how much I missed it until I got consigned to that barren barracks."

"You should get a girl," Vix advised. "Visit her off-duty. Bribe the right people, and you can even get permission to sleep out of the fort."

"There's already a girl I want." For a heady moment, Titus pictured a little cheerful room like this one: books in cases against the walls, fresh bread and fresh flowers, and Sabina lying across the bed crunching an apple and reading. Dimpling up at Titus when he came in . . .

"But she's in Rome," Titus concluded. And she'd never been *his* girl to begin with.

Not that he was still in love with her. If anything, he knew her far better than he had when he'd fallen head over heels at sixteen for a blue-eyed girl who'd been kind enough not to sneer at his very first attempt at a marriage proposal. She'd become someone to borrow books from; someone to take to the Campus Martius on the mornings her husband was busy; someone to share a couch with at dinner parties. Someone to make him secretly proud, when she glided along on *his* arm at the occasional social function. Somehow the other girls his grand-father kept trotting out as prospective wives looked flat, pallid, and passionless compared to Sabina.

No, he wasn't in love with her. But until he found a girl just as captivating, why settle?

"So you've got a girl in Rome," Vix was saying, oblivious. "Who cares? Have a girl here too. It's not like they're ever going to *meet*."

"I won't dignify that by arguing." Titus felt a warm weight against his side, and looked down at the brown-eyed little boy with his curly hair. The child had retreated warily when Titus first entered, taking his carved wooden horse and edging back into a corner to watch, but now he blinked shyly up at his mother's guest. "We were weeks on the road," Titus accused Vix, "out to the edge of the Empire and back, saving each other's lives—and you never told me you had a son! He's what, two years old?"

"Oh, he's not mine." Vix mopped out his bowl with a scrap of bread. "His father was a clerk the legate brought over from Bithynia a few years back. The clerk brought Demetra and the boy with him from his village, but he died the first winter and left 'em alone. German winters aren't for everyone." Vix punched Titus's arm, jostling the stew in his bowl. "Try not to cry when you get your first chilblains."

"I'll do my best." Titus ruffled the little boy's curls, the same dark-honey color of his mother's. "Good of you to look after him, with no father in the world."

"He's not much trouble."

"He shouldn't be bothering you!" Demetra swooped down and bore her handsome son away, scolding in soft Greek.

"So what else did the legate say when you made your report?" Vix reached for the clay jug on the table. "They'll mobilize the Tenth for sure; we're the best legion outside Gaul, and closer too." He still had mud on his boots from the endless riding of the past weeks, but he looked ready to throw his cloak over his shoulder and march for Dacia on the spot. "How long till we march, you think? Two weeks, maybe three—"

"More like three months," Titus said, and sipped from his cup. Cold local mead rather than wine; rotgut stuff, but he'd have choked it down if it had been vinegar. He hadn't felt so warm and welcomed since— well, since he'd come to Germania.

Vix sputtered. "Three *months?*"

"At least. I sit at the Senate a great deal—just listening at the back during public sessions when my grandfather speaks—and I hear a great many wranglings about the disposition of the legions." Titus picked at the mud flaking off his tunic. "It will take time to mobilize everything, send for reinforcements, call in additional legions. At least three months, and more like four."

"Mobilize?" Demetra said behind them, her brown eyes wide. "The Tenth, you mean—it's going east, sir? To fight?"

"Nothing's certain yet," Titus reassured her.

"There had better be a fight this time," Vix snorted. "Five years in the legions, and I haven't had a single good battle! That first go-round Trajan had at the Dacians, when I was just out of training? The Dacians ran before the fight even started, damn them. How am I supposed to get a battlefield promotion to centurion when the buggers settle everything by treaty?"

"Why on earth would anyone want to be a centurion?" Titus asked. "Haven't you seen how hard they have to work?"

"I want all of it," Vix said unhesitatingly. "The work, the rank, the battles; campaign tokens, looted gold, and a triumph in Rome."

"How grand," said Titus, amused. "For myself, I'm just hoping to make it through my tribune posting without anyone else trying to kill me. After that a quiet post looking after census records or inspecting the occasional aqueduct." With a quiet house in a garden, sturdy handsome children like Demetra's boy, and a wife who wasn't Sabina. Hard to fit Sabina into *any* fantasy of domestic bliss. Even in her own immaculate house in Rome, she'd never looked like a contented Roman matron. More like a cheerful but untidy guest who might float out the door at any moment and depart for the ends of the earth.

Well, no use musing.

"You might get that promotion to centurion," Titus said. "Somehow I don't think this go-round with the Dacians is going to end in a treaty. A few months before we move out, maybe, but—"

Demetra burst suddenly into tears, scooping up her son and running from the room.

Titus half rose as the door banged behind her. "What did I say?"

"Who knows? She cries when anyone talks about war. She cries whenever she thinks about me leaving. She cries when her bread doesn't rise." Vix mopped up the last of his stew, unconcerned. "She cries a lot."

"Shouldn't you go after her?"

"Why? Better to let her sob it off. I usually go sleep somewhere else for the night. There's a redhead I like on the street behind the big theatre . . ."

CHAPTER 10

SABINA

Two luxurious wagons had been provided for the wives of the officers traveling north—covered, cushioned, padded, and shuttered for maximum comfort. Within four days Sabina had the first wagon to herself and all the other wives found excuses to ride in the second.

"What on earth did you do to them?" Hadrian ducked his head as he entered.

"Left the shutters open so I could see out." Sabina looked up from the nest she had made for herself: a cushion for her back, a fur over her knees, a dog at her feet, and a scroll in her lap. "Enjoying the fresh air is apparently a criminal offense. I might also have told a few stories about cannibal German tribesmen who burned women alive in wicker cages."

"Did you have to do that?" Hadrian said mildly.

"After four days of listening to their complaints about disobedient children and thieving slaves? Never mind the German cannibals, *I* wanted to burn those wretched women alive in wicker cages."

Hadrian gave his faint flick of a smile, stripping off his gloves and giving them to the dog to chew. He already wore his legate's cloak and breastplate, and very handsome he looked in it too. "How's my old lady here doing?" he asked, reaching down to stroke the gray-muzzled hound curled in the furs at Sabina's feet. "She gets stiff in this cold—"

"Don't worry, I'm taking good care of your favorite girl." Hadrian had no great interest in the comforts of his slaves, but nothing was too much for his dogs. He'd brought the whole pack with him to Germania, insisting there would be good hunting outside Moguntiacum, and they loped grinning and happy behind his big horse—all but the graying bitch who he insisted was too old to run the whole journey, and consequently rode in luxury with Sabina. *Most men would have had her knocked on the head as soon as she couldn't hunt*, Sabina thought. But Hadrian stood tweaking fondly at the old dog's ears as her tail thumped the furs, and every evening he brought her the choice bones from the evening's meat. "I promise I'm looking after her," Sabina reassured her husband. "Do you want breakfast? Looks like we've got a halt before the next river crossing."

Outside the wagon, Sabina heard the cheerful bustle of their journeying party: the ox drovers swearing at their beasts; the young tribunes boasting and spurring their horses back and forth; the slaves dashing in search of food, cloaks, anything to keep their masters comfortable. The sky was gray and the road puddled, but their party of northbound officers, officials, and soldiers was cheerful and noisy. "Bread, honey, and grapes," Sabina said as the slave entered and began laying the cups and plates. "Your usual."

Hadrian's breakfast had to be arranged just so—new-baked bread, the crust not too dark; grapes in a cluster (never a bowl); and just a thimble of honey. Exactly the same whether he was breakfasting at home in their house on the Palatine Hill, here on the road halfway between Rome and Moguntiacum, or anywhere in between. On the day he landed in Hades, Sabina thought with amusement, her husband would demand that Charon the Ferryman bring him his bread, his grapes, and his honey. Half the baggage on this lengthy northbound train of wagons and mules was Hadrian's: the books he could not do without, the slaves essential for his comfort, the dogs and horses and bits of Greek sculpture . . . "And they say women pack too much!" Sabina teased him. "I was ready to leave with a trunk of clothes and a few books!"

"I may wish to see the world," Hadrian said primly, "but not without my library."

At least we are seeing the world now, Sabina thought. With every slow, ponderous creak of the wagon's wheels, they were retreating farther and farther from Rome, from duty, from Plotina's lecturing. Sabina had spent hours hanging out the window of the wagon, chilled to the bone but too fascinated to close the shutters, watching as tilled green fields and tidy vineyards slowly gave way to craggier rocks, deeper pines, darker shadows. Hadrian said they had passed into Raetia now, perhaps halfway to Moguntiacum and the legion that awaited him. Germania. What would it hold?

Hadrian made a face at the cup Sabina passed him as he settled on the bench opposite her. "What *is* this?"

"The local mead. I like it."

He passed the cup back. "I'll stick to Roman wine, thank you."

Sabina took another swallow, unrolling a new section of her scroll. "Lucius Nystericus didn't like the mead either, according to this."

"Who's Lucius Nystericus?" Hadrian sat reading through the correspondence that had already followed them from Rome. They hadn't been two days on the road before messengers on lathered horses began appearing with letter cases.

"Lucius Nystericus was a legate who served here under Augustus. I found a copy of his diaries; thought it might have something useful on the region."

"Anything interesting?" Hadrian reached out absently, scratching the dog's belly as she rolled on her back.

"'The natives are surly,'" Sabina read in a pompous bass. "'But ferocious fighters.'"

"They do look surly. I noticed as soon as we crossed the mountains." Hadrian's hand on the dog's belly slowed; she nosed him until he began to stroke again. "Let's hope they're not still ferocious. Leave the book out for me, will you?"

"Of course." Sabina curled her feet up onto the bench, tucking the fur lap robes in closer. "Any letters in that pile of correspondence for me?"

"From the Empress—"

Sabina took the scroll with Plotina's seal and tossed it out the window unopened. "Anything else?"

He slanted a disapproving brow but let it go. "A letter from your little sister, judging by the straggly handwriting. Perhaps I can leave you to it? The dogs flushed a stag in the woods earlier; magnificent rack of antlers, and since we're paused for another hour—"

"Go hunt." She waved him on. He dropped a perfunctory kiss on her cheek, and she felt the scrape of bristle. "You're growing your beard again?" So many senators had mocked him in Rome that he'd finally shaved it. He'd been out of temper about that for a full week.

Hadrian passed a hand over the stubble. "I think it will pass in the provinces."

"A beard suits you. Very philosophical." And it hid the acne scars he'd acquired as a boy—the real reason he'd grown a beard in the first place. *You're vainer than I am, husband.*

He smiled, touched her hair in passing, and looked down at the dog. "What do you say, old lady? Can you manage a short sprint after a stag?"

The dog uncurled with a happy pant and trotted after him as he ducked out. Sabina waved after them, then finished her mead and handed the cup to a page hovering outside the wagon. A beautiful page; dark-haired and long-limbed and well-muscled; an Antiochene youth of perhaps twenty. Hadrian had not taken as many slaves on this journey as dogs, but somehow all the slaves he'd brought were male and beautiful.

"Domina, will you be wanting to visit the other ladies while the wagons are halted?"

"Gods, no," Sabina said, going back to her book. The long-dead legate Lucius Nystericus had abandoned his complaining about the natives and was now reminiscing about his days stationed in Greece.

Maybe we should go back to Athens soon. Hadrian would like that—he was already complaining about the air here in the north, so damp and heavy on the lungs. Very far from Greece's violent white light and equally violent purple shades. But Sabina thought she might get to like the mists here, the deep stands of trees and the short days with their mole-dark shadows. *Things to be learned here, and work to be done,* she thought, and tossed aside the useless scroll with its prim views on native mead and native women. *No matter what Lucius Nystericus says.*

VIX

Moguntiacum was a different place with three and a half legions in it. Normally it was quiet enough—native women and children bustling through the markets in the daytime hours, taverns and brothels coming alive at night when the legionaries came off duty. Besides drinking and whoring there was a bridge over the Rhine, though what there was to do over the Rhine I didn't know, and there was a shrine to some long-dead Roman prince that drew worshippers from all over Germania, and there was a playhouse that Demetra told me proudly was the largest north of the mountains. I told her I'd seen theatres three times as big in Rome, but she didn't believe me. I'm not even sure she entirely believed in Rome. To Demetra, Rome was Elysium—it might exist somewhere, glittering and beautiful, but it had nothing to do with her.

Now, though, Mog wasn't nearly so sleepy. It was full, crammed, bursting with soldiers. That bloody Dacian king was in full rebellion, and the Emperor had brought in more legions to deal with him properly.

"Three months," Titus had said, and he'd been right after all—we were all the way through winter and into spring now with no sign of marching yet. Nor were the legions done pouring in—the Second Adiutrix had come first, swaggering and boasting that they'd take care of the king of Dacia without needing to stir us from our cozy fort; then the Fourth Flavia Felix came, swaggering and boasting of their lucky reputations without which nothing could be won, and just last week a division of the Sixth Ferrata had come as well, swaggering and boasting of their feats along the Rhine; and now there weren't enough women to go around in Mog, and the girls who looked like my Demetra had to be careful when they went out.

"How many legions do we *need?*" I'd snarled to the rest of my *contuber-*

nium one night when we were all out whoring. I'd dragged Titus along too, though he and my brothers-in-arms still regarded each other with wary bemusement. He was a tribune, after all, an officer even when off-duty, and they were my fellow soldiers, the four men with whom I bunked, slept, ate, trained, and fought. Usually a *contubernium* was made up of eight men, but we'd lost one to a Dacian spear thrust the year I entered the Tenth, and two more had died of camp fever last fall. The five of us left—Simon, Boil, Philip, Julius, and me—might as well have been brothers.

"Titus and I saw off three of those Dacian bastards," I complained. "I don't see why the Tenth can't handle the rest, outnumbered or no."

"Correction," Titus murmured around his mug of beer. "You saw those three Dacians off. I just hung on and prayed."

"It worked," I pointed out. "We're both still alive. Hey, why haven't you grabbed yourself a girl? It's why we came here."

"I don't really go whoring very much," Titus said. He cut an odd figure in that dim smoky little room among my brothers-in-arms: sitting with one heel crossed over his knee, sipping his beer as if it were fine wine as Philip on his right side sat dicing with two half-naked whores, Boil on his left fumbled under the dress of the girl on his lap, and Julius across the table was halfway into his signature tall tale about being descended from Julius Caesar. "Besides, there aren't enough women to go around with three and a half legions in town." He gave a courteous nod to the various half-naked girls around him, and they all dimpled back. "I'm sure the girls are overworked enough as it is."

"Too right," grumbled the redhead in my lap—my favorite for the nights I didn't spend with Demetra. "The men from the Sixth, they're arrogant bastards. Worst tippers in Mog—"

"Them and their lion-head banners," Simon sneered, cracking a nut between his mug and the table. "My sweet, why don't you bring me some more of that mead, and then take a seat on my knee and share it with me—"

"Don't you be sweet-talking me! You know what I cost, and I want coin in hand before I'm sitting on your knee or any other part of you—"

"I'm inclined to think well of the Sixth right now." I draped an arm around my redhead's neck, savoring the news I'd been waiting to drop all night. "Our centurion, in his infinite wisdom"—we all paused to spit and swear—"has decided that with the newest influx of our brothers from the Sixth Ferrata, the camp is becoming overly crowded—"

"We could have told him that!"

"Actually I did tell him that," said Titus. "He didn't listen to me either."

"—and those men who have arrangements in town might lodge there, provided they pay for the privilege." I tilted my chair back, smug. "So while you bastards are bunking with the Sixth and their lion-head banners, I'll be snug in bed with Demetra."

"Hey," said my redhead, poking my shoulder.

"Don't worry, love, I'll have plenty of time for you." I dragged her head down for a kiss. Simon pitched more nutshells at me. Julius, who liked to brag he was descended from the legendary Gaius Julius Caesar just because he had the same balding head and hook nose, made a rude gesture at me without coming up for air from his whore's breasts. "You'll be eating that swill from the legion cooks," I told them with relish, "and I'll wake up every morning to Demetra's bread—"

"Where's my javelin?" Philip asked his two giggling half-naked girls. Philip was a lean little Greek, small but quick, and the only time he didn't have his dice in his hand was when he had his javelin, and when he had his javelin you prayed to whatever god you had that he wasn't pointing it at you.

"You know where your javelin is, legionary!" his girls giggled. "Standing at attention like a proper little soldier, he is—"

"Of course you're all welcome to come eat bread and roast pork whenever you like," I concluded. "Didn't I mention that part?"

"Why didn't you say so?" Boil put down the knife he'd been preparing to whiff through my hair. "Tell her Boil's coming tomorrow after sentry duty."

"Boil, that's an interesting name," Titus said. "How did you get it?"

"Don't ask," I snickered as Boil scowled. He was the youngest of us at seventeen, a fair-haired Gaul as big as a stone outhouse, and when he'd first joined our *contubernium* he'd had a boil on his arse the size of an apple. In the legions you'll be dead before you ever get rid of a nickname like that.

My redhead was scowling at me. "So that's why you stay with that Greek girl. For the *food?*"

"Now, don't be cross with me—"

"You can find another bed warmer, Vercingetorix," she sniffed, and slid off my lap. "I think I'll find myself a *gentleman* for a change." She grabbed Titus's hand and hauled him up from his chair. "Want to see if I'm red-haired all over, Tribune?"

"I wouldn't dream of doubting a lady's word," he said politely. But she was already hauling him away.

"Didn't have to poach mine, did you?" I called after him, but he just gave me a rueful look as the redhead yanked him upstairs.

"Serves you right," Simon told me. Simon was senior man in my *contubernium*, a dark burly man of forty years or so, close to the end of his stint with the legion. He'd been the one to welcome me to the Tenth, when I first shipped north out of my training camp to Germania.

"Vercingetorix." He'd looked me up and down in my creaky new armor and clean sandals. "From Gaul?"

"Britannia."

He grunted and waved a hand at the lowest cot in the *contubernium*. "The recruits keep getting younger," he muttered in Hebrew.

"And the veterans keep getting older," I said back in the same language, and his heavy brows shot up.

"A Jew as well as a Briton?"

"No." I lapsed out of Hebrew, which was rusty for me. "My mother was, that's all."

"Then you're a Jew," Simon said firmly.

"How's that?"

"You're a Jew if your mother is a Jew. That's our law."

"Why the mother?" I wondered. "Why not the father?"

"Because too many soldiers like us have marched through Judaea to make anyone too certain of their fathers," Simon had grimaced. A good man to have on your shield arm.

Titus came down from my redhead's room a few minutes later, looking mussed. "Done already?" I jeered. "Quick work. Admit it, she was your first!"

"No, I just thought I'd come tell you to go home without me," he explained. "She's giving me a whole night free."

"I never get a night free," Boil complained. "What's your secret?"

"I said she had wine-dark lips. It's from the *Odyssey*, sort of."

"Poetry," Philip mused. "Never tried that before. Have you got any more quotes handy?"

"I'll have a list for you by tomorrow," Titus promised over his shoulder as he dashed back up the stairs. They liked him after that, tribune or no.

A long impatient winter, though it passed faster and warmer with Demetra's savory stews in my stomach and her long body in my bed. The other four in my *contubernium* came for dinner as often as they could get out of evening duty, and they got comfortable enough with Titus to start groaning openly whenever he quoted Cicero. Titus still made Demetra nervous, and so did Simon. "You're sure he's not a devil?" she whispered to me, watching him mutter his Hebrew prayers over his plate. "They say Jews mutilate their babies!" She cast an uneasy look at her little boy who tussled, solemn and absorbed, with his carved horse.

"Only their own babies, I think," I said vaguely.

"But *Vix*—"

"Stop fussing!"

She bit her lip, and I bit mine too. Demetra had a harder time of it with so many more men in Mog, after all—a girl who looked like she did couldn't even go to the market alone now without being harassed by off-duty legionaries. She'd tried to hide how relieved she was when I brought my pack to stay in her cozy little home, but she'd cried tears of relief the first time I'd tossed some drunken bastards from the Second out on their heads when they came pounding on her door. She'd been so happy that night, she even let me love her on top of the blankets in the firelight where I could see how beautiful she was. Her hair rippled over my hands like a fall of honey, and I pulled her down to the bed on top of me. She put her arms about my neck, but she was so plainly uneasy that I laughed and tugged the blanket over us both. "Have it your way, prig."

"I am not a prig! People don't make love in plain view where I come from."

"I'm a barbarian." I growled and bit her shoulder. "We do things differently."

"I know," she giggled, and kissed me. An easy lovemaking—she lay still beneath me, smelling sweetly of fresh bread, and afterward she lay against my shoulder chattering of little things. The gossip she heard from the bakeshop, the rumors that the Dacian king had a lion's mane and three horns, the new play coming to the theatre soon. She didn't expect me to listen, and I didn't, just dozed in the cradle of her hair. Dozed, and dreamed of glory.

Spring came muddy and early that year, none too soon because we were hearing more and more rumors of the Dacians massing in the east, and I hoped finally we might be marching. But our legate was ill, something quick and convenient that got him out of his post and back to Rome in a hurry where there were no more wars threatening. Wasn't *that* fun, defending the Tenth's reputation to the bastards in the Fourth and the Sixth and the Second, while their legates growled for war and ours went home to his house on the Tiber. But none of us was growling long, because the Emperor came.

PLOTINA

The House of the Vestal Virgins had been taken over by little girls. Hopping with excitement or round-eyed with awe, they clustered about the long pillared atrium with its tranquil pools and double lane of statues, the bolder girls making cautious forays toward the five white-robed priestesses surveying the scene, the shyer ones clinging to their mothers' skirts. But Plotina had no eye for the children.

"My dear, what a surprise!" She made a deep curtsy to the only woman in Rome who deserved her reverences. "I had no idea you were coming to see the new Vestal selected."

"One of my sister's many granddaughters is a candidate this year." Domitia Longina, Emperor Domitian's widow and former Empress of Rome, raised Plotina from her curtsy. "I came to support her."

"Always a pleasure to see you, of course." Plotina put an arm through her predecessor's, and their respective pairs of Praetorians fell to a tactful distance behind them. The former Empress rarely came to Rome these days—after Emperor Domitian's unfortunate assassination, she had retired to a private villa in Baiae, and made very few public appearances. "I had been planning to call upon you soon," Plotina said. In fact, there was a matter Plotina dearly wished to discuss with her predecessor—and now, the opportunity had dropped itself in her lap. *Doubtless Juno arranged it just for me*, Plotina thought. *I must remind myself to have a cow sacrificed in thanks.*

A little girl in a rose-colored smock ran up with a nosegay of violets and larkspur, looking confused about which Empress to give it to. Plotina made a demurring gesture, and the former Empress took it with a gracious nod. A tall woman, though not as tall as Plotina, with a calm, carved face and iron gray hair knotted demurely beneath a simple veil. She wore a plain pale-blue gown topped by a white wool *palla*, and not a jewel to be seen anywhere. A perfect picture of modesty, dignity, simplicity: Plotina had taken care to model herself in the same mold when she took the former Empress's place.

"Which one is your candidate for sixth Vestal?" she asked as they resumed their slow stroll along the reflecting pool. "Your great-niece, you said?"

"Little Drusilla Cornelia." The former Empress nodded to a blue-gowned little girl holding hands with a beaming grandmother from whom she had clearly inherited her deep dimples. "I'm not certain I want her to win—a thirty-year vow of chastity is something I hesitate to wish on a nine-year-old girl—but no doubt it's an honor to be considered."

"The new candidates are most carefully selected when a Vestal retires," Plotina assured her. "I attended to it myself this year, with the Emperor already gone to Germania. The Vestals, well, I don't need to tell you the importance of picking a girl of *unblemished* moral character." The six Vestal Virgins guarded Rome's eternal hearth, after all. Rome's morality, in a sense. "Not just any loose-kneed little giggler can fulfill such a task."

"I don't know about that. The best Vestal priestess I ever knew had a delightful giggle. And she wasn't a virgin at all."

Plotina blinked. A joke? But the former Empress's face was calm, pensive. "My dear—may I call you Domitia?"

"I don't go by that name anymore. Domitian conferred it on me; he fancied having a wife named after himself. Now he's gone, I find I prefer the name I was born with."

Impossible to read anything from her even voice. Certainly the former Empress always spoke respectfully in public of her dead husband, but one always heard whispers . . . the marriage had begun with a most scandalous elopement (while she had still been married to another man, no less!), and had not proceeded smoothly. Rumors of lovers, a divorce after a quarrel and then a speedy remarriage . . . and the rumor that would not die, the rumor that Emperor Domitian's assassination had been hatched, planned, masterminded, and executed by his wife. The tall woman who now stood at Plotina's side, sniffing at a rosebush.

Absurd, of course. Plotina of all people knew how people liked to tell tales about women in *their* position. Jealousy, not only of rank but of innate moral superiority. She had always discounted the rumors.

Though she did wonder why the former Empress never wore black for the husband she claimed to mourn.

"Marcella Longina of the Cornelii, I believe, is the name you were born under?" Plotina asked brightly. "I can see why you prefer it. Fewer painful memories."

Former Empress Marcella gave a curved smile. "Something like that."

The five Vestal Virgins were trying to corral the little girls now, herding them toward the temple. Chattering mothers and proud fathers followed in their wake, but Plotina put a hand to her predecessor's elbow as she turned to follow. "Perhaps I might speak with you, my dear Marcella? There is a matter very close to my heart . . ."

"Certainly." They lingered by a statue of some long-dead Vestal, doubled in white perfection in the surface of the pool below.

How to put it? Plotina wondered. Perhaps, with a woman she could truly call her equal, it was best to be blunt. After all, Marcella Longina had been the mistress of Rome too once, Empress of the seven hills, another sister to Juno in the heavens. Of *course* she would understand. "You know my husband's ward, Publius Aelius Hadrian?"

"Yes, a fine young man. He was kind enough to dedicate some poetry to me once. Amusing little verses, though I think he was miffed when I said so. A young man's pride bruises so easily."

"I had the raising of him," Plotina said modestly, "and I'm very proud of his achievements—for far more than poetry. Did you know he's been given a legion in Germania? I expect he'll cover himself with glory against those wretched Dacians. Naturally I hope to see him rise."

"Naturally." Empress Marcella began to walk again, her profile calm and regal against the pillars. Plotina tucked a confiding hand through her elbow and lowered her voice, though the chamber was now quite empty. Just two women—empresses, sisters, goddesses—having a little chat.

"It's a matter of the succession. Trajan refuses to name an heir; says it's morbid while he's in such good health. He won't hear any advice on the matter. *You* know what Emperors can be like." A little martyred sigh. "But I worry. For Rome, you know. I want to see the Empire in good hands. And there are none better than my dear Publius."

She waited for agreement. Empress Marcella raised her eyebrows. Plotina pressed on. "I brought him into the Imperial family by marrying him to Vibia Sabina. You'd think that would do the trick—it's not just family ties; Trajan thinks the world of her father. Marcus Norbanus, one of the most moral men in Rome—"

"Most of the time, anyway," Marcella murmured.

"—I thought that would be enough, you see. Enough for Trajan to give Dear Publius his due. But it wasn't. So now I wonder . . ." Plotina gave a little laugh, feeling uncharacteristically giddy. "Forgive me, I hardly know how to put it. What I mean is, how much can one *help*? A woman in my position, I mean. I know my Publius is best for Rome; I simply assumed everyone else would know it too once I drew him into the fold. But now I find people still need a little—push. How much can one push? A wife must keep out of such things, but an empress must also look after the empire's best interests." The question had gnawed on her for quite some time. *Wife or empress? Empress or wife?* "Which comes first?"

Plotina tugged her predecessor to a halt, feeling quite breathless. "You had a hand in seeing your husband become Emperor of Rome, surely. How much of a hand? I model myself on your example in all things, my dear Marcella, so I would model myself in this as well. How much can I do for my Publius?"

Empress Marcella looked her over with a long cool stare. "More scheming empresses," she said at last. "Marvelous."

"Hardly scheming," Plotina smiled. "I merely wish to know if one should . . . help. *Assist.* Under the circumstances, which seem very—"

"Since you seem to want my advice, here it is," Marcella interrupted. "No scheming. No plotting. No kingmaking."

"You don't need to put it like that," Plotina said, nettled. "It's for the good of Rome."

"Fortuna save me, a moralist," the former Empress muttered, giving a shake of her veiled head. "At least in my day, I never pretended I was scheming for anyone's benefit but my own. I didn't want to save Rome; I wanted to be a kingmaker. And for all your fine words, so do you."

"I do *not*—"

"Don't try to outscheme a schemer, my dear." Marcella patted her

successor's cheek. "I've been at this longer than you, and far more effec-
tively. My schemes landed more than one Emperor in his grave, but
they also nearly landed me in mine. Now that I'm old, I've given up
kingmaking. I advise you to do the same, before you even begin, and
let your Publius sink or swim on his own."

"I only asked—" Plotina felt herself floundering. *Me, floundering!*
She never floundered. "That is—"

"I don't wish to know." Empress Marcella held up a hand. "These days
I confine myself to the politics of the past rather than the present. I'm
writing a history of the Republic, and the only scheming I concern myself
with is on the page and at least a hundred years concluded. Give my regrets
to the Chief Vestal; I don't believe I will stay for the selection after all."

She turned and glided away unhurriedly from the sunny pillared
atrium to the round unadorned room that was the Temple of Vesta.
Plotina could only hasten after, swallowing a host of hot words. A trip
to visit the statue of Juno was going to be necessary today, but not for
sacrificial thanks—for commiseration. *Not a true daughter to you, Juno,
oh no. How you must have suffered under Domitian's reign, without a true
empress to guide. Those rumors are true, aren't they—that she slept with
actors and gladiators, that she had her own husband murdered. I am your
only true sister, your only equal.* Schemer indeed!

Plotina could see it clearly now. How foolish she had been, to ask
for guidance from such a woman. Did she not have a conscience of her
own? Didn't she *know* what was best for Rome? For Trajan? For Dear
Publius?

Empress, perhaps, was the title that must come before *wife*. If it was
her duty to help Trajan see clear to the right path, then she must help
him. And Dear Publius too.

The Chief Vestal called for quiet just as former Empress Marcella
reached the cluster of her family. Plotina heard her voice very clearly,
cool and faintly amused as she spoke to her sister: "Cornelia, perhaps
we should take your granddaughter home. Somehow I don't think she'll
be selected today."

CHAPTER 11

VIX

"Isn't he splendid?" I beamed. "Isn't he?"

"That's the Emperor?" Demetra had refused to speak to me all morning, but the sight of the Emperor of Rome riding through the streets right before her eyes had unlocked her pretty mouth from its stubborn silence. "He looks like a god!" she breathed.

"He *is* a god."

"I think I agree," Titus echoed, a skinny pillar standing on Demetra's other side. He wore his toga, for which he ditched his tribune armor whenever possible, and somehow even in all this crush the immaculate folds were unwrinkled. "There's no one quite like Emperor Trajan, is there?"

Our Emperor rode through the streets of Moguntiacum in a red cloak and full armor, vigorous and impatient on his black horse, waving and calling out to the crowd as they screamed for him. He could have been a god . . . or a man on holiday . . . or simply an emperor. An emperor the way an emperor was supposed to be. "I cut his arm open in a fight once," I said reminiscently. "He's probably still got the scar."

"You shouldn't tell lies," Demetra chided.

"I'm not lying! It was a good fight—if he'd had a shield he might have pinned me, but—" A legionary jostled me in the crowd, swearing, and I swung Demetra's little boy up to my shoulders to keep him out of the crush. He yelled, grabbing double handfuls of my hair in his excitement as the Emperor's Praetorian guards began filing past in immaculate red-and-gold rows.

"Maybe there won't be war now." Demetra shaded her eyes with her hand, peering over the packed heads before her. "Now the Emperor's here, maybe he'll make peace?"

"You might hope for that," Titus told her, "and so do I. But unfortunately, I think we're the only ones. No one else from the Emperor on down wants peace."

"Me included." I craned for a last view of Trajan's red cloak, vanishing now around a bend in the road and toward the fort. Normally I'd have received him in tight rows with the rest of the Tenth, but there were far too many legions to array us all together, so half of us had been released to welcome the Emperor in the crowd. The poor bastards at stiff attention in their ranks outside the fort must be finding it hard to keep discipline—I could hear the banging of spear hafts against shields from a mile distant. Suddenly I felt an itch to be back among them, cheering myself hoarse among the smells of iron and sweat.

"Sojers!" Demetra's little boy yelled, hanging on to my ears, and I yowled at him. Swinging him down, I made horrible faces until he giggled. "At least someone thinks I'm funny," I said pointedly.

Demetra looked at the ground, lips tightening. Titus looked back and forth between us.

"It's supposed to be a celebration today." I swung her son upside down, holding him by his heels as he gurgled and shrieked. The Praetorians had passed now, giving way to the wagons, the Imperial freedmen, the secretaries and stewards, the rest of the entourage that traveled wherever an emperor led. The crowd's cheering had mostly died off, though I could hear the banging of javelins against shields increasing, and the shouts mounting as well. The crowd about me had slowed to cheerful conversation, the passing of wineskins, the waving of pennants, and the business of making the day into a holiday. "It's a holiday, so will you stop sulking?"

"*Sulking?*" Demetra's voice wound up into a squeak. "If you think I'm sulking—"

"So," Titus interrupted brightly. "I thought you'd have sentry duty today, Slight. How did you get out of it?"

"Luck. Simon and Boil got stuck instead, poor bastards." I blinked my thanks at Titus for the interruption; he blinked back and turned to Demetra.

"Allow me to take your arm, can't have you crushed in this crowd—"

Demetra gave a shy bob of her head. Titus came to dinner often enough that she no longer dropped to her knees at the sight of him, but she still tended to get stiff and self-conscious in his presence.

"I don't see how you can say you're friends with an officer," she'd said to me, awestruck and a little disapproving. "Like should keep to like."

"According to who?" I'd shot back.

"Have you heard the news?" Titus continued. "It's just come from the *principia*, about the new legate—hadn't you better put him right side up, Vix?"

"The legate? Oh." I realized I was still holding Demetra's boy upside down by the ankles and hastily swung him back up before his face turned purple. Demetra took him, still jutting her chin at me, but the boy just grinned. A handsome little scrap, honey-haired and dark-eyed like his mother. "What about the legate?" I pressed. "Have we got a new one?"

"Just come from Rome." Titus beamed as if he'd brought the Legate all the way north just for my approval. "One of the Imperial cousins, at least by marriage."

"Just what we need," I grunted, applying my shoulder to the crush. Titus courteously cleared a path for Demetra as we fought our way out of the crush around the bridge and back toward the town's forum. "Another patrician sprat."

"I'm a patrician sprat," Titus protested. "We're not all bad."

"I still wouldn't want you leading my legion! The worst tribune in all Germania—"

"I'm sure you'd make a lovely legate, sir," Demetra said, anxious. "Vix didn't mean that."

"I did too! Who wants a sprig in a toga at the head of a legion? We need one of those rawhide commanders who worked their way up from centurion—"

"Someone like you? I'll put your name forward, Vix, but you might be a little far down the chain."

"Not so far down. I'll make centurion, then I'll make chief centurion, then prefect of the camp, then I get my own legion." We broke out into the forum, and I paused to buy a stick of savory roasted meat off a vendor. "Couldn't be simpler."

"Only those of, ah, senatorial class are appointed as legates," Titus pointed out.

"Then I guess I'll be the first exception."

"Not if you don't make *optio* first," Demetra snapped. "And you won't, not the way they all hate you—"

"Who wants to be an *optio*?" I bit a chunk of spiced meat off the skewer. "Gutless little weasels."

"Then you'd better make some friends who can bump you straight up to centurion without any intervening stops at *optio*," Titus advised. "Meet me at the *principia* this evening, and we'll circulate. The Emperor's having a dinner party to meet his officers—we won't get into that, but there's bound to be plenty of important people drifting about. If you don't look too grubby, I can introduce you to a few of them."

"It could be a great thing for you," Demetra insisted. "I don't see what you have against making *optio*. We could use the money. Especially this fall . . ."

"Not that again. I told you."

Demetra's face darkened, and she jerked her arm out of my hand. She snatched up her squirming son and began elbowing her way through the crowd again.

"Oh, hell," I scowled.

"What's wrong with her?" Titus blinked.

"The silly cow got pregnant." I tossed away the greasy meat skewer, scrubbing my hands together.

"Congratulations," Titus said at once.

"For what?"

"It's the traditional response, Slight. And surely it's an occasion for happiness? She's a beautiful girl, she's respectably born, and she cooks like a goddess. Actually I doubt goddesses cook at all, so she's better than a goddess. You're going to marry her, I presume?"

"*She* presumes." I stifled a belch. "She's been after me ever since she found out—we marry, we get bigger rooms, God knows what else."

"It's hardly a fate worse than death." Titus looked wistful. "I wouldn't mind having a wife to cook for me."

"You marry her, then."

"And raise a child of yours? I'd be driven to an early grave." Titus cocked his head toward where Demetra had stormed off. "Aren't you going after her?"

"Why? We already had this argument last night."

"She's carrying your child, Vercingetorix." Titus's voice was surprisingly stern. "She has earned your respect, if nothing else."

"Oh, hell," I grumbled again, and tramped after Demetra.

Her grand exit had been slowed by the crush, and I caught up to her as she squeezed out of the crowded forum and into one of the winding side streets.

"Don't flounce off alone just to make a point." I took her elbow irritably. "Too many soldiers around this afternoon looking for a little fun."

"Why should you care?" Demetra stared straight ahead as she bore down the street, color burning high in her face. "You don't want your own child, so why do you care what happens to me?"

"You know soldiers aren't allowed to marry! What's the point of starting a family? You work hard enough with just the one pup in tow!"

She didn't answer, just put up her trembling chin and towed me behind her by my grip on her elbow.

"I said I'd give you money, didn't I?"

"To get rid of it!"

"It's early days, it's safe enough. And I'll pay for the work you miss too," I added generously.

She started to sputter, lost her words, and lapsed back into her native Greek.

"What?" I raised my voice as she jerked her arm free and whirled up the street again. "What did I say?"

"Go away!"

"Oh, now you're telling me to go away," I yelled back. "But when your belly's under your chin you'll have your hand out, all right! Didn't you even *think*? Even try to be careful?"

"No!" She whirled around on me just as she turned onto the narrow street where her rooms lay above the bakehouse. I saw tears in her huge eyes, but her chin was still high. So beautiful, with her dark-gold hair loosening around her face in little curls and her cheeks like wild roses . . . Hell's gates, she was tiresome. "No, I didn't try to be careful. I'm not a *whore*, Vix, how would I know about things like that?"

"So you have to be a whore to think ahead?" I thought of Sabina, her pessaries and concoctions that had kept both of us free of having to worry about consequences. "You just wanted to hook yourself another husband, admit it—"

"I did not!"

There were a great many interested glances coming our way by now. I tried to bring my voice down. "Look, let's be sensible."

Demetra squeezed her little boy so tight he yelped, then flounced on her heel and disappeared into the bakeshop.

"You know I'm right!" I yelled after her. "I'll give you some money, and everything will be good as new."

"I don't want your money!"

Of course she wanted money—what else could she possibly want? What else did *any* woman want? "Demetra—"

She banged the door of the bakeshop in my face. I heard a loud sob from within, and then nothing.

I hammered on the door for a while, but she didn't answer, and soon I realized that half the housewives on the street were staring and giggling from their windows. I made a rude gesture and stalked off. Bloody women. I hoped the Tenth would be marching to Dacia very soon.

My furious feet took me back over the bridge, where the roiling river was swollen with spring floods and matched my mood perfectly, back along the well-beaten path to the camp. Two soldiers from my cohort called out to me, but I gave such a black scowl in return that they kept going.

I banged my way to the *principia*, scanning the notices pinned to the outer wall. News always came there first—promotions, demotions, holidays, upcoming inspections. Any news that the invasion into Dacia was beginning—hopefully tomorrow—would be posted here first. But there was no news posted, and I turned with a snarl and caromed off a tall figure in a toga.

"Watch where you're going!" I snapped.

"Better for you to watch where you are going, soldier," a deep patrician voice said, and I knew the voice before I looked up and recognized the handsome bearded face. I remembered the voice very well. I remembered another voice too, a voice from the slums that had snarled, "This is from Tribune Hadrian," before driving a fist into my face and a boot into my side.

Oh, how I wanted to hit the bastard. I could feel my hand itch. "Tribune," I said.

"Not anymore." His eyes flickered. "I know you." It was not a question.

"Could say so." I bowed, calculating just how many lashes I'd get across the back from my centurion for striking a superior, and if it would be worth it. "Sir."

I could see the honing of his glance as he retrieved the memory from whatever bank of scrolls it was that served him for a mind. "Vercingetorix. The Norbanus guard. I suppose it is to be expected that you joined the legions. What else is there, for those of your sort?" He twitched the folds of his toga across his chest. "Dismissed."

I bowed, and he whirled his purple-bordered folds and turned in the other direction. But I'd spied a trailing end of that fine toga, and surreptitiously put my foot down on it, and it snapped taut and caught him up. His foot slipped in a slick of spring mud and down he went.

"Sir!" I sprang into motion. "Allow me to help you, sir. My pleasure, sir." I managed to slip and get my own hand covered in mud before I held it out to him, then trip again and land him back in the worst of it. "So sorry, sir. Mud, sir, very treacherous in the springtime, sir."

He was expressionless as he finally rose: a broad smear of mud down one arm and along one leg, and another right across the rump. Across the *principia* I could hear a cluster of watching centurions snickering.

"Vercingetorix," he said, thoughtful. "I seem to remember you required a lesson from me in the past. Perhaps it was not stern enough."

"Sorry, sir. Can't remember, sir."

"Clearly it was not stern enough, then."

"Sir." I stood at my stiffest attention as he gathered his muddy folds about him and marched off into the *principia*. If that beetle-brained prig thought he could lay a finger on me while I was in the Tenth, he'd have a stern lesson coming *his* way. Only an officer of the Tenth could levy punishment on me, and only for violating the legion's own regulations. And if Hadrian got creative and tried to hire a beating for me, as he'd done in the past, he'd find I had a friend among the tribunes *and* four loyal brothers in my *contubernium*, all of whom would have my back clear down to hell.

Suddenly feeling more cheerful, I swung back into the rows of barracks toward my own.

"Heard the news?" Boil was lacing up his breastplate as I came into the little barracks room with its stacked beds that I shared with my *contubernium*. "We've got a new legate."

"Heard that already from Titus." I tossed my sword belt onto the cot that had been very little used lately. I had a feeling that with Demetra barring her door, I'd be seeing more of my barracks cot. Or at least of my redheaded whore. "Some cousin of the Emperor's?"

"Had some experience at least," Philip said from the floor, where he was casting another endless game of dice. "Tribune somewhere, a legate somewhere else—maybe the Fourteenth? Trajan doesn't promote generals who just stand around looking pretty, so this one must be decent if he's got the Tenth just in time for an invasion."

"Just hope he's not a flogger," I said. "Who are you playing against, Philip?"

"Myself, and I'm still losing." Philip cast the dice again, cursing. "Boil, you saw the new legate. What's he look like?"

"Tall." Boil stuffed a scarf under the neck of his breastplate. "He's got a beard—looks funny. How many patricians have you seen with beards?"

I suddenly felt cold. "What's his name?"

"Publius Aelius something. He married the Emperor's niece or something, that's how he's got so high up when he's not even thirty-five. Publius Aelius—Adrianus?"

I fell onto my cot with a moan, narrowly missing the sword. "Hadrian," I said hollowly. Our new legate, our general, the man who would be leading us into battle against the Dacians and have command over all our lives, was Sabina's husband Hadrian.

TITUS

"Titus!" Sabina straightened from a box of scrolls. "As soon as Hadrian said he got a legion in Germania, I prayed it was yours. Fortuna must have been listening."

She stood on tiptoe and kissed him on both cheeks. Titus hoped the lick of hair on the back of his head wasn't standing straight up. "You're still unpacking?" he said, and at once kicked himself. *What does it look like she's doing? Baking a cake?* Slaves bustled about with piles of clothes and armloads of cushions, rushing from this room to that, and boxes lay everywhere bursting with half-unrolled scrolls and trailing scarves and dozing dogs who lifted their heads at Titus's arrival and then went back to sleep.

"Yes, we only arrived a few days ago. Trajan started after us, and he still nearly beat us here." Sabina removed a bust of her father off a box, waving Titus to sit. "I'd offer you a chair, but I'm afraid this is the best I can do. I couldn't even find my own clothes this morning."

Titus perched on the edge of his box, trying not to stare. Sabina had skewered her hair at the back of her neck by jabbing a stylus through it, and she was wearing what was clearly one of her husband's tunics, which left her long legs bare below the knee. *Vix can have his blond Bithynian goddess*, Titus decided. *I like them blue-eyed and coltish.*

A slave girl hovered at Sabina's elbow with a questioning look. Sabina glanced at the crate in her arms and pointed. "Books go in the back. I'll organize them later. Did you bring a message, Titus?"

"A note from the Emperor. He wants to dine with all the legates this evening." Any of the aides or freedmen could have delivered it, but Titus had seized the excuse to take it over himself.

Hadrian stalked in then, brushing dried mud off his arm. "No progress on the chaos yet?"

"I've extricated the library, but the box with my clothes is still nowhere to be found." Sabina rose to kiss her husband's cheek with casual wifeliness, and Titus felt a shaft of pure envy go through his chest. "Goodness, what happened to you?" she added, eyeing the mud that literally daubed Hadrian's toga.

"An accident." Hadrian frowned, unwinding the muddy folds and presenting them with the tips of his fingers to a waiting slave. "One I shall have to give some thought to correcting. You have a dispatch for me, Tribune?"

"Yes, from the Emperor." Titus handed it over. He had met his legate formally a few days ago, during formal introductions to the young officers, and had been astonished to be singled out.

"Titus," Hadrian had said with a charming smile. "I had not thought to find a familiar face so far north."

"I'm surprised you recognize me at all, sir. I'm far too insignificant to be noticed by a man of your stature." Titus had met Sabina's husband many times in Rome, of course, at dinner parties and plays and formal occasions, but Hadrian had had little time then for some callow young friend of his wife's. He had merely nodded at Titus in passing and looked on to more important people. But finding Titus among his staff in Germania, he had smiled as if at an old friend. "Delighted to have you, Tribune."

He really did sound delighted, Titus had thought—and he looked pleased now as he took the dispatch from Titus's hand and broke the seal.

"We're dining with Trajan tonight," Sabina explained.

"He doesn't allow *me* to call him by name," Hadrian grumbled.

"But I get special privileges. I'm his little pet, after all."

"And I'm his ward! The closest thing to a son he has, or at least I should be." A slave bumped Hadrian's elbow, murmured an apology, and kept dashing with an armload of clothes. Hadrian looked at the chaos around him and shook his head, reaching down to dispense pats to the dogs, who had leaped up as soon as he entered. "I hope you can unearth a dinner synthesis for me out of all this mess, Vibia Sabina."

"Never mind your synthesis." Sabina rooted through the nearest box, unearthing a statuette, a single earring, and a bottle of ink. "If I don't find *my* clothes, then I'll have to show up naked. Wouldn't that make a splash?"

Titus did his best to dismiss the image that popped immediately to mind. At least until he was out of his new legate's presence. "How do you find your new legion, sir?" he asked hastily.

"The men are impudent," Hadrian frowned at the smear of mud along one broad arm.

"I assure you they can fight, sir."

"I'd prefer them both fighting fit *and* respectful." Hadrian directed a slave with a stack of writing tablets into his study. "None of your exploring, Vibia Sabina. Even a legate's wife isn't safe to walk alone among all these rough men. They haven't seen a proper Roman woman in years—no telling what they'd do if they came across you wandering about sniffing the flowers."

"No wandering," Sabina said. "I promise."

"Is it a promise you have any intention of keeping?"

"Not really, no," she confessed. "But I'll be careful."

"Minx." He smiled faintly. "Go and change. I'd rather not have you flashing your knees at my tribune, even if he has been good enough to keep his eyes away from them."

Sabina gave a little salute, blew a kiss at Titus, and disappeared into the next room. Titus cleared his throat, looking at the ceiling.

"Forgive my wife," Hadrian said, breaking the seal on Trajan's note and scanning it. "As you well know, she can be impossible at times."

"'Often the prickly thorn produces tender roses.'"

"I'd not thought to find a reader of Ovid in Moguntiacum."

"I brought as many books as I could carry north," Titus confessed. "Though I fear I've read them all by now."

"If you wish to borrow any of mine, you have only to ask." Hadrian's smile was aloof but friendly, his dark eyes keen. "Will you accompany us to dinner this evening with the Emperor?"

"Me, sir?" Titus blinked, wondering for a moment if Sabina's husband might be flirting with him. *Gods, wouldn't that be awkward.* But Sabina had confided before that Hadrian's taste ran solely to strapping young athletes, and Titus had only to look at himself to know that he didn't fit *that* mold. Besides, the warmth in his legate's gaze was friendly rather than flirtatious.

"I would appreciate the company," Hadrian went on. "The Emperor is a great man, of course, but conversation at his supper tables does tend toward siege tactics and war stories rather than philosophy and rhetoric. I would be grateful for a fellow lover of books to converse with when the others start refighting Philippi."

"Honored, sir." Titus went out whistling.

Thank the gods he didn't catch me looking at her legs.

SABINA

"I win," Hadrian whispered. Sabina made a face at him, but dropped a coin into his hand under the folds of his dinner synthesis. It had taken Emperor Trajan and his officers just until the second course to start refighting the battle of Actium, not the third as Sabina had wagered. The slaves, obviously used to their Emperor's ways, circulated the wine again and stood back against the walls rather than clearing away the picked-over dishes. They watched Trajan with undisguised fondness, as did Sabina: a celebratory wreath cocked over his graying head at a rakish angle, poking a gnawed goose leg at one of his other legates. "No, no, it wasn't like that at all—" and he swiftly rearranged the bones of the roast goose into a diagram of the Egyptian fleet. The Emperor looked far happier in this crude smoky triclinium in a far outpost of Germania than he ever looked stuffed into a toga and sitting at Plotina's side during one of her interminable Imperial banquets.

"Little Sabina!" he'd shouted when she and Hadrian entered that evening, enveloping her in one of his crushing bear hugs. She was the only woman to dine that evening; none of the other legates had brought their wives north to Germania. "Gods' bones, what is a little bit of a thing like you doing up in the arse end of nowhere?"

"Escaping your wife's good advice," Sabina said with utter honesty. Hadrian frowned at that, but Trajan threw his head back and roared.

"Maybe I'm doing a little of that too, eh? Come, come, sit by me—"

Trajan and his officers had moved on from Actium to Alesia. The roast goose bones had been rearranged to represent Caesar's legions, and a shank of roast boar had become the enemy fort. Hadrian, on Sabina's other side, had claimed Titus's attention and they were dissecting the tale of Aeneas, with Titus holding staunch for Virgil and Hadrian waving his arms in support for Ennius. Titus looked over from time to time, trying to draw Sabina into the conversation, but there was no interrupting Hadrian in full flow.

"No, no, far too polished and mannered. Good straightforward prose is what Roman literature needs, not these mincing tricks of the pen—"

"—that Dacian king, he'll go down faster for us than the Averni did for Caesar—"

Sabina slid off the couch. Neither Hadrian nor Trajan noticed as she tugged her *palla* up over her hair and sauntered out of the triclinium into the black German night.

Such stars! Were there stars like this over Rome, hidden by the smoke and the dust? Or did Germania have a different night sky altogether? So much bigger, so much blacker, stars flung across from horizon to horizon like an emperor's ransom in diamonds. Sabina wandered away from the circle of lamplight outside the Emperor's quarters, waving back the guards who started to tramp after her, and after some more wandering around the shadowy darkness of the *principia*, she found a patch of grass. The occasional legionary tramped past on his way to sentry duty, or an aide dashing with an armload of slates, but no one paid any attention to Sabina, so she flopped down on her back in the grass and stared skyward. If she closed her eyes, it felt like she was clinging to the surface of the earth by her fingertips. *If I let go, will I fly up there and never come down? Would I even want to come down . . .*

"Ow," said a male voice, and someone fell over her in the dark.

Sabina scrambled to her feet, tripping over a fallen spear haft. Someone else tripped over her foot, and nearly went down again. A large male someone, just an armored shape in the dark.

"Who goes there?" a voice demanded, finally straightening.

"The legate's wife," Sabina said, tugging the black *palla* off her hair. "Hello, Vix."

There was a long pause. "Oh, hell," he said finally.

"I thought I might run into you here," Sabina smiled into the dark. Clearly this was to be a night full of surprises. "Just not quite so literally."

"Lady." His voice was flat as he gave a jerk of a bow. "The Emperor's banquet is that way."

"Good, then you can take me back." She managed to find his arm in the dark, tucking her hand neatly into his elbow. "Trajan and his legates are busy refighting the Republic's wars, so I came out here to catch my breath from those smoky lamps—why does German lamp oil smoke so much? Now I'm not sure I know the way back."

"Straight left and up." Vix tugged his arm loose from her hand. "The legate's quarters are always on the far side of the *principia*. Every fort in the Empire, they're all laid out the same."

"Really?" Sabina said, interested. "I didn't know that. Tell me more."

"No."

But her hand had found his elbow again, and he was towing her resignedly back up the path between the barracks toward the Emperor's quarters. A yellow flash of torchlight cut across the path as they turned the corner, and he turned from an anonymous armored shape into—Vix. But a very different Vix from the tall boy who had shared her bed at eighteen. He'd finally filled into his height, all those long bones knitted together with a man's muscle. He looked brown and lithe and watchful, and he wore his breastplate and sword as naturally as a dragon wore its scales. She tilted her head up at him in frank admiration. "You look well, Vix."

"You don't," he said rudely. "You look haggard."

"I still read too much at night."

"Not much else to do at night, I reckon. Not with a husband like you've got." His eyes went over her as they passed another torch, and Sabina was glad she'd managed to unearth her black *stola* from the chaos of unpacking. She knew she looked well in it—the cloth woven so fine it shimmered and ran under the torchlight like dark water, and a single massive gold cuff shaped like a lion covering one wrist. Somehow she found herself still wanting to look well for Vix, even if he didn't care either way.

He lengthened his stride as if he were trying to leave her behind, but Sabina kept up, swinging the black *palla* over one arm. "Have you got a woman now, Vix?"

"Plenty of them," he shot back. "Lots of high-born ladies like a bit of rough."

She laughed. "Gods, I'd forgotten how you can glower. You're in the Tenth, aren't you? My father wrote your letter of recommendation."

"The Tenth's the best in Germania. We'll be the vanguard, when Trajan takes us into Dacia."

"I hear the Fourth wants the vanguard."

"The Fourth can bugger themselves on their own javelins."

"I'll tell them so for you, if I meet any."

"Don't care what you tell anybody. Here you are, Lady." They'd reached the legate's quarters that Trajan had made into his temporary home. The doors had been thrown open, slaves clustered with cloaks for their masters, and inside Sabina could see the tipsy guests saying their languid farewells in the atrium. "I guess they finished refighting Alesia," she said. "Or maybe they just ran out of chicken bones to build diagrams. You know the Emperor's declared a march? He announced it tonight at dinner."

"A march?" Vix halted in the act of turning away. "When?"

"Next week, if he can—how did he put it?" She cast her eyes up to the black, diamonded dome of sky. "'Put a boot to every legion's arse in time.'"

"He'll find the Tenth ready." The corner of Vix's mouth tugged upward, no matter how much he tried to stamp it down.

"I wish I could see it," Sabina confessed. "The legions on the move. I'm sure it will be a sight."

"Lots of swearing. Lots of mud."

"Other things too, I'm sure." She tossed the bundle of *palla* over one shoulder. "But there's no room for wives on the march; Hadrian's made that clear. Even legates' wives. I'd go back to Rome, but then I'll have to deal with Empress Plotina. I think on the whole I'd prefer the king of Dacia with his horns and tail." Sabina looked up at Vix. "Don't keep safe."

"What?"

"Don't bother keeping safe when you finally march off to war." She clasped her hands in front of her waist, the gold lion cuff catching a gleam from the yellow torchlight. "Safe soldiers don't win glory. If it's glory you still want?"

"Yes," Vix said at once. "And a laurel wreath, and a promotion to centurion, and then—" He caught himself, scowling. "None of your business. Good night, Lady."

"Good night, Vercingetorix." She grinned as she turned away, toward the triclinium where Hadrian and Titus still stood debating poets. "It *is* good to see you."

"Can't say the same for you," he shot back, and took off into the dark.

CHAPTER 12

VIX

I like route marches. Provided the sun is shining and there isn't too much mud, they're downright pleasant. My shoulders usually protested the heavy pack for the first hour or so, but after a while everything loosened up and I'd be swinging along in good humor, roaring out the marching songs that helped keep the legion in step. Marching songs varied—if you got a particularly pious or priggish centurion, then the songs all tended to be grim invocations to Mars, or leaden patriotic verses about the glory of Rome. But Emperor Trajan was a legionary at heart, and he liked his marching songs the dirtier the better, so we all had free rein.

We marched fast out of Mog. Half of us were leaving bad debts and pregnant women behind, and all of us were happy to be marching toward action. Slaves, loot, plunder—plenty of rewards, once we mashed down that Dacian king. Even the lowly soldiers like me could come out rich.

"I don't care about rich," Boil confided between marching songs as we proceeded arm to arm. "I just want me one of those Dacian women. Wildcats, they are. I'll bring her back to Germania with me—"

"And then she'll leave you for a tavernkeeper like the last one did," Simon teased.

"That was a long time ago."

"Four months! And the one before that left you for a lute player—"

"Slaves for me," Philip was saying on my other side. "A dozen big muscular warriors. Send them to my woman, she can feed 'em up and train 'em—"

"If they don't up and kill her."

"You ever seen my woman?" Philip shuddered. "She'll have 'em heeling like dogs. A fat profit on the market, that is. Gladiator schools pay well for barbarians—"

"Enough to stake your dice for a month at least," I agreed, and Philip whacked me over the head with his javelin. I shoved back.

"Order in the ranks!" Our centurion rode by, shouting, and we straightened hastily. "Step lively, now."

"Bastard has something to prove," Simon muttered.

"Don't we all?" Julius peered up the road through the dust, where the Fourth were trotting double-quick. "You want to see the Fourth get into Dacia first? As my ancestor the noble Julius Caesar was first across the Rubicon, we shall be first into the east."

We shifted our packs and quickened our steps. The Tenth Fidelis could easily make eighteen miles in a day—twenty-two if we hurried. Not bad at all for a fort-based legion that only did one or two route marches a month.

Though if I'd been commander of the Tenth, I'd have made it twenty-*four* miles a day.

I hadn't seen anything of Legate Publius Aelius Hadrian since the start of the march, when he'd sallied out on horseback, very noble in a red cloak. He rode far ahead with the Emperor and the rest of the legates, and as far as I was concerned he could stay there. A legion was a big place—more than five thousand men when we were up to full complement. Big enough to avoid even the man in charge if you were bent on it, and I was bent on it. That bearded bastard wasn't going to lay eyes on me for the entire campaign if I could help it . . . had I *really* made a point of pushing my legate into the mud in front of a cluster of snickering centurions?

Never mind. I had a legate who hated me, but I also had a war to fight and a ladder to climb. More than enough to deal with without borrowing trouble.

A long day's march. We cycled through most of our marching songs, and at the midday rest I learned a few new ones from a friendly clerk in the Sixth. Very dirty ones. "We were posted out in Syria for years," the clerk confided. "Nothing to screw up there but the cows. You think Dacia has any pretty girls?"

"Pretty," I said, "but they'll leave scratches down your back a mile long."

"Better than mooing," he leered. "You've got a woman?"

"One, and that's one too many." I'd patched things up with Demetra, mostly because Titus had gotten very stern with me. "She's carrying your child," he said, exasperated. "In plenty of traditions that makes her your wife, whether or not you stood before an altar and recited any vows—"

"Don't say it," I winced.

"—and a husband at least owes his wife a farewell before he marches off to war." For such a skinny self-effacing young sprig, Titus had a surprisingly flinty stare. "Do right by her, Vercingetorix."

In truth I cared more about keeping Titus for my friend than keeping Demetra for my woman, but the result was the same. I gulped under his gaze, fortified myself with a fair amount of unmixed wine and a good-bye cuddle from my redhead, and went to see Demetra the night before we marched. It was about as bad as I'd feared—she cried a lot, and I tried to be soothing, and she cried some more, and I made noises about having to be up in time for the dawn march, and that set her crying the hardest of all. "You'll be dead," she sobbed into my chest. "You'll be k-killed in Dacia by that king with the lion skin and the horns—you'll never come back!"

"None of that, now," I cajoled. "Takes more than a king with horns to kill me. I'll be back soon with a sack full of gold, you'll see."

"Really? You'll come back to me?"

"Really." Maybe. Maybe not. By that time I'd have promised anything to stop the weeping. Her little boy watched me from the corner with big brown eyes just like hers, only less red and blotchy.

"I'll have your son," she said, hands sliding to her still-flat stomach. "I know you'll want him when you see him, Vix. All men want sons."

"You could still, you know . . ." I hedged. "Before it gets dangerous. Then maybe we could get married when I come back. It would make everything easier."

Her answering smile was wan, and I smothered the spark of anger in my chest. Wasn't I doing my best here? Wasn't I *trying?* "We'll have a proper wedding," I said, watching the moon drift past the window carrying my last hours of rest with it. "With a feast and a red veil and everything."

"But my people don't wear red veils at weddings."

"Whatever you like." I leaned down and kissed her, edging her back toward the bed—it would be a long time marching, after all, and I would miss her smooth slim form in my bed, and maybe *that* would stop her crying—but there was another fuss and apparently the women of Bithynia didn't make love while carrying children, and all in all I spent the night before my march east holding Demetra on the bed, fully clothed, making soothing noises whenever she stopped crying, which wasn't often.

No wonder I was enjoying the march.

I thanked the clerk from the Sixth and headed back toward the rest of my *contubernium* with a water skin. Demetra had been very dignified when bidding me good-bye—the night's worth of tears had just made her eyes enormous and hollow and appealing. Maybe I *could* marry her when I got back. Titus was right; I wasn't going to find better than Demetra. If I married her, maybe she'd quit crying all the time. And there was no denying she was beautiful, docile, uncomplicated: all the things I liked. All the things Sabina wasn't.

It hadn't been hard to avoid my legate's wife, after that odd night stumbling into her outside the *principia.* Officers' wives didn't cross paths with common soldiers in the ordinary scheme of things . . . damn her, she'd looked well. I'd have liked to see her pasty and unhappy, but she just swung along beside me in her gold sandals, sinuous and unconcerned as ever. I couldn't help but wonder briefly if I might be able to bed her again—that would put a spike up Hadrian's arse and no mistake. But if my legate already loathed me, then bedding his wife wasn't the wisest move to make, and besides I'd already been burned once by that girl and I was damned if I'd do it again. Far better to just marry my Bithynian goddess and have done with it.

Another half-day's march. Emperor Trajan rode past the column, splendid in a red cloak, his face cheerful and boyish under the plumed helmet, bawling out the bawdiest marching songs with relish. His singing checked when we marched past a burned garrison just like the one Titus and I had reported at the end of . . . could it be just last fall? The Dacian king had sent raiders deep into Germania, thumbing his nose to show us how close he could get, and the garrison was hardly more than a heap of blackened timbers and scorched tiles. There was a skull set up in the ruined gate, a skull in a carved niche with sprigs of something stuffed in its eye sockets and rags below it tied in queer knots. Simon muttered a prayer in Hebrew as we passed, and I touched the amulet around my neck. The marching songs stilled of their own accord as we marched by, and in turn every aquilifer in his standard-bearer's insignia dipped the pole bearing the legion's eagle. From down the line the word passed that the Emperor had stared for long moments at the skull in the gate of his ruined fort, then speared it out of its niche with his javelin and crushed it under his horse's hooves. My heart nearly burst with pride. That was an emperor. That was *my* Emperor.

Nightfall saw us well past the ruins, out of reach of the ghosts, and there was a certain jockeying to see which legion could set up their camp the fastest. In my training days we'd done long aimless route marches through the hills to set up practice camps, tearing them down and setting them up again as many as three times before our time was satisfactory, but the Tenth had been in a fort too long and we were out of practice. Simon retrieved our tent from the wagons that came lumbering behind, Philip was herded off to start digging the camp's protective ditch, I squatted to lay a fire, and Boil went trotting away with an armload of long stakes to help lay the tall surrounding fence. He came back huge, perspiring, and disgusted. "Fourth got theirs up already."

"We'll get it tomorrow." I blew on the little flame I'd coaxed on the kindling. "Anyone got a wineskin?"

"Not so fast; they need more men for the fence. You want to be the last camp up? Better second than last."

Boil and I loped off, and we heaved stakes into holes as fast as they were dug, and cursed under our breaths at the surveyors who would rather stand and point at their maps than get their hands dirty. A mule kicked me, and by the time I was done hopping and cursing, I looked up and saw a bloom of campfires. Every *contubernium* had its tent and fire; every wagon had its dock; every mule had its picket. Legionaries trotted with their weapons, clerks with their scrolls, centurions with their tablets. A small and orderly city had gone up in less time than it took to seduce a reluctant woman—and it would fold back up into our packs and wagons tomorrow with no sign it had ever been there but a few fence holes and a scattering of manure.

Julius had a pot over the fire before the tent as I got back, and the others had hunkered down around it. I smelled mutton and hard wheat biscuits. "Want some?"

"Not if you're cooking." I ducked the ladle Julius threw at me. "I'll take a biscuit and turn in. I was up all night last night with a weeping woman. God help me."

"Maybe He'll have to." Simon gave me an odd look. "Cutting it close, aren't you?"

"What?"

The others were snickering. "Never thought you had two," Julius chortled.

"Two what?"

"No, three. You're forgetting his redhead . . ."

More snickering.

"Go get bent," I instructed them, and ducked inside the tent. And froze.

"Surprise," said Sabina.

SABINA

When Sabina had perched herself on Vix's rolled-up bedroll to wait for him, she'd resolved not to laugh. But one look at Vix's expression as he ducked into the tent and she was lost. "Oh, Vix," she giggled. "Your *face*." She threw her head back and kept laughing.

"Wait here," he said, and ducked out of the tent. Sabina saw his shadow looming against the fire outside over the other shadows that were his comrades. "You're all dead," she heard Vix snarl, and that sent her off again. She put her head down on her knee and laughed till tears came to her eyes, joining the torrent of snickers and hoots from outside.

"*Dead*," Vix repeated, and banged back into the tent, his face now a dusky maroon. Sabina had gotten herself more or less under control, but as he glared down at her, she could feel her shoulders start to shake again.

Vix folded his arms across his chest. "How did you get in here?"

"Not the most original opening line, is it?" Sabina swallowed the last of her giggles with an effort.

"I marched twenty miles today, and built maybe twenty more miles of fence, and I haven't slept more than two hours in the past forty. I'm too damned tired to be original. So, how did you get in here?"

"Don't blame your friends." Sabina looked around the tent. "All they did was tell me which bedroll was yours once I showed up."

Vix's eyes went over her. Sabina supposed she looked a far cry from the elegant legate's wife he'd met last week after the Emperor's dinner party. She'd borrowed a plain wool dress from her maid, roped her hair in a careless plait down her back, and strapped on a pair of hobnailed sandals. The kind of sandals built for long walking.

"I don't know what you're playing at," Vix said finally. "But you can get out of here and go home."

"I think this *is* home, Vix. Isn't that the point of building all the legion camps exactly the same whenever you're on march?" She looked around the neat sturdy walls of the tent, pegged immaculately into place. The bedrolls were already laid in a neat pattern, and a clutter of smaller possessions—dice, good-luck charms, private talismans—marked each square of personal space. Sabina picked up the whetstone that had sat by Vix's bed when he lived in her father's house and now sat by his bedroll here. "Home away from home wherever you are."

"Not your home." He snatched the whetstone out of her hand. "Go back to your husband's tent."

"You don't think we share quaters, do you?" Sabina raised her eyebrows. "He's quite cross with me at the moment, actually—he already has a nice arrangement with a tribune from the Sixth, *much* prettier than me, and didn't want me tagging along on this campaign at all. Dragging a wife to parts unknown; most unsuitable. But I begged the Emperor very prettily, telling him it wasn't really so unsuitable as all that—Emperor Augustus's granddaughter Agrippina followed her husband on all his military campaigns, after all. Trajan just chucked me under the chin after that, and said I could tag along as long as I didn't try to lead any charges like Agrippina did. So, here I am." Sabina wiggled her toes inside her rough sandals, pleased. "Hadrian makes me ride with the baggage train in a special wagon, and set up my own tent a good distance from anything interesting, but he couldn't send me away after the Emperor gave permission."

"Why *did* you beg to come along?"

She spread her arms wide, encompassing the tent and the camp beyond it. "To see the world."

"At the back of an army?"

"I think it will be interesting."

"Mud, blood, battles, danger—"

"Better than sitting around at home weaving cloth and ducking Empress Plotina's good advice. Besides, I can do some good here. I've only been traveling with the army for a day, and I can already tell you your supply trains could use an overhaul. Do you know your native auxiliaries don't get the same ration as Roman legionaries? I don't know if it's supposed to be that way or if your supply officers are cheating them, but I'm going to speak to Trajan."

Vix sputtered. "You're out of your mind if you think that bastard you married will let you traipse around with us common legionaries!"

"Who says Hadrian needs to know?" Sabina said airily. "He'll eat with his officers and sleep with his aide and dance attendance on the Emperor. I doubt we'll see each other more than once a day once this march gets underway. If I'm going to see a war, I plan on seeing it properly—on foot, and on the same level as you."

"And you thought I'd be grateful for the chance to be your guide?" Vix turned his back and started tugging at the laces of his breastplate. "You have no shame."

She grinned. "I'm glad you remembered."

"After everything you—" Vix struggled out of the breastplate, dropping it on the ground beside his helmet. "After the way you used me five years back, you really think I'd let you stay here with *me*?"

"Apparently I'd have to pay a tax to your four friends out there for the privilege," Sabina amended. "According to your friend Julius, anyway. Though he might be fibbing. He already told me some long yarn about being descended from Julius Caesar—"

"Get out!"

"If you want." She rose, brushing at the mud on her hem.

"You want fun with the unwashed soldiers, you can find someone else," Vix sneered. His ears still got bright red when he was angry, Sabina noted with interest. "There's always some smelly *optio* willing to share his bedroll with a whore."

"I doubt it will come to that," said Sabina, unruffled. "If you don't want me to stay, I'll go back to the baggage train and get a good night's sleep. I understand legions start early, and I've a mind to try walking the first leg. I may only be a legate's wife with soft feet, but surely I can keep pace with you legionaries since I'm not burdened down with a pack and two fence poles."

Vix stared at her.

Sabina picked up the dirty sheepskin she'd decided to use for a cloak instead of the fine wool *palla* that would probably just get her robbed once outside the sheltered circle of the baggage train and the officer quarters. "Are you going to let me by, Vix?"

He still stood square before the tent flap, looking down at her. She'd forgotten how tall he was. He bent, rummaging briefly in his pouch, and lobbed something at her. "Take that with you."

Sabina looked down at the heavy silver-and-garnet earring in her hand. "I thought you'd have sold it by now."

"No one would pay me what it was worth." He scowled. "Tried giving it to my girl, but she didn't see the point of just one earring. You might as well take it. I sure as hell don't want it."

Sabina felt something small and warm in the pit of her stomach.

"Why are you here?" he blurted out.

"I told you. I want to see the world. Maybe change it a bit for the better too."

"No, I mean—" Vix raked a hand through his hair, almost snarling. "Why are you *here*? Why do you keep bothering *me*?"

"If I'm going to see the world," Sabina said, "I'd rather see it with you."

He reached out and took her by the shoulders in his big hands, lifting her up so her eyes were on a level with his own. His face was cold and hard.

"I'm going to regret this," he told her grimly.

Then he kissed her.

"Hello," Sabina greeted the rest of the *contubernium* as she and Vix emerged from the tent. "I'm Sabina. I'll be sharing your tent in the evenings sometimes, but I'll always pay for the privilege. Let me know what I owe you. We'll try not to be too loud, at least not in future. Is that lentil stew? I'm hungry. Boil, however did you get that nickname?"

She helped herself to two bowls of stew, handed one to Vix, and settled cross-legged by the fire. The rest of the *contubernium* looked at her, then at Vix.

"Not a word," Vix warned, and put an arm about her shoulder as he settled in at her side.

TITUS

A week on the road marching with an army, Titus thought, and most legates were starting to show signs of wear. Mud on the boots, perhaps, or a stubble of beard on a once immaculately shaved chin, or puddles of water tracked into a tent. Most legates—but not Hadrian.

"If you will see these letters delivered, and then collect the next batch of correspondence," Hadrian told Titus, not looking up from a wax tablet where he was jotting rapid figures. "Send the prefect of the camp to see me tomorrow before march; I don't like the situation with the grain stores. Someone's skimming, and if it's not him, he'll know who."

He'd better. "And the report for the Emperor?" Titus reminded him, juggling an armload of slates and scrolls.

"I'll copy it out myself. Lucius, that report from the chief centurion about insubordination in the fourth cohort—"

Legate Hadrian's immaculate tent hummed like a beehive: an aide rummaging among the books stacked in their orderly cases, the desk tidily divided into stacks of completed work and half-completed work and work yet to be touched, the slave with the wine flagon perfectly matched to the slave with the pen case. Another tribune hovered, waiting with a batch of slates. A third tribune was just dashing out with a message, brushing past Titus. A secretary filed scrolls while a slave brushed mud from the boots the legate had worn that day and set out a second immaculate pair for the following morning. Another secretary took down a letter Hadrian was dictating—"Sign it *By the hand of Publius Aelius Hadrian*, will you?"—while Hadrian himself simultaneously finished writing his own report in perfect, unhurried script. The only one in the room not hard at work was the old dog lying asleep with her head on Hadrian's foot.

"The chief centurion sent a message." Titus waited for a gap in his legate's even dictation. "A reminder that you wished to inspect the second cohort tomorrow?"

"Thank you, I had not forgotten." Hadrian, as far as Titus could tell after a week's work on active march, forgot nothing. He attended punishment details and promotion ceremonies in person, no matter how lowly; he made a point of remembering the names of not only the higher officers but the centurions; and when the legionaries had a complaint, they learned they could take it direct to their legate, who would listen and pronounce judgment rather than shove such problems off on a tribune. Hadrian rode all day in full armor rather than be carried in a litter, as much a part of his big horse as a centaur; he worked far into the night wearing out secretaries, aides, and tribunes by the handful; and he rose in the morning as early as any legionary. All looking as calm, clean, and impeccable in his superbly polished armor and neatly trimmed beard as if he had just stepped out of a bathhouse.

"Lady Sabina sent a message as well, sir," Titus said. "She asks if she will be dining with you this evening?"

"No, I will work. Send my regrets."

Titus sighed a little. He'd been delighted to find that Sabina was coming along on the Dacian campaign—surely when he was working under Hadrian, he'd see her every day? But she'd hardly once stepped into Hadrian's busy whirl of a tent. And the last time he'd taken his horse back to her luxurious palanquin, she hadn't even been riding in it. "She's off exploring," her maid had said.

"You've got it comfortable, haven't you?" Titus couldn't help remarking. The maid lounged on her mistress's cushions, fanning the dust away with Sabina's plumed fan.

"Don't tell on me, will you, sir?" The maid grinned: a scrappy urchin of thirteen Sabina had plucked from a begging bowl and a street corner

in Brundisium, Titus knew. Sabina was always picking girls up in odd
places and offering them jobs in her household. Half of them robbed
her blind and ran away again, but it never seemed to discourage her
from picking up another one. "Lady Sabina told me she doesn't mind
if I take things easy here."

"I wouldn't dream of telling on you," Titus had promised. Still, he'd
hoped to see more of the girl's mistress on this campaign . . .

"Thank you, Tribune." Hadrian put his seal to the bottom of his
report, took a second letter from the secretary for signing, lifted a hand
for a fresh pen, and still found the time to look up at Titus with a smile.
"I think I've used you up quite enough for one evening. Dismissed."

"Used up is right," one of the other tribunes grumbled as he and
Titus left the tent. "Why couldn't the old legate have stayed? He never
made us do anything except keep his wine cup full."

"Oh, I don't know. I like Hadrian. Can't say he doesn't work harder
than we do."

"I still wouldn't mind a layabout. Legate Parminius's tribunes don't
spend all day dashing up and down the column with his correspondence. They get to hunt, ride in litters. I've got blisters!"

"Rub them with goose grease," Titus advised. A cure he'd picked up
from Vix. Perhaps he'd drop in on Vix's *contubernium* tonight—the first
time since they'd started the march that he'd had an evening to himself.

"I hope you didn't come for dinner." Vix looked up from the cooking pot he was stirring over the low fire. "Julius made this stew before
he went on sentry duty, and it tastes like boiled boots."

"I'll put up with the dinner for the company, Slight." Titus settled
himself by the fire, folding up his long legs under his tunic. He always
changed out of his tribune armor and insignia before coming to visit Vix
and his *contubernium* brothers, since it saved them the trouble of wondering if they had to salute him or not. They looked up at him—the little
Greek Philip tossing his dice and big fair-haired Boil half asleep by the
fire and bearded Simon whittling a stick—and they all gave friendly nods.
Titus nodded back, taking a bowl of stew from Vix just as they did, and

settling in to eat. Night had fallen by now, the last streaks of red sunset gone behind the line of trees, and the flickering light of the fire cast a pool of warmth in the black. A black broken by thousands of tiny pools, Titus thought as he looked out over the orderly expanse of camp. A field of fires in every direction as every *contubernium* in the Tenth settled to eat dinner, sharpen swords, doctor blisters, trade stories—and do it all the next day, and the next, until either they or a Dacian king was dead.

"You're right," Titus told Vix after a taste of the stew. "Boiled boots, I'm afraid, is putting it kindly. I suppose you're missing Demetra and her lamb stews now, eh?"

Simon and Philip let out identical snickers. "Not exactly," Vix said, rubbing a hand over the back of his head. "I've got another girl."

Titus raised a disapproving eyebrow. "Would it do any good to tell you that the mother of your child is due not only courtesy, but fidelity?"

Vix kept eating. "No."

"Then I won't bother." Titus had heard of the old saying about a man who could fall into a sewer and come out smelling of roses. Vix, he thought, could fall into a sewer and come out with a pretty girl on each arm.

A female voice sounded behind Titus. "Is there room for one more?"

Sabina?

Titus looked up in astonishment. His legate's wife, looking nothing like a legate's wife, with a sheepskin cloak and a sunburned nose and a rope of hair over one shoulder.

Did she come looking for me? But the flush of pleasure had barely started to spread through his chest when she took two steps forward and jumped up into Vix's arms.

For a moment Titus wondered if he was dreaming. Dreams were like that sometimes—people and places mixing up in mad ways, nothing like it was in real life. But it occurred to him that if this were his dream, then Sabina would be jumping up into *his* arms, holding her face up for *his* kisses. It wouldn't be Vix twining a hand through her hair and tipping her head back so he could set his mouth at the base of her throat. It would be Titus Aurelius Fulvus Boionius Arrius Antoninus.

Not a dream, he thought numbly. *No, not a dream at all.*

"Titus!" Sabina exclaimed as Vix finally set her down on her feet. "I didn't even see you sitting there. Since when are you and Vix such friends?"

He was surprised at how evenly his voice came out. "I could ask you the same."

She smiled and put a finger to her lips, eyes flicking sideways to where Simon and Boil and Philip had pushed their bowls aside for a game of dice. "Later, I think. Dear gods, Vix, don't tell me you let Julius make the stew?"

Titus felt a twist in his stomach at the casual way she used Vix's name. *Not so Slight at all, if you got a girl like that.* Because Sabina clearly came often to sit by this fire, from the way she teased Philip about cheating at dice and begged Simon to teach her the Hebrew prayer for bread. From the way she sat curled in Vix's arms, her head leaned back against his shoulder as he reached around her from either side to stitch up his torn helmet lining . . . Titus concentrated on his stew, very carefully spooning up every last drop and swallowing it down. He got another bowl, not tasting it at all, and that lasted him until Boil and Simon at last went yawning into the tent to sleep, and Philip finally staggered off to see if he could find a whore. Then, and only then, did Titus look up.

"Well?" he said.

Sabina smiled. "So how did you and Vix meet all the way out here?"

"He saved my life a time or two when I first arrived in Dacia." Titus took a deep breath. "And you?"

Vix and Sabina looked at each other for an instant, and then their eyes cut away as they both started laughing at the exact same moment. That was when Titus felt a shaft of pure jealousy bolt through him. Jealousy, he noticed in passing, tasted a sour yellow on the palate— yellow as bile.

"It's a long story." Sabina reached up and smoothed Vix's hair back from his eyes.

"I like long stories." Though Titus had a feeling he wasn't going to like this one.

"She couldn't resist me five years ago, when I was a guard in her father's house." Vix kissed the side of her neck complacently. "And she can't resist me now."

"Maybe it's not that long a story after all," Sabina concluded. "Though if we're talking about who couldn't resist who, Vix—"

Five years ago. *So when I was bringing her violets and Hadrian was quoting her poetry* . . .

Oh, dear gods. Hadrian.

"You're both utterly mad," Titus burst out. "You think Legate Hadrian won't find out? A legion is no place to keep secrets!"

"I'm not keeping any," Sabina said equably from within the circle of Vix's arms. They made quite a picture in the flickering firelight: utterly at ease, utterly content. Sabina had laced both her small hands through one of Vix's big ones, and his long hard fingers played idly with the ends of her plaited hair. "Hadrian already knows I explore more than I should. And he probably assumes I have a lover of some kind. He's made it clear over the years that he doesn't mind, as long as there are no inconvenient bastards and as long as I'm discreet."

Now you tell me, Titus couldn't help thinking. *If I'd known that back in Rome after you married* . . . He thrust that thought away, at least for the present. "Discretion or no, I doubt Hadrian would take kindly to learning you've chosen—well, a common legionary."

She tilted her head to gaze up at Vix. "Hardly common."

Titus looked at Vix too. "You'd be flogged. Maybe executed."

"Only if he finds out." Vix sent a cocksure glance over Sabina's sleek head. "Who's going to tell him, Titus? You?"

Titus considered that for a heartbeat. But only a heartbeat. "You're both mad," he repeated.

"Possibly," said Sabina. "Here, I brought a wineskin. Have something to drink before you faint."

Titus poured out a cup of wine and swallowed it unwatered for the first time in his life. He barely felt the burn as he offered the skin back to Sabina. "I didn't think you were the kind to take lovers," he said at last, quietly.

"Does it lessen your opinion of me?" Her smile faded to something gentler. "I'd be very sorry if it did."

"Why should it?" Vix hooted. "You know what Hadrian is!"

"I suppose only us old-fashioned sorts believe in fidelity anymore." Titus knew he sounded like a pompous ass, but he couldn't help it. "Fidelity to our wives, our husbands—and to the mothers of our children, Vercingetorix."

Vix sent a stare of grim warning over Sabina's head: *Don't you dare mention Demetra.* Titus wondered if he should.

Sabina was still looking at him, her face grave. "I'm sorry if I've disappointed you, Titus."

He sighed. "You haven't." Could one really fault any woman married to a man of Hadrian's tastes? Everyone in the Tenth knew Hadrian had an arrangement with one of Titus's fellow tribunes, not to mention a handsome young aide and an even more handsome engineer. "I don't think less of you," Titus said, and the smile returned to Sabina's eyes.

But couldn't you have picked—someone else? he couldn't help thinking. Someone besides crude, cocky, grinning, lying, unfaithful, uncouth Vix?

Or was that tall, strong, brave, ambitious, confident Vix, at least to Sabina? Titus looked down at himself: his legs, which still stuck out long and bony from his tunic; his skinny wrists, which had never been broadened by using a sword.

His hair was probably sticking up in back.

"So I'll have to work with my legate for the next six months or however long this campaign lasts," Titus said finally, just to be saying something, "and keep him from finding out that I spend my nights sitting around a fire with his wife and her legionary lover?"

"That's right," Sabina agreed. "Thank goodness you can keep a straight face. I think it's something to do with how we senatorial children are brought up."

"Excuse me," Vix objected. "The vulgar pleb is feeling insulted."

"Admit it! You can't hide your feelings to save your life—"

I can, Titus thought with a wrench. *And dear gods, I'm going to have to.*

CHAPTER 13

VIX

Memory is as full of holes as a wormy apple. I thought I remembered that Dacian campaign so clearly—even now, so many years later, I wake in the night smelling the tang of those dark pines. No other pines smell like that, at least not in any of the places I've traveled, and I've traveled most of the Empire at one time or another. I remember the pines as if it were yesterday, and I remember other things too, but mostly details. The larger things are hazy.

Trajan is gone now, long gone, and he has a column monument on the Quirinal Hill just north of the Forum Romanum. It's a pillar of marble decorated with friezes depicting his various campaigns, including the Dacian campaign, and at least once a week I pay it a visit. I look at the friezes and I can see that Trajan's army advanced in three columns, driving through Dacia toward the capital city of Sarmizegetusa. It's easy to see on the frieze, but when you're a common soldier all you see is the road at your feet and the sweaty sunburned neck of the man marching ahead of you. The road, the sting in the air, the road, the dust in your throat, the road, the ache in the feet and the small of the back, the road—nothing but the endless road. I had to go to the maps and the friezes to find out what I hadn't known at the time, that Trajan's first column had followed the path of the winding rivers, going from garrison to garrison, then joined with the second column, which had marched north through the valleys. They saw fighting, I heard from

the men who marched in those columns—hard and desperate fighting
from bands of Dacian warriors who harried the outskirts of the march.
But I marched with the third column, under Trajan, and I don't remember any fighting.

I remember sunny days, drying the dew an hour after dawn and
sending the dust up in white clouds under our hobnailed sandals. I
remember the steep-sloped mountains furred with those tangy pines,
falling abruptly into flat greenlands or glacial lakes. I remember Trajan's
red cloak as he rode, not safe behind his guards at the center of the
column but spurring restlessly up and down the flanks with his eyes
scanning the horizon.

There were villages destroyed in our wake, usually for giving aid to
the rebels, but I don't remember putting a torch to a single roof. I
remember one girl with a red scarf over her hair and the huge liquid
eyes all the Dacian women seemed to have, staring at us over the backs
of her sheep as we marched by. Boil fell head over heels for another
Dacian girl he met at a well, and brought her along with us for a few
weeks. She shared the tent at night for a while, adding odd vegetables
to our flat stews and teaching Sabina a few words of her own language,
but the girl left Boil and went home after a week too many of long
marches, and we ribbed Boil about it until he bellowed.

I remember watching the legion's eagle, mesmerized, as it flashed in
a shaft of sunlight. It rode proudly on a tall pole, carried by the aquilifer
who marched along just as proudly in a lion-skin cloak. The eagle looked
so regal and defiant, carried over the fields of alien grain, that I threw
back my head and gave a shout of joy, and my centurion, the bastard,
caned me across the shoulders with his staff as he rode past.

I remember my *contubernium*. Philip's brown fingers endlessly rolling his dice, Boil carving a bracelet out of silky beech wood for his
Dacian girl and then hurling it sullenly into a river when she left him,
Simon trying to figure out which way was Jerusalem. My brothers. Not
one of them alive now but me.

I remember Titus, who shouldn't have been part of our *contuber-*

nium because he was an overeducated sprat whose only ambition was to get home from this campaign and never go near a legion again. But he was one of us anyway, somehow, coming every few nights to our campfire after his duties to the legate were done, folding his long limbs inside his immaculate linens, telling wry stories of the other officers, telling the same stories over and over about Trajan because we couldn't get enough of them. I remember the face he made the first time he tasted *posca*, the sour soldiers' wine we got in rations. "What *is* this?"

"*Posca*," I grinned. "Made from the finest vinegar in the Empire. It doubles excellently for cleaning wounds. Drink up!"

"Pour it in your helmet first," Simon advised, "and soak your feet in it. Nothing better after a long march. A good foot bath in *posca* will peel off all the dead blistery stuff between your toes."

"Surely you don't drink it after that?" Titus said, horrified.

"You can strain it first if you're fussy," Boil allowed, and we all fell over howling as Titus poured his cup out into the earth.

I remember the first time I saw Hadrian dirty himself. The column had paused at the banks of a swollen river, and the surveyors were fussing with their maps about a ford that should have been there and wasn't. I sat down in the road, easing my pack off with a groan and stretching my weary feet in their sandals, and most of the other legionaries did the same, but the tribunes cantered their horses into a nearby meadow, shouting and playing foolish games. One of them flushed a deer from the trees, a stag with antlers like a crown. Hadrian had been sitting his horse some distance apart, a smirk on that bearded face as he watched the antics, but as he saw the deer the smirk vanished. Taut concentration replaced it, and he snatched a javelin from the nearest legionary. In a heartbeat he'd spurred his horse beside the fleeing stag, and in another heartbeat he'd brought it down in one beautifully placed stroke to the heart. A dark jet of blood spurted over his foot, but he only blinked slowly, as if the kill had brought him down to earth from someplace distant—and then he smiled. "He loves hunting," Sabina told me later. "Deer, boar, anything he can chase down on foot or horseback.

Strange, isn't it? You wouldn't take him for a hunter at all, since he loves animals and hates getting dirty."

"He doesn't love hunting at all," I said. "He loves killing." That's another image that wakes me sometimes in the night: Hadrian with his javelin, smiling at the spray of blood on his foot. The blood was dark, but in my dreams it glows scarlet.

I remember Sabina.

Her fine hair in a braid that was always coming undone. Her fingers ruthlessly rubbing and yanking and kneading my feet after a twenty-mile march until all my muscles were jelly. Her endlessly repeated "That's interesting" when Philip showed her how to palm dice, when Simon taught her the Hebrew prayer for bread, when Boil demonstrated how to scrub rust off a breastplate. Her short nose at first getting brown under the sun, and then getting freckled. I don't know if she bribed her maid and her guards or just swore them to secrecy, but she spent her days marching in the hot sun beside the wagon that was supposed to carry her in isolated comfort, and more than half her nights in my tent, where my friends didn't even realize she was their legate's wife. Once a week she put on silk and ate dinner with the Emperor, and she looked elegant enough to put on a temple plinth and sacrifice goats to—but the rest of the time in her wool dress and sturdy sandals she could have been any other muddy capable woman who followed her man to the legions. I'd heard stories of goddesses who walked the earth in disguise, and no one knew them for who they were either. Maybe my girl had a little goddess in her.

I remember laughing at her. At the face she made when she first tasted barley soup boiled over a cook-fire in a helmet; at the time she performed a flawless set of legion parade maneuvers around the empty tent wearing nothing but that same helmet and a very serious expression. I remember admiring her too—for the uncomplaining way she bound up her blistered feet until they toughened to the marching; for all the times she loaded up her luxurious wagon with camp followers and their children so they could cross a ford in safety instead of struggling against the currents; for the fight she picked with the Tenth's senior medicus. The legion's doctors didn't like treating the legionary women or their children—"They aren't supposed to be here anyway; we're not wasting medical supplies on them!" Sabina reduced the senior medicus to a quivering heap and reported him to Hadrian for a flogging. After that, the legion women and their children got treated for fevers and broken bones just like the soldiers.

I remember making love to Sabina under the blankets of my bedroll in the darkness of the tent, trying to keep quiet, not always succeeding. Philip once threatened to throw a bucket of water over the pair of us so he could get some sleep. "Go fuck a horse," Sabina advised him politely through the dark, and I laughed at that too, so hard I nearly died.

I remember Titus reminding me disapprovingly of Demetra, waiting for me back in Mog. "She'll be getting big by now with *your* child," he said in an icy voice, "and you didn't wait even one day to replace her. Do you ever give her a single thought?"

"No," I said honestly. "And don't you dare tell Sabina about her either." I tried to imagine Demetra, perhaps getting rounded in the belly by now as she kneaded never-ending lumps of bread dough and played with her little boy. Demetra with her queenly height and mass of honey-colored hair, so much more beautiful than Sabina with her slight body and little freckled face. I thought of Sabina, thoughtfully sounding out a new word of the strange Dacian language or reviling the *optio* in rough legionary slang, and I realized how much my beautiful, dutiful Demetra had bored me.

Who had time for guilt? It was summer; I had an emperor to serve and an enemy to kill; I had a long road to tire me by day and a lithe girl to tire me by night. That's what I remember from those months of the Dacian march, not the broader strokes of policy and strategy. You want a campaign history? Go to Trajan's column on the Quirinal Hill and read the goddamned friezes, frozen and colorless. The friezes might give you the facts, but they won't show you how splendid Trajan was, how restless and godlike as he marched on foot beside his cheering men. The friezes won't tell you the details, the little things that still wake up an old soldier like me in the middle of the night and make him realize that it was the best part of his life.

It was late summer before we reached Sarmizegetusa. That, unfortunately, is where my memory gets very clear.

PLOTINA

A letter from Dear Publius!

Plotina ran her fingers along the raised imprint of the boy's personal seal. His letters were far more infrequent than her own weekly missives, and of course they had to be. The distance was so great, the roads so unreliable, and after all he was a man of importance now with numberless duties to fill his time. Even the most devoted of sons must choose duty over their mothers. *Never let it be said that Pompeia Plotina was a clinging mother.* But he still found time to write, and in his own hand too. He knew what satisfaction it gave her to see his firm, perfect script. She had taught him that script herself, guiding his plump boyish fingers on the stylus. "Come along, girls," she called to her household, who looked up surprised to see their Empress so cheerful. "With such a beautiful day, we will take our work outside."

It wasn't such a beautiful day, really—autumn in Rome, blustery and gray. And the gardens were not at their best, the lilies looking a trifle draggled and the roses in the brown and clothy stage. She would have to speak to the gardeners about that. But later. Plotina swept her dark-purple silks over the dry grass, choosing a little grotto where a marble bench invited the viewer to sit for a moment beside a softly trickling fountain, and gazed over the vista of the Imperial gardens dropping below. Her women settled gamely around her—slaves with baskets of sewing, freedwomen with her correspondence, little girls waiting to run her errands. "Silence, if you please," Plotina called, and was pleased to see that they had already settled to their work in utter quiet. She had them well trained, but slaves, like dogs, needed constant reinforcement.

Without her sharp eye, they would dawdle and gossip over their sewing like hens scratching in the dirt. One last glance over her obedient household, and Plotina settled on her bench and opened the letter.

Yes, the dear boy was well. Working very hard, of course—he was too modest to say as much, but she knew the legion must be thriving under his leadership. Trajan, disappointingly, was still proving cool.

I can see you frown from clear across the Empire, Dear Publius wrote, *but I'm afraid I have been reduced to getting drunk with the Emperor and his officers in the evenings. You will disapprove, and certainly I have no love for unmixed wine and war stories, but it appears the only way to converse with Trajan in ease.*

Plotina did frown, but not at her Dear Publius. Trajan, such a far-sighted man in so many ways, but so blind about his own family. And still getting drunk and swapping dirty jokes with his men, as if he were a boy! Thank the gods Hadrian had gotten over *that* stage at a suitable age.

Your Imperial husband works hard, Hadrian continued, *and is to be emulated in all things. No detail of the march escapes him, but he still makes time to consider matters in Rome. You know how enthusiastically he took up that* alimenta *scheme proposed by Vibia Sabina.*

Another frown. Plotina still could not believe that Sabina had taken herself along on the Dacian campaign. A Roman woman, marching with an army? What notions had gotten into the girl's empty head, to give her such an idea? Dear Publius had not been pleased, though of course he was too charitable to criticize. Plotina did it for him, in her own letters. *She* understood.

"Daughters-in-law," she said to the plump Ethiopian woman whom she trusted with the Imperial household's fine sewing. "So troublesome, don't you agree?"

"Yes, Domina," the woman said without looking up from her needle. The Empress, they all knew by now, did not encourage response from her slaves even when she addressed them directly. Plotina nodded approval, tugging her dark-purple *palla* closer about herself against the brisk autumn breeze.

Speaking of the alimenta *scheme, Sabina wishes to make a contribution to help launch the program.*

The idea, Plotina supposed grudgingly, had merit. Imperial funds offering yearly living allowances for orphaned freeborn children—all well and good. But it had hardly been little Sabina's idea! Dear Publius had suggested a similar scheme to Trajan not two years ago, and been brushed off. Of course if it was *Sabina's* idea, her husband couldn't wait to endorse it. Anything for his little pet!

Sabina wishes to contribute one hundred thousand sesterces from her own private purse, to launch the alimenta *program. I knew you would be pleased.*

One hundred thousand sesterces? Plotina was not at all pleased with that. Oh, the girl might finally be interesting herself in some *respectable* charitable works for a change, rather than picking up whores out of slums and offering them jobs—but a token gesture would have been good enough. One hundred thousand sesterces; that was a quarter the fee a plebeian paid to be entered into the *equite* class! And this talk of her *private* funds. A wife had no private funds. That money belonged to Dear Publius, and he could hardly spare it. Public life was so expensive—the fees, the bribes, the public appearances, the entertainments. *She had far better spend that hundred thousand sesterces advancing Dear Publius's career.*

And of course the girl knew it. She did it only to irritate Plotina, whose advice she routinely snubbed, whose letters she ignored. Had she responded to even one of Plotina's many letters since the beginning of the campaign, letters intended to guide and mold, to give advice where advice was due?

She had not.

Plotina exhaled sharply, looking up from Dear Publius's letter. The little fountain splashed softly behind her, the double lane of cypress trees waved their bare black branches in the breeze, but the Empress of Rome took no pleasure in any of it. Her pleasure in the day had been spoiled.

"Niobe," she snapped at the slave girl just holding up a piece of household cloth, "unpick that seam and do it again."

"Yes, Domina."

I trust you to make arrangements for Sabina's donation, Dear Publius wrote, and went on to other things. A lighthearted account of the hunting he had been able to do now that Sarmizegetusa had been reached and the legions encamped around it in siege. But Plotina put the letter away. A waste to read Dear Publius's letters when she was in a bad mood. Besides, she had a better idea how to spend the afternoon . . .

The Empress of Rome sat still for half an hour longer, gazing at the spreading slope of the gardens, deep-purple *stola* blowing around her feet. The wind picked up, keen and cold, but none of her women complained, merely hunched deeper into their shawls and continued their work as she tapped her letter slowly against the bench.

"Fetch me my new undersecretary from Athens," Plotina said at last. "Bassus, his name is? I wish to consult with him about this new *alimenta* program."

Taking charge of the project herself would give her oversight, information, access. *I trust you to make arrangements for Sabina's donation*, Dear Publius had written. And she would. Surely there were far better uses for a hundred thousand sesterces than the feeding of a lot of lazy runny-nosed children in the provinces?

No doubt former Empress Marcella would call it meddling. Plotina called it duty.

"Come along," Plotina said cheerfully to her women, rising. "It's far too cold to work outside. Why did none of you say so?"

"Yes, Domina," her household muttered, and filed back into the palace in her wake.

SABINA

"You must not be riding much in your wagon," Hadrian noted. "You've gotten very brown."

Sabina looked down at her tanned arms. "Trajan likes it."

"I don't."

Sabina knew what Hadrian didn't like, and it wasn't her tanned skin. It was the Emperor's careless comment as he patted Sabina's freckled cheek at the last dinner: "You're taking to army life much better than that husband of yours, little Sabina."

"He wasn't mocking you," she answered Hadrian directly. "Just ribbing a bit."

"He has no cause to. I do my duties—I work three times as hard as any other legate in his army—"

"He knows that. He also knows you don't care for campaigning, that's all."

"Soldiers," her husband grumbled, shifting a pile of writing tablets. "All the same, Emperor to legionary. None of them has any use for a man who prefers a book to a sword!"

"Don't take it so hard," Sabina consoled her husband. As she had predicted to Vix, her path rarely crossed Hadrian's more than once a day now. But she did like to drop in now and then in the evenings and share a few friendly words. Especially now that the legions were camped about Sarmizegetusa, locked in the most dull and frustrating kind of siege warfare. Which, to Sabina's eye, looked a lot like plain waiting.

"—useless campaigns," Hadrian was complaining. "Of course the Dacian rebellion has to be contained, but once the siege is over, Trajan's talking about expanding the territory into Sarmatia. Sarmatia! How many years and how many millions of sesterces will that cost? These wars of expansion, they're costly and mostly useless. Rome is large enough."

"Oh, but we do love acquiring new provinces," Sabina said. "And isn't it better to keep all these legions busy rather than let them get bored and stir up trouble?"

"I'd keep them busy by other means." The pen was tapping thoughtfully in Hadrian's hand now. "A program of building, perhaps . . ."

"Trajan doesn't want to build. He wants to be Alexander."

Hadrian gave an uncharacteristic snort. "Every Emperor wants to be Alexander."

"You wouldn't?"

"Dead at thirty-two with everything I built coming to pieces around my bier? No. I would settle for being—Hadrian."

Sabina propped chin in hand. "And what's that?"

His eyes gleamed. "Something the world has never seen."

Sabina looked at her husband: his cropped beard, his heavy shoulders even more imposing in his breastplate, his hand restless and his eyes turned on some inner vision. What that vision might be, Sabina had no idea . . . but she sometimes wondered if her husband had been entirely truthful with her when he said all he wanted of the world was to travel it. He seemed to have other ideas too, ideas he didn't share so readily. "A pity we're stuck here until the siege is done," she said lightly. "It's such beautiful countryside in Dacia, I'd rather be exploring."

The thoughtful gleam vanished, replaced by the fire of enthusiasm she liked so much better. "Gods, yes. I've never seen better hunting country! Wolves the size of bears; the dogs bagged a pair last week that might have been Romulus and Remus in the flesh. I'm having the pelts cured; they'll cover my bed with tails to spare—"

"Legate." A tribune entered, saluting and removing his helmet. Sabina saw it was Titus. "Dispatches from Rome. Shall I bring them in?"

"Yes, at once." Hadrian gave a last sigh for the hunting fields of Dacia and returned to his writing tablet.

Sabina put her cup aside and rose. "Perhaps you will be good enough to escort me to my own tent, Tribune?"

Titus kept his eyes scrupulously away from her. "I would be pleased to do so, Lady."

Hadrian gave an absent good night, and Sabina took Titus's arm as they left. "Let's stop at the stream first," she said as soon as they were out of earshot. "I finally got Vix's tunic off him for washing—it's stiff enough from dirt to stand up all on its own."

Titus exhaled a long breath but kept silent as she retrieved a bundle of laundry from her wagon. Whatever disapproval he felt of her, he kept it to himself. After the look of blank shock on his face that first night, Sabina had found herself hoping, with an intensity that surprised her, that she wasn't going to lose him for a friend. But he still came to share food and conversation at the *contubernium* fire in the evenings, and if he averted his eyes from her and Vix, it seemed to be from courtesy rather than disapproval.

They had reached the stream, a winding bend of silver gone purple in the twilight. A dozen soldiers and a few women were scrubbing out helmet liners and tunics on its banks, grousing good-naturedly about aching feet and sore backs. Some looked curiously at Titus in his pristine tribune's armor, but none glanced twice at Sabina with her plaited hair and sheepskin cloak. Why would they? She could have been a slave or perhaps someone's freedwoman maid; just another tough and seasoned woman who followed after the legions.

Over the organized sprawl of the camp loomed Sarmizegetusa, which the men had taken to calling Old Sarm. Sabina looked up above the trees at the Dacian capital: a jagged crag of rock spearing into the dusk, crowned by a fortress. The legions had let out a dusty cheer in the road when it first loomed in the distance, and Sabina had shaded her eyes with her hand for a closer look. Rome was geometrically built, ordered around forums and hills and capitols. The Dacians had built a city that climbed almost vertically up the mountain, peaked roofs and steep streets winding around stepped terraces, crowned on top by the massive fortress where the Dacian king was now holed up with his wild-haired, wild-eyed warriors. "We'll have it down in rubble within the week," the engineers had boasted, but Sabina was not surprised to see the army still here a month later with no real dents put into those mountain walls.

She shook off her fancies and dropped to her knees on the damp sand of the stream bank, rinsing Vix's tunic in the chilly water. "I don't see many legates' wives doing laundry," Titus observed. "Why not have your slaves do that for you? Unless you enjoy scrubbing dirt out of clothes."

"No, not exactly." Sabina rubbed at a stubborn mud stain. "But there isn't much point in an adventure if you only do the fun parts, is there? Vix can't ask a slave to polish his boots for him or repair his breastplate, so why should I? That just makes me a dabbler."

"That settles it," said Titus. "I do not have the heart of an adventurer."

"You have the heart of a scholar," Sabina offered.

"Oh, not even that. I'm thoroughly ordinary. But I don't mind—'Diligence is a very great help even to a mediocre intelligence.'"

"Seneca?"

He bowed assent. "I'm happy to leave the adventuring and questing to greater men than myself. I'll be happy enough to get home from this campaign, and never worry again about keeping my tunics white."

"Give them to me, and I'll get them white for you." Sabina wrung out Vix's tunic, holding it up with some pride. "Laundry may not be the most interesting chore on earth, but I've gotten very good at it."

In truth, it was all interesting. More than that—it was *fun*. Walking alongside the wagon drinking in the smell of the pines was fun. Helping a cursing clerk to whack a stubborn mule along the path with a switch was fun. Helping some legionary woman carry her children across a river ford, one on each hip, was fun, even when her sandals squelched for the next hour. Picking up the cheerfully obscene legionary patois that was almost a different language—that was fun too. Vix's friends were fun: Philip, who had taught her to cheat at dice; Simon, who had cast suspicious glances when he heard her accent but since relented into gruff liking; Julius, who lied about everything and cheerfully accepted that Sabina was lying about a few things too; Boil, who had been head-hanging shy in her presence at first but now followed her around half-hoping she'd give up Vix and come be his woman instead.

And when the other legion women asked, "Which one's yours?" Sabina could point at a tall warrior—russet-haired, sun-browned, restless, and grinning—and say casually, "That one's mine."

That was the most fun of all.

"I hope that's all the mud." She gave the tunic one last rinse, holding up the dripping weight of wet linen. "I can't see it anymore, so it will have to do."

The legion had bloomed into a forest of campfires, and a thousand smells rose up into the dark toward the distant stars: smoke and oil, roasting meat and drying wool, leather and sweat and manure and steel. Sabina breathed it in deep as she and Titus threaded their way through the maze of tents and fires. *Does my husband love the smell of a legion on the march?* She thought not. Emperor Trajan, though—yes, he loved it. And as much as Vix might complain about the Tenth and its centurions and its traditions and its smells, he loved it too.

"You stole my tunic," Vix accused as she and Titus came into the glow of the *contubernium*'s campfire. "And now you're running off with a tribune. You girls, always going for the officers."

He sat cross-legged by the fire with his *gladius* across his knees. The firelight touched his hair from russet to gold, and the muscles leaped under the skin of his bare arms as he worked the whetstone back and forth. There was a trick to getting a sword sharp, Sabina knew by now. A small knife first, to scrape off any patches of rust, then a good hard session with a whetstone—long strokes for the cutting edge, small strokes to hone the point. Then oil to smooth the blade, tenderly rubbed in with a soft cloth. Anyone who thought men couldn't tend babies, Sabina reflected as she settled beside Vix, hadn't seen a legionary tend a sword.

"I brought wine," Titus announced, holding up a skin. "Would I bring wine if I were running off with your girl?"

"Give me the wine, and you can have her."

"Can I?" Titus asked. But Vix just put an arm around Sabina and snugged her in close beside him, kissing her temple.

"Where's Simon and the others?" Sabina looked around the campfire.

"Boil and Philip have sentry duty tonight, poor buggers." Vix picked up his whetstone again. "And Simon got picked out by the *optio* for some additional scouting. We have the fire to ourselves." *And later the tent*, his eyes gleamed at Sabina. *For once we can be as loud as we like.* Countless times sharing a bed, Sabina thought, and he could still clench her stomach up like a knot with one glance like that.

Titus gave a cough and poured out the wine into tin cups, and the three of them sat lazy in the fire's leaping shadows. Or rather, Sabina and Titus sat lazy. Vix tapped one foot restlessly against a stone and griped about the siege.

"—more catapults," he was arguing. "Build enough, and the gates'll come down."

"Build any more siege engines, and we'll be out of trees." Even in argument, Titus was mild. "For myself, I'd just *pay* to get those gates open. According to Cato, 'No fort is so strong that it cannot be taken with money.'"

"Cicero," Sabina said lazily. "Cicero said that." Titus's literary references tended to elicit blank stares from Vix and his friends, but she could usually top him quote for quote.

"A night attack, maybe," Vix was muttering, oblivious. He stared up at the black shape of Old Sarm where it reared with magnificent disdain over the surrounding detritus of camped legions, siege engines, and assault platforms. "Get a few picked men over those walls to open the gates . . ." He attacked his *gladius* again with the whetstone. Vix wasn't really meant for waiting—a month's worth of siege was a month too long, as far as he was concerned. Sabina came behind him and rose to her knees so she could knead at his shoulders, and his muttering broke off in a reluctant gasp. "Left shoulder, harder—I pulled something sparring today—"

"It's always the left that knots up on you." She dug her fingertips into the one particular muscle below the shoulder blade where he always carried the worst of his tension. "It's never liked being demoted to shield arm."

"They made such a fuss about fighting left-handed when I went to legion training, it was easier just to learn to fight with the right—ow!"

"Your left arm isn't happy with it, that's all I'm saying." Sabina slipped a hand under the neck of his tunic, kneading the shoulder. His skin was warm under her fingers, but not from the campfire. Vix never needed a fire to keep warm. His flesh was always hot to the touch, as if the blood inside ran close to boiling.

He captured her fingers in his own, rough from the sword and oily from the polishing cloth, and gave them a quick squeeze as he continued his rant against the Dacians. "Get me over those walls with a rope—"

"I give up." Sabina abandoned the massage. "There'll be no relaxing you now. At least not till later, when I can get the clothes off you." She crawled around to his other side, surveyed the sword lying across his knees, and stretched out to lay her head in Titus's lap instead.

"—have those gates open," Vix was still grumbling.

"Oh, Hades, give it a rest," Titus said. "The city falls, or it doesn't. Likely it matters very little."

"What do you mean it matters very little? I didn't waste a summer of my life marching through Dacia if all we're going to do is march home with nothing show for it!"

"Who says you have nothing to show for it? It's been a rather nice summer, full of fine weather and lovely scenery and vigorous exercise. It's even convinced me of the occasional pleasures of army life."

"Me too," said Sabina, her head still in Titus's lap. At the beginning she had been mortified to discover she could stand only an hour or two of marching before she had to climb back in the wagon to rest. She had rubbed her sore feet and bandaged her blisters and cursed at her own aching muscles, unable to believe how long and stolidly the legionaries could march—carrying weapons, armor, and heavy packs to boot. But slowly she felt her muscles strengthening as the campaign went on, and now she could walk all day on her tough new feet *and* have breath left over to sing a good dirty marching song. She sometimes made up obscene new verses and taught them to Vix and his friends.

"None of this is worth anything," Vix was proclaiming at length, "if we haven't got a few heads on spikes to show for it at the end. What else did I join the legion for—the canings and the pay?"

"You really are a barbarian," Sabina informed him.

"I concur," Titus agreed. He had begun to stroke Sabina's hair, very lightly, as if afraid she would brush him away. She closed her eyes instead, comfortable. "No need to do anything drastic about Sarmizegetusa, Vix—we know they haven't got a water source up there; sooner or later they'll get thirsty."

"Not when they've got pipes to bring their water in." Vix lobbed a new chunk of wood into the fire, sending another drift of sparks skyward toward the white sparks of stars in the sky.

"True, and there's a heated discussion about those pipes every night in the Emperor's tent. I stand in the back with message cases while he argues with all his legates." Titus was still stroking Sabina's hair—he had a lovely light touch. *His wife will be a lucky woman.* "Legate Hadrian wants to poison the water supply, but it's unreliable, and the Emperor wondered if the pipes might be big enough for a few men to slip through and under the wall at night, but the diameter is too narrow—"

Vix threw back his head and laughed, tossing his sword in the air in an exuberant overhand toss and catching it again on the way down. Sabina's heart squeezed, looking at him. "I love the Emperor," Vix said, still laughing. "And I love you, Titus. But you think too much like nobles. Poison, night raids—think like a barbarian for once! *Break* the damn pipes!"

"Only possible if you know where they come out," Titus said. "We don't."

Vix grinned. "But I do."

CHAPTER 14

TITUS

"You think we haven't considered breaking the pipes, lad?" Emperor Trajan sounded kindly as he looked at Titus. "There's no access."

"But there is, Caesar. I can show you on a map." Titus shifted from foot to foot. "One of my legionaries discovered it on night sentry duty—where the pipes come out. Smash the pipes; cut off the water supply. Not an elegant solution, but the simplest. Once the Dacians get thirsty enough, they open their gates."

The Emperor frowned, but thoughtfully. "Get my engineers in here!" he called, and there was a flurry of activity. Titus stood in the middle of it all feeling oddly exhilarated. He'd had to scrape up every bit of courage he had to dare approach the Emperor directly with Vix's mad plan.

"What am I supposed to do, present it myself?" Vix had hooted. "They'll never let a muddy-boots legionary like me in to see the Emperor of Rome. You'll have to do it for me."

"Me? I can't do that!"

"You've talked to him before, haven't you?"

"In passing," said Titus. "Once or twice. *Not* in depth. I don't like talking in depth with emperors, or important people in general. They look at me and I start to stutter, and all in all it's a scene I prefer to avoid."

"You take it to Hadrian and he'll just take the credit," Vix warned. "Then I'll have to beat you bloody for giving that weasel a career boost on *my* idea. Be a man!"

"You sound like my grandfather," Titus winced, and the following day he'd put on his best armor, applied the parade plume to his helmet, scrubbed everything to a shine, and applied to see the Emperor. Who was now looking Titus over with a speculative eye.

"What did you say your name was?" Trajan asked. "You're one of Hadrian's, aren't you—the one who quotes?"

"Yes," Titus said, resigned. "I'm the one who quotes."

"Good to see you've got more in that head than epigrams. Not saying this plan of yours will work, mind, but it's worth a try."

The tent was rapidly filling up now: aides spreading out maps, Trajan's staff officers already debating hotly with each other, engineers spouting technicalities in that superior nasal drone all engineers seem to have . . . the Emperor's quarters were confined to a tent as small and plain as any legionary's; the interior furnished with nothing more than a makeshift desk, a bedroll, and a few spartan camp stools, but Trajan's perpetual good cheer brightened any room.

"Hadrian!" he called as Sabina's husband came striding into the tent. "You've been keeping this Cicero-spouting young tribune from me. He shows promise."

Hadrian frowned. "I'm sorry if he disturbed you, Caesar—"

"Not at all. This notion he has about the pipes works, and I may poach him off you for my own staff. Tell us again, lad—"

"If it were that easy to cut off their water, we'd have done it already." Hadrian began shaking his head before Titus was even finished. "It won't work."

"It *will* work," Titus found himself venturing to his own surprise. "We know they don't have a water supply up there, not one that will supply the whole city. They rely on those pipes."

"Boy's right," one of the engineers grunted. "This place your legionary found, Tribune—he's sure he's seen where the pipes feed out? It's not on our maps."

"You see?" Hadrian dismissed. "If they were accessible, we would have known."

"Not necessarily; the spot's hidden. They took good care to keep it off our maps." Titus edged forward, pointing to the maps. "Here, let me show you . . ."

More muttering, more arguments and speculation and pessimistic grumbles, but the Emperor's optimism had already risen to fill the tent. He was making plans now, striding up and down in his battered armor, arguing with his officers, and Titus was content to drift back to the back of the throng. Unnoticed, just as he liked it.

Perhaps not quite unnoticed.

"You should have come to me with your notion, Tribune." Hadrian's voice sounded at Titus's shoulder, and it was distinctly cool.

"I'm sorry, sir," Titus said. "I thought—I thought I might just get shot down, so why bother making you look a fool."

"But instead you look very clever. Doubtless what you wanted."

"No, sir . . . I don't want much of anything. Just to get along in this world."

Hadrian cast him a disbelieving glance and moved off. "Caesar, perhaps I can draw your attention *here* on the map—my tribune and I had discussed the idea before, analyzing the weakness—"

No one ever believes me when I say I don't want much from the world, Titus thought. Hadrian, who wanted to rise to consul or even beyond . . . the Emperor, who wanted to conquer the whole world . . . Vix, who wanted his own army to help do it . . . Sabina, who wouldn't be content until she'd crossed every sea and horizon the earth had to offer. *So many movers and shakers,* Titus thought, *and in the middle of all those grand ambitions, me.* With no ambitions at all.

Except maybe to acquire a nickname someday besides "the fellow who quotes."

"Tribune," Trajan said at last, tugging on his gauntlets, "I'll be keeping an eye on you, to be sure. Any epigrams for the occasion?"

"'My tongue is palsied,'" Titus found himself quoting. "'Subtly hid fire creeps me through from limb to limb.' Catullus said it about a woman, Caesar, but that's how nervous I was trying to approach this tent."

Trajan laughed, giving Titus's shoulder a thump of Imperial approval that buckled his knees, and his retinue were quick to laugh with him—though Hadrian gave only a token shadow of a smile.

VIX

"So tell me." Sabina tilted her head up at me. The pipes were broken, and the days stretched out warm and idle again as the whole army waited for the Dacians to get thirsty. "Why *do* you dislike my husband so much? You must admit, he's a very good legate."

I grunted but couldn't really deny it. I might not like having Publius Aelius Hadrian as my commander, but he'd turned out better than I expected. He was even-handed, he didn't overmanage the centurions, he enforced discipline but wasn't a flogger. "He just models himself on the Emperor," I said scornfully. "How much brilliance does it really take to look for the best there is and copy it?"

"He does do that," Sabina admitted. "He watches Trajan very carefully. Picked up the same habit of greeting all the men by name and clapping them on the shoulder in that friendly way. It's a touch studied, but Hadrian's always a little stiff when he's first settling into a role."

"That's all everything is to him. This role or that one."

"But he plays them all very well, you must admit. Why are you so set against him? He's never done anything to you."

"He had thugs beat me up in an alley!"

"You have thugs trying to beat you up in alleys every day. You never hold it against them."

"Well, he's a supercilious lizard."

"Yes," Sabina conceded, "but so what?"

"See here, why are you defending him? Don't you hate him?"

"Of course not."

"But you don't love him." I groped for words. "So I thought—"

"Love or hate, with nothing in between?" She cocked her head at me, amused. "Is that how it is for you?"

I thought about that for a moment. "Generally."

She chuckled. "My husband's a bit more complicated than that. He's not lovable, perhaps, but he's interesting. We talk a great deal."

"About what?"

"Greek poetry. Syrian architecture. Hunting lions. The declining condition of Roman literature. Why Egyptians worship cats. The Sibylline Books and what could possibly be written in them. How to play the flute. The mechanics of oratory. The possibility of taking a river journey down the Nile some springtime. Whether paving stones should be made rectangular or polygonal for maximum stress displacement. The best way to build a trireme . . ."

"All right, all right," I grumped. "You're the best of friends." I didn't know what half those things she reeled off even were.

"Friends?" Sabina mused. "Mmm, no. Hadrian and I might be friendly enough, but we aren't friends. He might have comrades, but he doesn't really have *friends*. He doesn't like people getting close."

"And that's a nice husband?" I jeered.

"He's courteous, he's considerate, and we have some decent conversations over the dinner table. That's a good enough husband for me."

Allowable, I supposed—considering there wasn't much between Hadrian and Sabina *after* dinner. It was the first thing I'd asked her. "Hadrian was more nervous on our wedding night than I was," Sabina had chuckled, turning over on one side that first night in Dacia. "He's had periodic affairs with married women, but I don't think he'd ever had a virgin girl. What he assumed was a virgin girl, anyway . . . he was so relieved that I wasn't crying and bleeding all over the place that we stayed up the rest of the night talking. All about the *Iliad*, if I remember correctly, and how we both thought Achilles was a muscle-bound idiot. And a week after the wedding, I had my own bedchamber on the other side of the house. Nocturnal visits between the two occur a few times a year. Whenever Plotina gets tired of nagging me about providing an heir, and nags him instead."

A few times a year. That wasn't so bad.

"You can enjoy all the dinner conversation you want," I told her now, generously. "As long as there isn't anything else."

"Thank you for your permission," Sabina said. "I've been holding my breath." She tugged my head down for a kiss, tracing the back of my neck in a slow circle. She could rouse a flutter in the pit of my stomach now, whenever she did that. I picked her up suddenly and bore her back into the tent, where Boil was stitching a new liner into his helmet. "Get out," I told him around kissing Sabina.

"You get to finish my helmet liner," he warned, and got out.

"Better make it quick," Sabina murmured against my mouth as I tossed her down on my bedroll. "You're due for drills in fifteen minutes, and that *optio* will stripe you if you're late again."

"Bugger him." And bugger bloody Hadrian too. I grinned as I kissed the curve of Sabina's hip, thinking of the look on that supercilious bastard's face if he could see me now. Of course if he saw us I'd probably have to kill him, but I wouldn't mind that too much. Sling the body into the ditch and blame it on those Dacian sentries . . . and then I had Sabina all around me and I forgot about Hadrian. Forgot all about Old Sarm too, looming overhead in the dry, rainless days of summer and slowly dying of thirst.

The friezes on Trajan's monument make the Dacian surrender look like a simple thing. Gates open, and in you march in triumph. But it wasn't so simple as that.

The gates opened all right, and the legions were assembled cheering and scrambling into line. I jammed myself in between Philip and Simon, one sandal still half unlaced, my helmet perched on my head with the cheek pieces flapping, halfway through dressing in the dawn when I'd heard the triumphant blast of our trumpets. Philip was swearing in soft jubilant Greek, and Simon was whooping like a fiend. But the sun rose hot and messengers rode back and forth, and we stood shifting from foot to foot as demands were trotted up and down the mountain. It was full afternoon before a line of prisoners surrendered themselves and the legions ground their way up the winding mountain trek to the city—and before we'd got halfway up we saw smoke begin to billow into the sky in huge black waves, and realized that the Dacians had fired the city to keep us from sacking it. By that time Trajan was in no mood for mercy. "Where is your king?" he said harshly, and even all the way back in the legion's second cohort I could hear the rasp in his voice.

"Can you see him?" Philip breathed, shorter than me and craning over the helmet crest of the man before him. We stood arrayed before the temples, which had remained unfired although we coughed through watering eyes at the acrid smoke that drifted from the burning quarters of Old Sarm. "Their king shouldn't be hard to find—I heard he wears a lion-skin cloak!"

"He might have taken the cloak *off*, you idiot!"

The Emperor's voice snapped out again like a whip. *"Where is he?"*

The captives glanced among themselves, muttering. "We'll see about that," the Emperor snarled, and in another moment his cavalry were stirring, vaulting onto horses.

"Bastard must have escaped before they surrendered," Simon muttered at my side.

"No fight, then?" I said, disappointed, as the trumpets began to sound again.

"They've surrendered! Of course there won't be a fight."

"Oh." I felt flattened somehow, and I wondered if the Emperor did too. He was staring up at the fortress, maybe remembering the sacked Roman garrisons with their skull idols staring from the niches where the legionary eagles had once preened. "If they burned their city, we can burn this," the Emperor said curtly, and again we could all hear the snarl in his voice. "Destroy it."

Not long at all before more flames began licking at the sky. The Dacian warriors looked at them, and looked away.

A few centuries were led into the smoldering city to beat down flames and crush any resistance, the rest of us left arrayed before the temples. Roman temples were square pillared things, roofed and grand, splendid houses for splendid gods, but the Dacians apparently worshipped in stone circles beneath the sky, gray lintels propped on each other and carved with runes. There was a vast flat circle of stones all tightly fitted together like a stone disc lying on the grass, and I watched Trajan vault off his horse and stride toward it with a face like a storm cloud. He snatched the standard pole from our aquilifer, leaving the startled man in his wake, and stormed out into the middle of the stone circle. He stood for a moment, breathing hard as if he'd forgotten what to do or what to say, and then without a word he slammed the Tenth's pole into a gap between two stones, so our eagle glared proudly over the heathen circle.

I felt a sting in my throat and realized I was screaming, along with thousands of others. Trajan raised a hand as if to quiet us, but we banged our javelins against our shields, and the grim look began to leave his face. He grinned like a boy, and our eyes streamed from the smoke that the wind had carried from the burning city to eddy around our splendid, arrogant eagle.

The legion's augurs came out then, to pronounce a lengthy benediction and proclaim Trajan the lord and conqueror of Sarmizegetusa, but we kept interrupting the droning prayers with more cheers and they kept flapping their hands at us. Pompous fools—who needed their benediction? Trajan became lord of Old Sarm when he jammed that eagle down on the stone circle. I could see Dacians—a woman with her arms about a baby, an old man, a boy a few years younger than Titus—watching with helpless, sullen hatred, but I had no thought for them. Only for my splendid Emperor.

His bad temper had gone now. When the priests were done gabbling he looked up at the burning fortress and grimaced. "I'll rebuild

it," he said to no one in particular. "More splendid than before, I promise." He turned to us all, bellowing conversationally. "See your centurions for orders. Any of you poor buggers set for sentry duty, you'd
better show up sober. The rest of you can have the night to yourselves—
take what you want, if there's anything still unburned and worth taking,
but if any of you get caught with a Dacian woman who doesn't look
willing, I'll have your cock off with a dull sword!"

We roared again at that, javelins thumping. He raised a hand again,
the smoky breeze stirring his short hair.

"And tomorrow we go after that bloody king in his lion skin. I don't
care if he's gone to hide in Hades!"

Another roar.

"*Dismissed!*"

I contemplated going back down the mountain for Sabina—she'd be
chafing to see something new after the monotony of the camp—but
decided against it. Even with Trajan's admonitions, and his centuries
sweeping for mutinous Dacian soldiers, there would be violence tonight
in Old Sarm. Women would be raped, sacks of loot would be gathered
and fought over, slaves would be taken, and for every Roman found dead
in the street with a knife in his gut, there would be ten murdered Dacians.
Better keep Sabina out of that—it might be too interesting even for her.

Parts of Old Sarm had burned flat, but not all the fires laid by the
frantic Dacian rebels had had time to catch hold. I left the looting to
the others and wandered until I found a tavern still standing, on a street
of buildings only slightly scorched. I dragged Philip with me, fleeced
him at a game of dice, got fleeced back, and walked out with half my
purse and a considerably clearer head than he. The streets were dark
now, strange and winding instead of Rome's angled lines, and I knew
there were eyes watching my red cloak and crested helmet. I didn't fancy
a street fight on a swimming head, so I'd drunk sparingly at the tavern
and felt half-disgusted with myself. Was this the start of turning into
a cautious old man like the centurions, forever weighing the consequences of everything? My friends jeered at me, all roaring drunk them-

selves, but I still stopped at half a cup of strong Dacian ale and left the tavern early, thinking I'd get back to the camp for a night's sleep if we were marching in the morning. Being cautious again—even worse, being *responsible*. But though I might not admit it to anyone else, I knew I'd far rather spend the night sleeping next to my girl than getting drunk in a tavern. At least in the morning I could look forward to making merciless fun of my moaning, puking brothers-in-arms.

I crossed a narrow square in the general direction of the city gates. A clutch of legionaries bumped past me, whooping—the change of guard from the temple grounds where Trajan had sited the Tenth's eagle. I caught a glow of something pale in the temple grounds, hesitated, then turned my course back toward the Dacian temples again. Sabina liked new gods, even the strange savage kind with horns and claws that Dacians worshipped—if I could tell her all about something new and interesting, she'd be more delighted than she'd ever be with a diamond necklace. My strange girl.

The glow I'd seen from the dark street was the reflection of a three-quarter moon from the flat stone circle in the grass. The rings of standing stones and crude pillars had disappeared into the dark, but the circle reflected in the moonlight palely, and I looked up at the moon again and thought I could see that it would be right in line with the stone circle once it was at the top of the sky. "What's that?" I asked, collaring a man in breeches and a sheepskin cloak who was hurrying past me with a glance at my sword. "The stone circle."

He looked at me with sullen loathing. "A solar disc."

"What does it do?"

He grunted, twisting out of my grasp and disappearing into the shadows. I hitched my shield up over my shoulder and advanced into the grass, curious. The circle seemed larger in the moonlight, bisected by the looming shadow of the standard pole still planted in the center. The Tenth's eagle was black under the moon, but no less proud. Behind it the fortress was a heap of slag and ashes, still smoldering fitfully in the dark. I idly swacked my javelin through the grass, wondering. What was a solar disc for, anyway? Did the Dacians sacrifice rams on it when the sun was high overhead? Did kings get crowned there, princesses married there? Sabina would be sure to ask.

Three soldiers crossed the solar disc toward the eagle as I stood musing. They conferred with the guards on duty—no eagle would ever be left unguarded. I saw an exchange of salutes, and then the center man leaned down and wrenched the eagle standard from the stones with a grunt. Moonlight silvered the lion skin over his head, marking his rank as our aquilifer, and I watched him enviously. A legion's aquilifer bore the eagle into battle: the greatest honor that could be conferred on some brave soldier. He wore a lion skin with the paws crossed proudly over his chest; he was paid twice the wage of a lowly soldier like me; he ranked just below the centurions. If he lived long enough, he'd be centurion himself. Lucky bastard.

"Putting the eagle back to bed?" I greeted him as he descended from the solar disc and tramped through the grass.

He grunted, startled at the sight of me, and dropped back a step, hand flying to his sword hilt and the standard pole bracing. The two men at his back braced too, javelins rising, and I stepped into the moonlight to show myself. "Vercingetorix, second cohort, third century of the Tenth Fidelis. Easy there." Losing the eagle was the worst shame any legion could endure; an aquilifer and his surrounding guards tended to swing swords first and ask questions later. A humorless bunch, even if they were well paid. "Just out for a stroll."

"Dismissed," one of the spearmen snapped. "We've orders to take the eagle out of Sarmizegetusa back to camp."

I squinted at the man in the lion skin. "Since when does the aquilifer carry a Dacian shield?"

"Lost mine," he said gruffly.

"They'll dock your pay for it," I warned, and stepped aside as they tramped past. Behind us, the guards who had stood watch about the solar disc had mostly scattered in search of their own beds. "Put the eagle to bed gentle, now. She's worked well for us today."

"It has," one of the spearmen said over his shoulder, and that was when I loosed my javelin at him.

It clattered on his shoulder with a soft chiming sound, quite different from the sound steel made on a Roman breastplate. Mail, not Roman plates; the round shield instead of rectangular; and when the spearman turned on me with a snarl I could see the long hair spilling out from under his helmet, long hair no centurion would ever have tolerated on any man under his command.

"*Dacians!*" I bellowed at the retreating guards, who had just let a trio of enemies walk off with their bloody *eagle*, and threw myself at the first spearman.

He met me with a howl, javelin arcing at my face, and I brought up my shield. I heard a dull *clang* as the spearhead glanced off my shield boss, and spared a quick glance back toward the solar disc. A dozen guards had circled the eagle there, but they'd gone quickly enough in search of whores and wine—only two had heard my shout and turned back. Two, unsheathing swords with shouts as the other two Dacians spun to meet them. Three of us against three of them, and a Roman legionary was worth two of any Dacian rebel—Hell's gates, I was even starting to *sound* like my centurion now!

The javelin came jabbing at me again, and I hunched behind my shield. My *gladius* moved around its edge in short jabbing strokes, and I had a crazily clear memory of Emperor Trajan circling me in a torchlit garden and saying, *The point beats the edge, boy, the point beats the edge!*

The javelin's head struck my shield and stuck there. I gave the shield a savage twist, ripping the haft out of his hand, and he tore an ax from his belt and whipped it about in a short vicious arc that should have ended somewhere between my ears. It chopped a bite from my shield instead, numbing my arm. Behind me I could hear a bubbling shriek, and I saw that the Dacian in the lion skin had buried his own ax in the head of a fair-haired legionary. He'd run to help me so quickly, he hadn't had time to relace his helmet . . .

The top third of my shield disintegrated into splinters at another blow of the ax. I slung the shield at my Dacian with a yell. A tall man, burly under the red cloak he'd no doubt taken from some poor dead Roman. His eyes were black pits in the moonlight; all I could see was the gleam of his bared teeth in a thicket of dark beard as he came at me. I ducked the next swipe of the ax and flipped the *gladius* into my left hand.

I'd learned to fight as a Roman with my right hand, keeping in formation, keeping behind the shield, keeping in line. Short jabbing strokes; the point beats the edge; everything that had been drilled into me during legionary training. But the left hand had been trained by a barbarian, by Rome's greatest gladiator who also happened to be my father. The left hand had made my first kill when I was thirteen years old. The left hand recognized no rules, fought in no formations. *The point beats the edge*, the right hand knew. *Hell with that*, the left hand thought.

I touched the amulet about my neck that my father had given me, and then I tore my sword across the Dacian's chest in a stroke that would have ripped him open throat to belly if not for the mail. He staggered back a moment and I was leaping with him, roaring that his mother was a whore, that his father was a bucket of scum, that I'd kill him in pieces and piss on his bones. I chopped the crest off his stolen helmet, I stabbed through his knee and left him hobbling, I took half his shield off and half the fingers of the hand along with it. He dropped the ax, but he didn't plead, just stared at me stoically, and he'd been brave so I took his life in one fast stroke through the neck.

He fell at the same time as the second legionary. I spun just in time to see the man cry out, a spear below the edge of his breastplate. He fell, driven back across the grass by the man in the lion skin to the edge of the solar disc, and as I came forward I realized there were just the two of us left. Me and Lion Skin, silver under the moonlight.

He turned and saw me at the same moment, the standard pole in one hand and his ax in the other. I held my sword out, advancing, and he retreated with careful steps. The eagle still gleamed over his head.

To my surprise, he spoke. "You're the one who raised the alarm."

His Latin was good, barely accented. No wonder he'd been able to fool the sentries into thinking he was the Tenth's aquilifer.

I pointed my sword at the eagle, blood still roaring in my ears. "Give her back," I panted. "And the lion skin. They're not yours."

"The skin is mine. I speared the lion when I was twelve years old. My first kill."

Something clicked inside my head. An aquilifer wasn't the only man who wore a lion skin. I thought of the rumors I'd heard, rumors of a man ten feet tall who led armies against Rome and hid horns and a tail beneath a lion skin. ". . . You're *him*. You're the Dacian king."

He stared at me, impassive. He was taller than I, which didn't happen often, and he had a short black beard, a full mouth, an unyielding blade of a nose. The lion's coarse mane mixed with his own coarse black hair, and the lion's claws crossed over a broad chest. The eagle screamed silently overhead. My eagle, held in this lion's paw.

"They said you went east," I blurted.

He grunted. "I would have."

"There must have been easier ways to get out!" But even as I said it, I wondered. An aquilifer went anywhere he pleased. The guards at Old Sarm's gates would have taken one look at the eagle and maybe not bothered looking at the face under the lion skin as they waved the aquilifer through. He could have taken horses from the camp, stowed the eagle away, and ridden fast to Ranisstorium or anywhere else to renew his fight.

Not that the Tenth would have been part of that fight. A legion that lost its eagle was disgraced past any measure of redemption.

I raised my sword again, pointing at the eagle. "Give her back, and I'll kill you fast."

"Kings don't die fast," he said wearily. "They get marched back to Rome in chains, and then they die in your arenas. What do you call it, when you kill men there—the *games*?"

A tendril of uneasiness uncoiled in my stomach, and I pushed it down. "Give her back."

He moved back again with the same care, taking a step up without looking onto the moon-bleached stone of the solar disc. "Stay back," he said as I lunged forward. His ax was poised not at me, but over the eagle as he lowered the standard pole. "I can hack it to bits before you get near me."

"Why?" I spat. "You're finished."

"More than you know." He smiled, and I saw the effort it took. "But you took something of mine, didn't you?"

I looked at the smoking fortress behind him. "I didn't do that. I'm just—*here*. With the rest of my legion."

"Why?"

"Why what? I get orders, and I march. It's not complicated."

"Do you even know my name?"

I'd heard it a hundred times, something strange that twisted the tongue. Something I'd never bothered to remember. What did it matter?

I looked at the eagle in his hand. My blood still pounded in my veins, begging for a fight, but my tongue might have been stone in my mouth. Why couldn't Titus have been here to face this clever king? Titus could have talked him down in that soft voice; quoted something clever and moving about the nobility of surrender. But I wasn't any good with words. Never had been.

We looked at each other, the Dacian king and I, and suddenly he sat, more falling than lowering himself. He gave a soft grunt and lowered the eagle to the stones, but took his ax with a warning look at me and poised it over the proud wing.

"All right, all right." I lowered my own sword, sitting warily on the edge of the solar disc. The king pressed his free hand under his lion skin out of sight, the knuckles of the other hand clenching white on the ax haft. "Left-handed," I said. "So am I."

"I noticed. Pity. My son was never any good against left-handers."

"Your son?"

He nodded at the man I'd killed, then at the other Dacian who lay slumped in the grass with the dead legionary's *gladius* buried in his throat. "Both of them."

I didn't know what to say to that. The wrong thing, and my eagle would be lying in two pieces. I saw a black shadow beneath him, spreading on the stones.

"What *is* your name?" I blurted suddenly.

"Decebalus." His Latin was blurring.

"Good name." It meant *strength of ten.* Better than *slightly.*

The shadow under him grew, creeping liquid-black toward the eagle.

"What gave us away?" Decebalus said. "What made you attack?"

"You called the eagle 'it,'" I said. "To us, the eagle is always 'her.'"

"Ah." He lay down carefully on the stones, one hand still stuffed under the lion skin. I started to edge forward, but the ax in his other hand jerked up, and I froze. "Don't test me, boy."

I held up a hand, appeasing.

He looked up at the watching moon, now poised almost exactly overhead. "I was crowned here," he said to no one in particular. "But at noon. Such a bright day. I was crowned at noon, and now I'll die at midnight."

"Give me the eagle," I said.

He made an inarticulate sound through clenched teeth. Under the lion skin his fist clenched, and more glossy blood spilled across the stones. The eagle was drowning in it.

I rose, came toward him. His eyes rolled in his head. "Bury my sword hand."

"The Emperor wants it," I said helplessly. If the king himself wasn't alive to be marched back to Rome, then Trajan had vowed to have the head for identification—and the hand that had been raised against Rome.

"Take him my right hand. He won't—won't know. Not many left-handers, eh?" He chuckled, and his teeth were black with blood. One of the lion's paws flopped back, and I could see the horror of the wound beneath. The dead legionary had torn out half the king's guts before going down himself.

Decebalus dropped the eagle, and it rattled with a clang against the stones of the solar disc. He hugged the ax against his chest a moment, then patted it and fumbled instead for the dagger at his belt. His teeth bared again like a skull, and I remembered the garrison he'd burned on the fringe of Dacia, the four sentries he'd left dead in the road, the men who had been tortured inside, and the skull that had been set up in the niche of the gate.

"You should have stayed here," I said as he fumbled the dagger from his belt. "You should have minded your own business."

In the end, his fingers wouldn't close on the dagger's hilt. He might have had the strength of ten once, but the river of blood had carried it all away. He looked at me, and I took the dagger from his hand. I didn't know what to say, didn't know what prayers the Dacians had for their dying warriors, so I just touched the amulet at my neck, given to me by another warrior who'd had the strength of ten too, in his day. I touched the amulet, and then I put my hand on the forehead of the dying king and I cut his throat.

"Vix?" Titus blinked at me, as I stumbled into the immaculate little tent my friend called his own. "Aren't you supposed to be getting drunk up there in Old Sarm with the rest of the legion?"

"See that the Emperor gets this." I dropped a bundle at Titus's feet. A lion's paw with bloody claws flopped limply over his sandal. He looked gingerly into the bundle and leaped back.

"This too." I jammed the eagle's standard pole into the ground. "Take care of her. She's had a hard night."

"Vix?"

"She needs cleaning," I said, not too distinctly. "The eagle shouldn't be all bloody like that."

I stumbled out of Titus's tent. My sword needed cleaning too; it was covered in gore from all the chopping, and my centurion would roast me for putting it back in the scabbard so filthy. But my hands were shaking too much, and I swore and kept moving. Hardly anyone in the camp tonight—as Titus said, the rest of the legion was up getting drunk in Old Sarm except for a few unlucky ones posted as guards here below.

"Vix?"

Sabina stood before my *contubernium* tent with a water pail in one hand. She had a bundle of my tunics in the other—laundry. Of course. Laundry didn't stop just because wars had been won, or kings had died. "You know you're doing a hero's laundry?" I said.

She lifted her brows, putting down the pail. "Am I?"

I spread my arms, grinning. "I'm a hero." Why was the grin so hard to force? I'd killed the king of Dacia—I'd ended the war—I'd have a laurel crown for it, once the Emperor heard, and a string of medals for my belt, and why couldn't I smile?

Sabina was regarding me with the same grave caution that I'd seen on Titus's face.

"The Dacians have something called a solar disc," I informed her, slinging my helmet aside. The helmet crashed into the water pail and upended it, but I paid no attention. "A solar disc—did you know that?"

"No, I didn't know that." She took a step closer.

"It's something to do with measuring the sun, maybe the moon too. It's round, and it's all put together out of white stones fitted like tiles, and *why are you looking at me like that?*"

She opened her arms. I dropped into them, crashing to my knees. "Kings are crowned on solar discs," I said into her waist.

"Ssshh," she said, her fingers running through my hair.

My eyes were dry, but I was shaking. Head to toe I was shaking, and I didn't know why. I didn't know why. "Kings die on them too."

"Hush, my love. Hush."

I gripped her, drowning, and I loved her more than anything on this wide green earth.

CHAPTER 15

VIX

"—selfless devotion to duty, risking his life not for gold but for the legion's honor—"

Who was my centurion droning on about? Surely it couldn't be me. I didn't *get* compliments from centurions. I got nasty looks and the occasional caning.

"—attentive even off-duty to the treachery he saw before him, he reflected great credit upon himself in keeping with the highest traditions of—"

I shifted from one foot to the other, trying to keep my face solemn as the centurion droned on in his loud flat voice about all the good qualities I didn't have. I was struck with a sudden image of Sabina strutting around a tent stark naked, swinging a rolled-up bedroll for a swagger stick as she imitated perfectly the centurion's bellowing voice, his tone-deaf cadences, and his habit of adding a little sniff to the start of each new platitude.

"—killing two with his own hand, and one of those our greatest enemy, Decebalus himself." *Sniff.* I bit down hard on the inside of my cheek to keep from guffawing out loud and ruining the solemnity of the moment.

And it was a solemn moment. The whole legion had been arrayed, spit-polished and shined, the cohorts aligned with mathematical precision, and all eyes fixed front. The centurions stood stiffly with their helmets beneath their arms; the tribunes yawned and fidgeted as only bored patrician boys could yawn and fidget—although Titus's face was a beacon of pride behind them. I'd polished my breastplate till it gleamed, the stiff red horsehair crest stood up proudly from my helmet, and Sabina had flattened my spiky hair smooth with a few desperate applications of water and goose grease. "You'll do the Tenth proud," she'd judged, and my friends nodded agreement—Julius and Simon, Boil and Philip, who might still be my brothers-in-arms but who were no longer my *contubernium*.

The centurion coughed, and I realized I'd missed my cue. Hastily I removed my helmet, bowing my head as he reached up.

It was light—so light. Just a few twigs and leaves twisted into a wreath. It was too big, and I had to cock it back on my head or else have it slip over my ears. I felt it under my hand, the victory wreath I'd dreamed so many countless hours, and my solemnity cracked. I looked up, past the centurion to the Emperor, who stood in his breastplate and red cloak like any one of us soldiers, and I grinned at him.

He grinned back, infectiously, and strode past the centurion who was still droning. "Give me that," he ordered, and yanked the pelt from the hands of the hovering *optio*. "Quit smiling like a loon, boy, and bow your head. This is a serious moment, damn it."

I bowed my head, trying not to laugh, hearing chortles from the first few rows of legionaries who had overheard. Emperor Trajan swept the lion skin about my shoulders, the mane covering my laurel wreath, the yellowed fangs framing my forehead. He tied the paws across my chest, and I heard the claws click against my breastplate. I raised my hand to stop the pelt from slipping, and felt the coarse fur of the mane in my fingers. It smelled like dry grass and sunshine, like blood and sweat, and above all like a king who had died on a stone circle. Trajan had offered me a new pelt, but I'd refused.

A pole was thrust into my left hand, and then the Emperor grasped my right. "Congratulations, Aquilifer," he said, and spun me about toward the assembled legion. He raised my arm into the air, and the Tenth exploded.

I saw Sabina, immaculate in green silk, applauding with the polite formality of any legate's wife, but she had tears in her eyes. Hadrian stood at her side, my legate in the unpleasant flesh, putting his hands together exactly twice before he was done applauding. His bearded face was impassive as he stood there in a breastplate that had probably never been bloodied in its life. He'd opposed my elevation, I'd heard. The Emperor had been the one to override him.

Cheers swamped me. The Emperor gripped my shoulders, looking as proud as my father would have, and kissed me soundly on both cheeks. He shouted something I couldn't hear over the cheering and the banging of shields, and I looked up dizzily to see the eagle riding over my head, giving her imperious silent shriek. I wouldn't have to carry a legionary's pack anymore, just the eagle.

My eagle.

One of my better memories, that.

TITUS

"Lion skins are hot," Vix complained as Titus slowed his horse to pace beside the new aquilifer. "I don't know how the lions stand it."

"Barely raised to your new rank, and you're already grousing." Titus shook his head. "Honor is supposed to be the reward of virtue, you know."

"Who said that?"

"Do you really care?"

"No. But if I don't ask you get hurt feelings."

Titus laughed, flipping a lock of his gelding's mane back across its neck. He could feel sweat running down his neck even though it was barely noon. A cloudless blue dome of sky over a flat expanse of green and a dusty white ribbon of road, as if the world were celebrating along with the legion. Celebrating the fact that the Tenth Fidelis was going home.

Mog, thought Titus. It had seemed such a backwater mud-hole when he first arrived, drab and charmless with its endless taverns and raucous theatres and half-paved streets. Now all he could think was, *Real beds instead of bedrolls! Roast pork and grapes instead of barley broth and wormy biscuits! Clean linens instead of blankets with lice!* Mog sounded like a paradise.

The rest of the legion clearly thought so too, marching along double-pace and bawling out marching songs in tuneless good humor. The Emperor sang too, riding just ahead on a big black horse with his legates. Titus could hear his loud tuneless voice, joining into the marching song's more obscene verses. "Everyone looks like they can taste that homecoming wine already," Titus said. "From the Emperor on down."

"What they're tasting is the hero's welcome we're all going to get," Vix said with relish. "The girls will flop on their backs the moment they see us coming. Who doesn't like a victorious hero?"

"I think you have enough girls to contend with already, Slight."

"Just two!"

"Does Sabina even know about Demetra, or—"

"Oh, not Demetra. Sabina's my first girl. *She's* my second." Vix glanced up the length of the standard pole to the eagle who paced the air serenely over his head. "Of the two, I think she'll be the more demanding."

"And what about Demetra?" Titus gave a withering look from his horse's height. "Her child will be born soon, you know. *Your* child."

"I'll give her some money to take care of it." Vix whistled between his teeth, cheerful. "She'll find a new man soon enough afterward. No girl who looks like her will be lonely for long. You want to make her an offer? You're a rising man now—Emperor's tribune!"

"I don't really know what he promoted me for," Titus confessed. "I just *brought* him that head. Not like I had anything to do with collecting it. Maybe it was a reward for not throwing up all over him when I handed it over? I admit, that took a fairly heroic effort."

Vix pushed the lion's mane off his hair, looking at Trajan's big armored figure on the black horse up ahead. "I'd die for that man in a heartbeat." Frankly. "I think I love him."

"Quiet, or you'll make Sabina jealous."

"Oh, she knows I love her too."

He said it so lightly, as if it were no great matter to love a girl and be loved in return. *You're the lucky one, Slight,* Titus thought. *And not for the lion skin and the victory wreath.*

"I thought it would be different," Vix confided, shifting the standard pole to his other shoulder. "Like a fish getting caught—some girl finally gets her hooks into you. But this is easy. Like breathing."

"She makes it easy," Titus said without thinking, and kicked himself. *Stupid, stupid.* But Vix hadn't noticed his slip of the tongue.

"She just held me that night after I killed Decebalus. Never said a word. Most of the time she's talking nonstop, but she knows when to be quiet." Vix hesitated, his confident swagger slowing a moment. "I still don't know why—it was like getting hit in the gut, killing him. But I've killed men before and never thought twice about it."

"'It is proper to learn even from an enemy,'" Titus quoted. "You're not the first soldier to admire a man he has to kill. It's been troubling men since first there was war, I imagine."

"If I'd been born in Dacia, I'd have been one of those men following him." Vix fumbled for words, which Titus never heard him do. Vix's words might lack eloquence, but they were always unhesitating. "It's just an accident, isn't it? Where we end up getting born? But it controls everything. Put my parents a few hundred miles northeast, and I'd have grown up with a round shield—and a beard—and I wouldn't have ever fought in the Colosseum—and I'd likely be dead by that solar disc right now, next to my king."

"Did you do what he asked?" Titus asked. "Did you bury his left hand?"

"Next to the disc, in the grass. With his ax."

One of the legates called for Titus then, and he steered his horse away back to the head of the column. But he still brought a wineskin to Vix's fire sometimes when they made camp at night, as the weeks rolled on and the Tenth marched west. Dark pines were fading to open fields, and for the first time in what felt like months, Titus began to think of Rome.

I'll campaign for quaestor, he decided. *Senator Norbanus said he'd put my name forward. Public works and festival organization; I'll do that better than I ever led a scouting party.* Perhaps he would get his own apartments in the city as well. Not too far from his grandfather, but a home of his own. A man's home. He'd marched across the Empire, after all; he'd been to war; he had that first all-important line of "Tribune" on his list of accomplishments. *For dreams as modest as mine, that puts me halfway up the ladder already.* Maybe that was the good thing about dreaming on a small scale. Vix still had a ways to go if he wanted to lead a legion.

"By the way," Sabina announced halfway through Pannonia, perhaps a fortnight's ride outside Moguntiacum. "I'm being sent ahead on to Mog. That wagon I haven't sat in all summer takes me on ahead tomorrow."

"Why?" Vix looked down at her, sitting wrapped in the lion skin inside the circle of his arms.

"Because Hadrian wants me to go ahead, to greet the Empress and help make arrangements for the triumphant return." Sabina shuddered. "She's come all the way north to Germania, just to meet him and Trajan. And to unload a whole summer's worth of advice on me the moment we set eyes on each other. I wish I *could* just come skipping up behind the legion in my hobnailed sandals. Hopefully the shock would kill her."

"Hadrian too, and then we're shut of them both." Vix kissed her soundly. His eyes when he looked at her these days had a softer gleam than the old casual possessiveness, Titus thought. His hand twined automatically through hers whenever she came near, and his big thumb rubbed in a slow tender movement across the back of her knuckles . . .

I need a girl, Titus decided. *A nice mistress I can set up in that apart-*

ment in Rome. He could afford one on a quaestor's salary. Someone pretty who didn't mind boring quotes from Horace, and who could cook. Lamb stew . . .

"Damn it," Vix grumbled the following day, after Sabina had kissed him a very thorough good-bye in the morning and that afternoon been handed into her wagon with elegant formality by Hadrian to be sent on ahead—along with her escort of guards and slaves, who had gotten quite rich that summer for looking the other way and *not* guarding her. "I don't like sleeping without her," Vix complained. "The way her hair gets in my face. And the way she digs her elbow into my side every few hours and grumbles at me to for gods' sake turn on my stomach and stop snoring—"

"Get used to it, Slight, because this mad arrangement of yours can't possibly go on in Mog."

"Why not?"

Titus stared. "Do you have a death wish?"

"My girl can sneak and lie with the best of them. We'll manage."

"But Hadrian's primed for a governorship now." Titus had heard the news from the Emperor, helping to draft a list of future appointments. "Pannonia or Syria, somewhere far."

"She won't stay with him forever."

Titus fell back on Seneca. "'Is the gladiator formulating his attack in the arena?'"

"What's that supposed to mean?"

"It means, don't you *ever* plan ahead?"

"Oh, I've got a plan. Sabina divorces Hadrian. I buy entrance to the *equite* class with her money. I get a wife with a little more polish than I've got. That helps me get ahead, get my promotion to centurion, move up the ladder, eventually get my legion."

"I see. And have you shared any of these plans of yours with the lady in question?"

"Sabina lives in the present," Vix dismissed. "I'm the one with my eye on the future."

"Somehow I doubt it will be as simple as you think, Slight."

"Why not?"

Titus rolled his eyes. The Tenth rolled west.

SABINA

"You look very brown." The Empress's eyes swept Sabina up and down. "You should have taken more care with your sunshade. Come stand by me."

"Of course." Sabina followed after the dark-blue-clad figure with the deep-set eyes and the severe swept-back plaits. Those elegant streaks of gray had advanced even farther into the Empress's dark hair, but otherwise she looked in distressingly good form as she swept to the head of the temple. Not much of a temple—Jupiter's shrine here in Mog wasn't much more than a few steps up to a modest altar. "The monument of Drusus is much more splendid," Germania's governor had argued. "Surely a better site to welcome the legions."

But Empress Plotina had efficiently crushed that notion. "Jupiter's hand delivered my husband to victory," she decreed. "We welcome our legions back to his temple, and none other." The governor had looked peevish, but it hardly mattered what he thought anymore—Plotina had taken charge of everything the moment she arrived in Mog.

And after all, Sabina thought, wasn't every army's homecoming really about the women who welcomed them? The site didn't matter at all in comparison. From the pillarlike Plotina in her dark blue and diadem to the legates' wives who waited stout and dignified behind Sabina; from the centurions' wives with their lively chatter standing in the next rank to the common women who lined the street below in their gaudy beads and packs of clutching children—they all had the same look. The anxious scanning of the horizon, the craning of the neck as they looked for their men to come home.

Sabina wondered if Vix's other woman was here today, the one he hadn't told her about but had doubtless left behind in Mog when the legion marched. The one Titus had been almost visibly tempted to bring up.

The Empress sounded disapproving as she looked Sabina over. "That dress is very bright."

"I'm so glad you like it." Yellow silk, with a golden eagle pinning each shoulder. Bliss to wear soft silks again after a summer of scratchy wool. A great many things had been bliss, coming back to civilization. Sabina's luxurious palanquin and speedy escort had taken her swiftly ahead from the Tenth to Hadrian's quarters in Mog, and she'd had a week of much needed solitude. Sleeping late in a soft bed piled with furs, curling up to a breakfast of cold mulberry infusions and fresh fruit, soaking in the steaming hot pool of her bathhouse . . . Sabina's slaves had exchanged glances as they shook out the fleas her clothes had inevitably acquired on the road, and the bathhouse atten- dants raised eyebrows over the calluses that had to be pumiced off Sabina's feet, but no one had said a word. When the page bringing his mistress a stack of letters in the library yesterday found her crying silently into a scroll, he had left the letters and backed out with lowered eyes.

Not too many tears, though. In the morning Sabina rose humming, lined her eyes in gold leaf, and thought smiling of Vix as she pinned her yellow silks into place with the eagle brooches.

"That dress is *too* bright." Empress Plotina's deep voice made the decree like a judge. "You must change, Vibia Sabina."

"But I think I hear the legions approaching. Three and a half legions make a great deal of noise, don't you think?"

That got her a Look from the Empress of Rome, a Look Sabina hadn't missed one bit during the last six months, but the roar had already begun in the distance, and a ripple spread outward through the women clustered in the street. More ripples, more murmurs, and sud- denly a shriek of excitement sounded and Sabina didn't have to be told the eagles had been sighted.

This was nothing, she knew, compared to the triumph already being planned in Rome. "White bulls in sacrifice to Jupiter," Plotina had ruled. "Black bulls to Minerva, more to Mars and Hades. Chariot races, gladiator bouts, perhaps a Colosseum reenactment of the final siege . . ." Trajan would ride along in a chariot with a laurel wreath over his head, his face daubed in celebratory red paint, and no doubt Vix and the other standard-bearers would be brought back to Rome too, to march with their eagles as millions screamed. But Sabina thought this was the real triumph, the triumph of the living coming back to their women, and the women screaming and waving pennants and barely restrained as the beaming, strutting soldiers swaggered back into Mog.

Trajan led the parade in his red cloak, vaulting off his black horse like a boy and bounding up the steps of the Temple of Jupiter with a grin to split the sun. Plotina unbent enough to smile in return, extending her hands in welcome. He moved with shouts of greeting to the governor of Germania, to the other officials who stood hopeful for his attention. He barely contained himself as the priest droned a blessing and sacrificed a bull, and when he waved to the crowd the screams drowned the blessing. He picked Sabina up in a bear hug, smearing her with bull's blood, but she just laughed and kissed him on both cheeks and he dropped her into Hadrian's arms with a shouted, "Here's the man who's been missing you, and after just a week too!"

Sabina smiled as Hadrian righted her. "Hello again."

"Vibia Sabina." He kissed her hand as formally as if they had not met for months—which they scarcely had. "You look considerably cleaner."

"Yes, I stayed days in the bathhouse when I got back to civilization. You look very splendid yourself." His formal armor suited him, and he had dismounted his big horse with a flourish not one whit overdone. No one sat a horse as magnificently as her husband, not even the Emperor. Maybe it was because horses adored Hadrian—even now, the big stallion was nibbling at his sleeve. "I've missed you," she said, and surprised herself by meaning it. They might have met once a day for a cup of wine or the occasional dinner, but their long conversations had withered away under his duties as legate and her hours with Vix.

A crinkle of surprise showed between his brows, but it quickly smoothed out as Plotina came forward. "Dear Publius." She kissed his forehead possessively. "It's been too long."

"Much too long." He took her arm. "Do I have you to thank for my new governorship?"

"Of course, dear boy." The Empress waved politely to the troops below, getting a swell of applause. "I'd hoped to get you Syria. You aren't disappointed?"

"Not at all. Pannonia will provide ample opportunities."

"Pannonia?" Sabina lifted her eyebrows, turning to Hadrian. "You didn't tell me!"

"Confirmed only yesterday," Plotina said, sounding complacent. "Of course Publius must not leave until after the triumph in Rome. You must be at the Emperor's side for that, he'll have it no other way—"

Will he? wondered Sabina. Hadrian might have ridden at the Emperor's back in the parade, but he'd certainly not been singled out from the other legates. Even now Trajan was roaring and backslapping among his tribunes rather than standing, waving, and bowing with his wife and her protégé.

"Wave and smile, Sabina," Plotina called to her. "It is expected."

"I doubt the men care if I wave at them," said Sabina. "They just want to be dismissed so they can go get drunk with their families."

"Let us hope they spend the day in sober thanks for their victories," said the Empress.

"You're lucky if they're sober for the victory itself," Sabina snorted. "Much less the celebration after."

"That dress is very bright." Hadrian flicked a speck of dust from her shoulder. "And eagles are really better suited for a standard pole than a brooch."

Trajan came bounding back, raising his arm to another wave of cheers. He spoke a few words of thanks that had the legionaries cuffing their eyes, but not too many words—Trajan, Sabina had observed before, knew how to keep things brief. "Keep your battles short and your speeches shorter," he often said. Hadrian, observing how well it worked for the Emperor, was now modifying his own speeches to suit.

"Your officials expect to speak with you," Plotina said the moment Trajan rejoined her side. "Preparations for the celebratory banquet this evening—"

"I'll be wanting to speak with them as well." Trajan waved a good-natured hand. "They're to invite the tribunes to join us this evening as well as the legates. Camp prefects and first centurions too."

"Husband, surely not. They are very rough."

"Gods' bones, at least they'll liven things up! And we'll have some-one else too—" Trajan spoke a brief word to his aide, who went dash-ing off into the throng. A few moments later he returned, dragging along a man in a red cloak with a lion's mane over his hair and a stan-dard pole in his hand.

"Caesar." Vix dropped to one knee, but Trajan raised him with a wave.

"Here's the man we have to thank for killing Decebalus! You'll plant that head before the Senate house at the triumph, boy. With your own hand."

"I believe the governor requires your attention," Plotina sniffed.

"Oh, very well. You'll come to that banquet tonight, Aquilifer—that's an Imperial order."

"Yes, Caesar." Vix grinned, snapping off a salute.

"Good, good." Trajan held his arm out for his wife. Just before they vanished into the hovering throng of well-wishers, he gave Sabina an approving glance over one shoulder and shouted, "I like the eagles!"

Sabina laughed. Hadrian made a motion to follow the Emperor, but Titus approached, tall and impressive in the toga he had donned the moment he could get out of his armor. He had always been skinny, but a summer's marching had filled him out to a pleasant leanness. He looked like a handsome young man now, not an uncertain boy.

"Legate, I had just heard news of your governorship." Titus's eyes had a brief flick of horror to see Hadrian, Vix, and Sabina all converged together, but his polite mask never faltered. *You will make a good politician*, Sabina thought. "My congratulations, sir."

Hadrian nodded his thanks, utterly ignoring Vix, who stood behind the eagle standard doing his best imitation of a post.

"At least on our march we had a chance to pass through Pannonia," Titus continued, keeping his eyes scrupulously away from Vix. "Very fortunate, sir."

"I've heard the Pannonians wear wolf-skin breeches and sacrifice to horned gods," said Sabina, "but you can never be sure about these rumors. I certainly didn't see any horned gods lying around when we were marching through to Dacia. And come to think of it, we heard the same sort of things about Dacians too, and they were all quite civilized. Solar discs and piped water rather than blood rituals and human sacrifices . . . I can't wait to see how the Pannonians turn out on a closer acquaintance."

"You will be accompanying the governor to Pannonia?" Titus addressed her as formally as if they had never shared a wineskin around a campfire in their lives.

"Oh, I wouldn't miss it," said Sabina. "New provinces, new horizons. I can't wait."

Under the lion skin, Vix's chin jerked.

"I see," said Titus, and offered Hadrian another bow. "My congratulations once again, Governor."

A second bow to Sabina, and a nod to Vix in which horror and amusement were blended just about equally. Sabina repressed a smile, but Vix was not smiling.

"You're going to Pannonia—Lady?" he demanded, barely remembering the honorific.

"Of course." She waved to someone nonexistent on the other side of the steps, angling them both away from Hadrian, who was perusing his pile of wax tablets again. "My father will probably send me three scrolls on Pannonia's recent history, a list of recommended reading, and a request that I please check up on the new aqueduct the Senate paid for and tell him if it's being built on schedule. He says it's been very useful having a daughter who travels—gives him an extra pair of eyes all over the Empire, as it were."

"So you'll be staying a while in Pannonia?" Vix lowered his voice. She could see his big hard fingers tightening on the standard pole.

"I don't know." She tucked a lock of hair behind one ear. "Most governorships last a few years."

"Years—" His jaw hardened. "Never thought to ask me about that, did you? When you made your plans!"

"I *didn't* make any plans," she pointed out. "I only found out about Pannonia two minutes ago."

"But you were going to stay with the Tenth!" he hissed, barely audible. "With me!"

"Never thought to ask *me* about that, did you?"

His fingers had fused around the standard pole. Sabina hoped he wouldn't crack it in half. "You bitch," he whispered.

"Why?" she asked, puzzled.

"I told you I loved you," he said in a ferocious whisper. "I went spinning dreams about the future and now you tell me you're just—"

"Is something amiss?" Hadrian's voice slid coolly between them.

"Not at all." Sabina turned her head toward him. "A moment, my dear."

He frowned, turning to his aide with a list of instructions. She gave a bright social smile to Vix, fading to something truer as she angled herself between him and her husband.

"I love you, Vix," she said frankly. "But whatever made you think I want to follow your stars, and not my own?"

He stared at her.

"I think you had best go now, Aquilifer." Hadrian's hand took possession of Sabina's arm, and he looked at Vix with cool displeasure. "As little as you are used to ladies of good birth, you must be aware it is rude to stare at them. Your time might better be served in finding a suitable costume for this evening's banquet, since the Emperor seems so determined to have his . . . pets."

Vix's face had a hard stillness that Sabina recognized. He stared at Hadrian, expressionless, and his eyes were flat, murderous stones.

She stepped between them, fast. "Hardly a pet," she said lightly, and dropped a congratulatory hand over Vix's on the standard pole. "A hero of Rome, as we saw ourselves. And likely to be an even greater one, someday."

"I doubt that," said Hadrian. "I doubt that highly."

Vix stared at him over her head for another long moment, the man in the lion skin and the man in the breastplate, and there was something in their gaze that excluded her.

Sabina squeezed Vix's hand over the standard, warningly.

Another suspended breath, and then the murder banked in his gaze. He jerked his hand from under Sabina's and turned in a swirl of red cloak, gone into the crowds. Sabina could see the eagle on its long pole marking a swift, brutal path through the throng of revelers.

"I wish you would not flirt with common soldiers," Hadrian frowned.

"I might say the same to you." Sabina made an effort to speak lightly. "Besides, I've known Vix for years. One of my father's household guards, you know . . . Why did you suddenly look so black and furious at him?"

"I dislike his type, that is all." Hadrian flicked a hand as if flicking Vix from his attention. *Back to what place in the mental files?* Sabina wondered.

"Flirt with the governor of Upper Germania this evening instead." Hadrian took her arm, following in the wake of Trajan and Plotina. "I will need the governor's support when I reach Pannonia."

"Do you think they really wear wolf skins there?"

"I devoutly hope not. Don't wear yellow tonight." His eyes swept her. "Or those eagles."

CHAPTER 16

VIX

That bitch.

That cool, calm, collected, two-faced whore.

I stamped back to the fort in a white rage, kicking everything that got in my path. *Fight me*, I hoped, *somebody pick a fight*—but the whole bloody Tenth was in a good mood and no one was drunk enough yet for fights. I saw a centurion hugging his woman in one arm and his son in the other, the boy wearing his father's helmet—I saw a cluster of shouting swaggering legionaries push toward the nearest tavern and get sidetracked by a pair of admiring girls tossing flowers at them from an upper window—I saw everybody happy, everybody but the bloody hero.

A horribly cheery clerk greeted me at the *principia*. "The new aquilifer? I've heard of you. Yes, you can leave the eagle with me."

I surrendered her over. She'd live in the chapel now with a permanent guard, keeping her haughty watch over the bust of the Emperor and everything else that the legion held precious. I'd carry her out only if we did a route march or went on campaign again. I looked up at her as she was planted in place, and she stared arrogantly down at me.

Sabina had worn an eagle brooch on each shoulder, with the same proud tilt to their gold heads. Why had she done that?

"Are you the one who killed Decebalus?" the clerk asked, and recoiled at my snarl.

I shoved out of the *principia*, still glowering. I didn't want to get drunk, I didn't want a celebration; I just wanted another fight. No, what I wanted was another *war*, something long and savage and preferably bloody. My feet took me halfway to my old quarters, but I stopped and realized that they weren't my quarters anymore. I didn't have a *contubernium* now, just an eagle with the double pay and double danger that came with it. I had no idea where the aquilifer slept when at home in the fort.

I contemplated going back to the clerk, but one more look at his cheery face and I'd probably break it, and then that bastard Hadrian would have me flogged. I had another wave of rage as I thought of his cold black gaze, meeting my eyes over Sabina's sleek head. He'd probably screw her tonight—one of his yearly visits. Turn her over and pretend she was a boy, and then they'd go swanning off to Pannonia together. "*How interesting,*" I mimicked, and got a puzzled look from the gate guard as I slammed through. "What are you looking at!"

"Nothing," he said hastily. "You're lucky, that's all. Having the day to celebrate. Someone had to draw sentry duty, and wouldn't you know it's me—"

"Fuck you," I growled. A whole city celebrating, and I had nowhere to go. Nowhere to go for years, probably—what other action would the Tenth see, now that Dacia was quiet? Guard duty at the fort, and the occasional route march so we didn't get rusty. There'd be the triumph first, and I'd even get to go to Rome to march in it with the eagle over my head, but after that it would be back to Mog, to sit in the fort and *rot*. Had it really seemed possible, just this morning, that I'd be a centurion soon, that I'd even do the impossible and get my own legion someday? What a joke. I was going to rot here in Mog for the next twenty years. I'd taken the oath and signed those years over, and now they yawned before me like a grave.

And no doubt Sabina would be gallivanting around Pannonia, checking out aqueducts for her father and seeing all the new horizons she wanted. I hoped the Pannonians cooked her over a campfire and ate her.

Suddenly I felt absurd in the lion skin. I unknotted the paws about my neck and yanked the mane from my hair. I balled the pelt into my pack, and a handful of centurions brushed by me roaring a filthy drinking song, waving wineskins jubilantly overhead. I couldn't even get drunk like them this afternoon—I had that bloody banquet tonight with the Emperor's guests, and even if I didn't care two shits for any of them, for *his* sake I'd have to be clean and on my best behavior. Besides, Sabina and her bastard husband would be there, and I'd rather have been cooked and eaten myself than have them think I slunk away. I'd come and stare at Sabina all night till she dropped *her* eyes for a change. Maybe I'd tell bloody Hadrian whose bedroll she'd been sleeping in the past six months while he thought she was in her own tent.

But I thought of Hadrian's cold stare and didn't want to cross it. Maybe the chances weren't so good I'd ever be a centurion, but they'd drop to nothing if I told my commander I'd been mounting his wife.

I stood with my hands hanging at my sides in the middle of a celebrating city and felt like howling. That calculating little vixen. She'd burned me once, and had I learned? Stupid barbarian, tangling with a patrician girl. No more patrician girls for me. No more clever girls; no more adventurous dreaming girls or girls who talked my ear off deep into the night. Nice simple girls, that's what I'd stick to from now on. Even stupid barbarians like me knew better than to get burned a third time.

Demetra.

I hadn't thought of her in months, at least not for longer than it took to shove her right back out of mind, but now she filled my head. Her dark-honey hair, her gentle mouth, her slim body. Her wide brown eyes, always so admiring when they looked at me. Her sweet voice, when she chattered on and on about laundry and the market and the day's baking . . .

Hell's gates, she was beautiful, but she'd bored me.

I wondered if she'd had the baby yet. My child. It was six months since I'd last seen her. She might be swelled up like a melon, or maybe she'd have something small and screaming on the breast. Or maybe she'd seen sense and done something to empty her belly out before it got big at all.

Hadn't I told Demetra I'd marry her when I came back?

I groaned aloud but kicked my feet into moving. Baby or no, I wasn't getting married. Just because I'd gotten burned by a scheming patrician snake of a girl didn't mean I was going to run right back to Demetra. I'd pay her a visit, take a dutiful look at the baby, leave her some money—maybe get a bounce in bed for old times' sake . . .

The street looked no different than it had when I'd left. More riotous, with soldiers drinking or dicing or swaggering past every third door, but the same. I pulled my lion pelt back out of my pack and draped it over one arm. Demetra wouldn't want to hear war stories, but she'd be impressed I made aquilifer. Her eyes would shine admiringly. Sabina never looked at me like that—she just looked at me like she *knew* me, right down to my bones, and that had been damned uncomfortable sometimes.

I didn't want to think about Sabina.

"Who are you?"

I blinked at the face that answered my dutiful knock at the door of the bakehouse. An old woman's face, thin and sour. "I'm looking for Demetra?"

"Never heard of her," the old woman snapped. "No trollops here for soldiers, you be on your way!"

I jammed my foot in the door. "The girl who lived over the bakeshop—a Bithynian girl? Long blond hair?"

"That one died last week when she birthed," the woman said. "Woman across took the child."

She kicked my foot aside and slammed the door. I stared at the panels just inches from my nose, stunned.

"Aquilifer, fancy a drink?" a drunken voice shouted from a passing party of legionaries. "Heard you killed the Dacian king; is it true he had horns?"

I shoved through them, kicking blindly across the street. I hammered on the door of the tenement opposite Demetra's. Another woman answered the door, tired and gray, a dirty child on one hip and another at her skirt. "Do I know you?" she asked, vague-eyed.

"Demetra," I said. "Where's Demetra?"

"That hag across the street didn't tell you? She's a worse neighbor than your girl, I'll say."

"*Where's Demetra?*" My heart thudded.

"Dead," the woman said. "The baby came early. It happens."

I winced. "The hag said you took it."

"The baby? No, that died too. I took her other one, the little lad."

"Was the baby a girl or a boy?" I'd never wanted it, hadn't thought about it for months—but suddenly I had to know. I had to know if my child had been a son or a daughter.

"How should I know?" Indifferently. "I wasn't there."

Would I ever know? Did it even matter? Boy or girl, it was dead. My firstborn.

I found myself wondering if it had had my reddish hair, or Demetra's blond.

"I don't much mind taking the other little 'un." The woman bounced the child on her hip, and for the first time I noticed Demetra's boy. "He's quiet enough, and what's one more when you've already got five? Besides, he might grow up as pretty as his mother, and that could be useful."

I shoved some money at her and got the hell out of there.

PLOTINA

"I don't mind telling you, my dear boy, that I shall be *ecstatic* to leave Germania," Plotina confided to Dear Publius. "Crude, cold—and these

slave girls they sent to wait on me are all thumbs! Sticky thumbs at
that; I'm sure they'd steal anything I turned my back on. You may go,"
she added to the girl brushing her gown.

The flat-faced German maid left the Empress's quarters, muttering
darkly, and Plotina reached behind her own neck to fasten the clasp of
her amethyst necklace. "Very regal," Dear Publius approved from his
corner where he sat keeping her company as she finished her dressing.
"Very regal indeed."

"I can hardly say the same for your wife. Did she use her sunshade
once, marching through Dacia? Brown as that German slut who just
left—"

"My dear lady." Hadrian's voice had a note of humorous warning as
he pinched a crisp fold of his tunic into better alignment. "I know you
disapprove of Sabina. But I do not, and surely that is what matters."

"Disapprove," Plotina sniffed. There was very little in Moguntiacum
of which she *approved*. The town was dirty, the slaves insolent, and
these quarters she had been assigned barely adequate for decent living.
Rough walls, garishly colored cushions on the couches, and those German lamps that smoked day and night. She had brought her own modest luxuries—the polished steel mirror at her table, her little writing
desk where she attended so much Imperial business; the appurtenances
expected and due one of her position. But oh, how glad she would be
to return to Rome! There was nothing about Moguntiacum that the
Empress of Rome found pleasing.

Least of all the rumors she had uncovered—all right, the rumors
she had made sure she uncovered—about Dear Publius's little wife.

"So Vibia Sabina invited herself along on the campaign," Dear Publius
was saying. Lovely to see him in a dinner synthesis for once, handsome
and formal and bearded, rather than the ever-present breastplate. Plotina
sometimes thought herself doomed to spend her whole life surrounded
by men in armor. "I admit I was displeased at the outset, but she did not
inconvenience me. She may even have assisted me. She was useful in one
or two matters—a problem with the supply officers she brought to the

Emperor's attention, and another matter with my senior medicus. Trajan grew very fond of having her at his dinner table, and therefore me as well. And there is no doubt she enjoyed herself on the march."

"Yes," Plotina said significantly. "I hear she did."

"What do you mean?"

Plotina raised her eyebrows, taking her time as she put on her amethyst earrings. Hadrian wandered up behind her, surveying his own reflection in her polished steel mirror.

"So good to have a proper barber again," he murmured, fingering his beard. "One hates the feeling of stubble growing halfway down one's neck, but Trajan lets these things slide on campaign, and it seems best to follow his example . . . I suppose you mean, my dear Plotina, that my wife took a lover during the campaign?"

"I'm surprised to hear you say it so lightly."

Hadrian shrugged. "A wife can call her bed her own, as far as I am concerned, so long as she is discreet."

"I raised you to think better than that," Plotina said tartly. "But we will leave that matter for the moment. Discretion is all, you say? I don't believe Vibia Sabina *was* discreet. I have heard disturbing rumors from slaves, from the legion's aides, even from junior officers. The girl spent her evenings . . . well, I don't like to say . . ."

"I think you had better not." Hadrian glanced at the slave standing with a flagon of barley water in one corner, the other slave folding Plotina's silks into their casket.

Plotina did not dismiss the slaves. She wanted them to spread a few whispers around. Not that one liked to see rumors circulate about a member of the Imperial family, but it was time to strip a little gleam off that adventurousness of Sabina's that Hadrian found so charming.

Trajan too. It was Dear Publius he should be finding charming, not Sabina.

"Common soldiers," Plotina said regretfully. "Legionaries. Those were Sabina's . . . companions . . . during the march."

Hadrian's chin jerked. "She has always had a taste for making friends in low places, but—"

"More than friends this time, dear boy. I hate to be the bearer of bad news—" Not precisely true; oh, well. Plotina bent her head to twist a ring into place, hiding her satisfaction. "Your wife was seen once or twice looking *very* intimate with common legionaries. Rough men, of the lowest sort. I need hardly remind you what people would think if *that* got around Rome."

Dear Publius stood quite still, turning his seal ring around and around his finger.

"I know how fond you are of your wife." Plotina gave a final comprehensive glance into her mirror, pleased at the severe vision in Imperial purple who gazed back. Juno herself would approve. "But perhaps it's time you brought little Sabina to heel?"

"You look very well." Hadrian offered his arm, expressionless. "Shall we go in to the banquet?"

VIX

"Cheer up," Titus implored as he dragged me toward the spill of lights and noise and music. "Don't you want to enjoy the occasion? It's your first Imperial banquet!"

"No, it isn't," I said. "There was another banquet once where I tried to kill the Emperor."

Titus blinked as we joined the line of guests waiting to be admitted. "You tried to kill Trajan?"

"Hell's gates, no. Another Emperor. Crazy as a loon."

"We've had a few of those. Are you making up stories again?"

"Maybe. Maybe not."

"I can never tell when you're joking. Don't tug at that synthesis."

"It's too small." I yanked at the fine white folds of the dinner tunic he'd lent me.

"Well, it's the best I could do at short notice. Otherwise you'd have had to show up naked under that lion skin."

"Bet that would make all these fine ladies sit up."

The Imperial steward descended on us then, recognizing Titus's name and rank, offering me a blander glance, and ushered us through. The finest villa in Mog wasn't much compared to the ones I'd seen in Rome, but it had been commandeered for the Empress and her entourage when they arrived—and now it hosted the Emperor's victory celebration. The floors might be crude stone instead of supple mosaics and the dining couches might be soldered metal instead of carved silver, but the Emperor stood in the center drinking and roaring campaign stories with his officers, and his happiness had spilled over everything and turned it to pure gold. The music was bright and the laughter from all those guests crowded around him was brighter, but everything looked off-color to my eyes. I could have taken Demetra to this, and she'd have put all these powdered patrician beauties to shame. I grabbed a goblet of wine from a pretty little half-naked cup-bearer who beamed at me as if she'd marched to defeat the Dacians too—but I couldn't drink. There was a bubble in my throat, hard and unyielding.

"What?" Titus asked me. "You look grim all over again."

Demetra's dead, I nearly told him. *My child with her.* But I didn't. He'd have covered me with his warm sympathy, thinking that was why I couldn't enjoy the banquet, and I couldn't have borne it. He'd have thought I was grieving, and I couldn't have taken credit for that. The bubble in my throat that wouldn't burst?

It was . . . relief.

No child. No wife. Nothing to weigh me down or drain my purse or stop me from following my stars. Poor, dull, beautiful Demetra was dead, my child was dead, and what did I feel? Some sadness . . . but mostly a twisted, shamed relief.

What a bastard I was. No wonder Sabina hadn't wanted to stay with me.

I'd seen her at once, as soon as I entered the room, but I didn't look at her. I forced my wine down and held out my goblet to another cup-bearer, who promptly filled it. A good wine, far better than the sour *posca* I'd had to drink on campaign, but who cared? "Let's get drunk."

"Better bow first to your hostess," Titus advised, steering me toward the little dais where the Imperial couches had been laid. "Empress Plotina does not approve of drunkenness. One wonders if she approves of anything, to be honest."

We pushed through the happy throng, and then Titus made a graceful speech of thanks to the Empress and I got away with jerking my head in a bow as the ladies stared at me in idle curiosity. Trajan's wife in her severe purple *stola*, a clutch of legates' wives—and Sabina, youngest of the women there, watching the crowd of guests as if she'd rather be whooping it up with the soldiers than sitting among all the disapproving old women who reclined so stiffly and properly on their couches. Maybe she'd gotten a taste for low fun in the time she'd marched with the Tenth. Her eyes drifted to me as Titus made his graceful introduction, and for a moment I just wanted to flee. But I hadn't fled the fucking Dacians and I wasn't going to flee any well-born whore, so I clamped my jaw tight and stared back at her as rudely as I knew how. No more flamboyant yellow like she'd worn at the parade— the Empress had clearly gotten hold of her and laced her into a white dress with a high draped neck. But she still didn't look right in it, no more right than I looked stuffed into Titus's synthesis. Her skin had gone dark gold from all the marching under Dacia's summer sun, and her slim arms were brown and exotic against the prim white. I remembered all that golden skin spread out on my bedroll, and tasted hatred sour and metallic in my mouth. Probably just like the taste in the mouth of Trajan's immaculate Empress, who was clearly thinking that a stuffy white dress and a stuffy linen synthesis hadn't succeeded in changing either me or Sabina into anything she wanted at *her* dinner party.

"Your loyal service is noted," the Empress decreed with one of her judicial nods, and I took it for a cue and bolted. Not noticing, not noticing at all, the grin Sabina shot at me behind Plotina's frown.

"More wine," I said instead, and looked around for the cup-bearer.

"Not unless you promise you can keep your eyes off the legate's wife." Titus steered me behind an ivy-draped column, regarding me bluntly.

"Not that it's any of your business," I snapped, "but I told her this morning that I was done with her."

Titus raised his eyebrows. "Good," he said at last, though his tone was peculiar. "I'd rather not see you dead and her exiled. Which could still happen, if the wrong person finds out what the two of you were up to this summer. Hadrian could kill you—adultery between a married woman and, if you will excuse me, a commoner is not taken lightly."

"I suppose you could hump her all day and get away with it?" I snarled. "You bloody aristocrats all stick together, don't you?"

"No, I couldn't hump her all day, as you so colorfully put it, and I'll tell you why. Because I served Hadrian for more than six months on that campaign, and I admire him. I wouldn't dream of poaching the wife of a man I admired, no matter how much I wanted her. Not to mention the fact that he's an odd cold fish who holds grudges. I wouldn't want to cross him and neither should you, even if he wasn't your *legate*." Titus rolled his eyes. "Your legate's wife—not one of your brighter ideas, Vercingetorix."

"Shut up."

His eyes danced. "I'll bet she was the one who broke it off."

"You're looking awfully pleased about all this," I accused.

"Yes, frankly. You got everything on this campaign, Vix—the glory, the eagle, the promotion, the Emperor's favor. It's a rather low feeling, but I can't help a touch of satisfaction that you didn't also end up getting the girl."

I thought of Demetra, and shoved the thought away. "What, are you jealous? I didn't think you were the sort."

"I'm not jealous of the promotion and the glory, that's for certain." Titus surveyed me. "You already got wine all over my synthesis."

"Sorry."

"Let's get out of here," my friend suggested. "Perhaps we should go get drunk? I confess I've never been completely swacked before. Surely tonight's the occasion for it. 'Seize the night; trust as little as possible in tomorrow,' as Horace would say."

"I'll get swacked, all right," I promised. "But I'm staying right here. She's not going to run me out of any good party."

"Oh, good gods be damned," I heard Titus swear as I lurched out into the crowd.

There was a lot of wine after that, and I wasn't the only one swilling it down. It was a party I could have enjoyed, if I'd been in the mood to enjoy anything. The Emperor got drunk, as cheerfully as he did everything else, and at one point he saw me and clapped me on the shoulder and told the whole story of my fight with Decebalus to a rapt audience while I stood shifting from foot to foot. Half a dozen of his generals congratulated me after that, some of them men as rough spoken as I was, and at any other time I'd have hung on their every word. The Emperor's Praetorian Prefect even gave me a nod of approval and I should have been flushing with pride because he was everything I wanted to be—a blunt-spoken soldier who had risen through the ranks and was now Trajan's right-hand man. Instead I just grunted at him, and then grabbed another cup-bearer and told him that he'd better be within arm's reach of me all night or I'd pound his nose through the back of his head.

"Don't you want to leave now?" Titus asked hopefully.

"No."

Slaves began trooping in with heaped platters—vast joints of roast ox, stuffed boar, goose cooked in its plumage. The Empress gave a signal for the guests to take their places at the dining couches that had been arrayed in graceful semicircles about the room, but nobody was paying any attention. The Emperor just grabbed a wing of roast goose from the nearest platter going past, waving it to illustrate some story he was telling about the siege of Old Sarm, and the rest of the guests dragged the couches out of their semicircles and flopped on them any which way as they grabbed food from the passing platters. The Empress gave a patient sigh and withdrew as soon as the troupe of half-naked dancers came in. Trajan waved her out cheerfully and then grabbed the tallest of the male dancers to sit beside him.

My head was whirling, and the room's heat stifled me. I yanked the wine flagon away from the startled cup-bearer and stumbled out of the noisy hall to the atrium. Torches had been lit in brackets around the walls but they'd mostly guttered out, and somehow I managed to fall in the little tiled pool at the atrium's center. "Hell's gates!"

I was wet head to toe, but I'd managed to save the wine flagon. Still sitting six inches deep in water, I tilted my head back and took a long drink. The stars sparkled coldly overhead through the open roof. My stars—or so I'd thought. Where were they leading me now?

"Do you realize you're sitting in a pool of water, Vix?"

"Never occurred to me." I drank again, blocking out the image of the figure in white approaching from the other end of the atrium.

Moonlight splashed across her face from the open roof. "Do you need a hand up?"

"Maybe I like it in here." I splashed a wave of water at her, wetting her white hem.

"Gods," she sighed, "but you're a child sometimes."

"I wasn't a child when I was screwing you." Tilting my head up at her.

"Go home, Vix. You're drunk."

"And you're a bitch."

She turned away, back toward the half-open doors where music and rowdy shouts eddied through. My hand shot out, seizing the hem of her dress, halting her.

"You said this morning you didn't want to follow my stars, Lady. Fair enough. But at least I've got stars. What have you got? Following whatever looks *interesting*, as long as it's forbidden? There's a word for that, you know." I bared my teeth up at her in something that might have been a smile. "They call it slumming."

With the moonlight falling over her white dress she looked like another marble column. "They should call it 'duty,' Vix. I'm not as free as you seem to think I am. Maybe I *would* rather stay with you; spend my life 'slumming,' as you call it. But I still have a duty to others. To Hadrian, who's always been fair to me. To Rome, for giving me a good life. To the world—because if I get to spend my life seeing it, I should spend my life improving it too, in whatever way I can. I push my limits as far as I can, get away with as much adventure as I dare, but there's still always duty waiting." She looked at me, level. "When did you ever feel a duty to anything but yourself?"

"I have a duty to Trajan," I shot back. "I owe everything to him—he'll be the next Alexander, he'll conquer the world, and it's my duty to help him do it."

"That's rot, Vix." Sabina's voice was tart. "You're in this for the adventure, and don't try to pretend otherwise. If your duty to Trajan meant sitting behind a desk day after day, you'd be a lot less keen to serve him. Real duty means giving *up* the things you want. I've had to walk away from you twice, but you don't hear me whining about it."

"You're all about patrician duty now, are you?" I spat. "Where was that the last few months you spent in my bed?"

"I didn't hear you complaining, Vix. Not as long as you got what you wanted."

"What about the next time *you* want it?" I rose, dripping all over but not feeling the cold at all. I was never cold in the middle of a fight. "What happens the next time you get the itch you can't scratch? It won't be me scratching it. I might be a stupid barbarian, but even stupid barbarians know better than to get burned three times."

"I don't think you're stupid at all." Her eyes had gone cool as those of a marble statue, and I felt a flick of savage satisfaction that I'd finally cracked that serene shell. "You're clever enough to keep your options open. Tell me, did your girl take you back—the girl you kept here in town, the one Titus hinted about? You were quite careful not to tell me about her. Making sure you had something to come home to, in case I didn't work out?"

"She's beautiful," I spat, forgetting for a moment that she was also dead. "She makes you look like week-old fruit at a village market."

"Not beautiful enough to keep you faithful, apparently. Who says I'd hold you any longer? Are you angry I left, Vix? Or are you just angry because I left first?"

I picked up Sabina and dropped her in the pool. Water slopped over the tiled edges, splashing her shoulders, and her white skirts went floating about her wet knees as she stared up at me.

"Better enjoy it," I said. "That's the last time I ever get you wet."

I turned and left her there, stamping back into the noise and music of the banquet, clawing my wet hair back. The bath and the fight had left me stone-cold sober again. A drunken tribune bumped me, staggering past, and I shoved him into a statue of a bathing nymph. The nymph crashed over, and the tribune hiccupped at me happily. Everyone looked happy. The Emperor lay sprawled on a couch with his arm around an adoring slave, pounding his free hand against his knee in time with the music. The lute players banged cheerfully at their instruments, sawing out filthy songs as half the soldiers roared along with the choruses and the other half lay passed out among the couch cushions. Even that bastard Hadrian looked as if he were enjoying himself as he watched a team of boy acrobats tumbling across the mosaics—though the enjoyment disappeared quickly enough as he looked at the door. He put down his wine cup and crossed the room quickly, brushing past me.

"Vibia Sabina, you look a mess."

"An accident with a drunken soldier and an inconveniently placed fountain," her voice came behind me from the hall's entrance. I leaned one shoulder against a pillar, pretending to watch the acrobats but keeping Sabina in view at the corner of my eye. She looked very nonchalant and very, very wet.

Hadrian's eyes flicked over her, and he moved to block the view of the rest of the guests. "That dress is indecent."

"Really?" Sabina plucked at the white folds, half transparent now with water and sticking to her brown limbs. "Surely not, since Plotina chose it. She'd never do anything so interesting as to be indecent."

Hadrian blinked. "Are you drunk?"

Sabina laughed, her hair coming down her back in a wet tangle and her dress slipping off one shoulder. "Perhaps I should be. Everyone else is."

"Go home at once!"

"I was going to, Hadrian. You really think I'm going to rejoin the party dripping wet?"

"I don't know half of what you do anymore." His voice was suddenly cold. "I heard a great many rumors about your behavior throughout this campaign. Normally I would pay no heed to vicious gossip, but when my Empress has to tell me you have a taste for the company of common soldiers—"

"I believe you've dipped a toe in those waters yourself, Hadrian." Her voice was still light, teasing. "More than once these past months I came to your tent and found a handsome half-naked legionary waiting on your presence."

"That is not the same!" He lowered his voice and I shifted from one foot to the other, still pretending to ogle the acrobats. "Discretion is all in such matters. It is hardly *discreet* for a Roman matron of senatorial birth to appear at an important occasion like this soaking wet and half naked for everyone to ogle! Or to seek out the company of common soldiers for amusement. My career is just beginning to bloom, and I cannot afford scandal. Plotina thinks—"

Sabina's smile disappeared. "Yes, Dear Publius, let's hear *all* about what Plotina thinks."

"She thinks it is time you started behaving yourself. And so do I."

I risked a glance at that. Hadrian and his wife stood nose to nose, unmoving, until Sabina took the wine cup out of Hadrian's hand and drained it. "No more wine for you tonight, husband. It's making you quite fanciful. I shall see you at home."

She turned and disappeared back into the atrium, walking with slow insolent grace. I could see the curve of her brown hip very clearly through the wet silk, the point of her shoulder . . .

"You will keep your eyes off my wife." A cold voice stung me, and I saw Hadrian tall and icy before me. "I have observed it in the past, Aquilifer. She is not a whore for the likes of you to gawp at."

"According to what you were hissing at her just now, she *is* a whore." My mouth decided to jump in without consulting my brain first about whether it was a good idea. "And from the things I've heard around the Tenth, Legate, you aren't far wrong. Lady Vibia Sabina, everyone knows she likes a rough—"

His broad palm crashed against my cheek. He had a hard hand for a man who had never fought in a real battle in his life; the blow sent me back against the wall. Incongruously I remembered watching him take down the stag in Dacia, how he had slain it with one sure blow of a javelin and then smiled at the blood that sprayed his foot.

I straightened, my cheek stinging. Tomorrow I'd be sporting a hand-shaped bruise. "That's the first time you've struck me," I said, and was surprised how quiet my voice came out. "There won't be a second."

"No?"

"No."

I saw his fingers twitch at his side, and his bearded chin jerked up. I could see him itch to hit me again and felt my own fingers curl. The party was still roaring around us—the Emperor and his Praetorian Prefect were slamming back cups of unmixed wine in some uproarious drinking game—but I felt like I'd been placed in a ring of ice. There was nothing in the world but the bearded face looking back at me with cold, blazing eyes.

"Legate Hadrian, have you made plans for your journey to Pannonia?" A courteous voice slid between us. "Surely you will return to Rome first for the triumph. I'm certain it will be a splendid occasion."

"Very splendid," Hadrian said, eyes leaving mine for Titus, who stood attentive and polite at his elbow, and I wondered if I'd imagined it—that moment of sheer, clawing hatred.

I hadn't imagined it.

"If you will excuse us, Legate? The Emperor wants a word with our aquilifer."

"The Emperor may have him."

I blinked as Titus's hand took my elbow and steered me away. "The Emperor wants to speak with me?"

"Of course he doesn't, you fool. I had to say something to remind your legate that you have Imperial favor. He looked ready to strangle you on the spot. Did he find out about his wife?"

"No. It wasn't that." I looked down at my synthesis, stained with water and wine. "Sorry about your tunic."

"Forget the tunic. We're leaving. Gods in hell, keeping you alive is a full-time job. I don't know why I bother." Titus grabbed his cloak from a sleepy slave girl and steered me back through the dark atrium. The moon had moved on overhead, and the little tiled pool under the open roof was now in black shadow.

"I dropped Sabina in the water there," I confided.

"I don't want to know why," Titus groaned. "I suppose that's why Hadrian wants to kill you?"

"No. He just hates me." My tongue felt heavy suddenly, and my feet heavier. I stumbled over the threshold, and Titus steadied me. "I may have to kill him," I mused.

"Shut up."

"In fact, I'm quite certain I'll have to kill him."

"Shut *up!*"

"It's going to be him or me." I felt that quite strongly. This morning when I'd marched into the city, I'd had a lover. I'd lost her. But I'd found something else.

An enemy.

A week later, calling myself all sorts of fool, I went back to the squalid tenement across from the rooms that had been Demetra's.

"You're here again, are you?" the tired-looking woman greeted me shortly. "Aren't you grand."

I'd worn my lion skin and breastplate, hoping to impress her if I needed to. "I've come about the boy. Demetra's son."

"What about him?"

"Let me see him."

She vanished into the second room. The one I stood in smelled of grease and stale food. Two children playing in the corner with a pile of sticks looked up at me, and I saw watery eyes, dingy hair, tunics spotted with food. Not much like Demetra's little oasis of scrubbed cheer.

The woman reappeared, with the boy in her arms. "Here he is."

I looked at him. He was bigger, nearly three years old now, wearing a dirty shapeless smock. He had his mother's dark-honey hair in curls all over his little head, and I thought I could see the start of her beautiful bones under his round cheeks. He gazed at me silently.

"He's a looker, isn't he?" the woman said. "He'll be a beauty when he grows up."

She'd said that before, last week, and somehow it had preyed on me. Bothered me. "You'll raise him?" I said.

"Like my own."

Titus would have believed her. I'd finally told him of Demetra's death, and my child's, and his sympathy had been as warm as I feared. "Gods, Vix, I'm sorry. No wonder you've been in such a foul mood. What about her son, the little boy?"

"A neighboring woman took him," I'd grunted. "Got five children of her own already."

"That's good," Titus had relaxed. "A new family for the poor little sprat, if he has to lose his mother. Gods keep her soul, she was a good woman. She'll be glad to know her son is well looked after."

Would he be well looked after? I gave the woman a hard stare and saw the way her eyes shifted sideways. I wasn't Titus, believing the good in everyone. I'd been raised a slave—and I knew what could happen to pretty little boys in the wrong hands. It might have happened to me, if I hadn't had kind masters. If I hadn't had a mother to shield me.

Demetra's boy, growing up in this sinkhole looking like her? He'd be dancing for dirty old men and bleeding from the arse by the time he was ten years old. I remembered the bald man who had offered me oysters and then tried to bugger me; how he'd screamed when I broke his fingers and ran.

Demetra's little boy looked up at me for the first time, tentatively.

He's not yours, something in my head whispered. *Not your blood, not your responsibility.* My responsibility had died. I'd gotten away clean.

The boy pointed his chubby finger at the maned pelt over my head. "*Yion!*" he crowed. "*Yion!*"

"Oh, fuck," I said, and grabbed him out of that dirty cow's arms.

"Hey!" she squawked.

"Hands off," I snarled. "He's coming with me."

"What, you're going to raise him? You with the legion and all?"

No, I was not bloody well going to *raise* him. What did I know about raising children? I had no idea what I was going to do with him. I just wasn't leaving him here. He was a very solid little weight in my arms, not crying at all.

"Yion," he said, petting the tawny pelt over my head as I carried him out of that dingy greasy room.

"Yion," I agreed, swinging him around so he could ride my back. He crowed with delight, clinging to the lion's mane. "You aren't much trouble, are you? I can pay some nice family to look after you. Drop in every few months to check in."

"*Yion,*" he shouted happily.

"Oh, fuck," I said again, and started up the street.

PART III

PARTHIA

CHAPTER 17

TITUS

"Ennia!" Titus looked around for his housekeeper. "Ennia, my graceful Terpsichorean nymph of the matchless gaze—"

"Never mind the pretty words, Dominus." His skinny black-haired freedwoman crossed her arms over her breasts. "What do you need?"

"Dinner for six, as soon as you can see it ready. I will be in your debt forever."

"Six?" Her gaze went from Titus to the armored figure with the dusty cloak and dustier russet hair, looming large and out of place in the narrow entry hall. The passage of three or four years had hardly changed Vix at all: a little browner, a little tougher, a little more weathered from the sun, but the same. "There's more of him coming?" Ennia asked unenthusiastically.

"No, just him, but he eats enough for five."

"Give me an hour." She disappeared toward the little kitchen, yelling for the slaves.

Vix was gazing around the small atrium: blue-tiled, modestly vaulted, narrow enough to cross in a few strides. "Can't a quaestor's salary buy something bigger than this? I thought you had a family villa taking up half the Palatine Hill."

"My grandfather retired there. I could stay with him if I liked, but I'm a man grown now—I've got a post, I've got some money of my own. No excuse to be living off my family, not with my mother gone and both my sisters married with their own households. So I took my own apartments." Not large apartments; just a bedchamber, a study, and the atrium, which doubled to hold his occasional modest dinner parties. "It's not much," Titus said happily.

"Seems to suit you," Vix approved, looking Titus up and down. "That toga fits better than armor ever did. Quaestor now, eh? I got your last letter—"

"No more marching, no more mud," Titus relished. "Just good clean scheming and backstabbing."

Vix hissed and booed. "Don't tell me you're turning into one of those cold political lizards like Hadrian!"

"Not yet. Then again, 'No man ever became thoroughly bad in one step.'"

"Hell's gates, I've missed you quoting at me. Cato?"

"Juvenal. Why did you say Cato?"

"Because half your quotes are Cato, you sod."

At Titus's direction, Vix hauled two couches in from the study, one over each shoulder, and soon they were both plunging into plates of stuffed salmon, roast pork, new bread, and ripe peaches as Ennia bustled in and out with the dishes. "What brings you to Rome, anyway?" Titus asked belatedly, after Vix had finished inhaling half a shoulder of pork. "Did I forget to ask?"

"Quarterly legion reports for the Emperor." Vix washed the last mouthful of pork down with a swallow of wine. "The First Spear wanted me out from underfoot. Bastard hates the sight of me."

"What did you do now?"

"I'm just after his job." Matter-of-factly.

"Then wash your hands between each dish instead of just plunging in." Titus raised his eyebrows as Vix tore another hunk off the loaf of bread. "Because you'll never make First Spear without a little civilization."

"I'll have to make centurion first. Next spot that opens is mine, now I've reached thirty."

"Did Simon from your old *contubernium* ever make centurion? He was well old enough—"

"No, he's out of the Tenth now—retired back in Rome, if you can believe it . . ."

That led to a discussion of all the Tenth's news: the new legate—a flogger or a layabout? Julius—was he still claiming descent from the great Caesar? Boil—had he ever found a girl who didn't leave him for the nearest flute player or tavernkeeper?

I miss it, Titus realized. Not the life of the army; he could do without that. But the easy companionship of the men he'd known in Dacia—in politics there was nothing like it. Everyone was far too busy looking out for his own career. To have a friend here was to have someone who might cut you out in the next appointments for praetor.

Ennia came bustling in then, surveying the picked-over detritus of plates and bones. "You weren't joking, Dominus," she commented. "He does eat for five."

She bent a slightly more approving gaze on Vix as she cleared the table, and Vix openly admired her as she swung out, the end of her black plait switching against her waist. "You like your housekeepers pretty."

Titus ran a hand through his hair, self-conscious. Ennia had been a freedwoman in his grandfather's house—black-eyed, twenty-five years old, with a thin pretty face and a tart lash of a tongue—and when Titus had left to make his own living arrangements, he'd made her a certain offer. "It won't be a large house to manage," he told her. "Just a few slaves, enough to handle meals and laundry for a man on his own. But you'd be in charge, not just one of the crowd of freedmen in this house."

"Housekeeper," she said in her brisk way. "Bedwarmer too, Dominus?"

"Well, if you don't mind. It's not a condition of the job, but you're very pretty." A little shyly. "And I really would rather have that side of things settled . . . I haven't got a wife yet, I don't care for brothels, and I can't really afford courtesans."

"I don't hold with orgies, and I don't service your friends." She gave an emphatic scowl. "What's the pay, Dominus?"

He named a modest but reasonable salary. She sniffed. He raised the offer. She lifted her eyebrows.

"I'm afraid that's all I can afford," he said firmly. "What if I throw in two new gowns a year and a present at Saturnalia?"

"Done." She nodded. "I'll stay till you marry. That should see me enough to retire on."

Easy as that, he had acquired a mistress. "You don't know much about women, do you?" she'd said, and undertaken his education with the same energy she took to reorganizing his household. Both Titus and the household had been happy for the improvement.

"I thought you'd be married by now," Vix was saying, unconsciously echoing Ennia. "Some pretty bit of fluff should have mounted your head on her wall."

"I came close last year. A legate's daughter—she had red hair."

"I like a redhead," Vix whistled.

"I do too, but Vibia Sabina warned me off her. She said to just look at the girl's slaves, and did I want to see the same cowed expression looking back at me from my mirror."

Vix paused in the act of slicing a peach in half. "You still see Sabina?"

"When she's in Rome." Which hadn't been often, since Hadrian had taken his wife with him to Pannonia. Titus cored an apple with a little silver knife, feeling a thread of mischief uncoil. "She's back in the city now, you know." Casually.

"Don't care." Vix scrubbed peach juice off his hands onto a napkin.

"'It is difficult to suddenly give up a long love,'" Titus remarked to the ceiling.

"Don't care, Cato."

"Catullus. In any case, Governor Hadrian came back from Pannonia, and she's with him."

"Don't care about Hadrian either. Just glad to have him out of my legion."

"Mmm. You've heard he's consul now?" Last week Titus had accompanied the consul and his wife to the theatre; Hadrian had spent most of the play being pestered by messengers and secretaries, and it had been Titus and Sabina who put their heads together in a happy critique of the actors and the verse. Sabina might have come back from two years in Pannonia with an armload of native bracelets and woad painted around her eyes (at least whenever the Empress was there to be shocked by it), but the old friendship Titus had enjoyed over Dacia's fires had not altered a whit. *Perhaps I'm luckier than Vix.*

Vix had clearly done away with the subject of Hadrian and Sabina and was looking around the airy atrium again with the sky showing black through the open roof and the fountain still trickling gently in the corner. "All this domesticity," he complained. "Give me a tent and a bedroll any day."

"Really?" Titus regarded his friend. "I think you're lying. You've got that look."

"What look?"

"*The* look." Titus saw that Ennia had her hands full lighting the lamps and rose to help her. It was full dark outside now, a noisy Roman night full of creaking cart wheels and yowling dogs and the occasional burst of passing laughter or patter of footsteps. Very different from Germania's rustling trees and black silences—Titus remembered the suddenness of the contrast, when he'd first come back from the north. "You need a woman, Slight."

"Always," Vix agreed. "You know any good whores here in Rome? The ones I knew years back are likely gone by now—"

Ennia snorted into the lamps.

"You don't need a whore," said Titus. "You need a wife."

"Legionaries can't marry!"

"Officers can, and you're one step from centurion," Titus pointed out. "Vercingetorix the cynical, a husband. Maybe a father too? You've had some practice, with that little sprat you adopted."

Titus had been the one to help when Vix turned up on his doorstep after the Dacian campaign with his Bithynian beauty's little boy clinging to his shoulders. "Help me find someone to raise him?" Vix had pleaded. "Hell's gates, I'm no one to raise a child!"

"At least we agree on that," Titus had said, and found a grocer in Mog willing (for a monthly allowance from Vix) to raise another child with his own three boys.

"He seems happy there." Vix reached for the bowl of fruit again when Titus asked about Demetra's handsome little son. "I drop in now and then, make sure he's cared for."

"See? Practice for when you have your own sons."

"Don't want any. *Or* a wife. And who are you to be giving me marriage advice? You're managing well enough on your own." Vix watched the swing of Ennia's hips as she retreated into the kitchen. "Or maybe not quite on your own . . ."

"I'm too busy organizing the Emperor's building projects to get married. I've got so much marble dust in my hair when I get home, no wife would put up with it."

"You helped with the triumphal column?" Vix asked eagerly. "I haven't seen it yet—"

"If you think the column's impressive, wait till you see the public baths Trajan commissioned. The biggest you ever saw. He wants them done tomorrow, but I wager they'll keep me busy for the next five years."

"Such a waste." Vix fiddled restlessly with the hilt of the knife at his waist. "He should be conquering the world, not building bathhouses!"

"I'm not certain I agree with you there, but Emperor Trajan might. One hears he's considering an invasion of Parthia."

"Parthia?" That perked Vix up visibly. "Don't suppose the Tenth will go. Damn, but I'd like to see Parthia. Brown women and hot skies—hot battles too, I imagine . . ."

Vix and Titus conquered Parthia over another cup of wine, toasting imaginary victories. Halfway through a dreamy invasion of Babylon Vix began to yawn; by the sacking of Hatra he was fast asleep with his head on the table.

"See?" Titus dragged a blanket out from the bedroom to throw over his friend. "You need a wife. Then she could do this for you, and not me."

But Vix was already snoring.

SABINA

Sabina couldn't remember when she'd had to start timing her moments to be sure of catching her husband in a good mood. The only time a good mood seemed certain was right after he had killed something.

"A good hunt?" she asked as he came into the triclinium, slapping a pair of bloody gloves against one hand. It was early still, the white marble walls on the triclinium stained pink through the east-facing windows.

"A deer." He moved as restlessly as the pair of hunting dogs weaving and growling about his feet, as if they were all three still smelling the morning mist, the fleeing prey, the spurting blood. "Only a doe, but one settles for what one can get."

"I didn't think you liked settling for anything, Hadrian."

He gave a wintry flick of a smile, already reaching for the pile of scrolls and tablets that awaited him for the morning's business. He'd washed before coming to the breakfast table; his toga was pleated into crisp folds along one shoulder, his beard was trimmed, his hands clean. Quite different from the man Sabina had watched from her window at dawn, steering his horse into the yard with a rough hand, splashed head to toe with blood and mud as his retainers trooped behind him with the deer's carcass. No doubt Hadrian had dismounted his horse to cut the doe's throat with his own hand. He preferred to finish off his kills up close.

"We've already got more venison than we can eat," Sabina said. As much hunting as he did, their slaves and tenants were awash in game. "I'll have this one carted off to one of your clients as a gift."

"As you please." Once the kill was done, Hadrian had no interest in what he'd bagged. "I won't be back for dinner tonight. I dine with Senator Ruricus."

"How lovely for you." Sabina gave a swift, teasing glance. "He has such pretty freedmen."

Another glance, considerably more wintry. *When did I lose the ability to tease him?* Sabina wondered. A few years ago such a comment would have won her a reluctant smile, or at most the faintly irritated flick of an eyebrow. Now, his voice could have frozen the barley water in her cup as he spoke. "I do not question your activities, madam."

"Actually, you question my activities frequently." Another change, in recent years. *Where did you go? Whom did you see? Why did you smile?*

"I don't question your activities," Hadrian returned. "Merely your discretion." He rolled up the scroll with a snap and reached for another. Sabina sipped her barley water, watching him thoughtfully. The pink light on the walls had gone to gold; down in the street below she heard the creak of wheels as carts began their daily rumbling past.

Hadrian glanced up again. "I wish you would not wear that." He indicated her wrist, where she'd looped an oddly interlaced little charm of thin knotted rope.

"I like it."

"It looks heathen."

"It is heathen." Given to Sabina by a witch in Pannonia, in fact. She'd liked Pannonia. Vast forested plains, deep rushing rivers, tribesmen with unreadable eyes drinking the lethal local *sabaea* as if it were milk. A great many mysteries to be found in Pannonia—and a great deal of work to be done, no doubt about it. Sabina had wheedled, begged, and browbeaten the funds out of Hadrian to build a hospital in Vindobona; the foundations were just being laid when it came time to return to Rome. She'd been sorry to leave it for Hadrian's tall narrow house on the Palatine Hill with its white marble walls and geometric friezes and silent slaves.

"I bought a book yesterday," she said. "The new verses from that poet everyone's been talking about, Ammianus. I think you'll hate his metaphors, but he does turn a pretty phrase."

Hadrian made rapid notes on a writing tablet. "I have no time for reading."

"That's not like you."

"I am consul now. I have many more important responsibilities."

"You always had time to read before, no matter what rank you held."

He did not answer, smoothing the wax on his tablet and starting again. He had a tiny splash of blood beneath his thumbnail, and Sabina wondered if the doe had looked up at him mutely as he reached down to cut her throat. When they had first married, Hadrian went to hunt perhaps once a week, tracking deer in his chariot. In Pannonia he had hunted for wolves every other day, maintaining an entire pack of ferocious Pannonian hunting hounds. Now he didn't have time to read his beloved Greek poetry, but he hunted every day without fail . . . and without quite knowing why, Sabina had started getting up with the dawn to watch him return, thoughtfully regarding her husband's blood-splashed, smiling face.

"Has the Emperor said anything to you regarding Parthia?" Hadrian asked abruptly.

"He means to go next year." Sabina tucked a lock of hair back behind one ear. "He told me he's still deciding which legions to bring."

"He didn't tell *me* that," Hadrian snapped.

"I'm sure he's getting round to it."

"Since you and he share so much conversation, you can tell him I want a legion to command. Preferably the Third Parthica."

"Why?" Sabina tilted her head. "I didn't think you liked the idea of invading Parthia."

"I don't," Hadrian said. "It will be a waste of time and money. But it will put me in position to take over the governorship of Syria."

"Syria?" Sabina propped her chin on her hand. "That would be something to see. The mountains, the heat . . . and I'm longing to see Palmyra. You once told me Palmyra is called the Bride of the Desert, remember?"

"I will not be taking you to Syria." Hadrian made a note on a slate and set it aside. "Not unless you promise better behavior than you showed in Dacia and Pannonia. All that tramping about the country-side, getting your feet muddy and chatting up inappropriate people—you embarrassed me. The wife of a governor must behave with decorum."

Sabina set down her cup with something of a bang. "You used to like tramping around the countryside right along with me. Seeing things up close; seeing what could be done."

"A consul must behave with greater decorum. As must his wife. And Syria is far less backwater than Pannonia. Many more eyes will be on us."

"If we get there." Sabina kept her voice even. "I suppose I can drop a word to Trajan about getting you a legion, if it means so much to you. But he may not listen to me. Lusius Quietus is pushing for the Third Parthica too, and he wants it badly."

"He also wants you badly."

"Does he?" Sabina felt her attention sharpening, her fingers stilling around the cup. A deer motionless in the shadows as the hunter approached.

Hadrian did not look up from his slates. "Quietus could hardly keep his eyes off you at the Emperor's last banquet."

"So?"

"Perhaps you could do something for me there."

Sabina raised her eyebrows.

"He's a Berber," Hadrian said, scanning his scrolls. "Berbers are hot-blooded. A word dropped in the ear over a pillow could bear fruit."

She sat still for a long moment after that.

"Whoring out your wife," Sabina said finally. "What would Empress Plotina say?"

"She would be appalled, of course. But she is a wife of exceeding virtue. Since I don't have one of those, I might as well use your other talents to my advantage."

"If I choose to be whored."

"You seem indiscriminate enough in other respects." Disinterestedly. "What, isn't a Berber exotic enough for you?"

Sabina slid off the couch, handed her goblet to a slave, and walked out.

"He didn't!" Calpurnia's eyes widened. "Oh, the pig. Didn't I tell you not to marry him, Vibia Sabina?"

"You did." Sabina coiled her hair up off her neck, jabbing pins with more force than usual.

"I never liked him." Faustina couldn't help sounding satisfied. "Did you slap his face? When he said *that*, I mean. I certainly would have slapped his face."

"No," Sabina said briefly. "But it was a close thing."

She slipped the gown off her shoulders and walked ahead into the billowing steam of the *caldarium*. Her stepmother followed suit, and her little sister trailed behind more modestly wrapped in a towel.

"Well?" Faustina pressed. "Tell us more!"

"Not in front of your sister," Calpurnia interjected. Sabina's stepmother had grown comfortably plump from her string of babies, but her fair hair was still bright and her unlined mouth as quick to laugh as ever. "I don't want to discourage Faustina from marriage altogether."

"I'm not discouraged," Faustina said. "In fact, Sabina, you can tell Mother to let me get married now instead of making me wait another two years."

"Sixteen! Far too young. Sabina was nineteen when she married."

"But doing plenty before that," Sabina agreed, thinking of Vix.

"Were you really?" Faustina looked speculative: a tall girl now, with their father's dark eyes and Calpurnia's fair hair. A beauty too—after just a few years of absence, Sabina still had to adjust from the memory of a skinny little girl to this statuesque young Venus. *Just yesterday she was trying on my dresses and praying she would grow as tall as me.*

"I can see you girls are going to gossip no matter what I have to say about it," Calpurnia announced. "Try not to get yourselves too over-heated. For myself, I think I'll take a splash in the *natatio* pool."

Faustina pounced the minute her mother was out of earshot. "Tell me everything," she begged. "Your husband is trying to whore you out to his friends—did I mention I never liked him? Now, tell me every detail."

"Aren't you even a little bit shocked?"

"Oh, tremendously. But can't I still be curious? The most interesting things always happen to you, and nothing exciting *ever* happens to me."

"Having your husband try to whore you out is not exciting, Faustina!" Sabina looked at her little sister—little no longer, really, though she still wore the heart-shaped gold amulet of unmarried girls about her neck. That amulet would come off on the morning Faustina married. Maybe she should know, before that day, that there was more to husbands than a red veil and a few vows.

"Hadrian worries me," Sabina admitted, gazing through the billows of steam. At one end of the *caldarium*, a cluster of naked elderly matrons gossipped over cups of rose wine. At the other end, a pair of girls whispered about their lovers. More secrets got traded in the hot confidential steam of the bathhouse, Sabina thought, than anywhere else in Rome. "He's changed."

"How?" Faustina lifted the damp blond curls off her neck.

Such small things. Saying them out loud made them absurd. "He doesn't talk to me anymore," Sabina said slowly. "And all he used to want to do was read philosophy and sketch architectural designs and travel to Athens, but now he's scheming to be governor of Syria. Empress Plotina has been pushing that kind of post on him for years, but now—now he's *letting* her push him."

"Ambitious mothers." Faustina nodded. "Mother warned me about them when I started getting suitors. Pick a husband without a mother, she told me."

"Empress Plotina isn't even his mother."

"That makes it worse, doesn't it?" Faustina sounded worldly. "A mother has to work with what she's given birth to, but these childless women just pick out some young man they can drive around like a chariot. Don't you get the feeling they'd really like to take lovers, but instead they just take protégés?"

"When did you get so worldly-wise?"

"Have I impressed you? Oh, good. I mean to be tremendously sophisticated and all-knowing, just as soon as I can manage it." Faustina swung her feet, pleased. "What I want to know is—can Empress Plotina possibly be as well-behaved as she seems? Surely no one could manage to hold that pose for so long without falling off the pedestal once or twice."

"No sign of a fall yet," Sabina said, regretful. "Certainly Plotina is *very* virtuous. So is Hadrian, now. She expects it of him." Only now he hunted every day instead of once a week, and reproved his wife for being indecorous but set her to seduce his rivals . . .

"I don't really see your problem," Faustina was saying decisively. "You don't like Hadrian anymore? Divorce him. The Emperor's so fond of you, he'd surely give permission. You could come live back home with us again. Help me pick *my* husband."

Sabina hesitated, tempted. Stay in her old bedchamber again, gossip with her sister, get to know the three tumbling half-brothers Calpurnia had produced after Faustina and Linus. Discuss books every evening over dinner with her father, who was getting a trifle frail now, though he was still a force to be reckoned with in the Senate. "I'm afraid I can't."

"Why?" Faustina looked around for eavesdroppers, then leaned close. "Is it a lover?" she whispered.

Sabina cocked her head, amused. "What rumors have you been listening to?"

"According to gossip, either you're a Vestal Virgin or you've slept with a whole legion," Faustina said frankly. "I can't wait till they start making up juicy rumors about me."

"A whole legion?" Sabina wondered. "When do they think I have the time? There haven't been very many men outside Hadrian, really."

"You have to tell me now, you know." Faustina held up a hand in promise. "I vow never to tell Mother and Father."

"Good. There are some things one's parents should not know." Sabina looked up at the ceiling. "Let's see. There was a praetor with a lovely gift for declaiming poetry. The poetry he wrote wasn't quite so good, but he could certainly recite other poets to perfection. He had a beautiful voice. Then there was a certain very intelligent colleague of Father's in the Senate, whom I won't name—"

"I think I know which one!" Faustina's eyebrows flew up. "He's thirty years older than you!"

"So? Gray hair and a devastating wit can be very attractive." Sabina smothered a laugh in favor of a nonchalant, sophisticated shrug. If Faustina saw her as the wicked older sister, she might as well play the part. "Before the senator, there was a very handsome priest at Delphi when Hadrian and I went to Greece. He let me chew laurel leaves and breathe the fumes like the Pythia did, and it made me very light-headed. After that he took me to an orgy with a variety of worshippers."

Faustina's eyes went round. "You went to an *orgy?*"

"I don't recommend it," Sabina advised. "After about three variations, group fornication gets tedious. What's that, three lovers? There was also a soldier. My favorite of the four." Better leave *that* story for another time—Sabina didn't want to give her little sister the idea of seducing any household guards. One scandalous daughter in the family was quite enough. "Are you very shocked at me?"

"No." But Faustina blushed.

"Even Calpurnia wasn't always so matronly and respectable, you know," Sabina pointed out. "She moved in with Father a full three weeks before they were married. That had all the old cats in Rome hissing."

"Mother?" Faustina marveled. "I suppose even old people broke rules when they were young."

"Calpurnia is hardly old—only forty-five, you know. Forty-five isn't ancient!"

"It's primordial," the girl of sixteen dismissed.

"I suppose all mothers look old to their daughters," Sabina conceded. "Except mine. But she was also the most notorious whore in Rome since Empress Messalina."

"Was she really?" Faustina wondered. "No one ever talks about your mother. Except the slaves, and from the way they whisper you'd think she was Medusa."

"She was worse than Medusa *and* Messalina. Combined. Why do you think everyone's so eager to call me a whore? 'Like mother, like daughter,' that's why."

"Four lovers in ten years does not make you a whore." Firmly. "Not given Hadrian's tastes."

"And what do you know about his tastes?"

"I gossip with all the slaves. Yours too. The best way to keep informed." Faustina hesitated. "Hadrian—does he mind? Those other men, I mean."

"He didn't use to." In their earlier years of marriage, he had never once questioned Sabina's private life. As far as Hadrian was concerned, a wife who was discreet and brought no shame on her husband's good name with an unexplained bastard or a public scandal could call her bed her own—and he hadn't even insisted that she produce a few sons first, the way most husbands would. But after Dacia, the topic of discreet love affairs had somehow become sore. "Did you share your tent with common legionaries while we were on campaign?" he had said bluntly, two granite-carved lines suddenly bracketing his mouth. That had been the night of Trajan's celebration in Mog, after he'd told her to start behaving herself and she'd stalked out in her wet dress. "A tribune or an officer, a man of your own stature—that is one thing, but low-born soldiers are beyond all propriety or shame. *Did you?*"

"No," Sabina had said, not lying. She had not shared *her* tent with anyone, after all; she'd slept away from it most nights. And never with more than *one* soldier. The key to telling good lies was telling as much truth as possible. Hadrian had turned away without comment and never mentioned the subject again.

But maybe that's when the questions started, Sabina thought. *Where did you go? Whom did you see? Why did you smile?*

"So tell me again," Faustina was saying. "I don't like Hadrian, Father doesn't like Hadrian, Emperor Trajan doesn't like Hadrian—so why did you marry him? You could have had anybody."

"I'm not altogether sorry I did marry him." Sabina rose, stretching in the steam. She kept her voice light. "We used to have such wonderful conversations. And even now, at least you can't say life with Publius Aelius Hadrian is dull."

Faustina looked at her quizzically. "Is that all that matters?"

Calpurnia bustled back into the room, cheeks glowing from the cold water of the pool in the next room. "Are you girls done with your gossip now? Sabina, if you've persuaded Faustina to either become a Vestal or elope with a gladiator, I'm going to be very cross with you."

"Not at all." Faustina sounded demure. "Sabina's given me some very useful advice about marriage. A girl should learn from her older sister, don't you think?"

"Not too much," said Sabina. "So, you have suitors now? Tell me all about them . . ."

They passed out of the steam of the *caldarium* into the next room, where they all stretched out on marble slabs and gestured for the bathhouse attendants. Sabina stretched on one side, looking at her half-sister as Faustina chattered under the masseuse's dextrous fingers. "There's one suitor I call the Dribbler, and there's a praetor I used to call Pretty because, well, he is. But then he tried to kiss me, and by kiss me I mean stick his tongue so far down my throat I almost gagged, so now I call him the Gagger . . ." Maybe Faustina did look like a young Venus, but her dark eyes had a shrewd gleam like their father's, and all that blond hair concealed a well of common sense just like Calpurnia's. Faustina wouldn't need help choosing a husband when the time came— she'd land on someone good, someone honest, someone without tricks and schemes, someone to value her.

I should have been born like that, Sabina thought. *Straightforward and sensible. Instead, I fall in love with brash ex-gladiators . . . and then leave them to marry cold stiff politicians with meddling would-be mothers.*

Hadrian wasn't always like that, another part of her mind whispered. But she had no idea what had changed him.

CHAPTER 18

VIX

No one tells you the depressing parts about getting older. Oh, I knew to expect gray hair and stooping shoulders by the time I hit the ancient age of fifty or so. But it seemed unfair that two cups of wine at age thirty could give me a pounding headache in the morning when at seventeen I could have slept off two jugs without a qualm. A whole clutch of blacksmiths were pounding an anvil chorus in my head the morning after my night of reminiscing with Titus, when I laced into my armor, added the ceremonial crest to my helmet, and dragged myself to the palace with the courier and his dispatches to see the Emperor.

I hadn't seen the Imperial palace for a very long time, and I can't say I wanted to see it now. I'd spent some bad months there when I was thirteen as a kind of semivoluntary house guest (never mind why) and I'd have been just as happy never to see it again. But the marble corridors were cheerier than I remembered, or maybe it was just that the bustling slaves and freedmen and even the lines of petitioners didn't wear terrified expressions anymore. "Name?" a supercilious freedman sniffed as the courier and I presented ourselves in the long hall.

"Vercingetorix, aquilifer of the Tenth Fidelis of Moguntiacum, and courier." I thumped my dispatch case, embossed with the legion's seal. "Dispatches for the Emperor."

The freedman waited expectantly, but I didn't press any coins into his hand so he sniffed again. "You'll have to wait. There's a considerable line ahead."

It was afternoon before we got in, and by then the anvil chorus in my head was thumping double-time. But I couldn't help a grin as I saw the Emperor—brown, broad, dressed in an ink-spotted tunic, jotting figures on a tablet as a team of secretaries hovered about him. And damn me if he didn't grin back.

"Vercingetorix of the Tenth!" Trajan flung down his stylus. He remembered everyone's names, even to the lowest soldiers—another reason the legionaries loved him. "Gods' bones, aren't you a centurion by now?"

"When the next opening comes along, Caesar. Or so I'm told."

"Good, good. I told the legate to boost you up as soon as you were dry behind the ears. You'll make a good centurion."

Would I? It was all I'd dreamed of for years—the side-to-side helmet crest, the embossed greaves, the sword worn on the other side because I'd no longer have to draw my weapon locked in formation. I'd ached for promotion ever since I'd first been made aquilifer, and now the thought made my palms sweat. Eighty men under my command. Would they have rude nicknames for me behind my back, call me a flogger or a pudding? Would they grumble when they saw me coming, or straighten eagerly? Brag me up among the other centuries, or make obscene gestures and spit?

Never mind. Trajan thought I'd make a good centurion, and for him I'd become one. Even if I had to turn myself inside out to do it. "I'm very grateful, Caesar," I started to say, but he cut me off with a wave.

"Nonsense, I need good officers. Especially now I've got my eye on Parthia. Want to come get it with me?"

His eyes were warm and steady, impossible to look away from. "Just say the word, Caesar."

"Good, good. You've got dispatches? Let's have 'em." He broke the seals and began scanning lines rapidly. "Not too dull in Mog, I trust?"

"Not too dull, Caesar." I'd feared stagnating in the German mud once the Dacian campaign was done, but there had been just enough raids from the sullen Dacians over the past few years to keep things interesting. "I managed to get a few scars."

He insisted on seeing them, and I shoved back my sleeve to show off the broad weal where I'd taken a short spear through the arm two years before. Trajan admired it. "Good old Dacia. We'll have to see if Parthia proves as much fun."

"Take the Tenth, Caesar. We'll win it for you in six months."

He waved me out shortly afterward, telling me with a wink to take my time before heading back to Mog. "Take a month's leave here in the city. I'll have dispatches for the Tenth, eventually, and you might as well carry them back for me."

"Yes, Caesar." I gave my sharpest salute and wheeled about, headache receded to a manageable throbbing. Trajan's infectious enthusiasm was more reviving than a draught of cool water on a hot day.

"Emperor's pet," the courier smirked as we made our way back through the hall crowded with its lines of petitioners. "That's the real reason the legate agreed to let you go along on this delivery, you know— thought that if the Emperor had a chance to bugger you, he'd be quicker to grant that request for more engineers. *Is* he buggering you?"

"No."

"I don't believe you!"

"I don't care if you believe me or not." Everyone knew the Emperor liked handsome young men, and married to Old Stoneface Plotina, I couldn't blame him.

I could have been one of the Emperor's more intimate friends, if I wanted. Right after I'd been made aquilifer, Trajan had paused one night in Dacia to give me his usual greeting as he headed back to his tent for bed and I headed the opposite direction with the eagle. He'd clapped me on the shoulder as he usually did, but his hand lingered a moment and he smiled a little and quirked one eyebrow in cheerful invitation. I'd had a hard time turning him away—not because I'd ever bedded a man or wanted to, not even because he was the Emperor and I feared what he'd do if I refused—but because I loved him so dearly as my Caesar and my general that I found it hard to refuse him anything. But I mumbled something about duties to attend to, sliding my shoulder out from under his hand, and he'd thumped me on the arm, not at all annoyed, and gone off to one of the many other young officers who happily shared his bed. Not all Emperors stayed so sanguine when you refused their whims—I remembered the last Emperor I'd attended in this palace, a cheerful and not very sane sort of person who liked to stick flies on pens. I didn't care much for serving Rome, but it was all different—it was all right—as long as Trajan was at the helm.

In truth, I wasn't Trajan's pet because I was special, or because I was unusual, or even because he liked my looks. I just happened to be the type he liked to have around him: an energetic young soldier who wanted nothing more out of life than a fast hard march and a fast hard fight at the end of it. The Emperor had hundreds of favorites like me, scattered through the legions and the Praetorians and the Empire. Even now I can always spot a Trajan man—an alertness in the eyes, a spring in the step, even now that we're all mostly old and gray. A little extra shine that came from having served such an emperor.

And now he'd given me a month's leave.

I stood in the shadow of the gate as I left the palace grounds and took a moment to look out over the teeming city. Last night I'd been too tired from the road, too eager for a meal and a friend's company to pay attention to my homecoming, and this morning my head had been pounding too hard to absorb the city's sights, but now I paused to take a look around the raucous streets. The buildings crowded me in, crammed so close together and leaning over the street—strange, after so many years of Germania's muddy tracks and tree-choked horizons. I was sweating freely under a brass coin of a sun, and that was strange too. Midsummer in Mog was wet.

I hadn't exactly missed Rome during my ten years in Germania, but now I took a deep hungry whiff of city air. "Hello, you old bitch." I smelled pitch and ale and spiced meat, unwashed bodies and perfume and *life*.

"What's that smell?" said the courier.

"She does stink, doesn't she?" I said, cheerful. "Nowhere like it. I love this city."

"Too hot," the courier complained, and soon tramped off to find himself an inn. "Coming?" he called over his shoulder.

"No, I've got a call to pay."

An old freedwoman in a headscarf answered my knock at her door, looking me dubiously up and down. "Yes, sir?"

I doffed my helmet, introducing myself, and halfway through my explanation her walnut face split in a semitoothless smile. "Of course, of course!" Ushering me into a tiled entry hall. "He's been expecting you, just wait here—"

I didn't have to wait long. "Hell's gates," I sputtered, fighting off a bear hug. "What happened to you, Simon?" I cast an eye over my former brother-in-arms, the first man to leave my old *contubernium* in retirement. Simon had grown a full curly beard, his hair was halfway to gray and covered with a cap, and he wore a tasseled cloak in the eastern fashion instead of the breastplate that had so long been a second skin on him. "Where's the man who taught me to spar with my right hand?"

"Gone forever, and good riddance to him." Simon dragged me out of the entry hall and into the house. I had a pleasant impression of a sunny open-roofed atrium, no different from any other Roman house, with orange trees in small tubs and broad carved doors leading to other airy rooms. People instantly began flooding through those doors, staring at me curiously.

"Didn't think I'd see you so soon." Simon thumped me on the shoulder, still grinning. "You must have just arrived!"

"Boil and Julius and Philip would eat me alive if I let another night pass without checking in on you." I cast a glance around the growing crowd of people, seeing variations of Simon's bearded face and dark eyes. "This is all your family?"

"Every one! This is my niece Mirah, that's her brother Benjamin—" A pretty freckled girl came forward with a little black-haired boy, who Simon promptly tossed in the air. He patted the freckled girl's cheek, saying something in Hebrew, and then switched back to Latin. "And my brother Isaac, his wife Hadassah, my cousins—" More names, more welcoming faces and words of greeting. I felt oddly wistful as I nodded to one friendly face after another. I wondered what my own sisters looked like: the one I'd seen only as a baby and the other one I'd never seen at all. I wondered if my father's hair had gone entirely gray yet, or if my brother had grown up looking like me. I sent letters out to my family whenever there was a messenger going to Britannia, and even more rarely I got a crumpled letter back in my mother's oddly elegant writing: Last I'd heard, life was still serene on their mountaintop, my father busy torturing his garden and teaching my brother how to spar, my sisters lengthening into coltish half-grown girls. Who knew when I'd see any of them again? There was more than a decade left on my term of service. By then, my mother might not be alive to welcome me home with kisses.

"Vercingetorix," an older woman greeted me. "My Simon tells me much about you. You must join us tonight for Shabbat, of course. Simon says you are a Jew as well?" Her eyes lingered on the tattoo on my arm, a crude eagle with wings spread and beak open in a cry of triumph. I'd had her inked into my flesh after the Dacian triumph.

"My mother is a Jew," I confessed, aware that a number of cousins and uncles were listening.

"Then so are you," she said firmly, and that was that.

I think I expected something exotic from a Jewish household. Several legionaries I knew in the Tenth had served in Judaea, and they did a good deal of dark muttering about that hot place with its hot-tempered people—though I discounted the wilder rumors like the one that Jews cut the pricks off their baby boys as soon as they were born. Still, I'd expected something different, something eastern and exotic. But Simon's family, once you got used to the sheer number of them, seemed much like any other Roman family I'd dined with over the years. The house was the same, built around the hollow square of the atrium; the airy triclinium was the same with its stylized friezes of grapes and urns about the walls; the freedmen servants who took my cloak were the same. Perhaps more of the men were bearded, and the women tended to cover their hair with bright scarves, but otherwise they looked no different from any prosperous Roman family.

Still, I couldn't help but see a division. I was shown to a place of honor at the table, but the various wizened aunts and grandmothers regarded me as if I'd come from another species, and the children stared like my head was sprouting antlers. A squirming little boy pointed at me and was quickly hushed by the pretty girl Simon had introduced as his niece. Her eyes met mine but dropped at once like any good girl's. I hadn't had much dealing with good girls in the past years, just the cheerful rough-voiced legion wives and the friendly German whores whose time I bought in Mog.

The couches were drawn up in an arch as at any common dinner party, though there were places for the children, which wouldn't have happened in most Roman homes. Servants came around the couches with wine and platters of food; I started to reach for the bread, but Simon nudged me and I realized his mother was intoning some prayer in Hebrew and doing something ceremonial with candles. I bowed my head hastily, but the prayer was short.

There was fish, there was roast lamb, there was more wine. More prayers were uttered at intervals, and I half recognized the Hebrew words. For my sake the family spoke in Latin—and as the wine kept circulating, several of the younger nephews spoke more heatedly about Judaea and how she had been wronged by Rome. I wondered if Rome was so terrible, then why were they living here in such comfort, but Simon was nodding along with them and looking a bit more like the fierce fighter who'd been such a rock at my right side during drills.

The conversation turned to the possible rebuilding of Jerusalem, and I dipped a toe in the water. "You might get your chance," I addressed one of the bearded young nephews. "The Emperor will be taking himself to Parthia soon, so I doubt he'll be much concerned with what anyone does in Judaea."

"Oh?" The nephew looked pointedly at the eagle on my arm. "What has Parthia ever done to the Emperor, that it deserves invading?"

I couldn't speak for Trajan, but I wanted to invade Parthia because I was bored. This didn't seem the place to say so, however. I took another bite of roast lamb rather than answer.

"So now it's Parthia that gets to fight off Rome." One of the other nephews sloshed more wine into his cup, despite a quelling look from his mother. Apparently even good Jewish boys got drunk at the table and disappointed their mothers. "They'll find out what that means. Masada, that's what it means."

I picked my head up sharply. Masada was a name I knew, and very well. There were sighs about the couches; Simon looked heavy and his pretty freckled niece made a gesture that reminded me sharply of my mother: a gesture to ward off sorrow.

"Masada was a tragedy," Simon's brother said ponderously from his position at the head of the table. "It is not to be mentioned at Shabbat."

"It wasn't just a tragedy," I said.

They all looked at me. I took another bite of lamb, defiant.

"An entire city dead because of Rome." The black-bearded nephew looked at me coldly. "Dead down to the last child. That isn't a tragedy?"

"Not *just* a tragedy. It was a triumph too."

"What would you know about it?"

"My mother was there."

Silence spread out. I looked up from my lamb, around the frozen couches. "What?"

"No one survived," Simon said finally. "No one. It's known."

"My mother survived."

The silence deepened, and again I felt the line that separated me from them. Even the servant girls seemed frozen in place with their decanters and platters.

No one said a word, but their eyes never faltered. I pushed my platter away, leaning back on one elbow. I'd heard the story only once, when
I was ten years old or so. My mother hadn't told me, but I'd been playing behind the table where she sat talking softly with a friend. I remembered her words.

"Masada—it was strong. Stuffed full of Jewish rebels, of food and
water. It held out a long time, sieged by Roman legions. The Romans
couldn't starve them out, so they built a great ramp up to the gates, and
a siege tower. They used Jewish slaves to do it, so the rebels couldn't
throw down pitch and stones to kill them."

Simon's niece rose abruptly, picking up the little boy on her couch
and putting him over one hip, beckoning to the other children. They
trailed out and I paused for a moment. She returned and sank back
down onto the couch. "Mirah," her mother began. "This isn't fit for your
ears either—" But the girl darted her fierce eyes around the couches
and looked back to me. I found my voice again. It came out very flat
and tight.

"The Romans were celebrating below. They'd take the city in the
morning, and they'd burn it, and they'd take all the rebels back to Rome
in chains. To be sold for slaves."

The black-bearded nephew spat.

"Inside Masada, the Jews met. All of them, men and women. My
mother wasn't there; she was only six years old. But she figured it out
later, from what happened. Her father came home, and he talked for
a long time with her mother in the bedroom. He came out, looking
very white. There was a body behind him on the floor—"

My grandmother. I'd never thought of that before, somehow.

"He was crying. He told my mother and her sister to come to him
like good girls, and my mother saw the knife in his hand and ran. Not
before she saw her sister go to him—he couldn't do it, so her sister took
the knife and stabbed herself. She was fourteen."

She'd have been my aunt, if she'd lived. Across the couches, the girl named Mirah put a hand to her mouth. She was surely only a few years older than that dead girl had been.

"My mother ran to the next house," I continued thickly. "But it was the same. In all the houses. By agreement—they all agreed, the men and the women—the fathers came home and destroyed anything they had of value . . . and killed their families. After that was done, the men met in the square, and drew lots. Ten men were chosen to kill the rest. They drew lots again, and one man killed the other nine. Then himself. So when the Romans came in, there weren't any homes to plunder or any women to rape or any rebels to chain up and parade back to Rome. There was only a dead city, still full of food. The Jews left that, to prove they didn't kill themselves out of starvation." I looked around the couches. "They killed themselves out of defiance."

"We hold suicide a sin," the black-bearded nephew said. But the anger had leaked out of his voice.

"Which is why they drew lots for the killing," I answered. "So only one man would have to kill himself." Though I wondered how many had had to stab themselves, like my young aunt, when their fathers couldn't do it. I imagined putting a sword to the throat of Demetra's little son, his face turned up eagerly to mine, and I shuddered.

"It was still a sin," the nephew said stubbornly. "They should have lived."

"To be slaves?" I looked at him until he looked away. "My mother was a slave. Her and a handful of other children who somehow escaped. They all died young except her, and there were plenty of times afterward she wished she *had* died." I looked around the table. "I was a slave too. It's no life."

Another silence. Beside me I could feel Simon's tense body. I felt sorry for ruining his dinner. I never got anything right.

"Perhaps we've talked enough of this," his mother said brightly. "It's Shabbat."

"We *should* talk of this because it's Shabbat." The freckled girl named Mirah spoke up from the couch across from mine. Her voice was low and strong, though I could see tears in her eyes. "He's right. Masada was a triumph."

"Not exactly . . ."

"They died as they wanted, and Rome got no victory. Isn't that a triumph?" Mirah looked at me. "What happened to your mother?"

"She won her freedom," I said slowly, picking my words. "She's on a mountaintop now, with my father, and more children besides me. She lives."

"Then Masada lives too." Mirah lifted her goblet, and I lifted mine. There was a moment of silence, and then Simon lifted his cup and said something in Hebrew. The words sounded harsh, but I looked over at him and saw his eyes glittering like brands.

Shabbat was over, but Simon's family lingered afterward—and they lingered around me. Old women clutched my arm; the firebrand nephews pressed for more details of the Jewish defense; even Simon's stern patriarchal brother gave my shoulder a squeeze. Simon's mother had tears in her eyes as she invited me to join the family next week when they left for their villa outside Rome. No more of that polite space separating *me* from *them*.

"I'm sorry," I muttered to Simon when I got a private moment. "Didn't mean to spoil your Shabbat."

"No," he said fiercely. "You spoke well. Over ten years I've known you, Vix—I've never known any of that."

"It was a long time ago."

"*It was yesterday.*"

My brows flew up at the heat in his voice.

"If Rome did that to your family," my friend demanded passionately, "why in God's name do you fight for Rome?"

"I'm no good for anything but fighting," I said, uncomfortable. "For a man like me, it's either the legions or the arena. And I'll never be a gladiator again."

Simon gazed into the dark atrium, and I didn't think he was seeing the orange trees. "Those poor bastards." His voice was proud and savage. "They left the world on their own terms, didn't they?"

"Yes."

"What more can any of us want than that?"

I looked around the dark atrium, lit with warm yellow light from the lamps and sweetly scented from the potted orange trees. It seemed to me there was a lot more to want from life than *that*, but I knew better than to argue with Simon in these moods. I thought of going back to Mog, living in my barracks that smelled like sweaty leather and waiting for the Parthian invasion to happen, and felt tired.

A hand caught my arm in the dark, and I looked down at a pretty face with a scattering of freckles across the nose. Simon's niece Mirah had a wide mouth, large eyes, and her head in its neat white scarf came to my shoulder.

"Thank you." She tried to say something else but shook her head. Giving my arm a mute squeeze, she turned and retreated down the lamp-lit hall. I watched her go, and wondered what color her hair was under the white scarf.

PLOTINA

The man was sweating. Plotina liked that. Men *should* be nervous in the presence of goddesses; it was only fitting. And it made things so much easier on the goddess.

He moistened his lips. "I don't understand, Lady."

"I think you do, Gaius Terentius." Plotina pushed a slate across her desk at the plump bewigged little official. "My secretaries brought the discrepancy to my attention, and I checked the numbers myself. You have been skimming money from the building funds for the Emperor's public baths."

The man's eyes hunted around the walls of Plotina's private study. She had stripped away the cheerful woven wall hangings last year to reveal the dark African marble beneath, stark and pristine as any temple. She suspected all that black marble was starting to close in on the sweating little official. "Lady, I assure you—"

"Spare me the protestations of innocence." She waved a dismissive hand, her wedding ring catching the lamplight. "A cartload of timber here, never delivered; an order of marble there, never arrived. Quite a few sesterces you've managed to pocket, Gaius Terentius."

A bead of sweat rolled openly down his neck. Plotina's lips curved at the sight of it.

"I shall resign my position at once, Lady," he whispered. "I shall leave Rome—"

"Now, have I asked you to do that?" The Empress caught a glimpse of herself in the glass hanging behind the little fraud's chair, and was pleased by her own reflection. She'd got the expression exactly right—aloof, regal, disapproving, yet not without mercy as she looked down from the height of her carved chair. A posture not unlike Juno's in the Temple of Jupiter Optimus Maximus, looking down at her supplicants. *Really, all I need is a diadem.*

"You may keep your post, Gaius Terentius," Plotina went on. "I shall require something else of you."

He fell to his knees before her. "Anything, Lady!"

"A share in what you take from the bathhouse funds." She allowed just the corners of her lips to turn up at his startled expression. "Shall we agree to half? Running this Empire is so expensive, you know."

A few more moments discussing details, and the sweaty little official was ushered out. Plotina picked up a separate tablet on her desk and made a neat line through the name of Gaius Terentius. There were other names, but she set those aside for now.

She'd been nervous the first time she tried this. But it was getting easier all the time. And how could it be counted as wrong, to squeeze a corrupt man for a worthy cause? Had she been working for her own benefit, that would have been quite inexcusable. But this was for *Rome.*

Plotina looked up at the mirror again. "One could say it's my duty," she told her own reflection. "After all, it costs a great deal to support Dear Publius in proper style as consul."

SABINA

Sabina waited until the black-haired Antiochene freedman with the shoulders like Apollo slipped out of her husband's bedchamber and padded down the hall. Then she struck the door open and walked in.

Hadrian blinked. He lay in bed propped up by pillows, a film of sweat still sheening his bare shoulders. A lamp cast its warm light over the rumpled blankets, the high corniced ceiling, the statue in the corner of a Greek warrior carved in the act of throwing his spear. "This is unexpected," Hadrian said at last.

Sabina crossed the floor, white robe whispering around her feet, and sat down on the edge of the bed. "Let's go to Athens."

She saw she'd managed to surprise him twice in as many minutes. "What?"

"Forget the Parthian invasion," she said. "Forget becoming governor of Syria. Forget your consular duties. Let's go to Greece. That tour we always planned: Athens and Corinth and Sparta, the little islands with those white cliffs and jewel-blue seas. Let's take ship and keep going all the way to Troy. Let's just get out of Rome."

For a moment she thought she saw a gleam in his eye. The old gleam, from the Hadrian who waved his arms in the air when enthusiasm for the world's mysteries carried him away. But then he looked down at the bedclothes, straightening the crumpled folds precisely, and his businesslike frown returned. "In the future, perhaps. Not now."

"Why not? Don't tell me you'd rather be arguing with stubborn old men in the Senate house than riding a mule up the hills of Delphi to see the Oracle."

"It isn't what I want that matters."

"So it's all about what Plotina wants instead?" Sabina lifted her eyebrows. "I thought you were your own man, Publius Aelius Hadrian."

"It isn't about Plotina at all. She merely helps me to achieve what is mine."

"And what *is* yours? The Third Parthica? The governorship of Syria?"

"Among other things."

Hadrian reached for a book he'd placed on the table by the bed, unrolling the scroll. Sabina leaned closer and put her hand over the page, blocking his view. He exhaled a short breath through his nose.

"You know this is the first time I've seen you reading in weeks?" Sabina said lightly.

"I have been busy."

"You were never too busy to read before." She kept her voice gentle. "What's changed you?"

"Have I changed?"

"You used to talk to me."

"You used to interest me."

"Don't think you can distract me by hurting me, Hadrian. I don't love you enough for you to be able to hurt me." She reached out and took his big hand between hers. "But I do care for you. And I know you aren't happy."

He disengaged her hands and rose abruptly. Sabina watched the muscles move under the skin in the warm lamplight as he shouldered into a tunic to cover his nakedness. He was a fine figure of a man, her husband. So much hunting kept him strong and fit.

"Perhaps I am not entirely happy," he said at last, yanking the belt of his tunic with a *snap*. "Perhaps I would rather go to Greece with you than battle Lusius Quietus for command of the Third Parthica, all so I can take part in a war I believe pointless. It doesn't matter in the slightest."

"Doesn't it?" Sabina drew up her legs until she sat cross-legged on the bed. "Tell me why." *Tell me anything, husband. Just talk to me.*

"I am not destined to spend my days wandering Greece and reading books." He folded his arms across his chest, looking down at her. "That is all."

"Yes, destiny. You told me you'd always known what yours was."

"I am going to be Emperor of Rome."

Sabina stared at him. His hair and beard looked almost black in the lamplight, and the blade of his nose threw a deep shadow across his cheek. His gaze was steady, his expression neutral, his body as relaxed as if in sleep. He looked quite calm.

"I had my horoscope drawn up when I was a boy," Hadrian continued as conversationally as if they were discussing the weather. "The astrologer said—"

Sabina burst out laughing. Hadrian's face stiffened coldly and she choked the laughter off, but she could still feel it bubbling in her throat. "An astrologer? You've based your life's decisions on a *horoscope?*"

"A great many astrologers are frauds, but Nessus was different," Hadrian snapped. "I never heard him get a word wrong when it came to the future."

"Emperor Domitian's astrologer; you told me." She knew the name well, though the famous seer was long retired. "You told me he predicted you would see more of the world than any man in Rome."

"He did tell me that. He also told me I would become Emperor."

"And that's why Plotina is always trying—"

"I never told her about the prophecy. I've never told anyone." A peculiar note crept into his voice. "I don't know why I'm telling you now."

"It's not much of a secret," Sabina pointed out. "One prophecy— how many astrologers have whispered thrones to ambitious men, hoping for a few extra coins?"

"Not just one prophecy. Ever since the day Nessus made his prediction, I made my own study of the stars and how to read them. Every year I draw my own horoscope, and every year I have to burn it. Because they *all* say that I will be Emperor."

Sabina laughed again but more quietly, shaking her head. "And I always thought you such a man of logic."

"It *will* happen. I can feel it."

"But do you even want to be Emperor?"

"Does that matter?" He shrugged. "I will be, whether I wish it or not."

She stared at him. "You're serious."

"When do I joke, Vibia Sabina?"

He looked down at her, arms still folded. Sabina put her fingertips together under her chin, feeling like she'd descended a step she hadn't known was there and snapped her teeth together on her tongue.

"Before I married you," she said at last, "I asked if you meant to live your life as Plotina wanted you to—politics and scheming and striving toward the top. You said no, that there were too many things to see in the world. Like the Nile in flood and the Temple of Artemis in Delphi—"

"All true." Hadrian nodded. "The key to telling a good lie, as you yourself have often said, is to tell as much of the truth as possible."

It was a hot night outside, the air from the open shutters heavy and blossom-scented from the gardens, but Sabina felt suddenly chilled to the bone. "Why would you wish to tell me such a lie?" she asked levelly.

"To win you," he said in surprise. "Though it did take me a while to puzzle out the best method of doing so. Most girls would be won by the promise of a crown, not the promise to avoid one."

"Then you should have proposed marriage to one of those girls, Hadrian. Not to me."

"I would have," he agreed. "Had there been another suitable candidate. But such are not thick on the ground. I require a wife with breeding and bloodlines, with a close blood tie to the Emperor, a sizable dowry, and connections to the powerful families of Rome. A wife with style and intelligence, educated beyond the common. A wife with a gift for charming people of all stations in life—my own character may lack spontaneity, but yours has been useful in making up the deficit. No, there were no other candidates. Providing you can control your taste for adventures in low places, Vibia Sabina, you will make a credible Empress."

"Well, I can't say the idea doesn't have its attractions." Sabina was no longer sure what might come out of her mouth once she opened it, but the roiling in her stomach made silence impossible. "However, I fear I will have to pass. Maybe you weren't listening when I told you the first time, Hadrian, but I don't particularly want any job that lasts for life. Still too unclear? *I don't want to be Empress.*"

"My dear," he smiled. "Why does it matter what you want? It is going to happen anyway."

"Will it?" asked Sabina. "Will it still happen without me?"

He turned sharply. "What do you mean?"

But she was gone.

CHAPTER 19

VIX

As far as I could see, Tu B'Av was a kind of Lupercalia for Jews. A lover's day, a day for the unmarried.

"Why should you want me along?" I protested when Simon dragged me out of the house. "I've mooched off your family the last week." The week after my Shabbat dinner with Simon's family, they had left for their modest villa outside the city and had almost forcibly dragged me with them.

"No, no, we're happy to have you to celebrate." Simon waved an expansive hand about the villa. A pleasant place, not grand like Senator Norbanus's summer home in Baiae, but pleasant. Just a big sprawling house where dogs ran in and out and hens scratched in the yard, and all around the vineyards stretched with a smell of dusty grapes. "The hero of Masada is always welcome here!"

"Look here," I complained, "I'm not the hero of Masada. I've never even been there."

"But you're the last bloodline from it." Simon gave my arm a punch. "Your children will be the heirs of Masada, Vix. Proof that Rome can never win."

"Rome *has* won." I pointed to the horizon where the city lights could still be seen every night, to the cultivated fields that spread out all around us. "You *live* in Rome. Not to mention fighting for Rome for the past twenty-five years."

"All gone in a heartbeat," Simon dismissed his time with the Tenth. "This is the real time. Now, I'll wager you've never seen a Tu B'Av celebration—look, there they are!"

"Who?"

A cart came rumbling up to the door, decked in flowers. A slave with a wreath perched rakishly on his head handled the mules, and in the back were a dozen giggling girls in white. The door to the house opened and another trio of girls dashed past us, also in white. I caught sight of Mirah's neat ankles as the other girls handed her up into the cart with much squealing.

"The unmarried girls dance in the vineyards on Tu B'Av," Simon explained. "It's supposed to bring them husbands."

"Does it?"

"Well, all the men come to watch," Simon grinned, "so marriages do tend to come out of it." He ducked ahead to link arms with his two younger brothers as the cart creaked off toward the vineyard. The procession already had the air of a festival, jugs of wine being passed back and forth among the younger men, the girls in the cart giggling under their lashes, the mothers and fathers walking arm in arm with more wreaths perched on their heads. I slouched along behind, liking the smell of the deep red earth under my sandals, the scent of the vines and the grapes all around.

"Don't fall behind, Vix!" Simon's mother caught my arm and pulled me ahead. She'd gotten fond of me the past week, which made me blink. Mothers were normally more inclined to warn me off their daughters and their clean floors, not stuff me with roast goose and urge me to sleep late in the mornings. "Goodness, it seems just yesterday I was dancing at Tu B'Av. Simon's father, he chose me that same day. Let's hope Simon does the same. He needs a wife. It seems quite foolish to me, this rule about how you soldiers can't marry. Who needs a wife to come home to more than a soldier?"

I gave a half-smile, still watching the cart full of girls.

"Let's hope this is Mirah's last time dancing at Tu B'Av," Simon's mother said, and I jumped a little guiltily. "Her third time! She could have had a husband at sixteen, but my son is lenient with her, and she keeps turning up her nose—"

I'd untangled a few of these family ties after a week. Mirah was Simon's niece, nineteen years old, and she had a low soft voice and cooked a roast goose that melted in your mouth. "At least they'll have a fair day for their dancing," I said, looking up at the cloudless blue sky.

"And maybe you'll find a wife here!" Simon's mother teased me over her shoulder as she moved off. "Better a good Jewish girl who can cook than some little Roman hussy who sacrifices goats!"

I looked at the cart full of girls. Two of them caught my eye and immediately collapsed into giggles behind their hands. No doubt about it; I had been marked for the chase. Funny, that feeling usually made me itch to bolt for the hills. Not now.

Not much, anyway.

The cart pulled up with more squealing from the girls, and the men came forward to hand them down. The older women began unpacking hampers of food and more jugs of wine, fussing about whether there would be enough as mothers seemed to do the world over. A cluster of little girls too young to dance among the vines descended on the patient mules and began braiding ribbons into their manes.

"Vix, give me a hand down?" Mirah tilted her head at me from the wagon. I came forward and put my hands to her waist, lifting her down from the tailboard. She wore a fine white shift, and I could feel her skin warm and smooth through it.

"Why are all you girls in white?" I asked, and took my time releasing her.

"So no one can tell the rich from the poor." Mirah put a hand on my shoulder to balance as she leaned down and stripped off her sandals. "It's a day for love, not haggling over dowries."

"That's sensible."

"I don't know," she said, thoughtful. "All the young men here have known me forever. They know what I'm worth, regardless of what I'm wearing. But it's a nice custom, anyway."

Half the girls had let their hair loose, but Mirah wore a white scarf over her head. It suited her, but I still didn't know what color her hair was.

She straightened, tossing her sandals into the wagon, and smiled up at me. Then she let out a piercing war whoop and dived into the vineyard. The other girls went giggling and squealing after her. Someone behind us began to play at pipes, and the little girls twirled wistfully as they watched their big sisters join hands among the vines and went ducking, dancing, swirling through the grapes. The men came up to watch the dancing with casual jests and intent eyes. "Pretty sight, aren't they?" Simon said at my elbow.

"Pretty enough. Which one have you got your eye on?"

"Don't know," he said, though his eyes followed an olive-skinned girl with a gentle face.

I nudged him. "She's pretty!"

"Well, I need a wife," he said, a little self-conscious. "It's time I started a family. I'm to get my land grant soon—I'm hoping for something in Judaea." All legionaries who made it through their twenty-five years were rewarded with a packet of land somewhere in the Empire for farming. Though I'm not sure who had the idea that retired soldiers would make good farmers. I didn't know a plow from a streetlamp, and as far as I knew, neither did Simon.

"So you'll take your new wife and move to Judaea and spend your days plowing?" I hooted. "You've never even seen Judaea!"

"I don't have to see it to love it," Simon said intensely, and I let the matter drop.

The girls began whirling back, tossing grapes or flowers to the men who watched them, and I saw mothers nodding approval. A middle-aged man with gray shot through his beard stood watching Mirah greedily—his third wife had just died, I knew—and I felt the sudden urge to pound him. A moment later he staggered and blinked as a cluster of grapes hit him in the chest, and Mirah ducked bright-eyed and innocent-faced back behind the vines.

I managed to catch Mirah's eye, and her mouth quirked at me. Then she yanked the scarf off her hair and waved it over her head like a banner as she pelted down the vines. Her hair was braided with sloe blossom, and it was a bright chestnut. Like mine.

I didn't know it before, but Jews got married under canopies. I stood under one myself a month later, when I married Mirah.

TITUS

"The *apodyterium* with changing shelves for clothes will be there." Titus pointed to a team of workmen laying brick under the noon sun. "The *frigidarium* with the pool, here." He pointed to another team of workmen pouring concrete and swearing. "The *laconicum* there—see the deeper trenches being dug? That's for the kilns, to keep the steam hot. The *tepidarium* there, with massage tables and refreshments." He turned to face his guests, feeling oddly nervous. "Well?"

Senator Marcus Norbanus and his younger daughter, Faustina, looked around them at the vast building site. Brick dust lay heavy in the air; workmen tramped past with shovels and loads of stone. The sound of hammers, axes, shuffling sandals, and muffled cursing filled the air. "I believe Emperor Trajan estimated three years to finish the baths when he proposed the project in the Senate?" Marcus drew a fold of his toga up over his gray head as a shield from the sun. "From the sight of all this, I'd estimate four."

"At least," Titus agreed. "And I'd guess five. Now's the time to make changes in the design—after this it's all set in stone, so to speak. I already know what Roman men want in a bathhouse: a gymnasium, a steam room to sweat off the exercise, and plenty of pretty slave girls for massages."

"I don't care if they're pretty." Marcus rubbed his crooked shoulder, rueful. "Not as long as their hands can take the aches out of these feeble old bones of mine."

"You're not feeble," Faustina protested, giving her father's arm a playful little shake. "You just play it up so people will underestimate you in the Senate!"

"Sshh," Marcus hushed her. "Not too loud, please. I've got Ruricus's claque convinced I doze off whenever the new road project comes up."

"Knew I was right." Faustina tossed her head, pleased, and turned back to Titus. "So why did you insist I come along?"

"To give me a woman's opinion." Titus bowed, flourishing his sun hat. "What do the women of Rome want in a bathhouse? These are going to be the greatest baths in the Empire; the voices of Rome's women should be heard. As represented by you."

"Me?" Faustina tilted her blond head at him. "Not my sister?"

"I did ask her, but I fear she was no help at all. She told me that the best bath she ever had was naked in a stream in Pannonia. I can provide a lot"—Titus waved an arm at the huge work site—"but not a stream in Pannonia."

Faustina laughed. She looked like a sheaf of hyacinths in a crisp blue linen dress; taller and prettier than even Titus had anticipated when he'd predicted to her eleven-year-old self that she would grow up a beauty. "So let's go see the greatest baths in Rome."

"I may not be as feeble as some of my colleagues have been allowed to think," Marcus announced, "but I am far too old to go scrambling over heaps of stone. Take my daughter, Titus, and I will sit here in the shade and ponder your architectural plans. You've got space here for a very nice archive, I think. Some of us would appreciate a bookshelf or two at the baths, not just racks of weights . . ."

Titus offered his arm to Faustina as the gray-haired bent-backed senator settled himself on a block of undressed granite. He didn't know how he would have survived his first months as quaestor without the advice of Sabina's father. His own grandfather was so frail now,

Titus hated to disturb him in the peace of retirement—but Senator Norbanus never seemed to mind giving a tactful piece of advice when Titus asked for it. "Gods, yes, the military payrolls are always in a snarl. But it will give you the best training in Rome when it comes to sniffing out new schemes of graft. And there are *always* new schemes of graft . . ."

Marcus waved him off, already deep into the architectural plans, and Titus offered his arm to Faustina. "Mind your step," he warned as he led her about the work site. "There's rubble everywhere. Not to mention staring stonemasons who haven't seen anything as lovely as you up close in their whole lives. Now, here's the gymnasium . . . the *lavatoria*, brass fittings for everything, even the flush handles . . . Phrygian marble in the entryway; Carrara marble is more famous, but I think the Phrygian has a better sheen when damp and these walls are going to be damp a good bit of the time . . . Five hundred lamps to light the *caldarium* . . ."

He caught himself, realizing he was chattering. "Forgive me, I do go on about my work. A real quaestor doesn't enjoy his work, or even do it if possible. He's too busy scheming to be praetor."

"I didn't think building projects fell into a quaestor's duties." Faustina peered into the excavated hole that would soon, Titus assured her, be a pool tiled in blue with dolphin mosaics.

"Normally, this would be outside my duties. But Emperor Trajan set me to the job. I worked with the architects on his triumphal column for the Dacian campaigns, you see—he wanted someone who'd actually *been* to Dacia, who could tell the relief-carvers how everything really looked. Everyone else who fought in Dacia had important jobs by the time the column started going up, so the task fell to me. Trajan must have been happy with the result, because he set me to oversee some of the work on these baths next."

"It sounds important."

"Not terribly," Titus confessed. "Mostly I keep Consul Hadrian and the architect from killing each other. Hadrian oversees the project too, you see, and since he has a great interest in architecture he has a great many ideas how to improve the plans . . . he didn't take it very kindly when the architect told him his domes looked like gourds. So I'm a kind of buffer state between them—like Pannonia between Germania and Dacia. I may get trampled on a lot, but I'm fairly essential if you want peace."

Faustina was squinting at the foundations of the *apodyterium*. "What kind of brick are you using here?"

"From Tarracina." He named the suppliers and factory.

"You've been given sun-baked bricks instead of kiln-fired," Faustina said. "Buy brick from me instead."

Titus blinked. "From you?"

"I own four brick factories," Faustina explained. "Mother gave them to me for my dowry, but only if I learned something about how they operated. I know about brick. And those bricks have been baked in the sun instead of fired in a kiln. Water wears away sun-baked brick faster than fired brick, and there's a lot of water in a bathhouse."

Titus made a note. "Anything else?"

Faustina turned a circle in the partially excavated *apodyterium*, hands on hips. The sun shone momentarily through her thin blue dress, and Titus had to motion his workers not to stop and leer. "You've got shelves for people to leave their clothes when they change?"

"Yes, made of pine."

"Alder would be better; it doesn't rot when it gets wet. I've got a timber yard as part of my dowry too," she said, forestalling his question. "And you should have pegs as well as shelves. Women would rather hang up their clothes than fold them."

"They would?"

"Fold up a linen dress like this one," Faustina offered a pinch of her skirt, "and you'll need an iron to press it back out. No woman wants to leave a bathhouse in wrinkly clothes."

"That is exactly why I wanted a woman's opinion in the first place."
Titus made another note on his slate. "Anything else?"

"Every bathhouse in Rome has naked mermaids in the mosaics.
Women don't want to look at naked mermaids who have better breasts
than we do. Keep the mermaids for the men's gymnasium, and put
something else in the room where women get massages. A sea god with
a nice bare chest, for example."

"No naked mermaids," Titus promised. "Not in the best baths in
the world."

Faustina fanned brick dust away from her face, tilting her chin up
at him. "This is important to you, isn't it? Even if it isn't strictly part of
your duties."

"I suppose a bathhouse isn't really important in the great scheme
of things." Titus ran a hand over a half-erected wall, double-thick to
contain the heat from the steam rooms. "But it will be the biggest baths
in the world. Eight million units of water in the cistern. And when it's
done, with naked mermaids in the gymnasium and naked sea gods in
the women's *tepidarium*, with gardens and flowers stretching all
around"—his eye could already see them spreading around the dusty
arid work site like a green oasis in the middle of the city—"then they'll
be known as the Baths of Trajan, because he commissioned them to
begin with. Or maybe the Baths of Apollodorus, because he designed
them, or the Baths of Hadrian because he really does have good architectural opinions to contribute even if his domes look like gourds. So
they won't be my baths. But I'll be able to look at them, and know I
helped build them. Know that I helped make Rome beautiful." Titus
turned away from the imagined gardens. "That's all I'd do, if I could.
Make Rome beautiful."

Faustina smiled at him from under her sunshade. "Then take me
around again. Father said something about adding an archive, and I
think you've got room on the eastern side. Maybe a library?"

"I fear your nose is getting pink."

"Bother my nose! I want to make Rome beautiful too."

SABINA

"Damn it," the Emperor grumbled, "I hate theatre."

"It's *Phaedra*," whispered Sabina.

"It's some fool woman mooning all over her stepson and then wrecking his life. I've seen *that* happen, and it's not art." Trajan's fingers drummed the arm of his chair. "It's a bloody mess, and I do mean bloody."

Empress Plotina turned to stare at them both, reproving. Trajan made a face like a guilty schoolboy, and Sabina made a point to laugh aloud. Plotina's disapproving stare deepened, and then she turned her attention back to the stage where the actors declaimed through their masks. The Theatre of Marcellus's tiered seats were crammed full, the plebs packed close in their woolen cloaks. Sabina could see the musicians sweating as they puffed and plucked at their instruments in the little *cavea* below the Imperial balcony.

"Don't worry, Caesar," she whispered as Trajan's fingers began their impatient drumming again. "You'll be out of here and killing Parthians soon enough."

"Gods willing."

This time Hadrian was the one to turn and glare from his position beside Plotina. Sabina returned his gaze levelly until he looked away—not back to the stage, but to his work. *If we'd come to the theatre alone,* Sabina thought, *then he might have watched the play.* Rigid with concentration, lips moving soundlessly along with the actor declaiming Phaedra's speech—paying attention to every gesture as he used to do; every word of the liquid sonorous Greek. But with the Emperor in attendance Hadrian was making a great show of consular diligence, rustling among a stack of scrolls and slates, dictating letters in a discreet murmur to a hovering secretary. Any glances he had to spare weren't for the stage, but for the ornate chair behind him—to see if Trajan was observing his industry.

Sabina could have told him that Trajan *had* taken notice, but not of the industry.

"Gods' bones, can't the man ever look happy?" Trajan growled, eyeing his wife's protégé. "I've gotten tired of that sour face these past weeks."

"I'm not sure he's ever happy," Sabina said. "At least not lately. But he's more sour than usual, Caesar, and that's because you gave the legion he wanted to someone else for the Parthian invasion."

"Well, I don't want him at the head of any of my legions."

"Why not? He's a good legate." In all fairness, Sabina couldn't deny that. "He has a good eye for maps, he reads terrain well, he's even-handed with the men—"

Trajan slanted a look at her. "Did he send you to plead with me?"

"Yes," Sabina said. "But I'm not doing it. I don't care if he gets a legion or not. I'm just curious why you're leaving him out."

"Because he expected to get a legion, and Plotina expected it, and the trouble with being a good-natured sort like me is that everybody starts expecting you to do what they want. It does them good to be disappointed now and then. I'll find a post for him in Parthia, but not until I feel like it." Trajan peered down at the stage, where a figure in a yellow-curled wig was beating its breast and wailing. "Will that woman never shut up?"

"It's not a woman, Caesar. It's an actor in a wig."

"Well, what's the point of a man who looks like a woman?"

"You don't see the point of women at all, Caesar!"

"I do think you're a nice little thing, Vibia Sabina." Trajan pinched her cheek. "I'll miss your company when I go to Parthia."

"I wish I were going. I hear the Parthians worship snakes."

"Why do they do that?"

"I could find out if I were going along on the campaign."

"You can come visit once I've conquered it."

On the stage, Phaedra was dead.

"What happened to the stepson?" Trajan whispered.

"He's dead too."

"Are there any plays that don't end in a heap of bodies?"

"I thought you liked heaps of bodies, Caesar."

"Only on battlefields."

Hadrian's attention was still rapt on his paperwork as the final spurt of applause burst out, but the Emperor had no time for either applause or the diligence of his consul. Trajan rose with all haste, and Sabina picked up her own cloak—pale green wool pinned at the shoulder with a silver arrow—and hurried after him with the line of Praetorians and the rest of his retinue. Like Vix, Trajan never slowed his pace for mortals with shorter legs.

The waiting crowd cheered as soon as he emerged, and the Emperor waved back cheerfully like a boy at a festival. Empress Plotina paused behind them to nod and bow more regally, Hadrian poised attentively at her side, but Trajan slung an arm about Sabina's shoulders and set off into the crowd. They made way for him: vendors hawking crude portraits of the theatre's actors, urchins with their begging bowls, an old soldier missing a leg; all of them beaming. Trajan paused to speak with the crippled soldier, raising the man up when he tried to bow. "You get far too close to these plebs, husband," Sabina had heard Plotina say time and time again. "A madman with a dagger could end your life anytime he liked!" But Trajan always ignored her, and Sabina admired him for it. What other Emperor could walk all over Rome without his guards, and have no fear at all of being murdered?

Sabina tugged her green cloak closer about her chin. The late afternoon was still bright, sunlight falling in hard bars over the theatre's marble roof, but a keen wind had picked up as evening approached. The crowd was thinning. Plotina had already swept out of the theatre, allowing one of her Praetorians to help her into the curtained silver litter. The litter rose on the backs of six Greek slaves, swaying like a ship, and the Praetorians cleared a path toward the palace. "Caesar?" Hadrian called after the Emperor, but Trajan waved one hand in dismissal and continued to walk with Sabina. She felt a mean little spurt of pleasure at her husband's set expression as he climbed into his own litter and directed it after Plotina's in a tight voice. Since the scene in his bedroom, they had not spoken one word to each other beyond what was necessary.

"Are you as cold as I am, Vibia Sabina?" the Emperor's voice sounded at her side. "Or is it just my frail old bones?"

"It's cold," Sabina agreed. "I think autumn is finally coming. Shall we walk to get warm, Caesar? You can lean on me if you get tired."

"Nonsense." Trajan waved his Praetorians well behind him. "You're too little to lean on."

"My father isn't tall either. But half a dozen Emperors have leaned on him."

They walked arm in arm, well away from the crowds now, Trajan's retinue trailing obediently behind. A few citizens paused to recognize their Emperor, and Trajan had a cheery wave for them all. "No smile?" he said, glancing down at Sabina. "Don't tell me that dreadful play made you mopey."

"No, it's not the play. Just memories." Time was, she and Hadrian would have walked home from the theatre together and argued the whole way about which actor was the better speaker of verse and which one had wooden gestures. Then Sabina would have declaimed the best speech in the play, and Hadrian would have interrupted her midway through to do it himself.

"Memories can ambush you," Trajan agreed, and tugged up the hood of his cloak. "Gods' bones, I *am* getting old. The wind saps me more than it used to."

Sabina tilted her head up at him as they walked. Trajan's hair had gone from gray-sprinkled to entirely gray, and his nose was sharper. Years of campaigning under foreign suns had graven deep lines about his eyes and mouth. *He is sixty*, Sabina realized with a start, *and he looks it.*

She took a deep breath. "May I ask something of you, Caesar?"

"Ask away. I'll even give it to you if it's reasonable."

Sabina redirected their feet away from the street, toward the Gardens of Antony, which wound beside the Tiber, and the Praetorians trailed obediently behind. They passed a row of spruces gracefully pruned to offer glimpses of the silver river, then a marble Diana in full sprint with her hunting hounds, as Trajan looked amused.

"Out with it," he said at last. "You want an emerald necklace? A house in Capri?"

"I want a divorce."

He paused midstride. "What?"

"I am thinking of divorcing my husband." The idea had danced at the edge of her mind for weeks now, ever since Faustina had suggested it at the bathhouse . . . and especially since Hadrian had announced his intended destiny. Having the words out made Sabina almost giddy. "If you please," she added.

"Well, it doesn't please," the Emperor of Rome said shortly. "The answer's no."

Sabina blinked. She'd heard Trajan's military voice before, on the rare occasions he got irked with droning bureaucrats or stubborn senators. But that snap of impatient authority had never been directed at herself. "May I ask why, Caesar? I didn't think you were so fond of him."

"And you need fondness all of a sudden in marriage? Who needs that? Plotina and I—" He broke off, looking irritable. "I may not have given Hadrian a legion in Parthia, but I'll need him in the invasion, make no mistake. Hardly fair to kick the man out of my family, then ask him to run my supply lines."

"Perhaps not. But—"

"No buts! Plotina and Hadrian aren't the only ones who expect me to grant their every desire, Vibia Sabina. What do you all think an emperor is, a wishing well?" Trajan scowled at the sunlit river. "It's enough to turn any good-natured man into a dictator."

She'd never heard him so short-tempered. *Is his age hurting him more than he lets on?* Frightening thought. Rome without Trajan . . . it couldn't be imagined.

"You *are* a dictator, Caesar," Sabina ventured. "Just a very good-natured one. I suppose we do take advantage of that."

"At least you admit it," Trajan said grudgingly.

"Are you sure you won't consider—"

"No! I may be fond of you but gods be good, girl, I've got an empire to consider! You think your whims stack up against that? I've got a duty to Rome, and so do you! If I ever do let you divorce Hadrian, it'll only be to marry you off to someone more useful!"

"I'll take that," she cajoled. "I know my duty, Caesar. Go ahead and marry me off to someone else; you won't hear a peep of protest from me."

"Don't hold your breath waiting, Vibia Sabina. I need Hadrian, and I need him in a good mood."

"Yes, Caesar," Sabina said meekly.

"Don't be abject with me, it doesn't suit you." Trajan gave her chin a fierce tweak. "Why don't you just ask for emerald necklaces and diamond rings, like most women? I'd be happy to give you those."

"No diamonds needed, Caesar. But you could give me something else. Not a divorce," she added hastily. "I promise I won't keep nagging on that score. This is something different."

His voice was very dry. "What is it?"

Sabina took another breath. This really was much harder than she had anticipated. "Don't make my husband your heir."

A pause, as Trajan halted and glowered down at her.

"I'm sorry," said Sabina. "That wasn't very tactful, was it?"

"Implying I might die someday? No, it wasn't, but I'll forgive you." He started walking again, perhaps leaning a little harder on her arm as they rounded a bend in the winding path. "I suppose it's possible, after all."

"Please—don't make Hadrian Emperor after you. *Please.*"

"Why?" Trajan looked grimly amused. "I thought all women wanted to be an empress."

"I don't. I've never seen an empress yet who got to have any life of her own."

"Plotina could have one if she wanted." Trajan sounded defensive, and Sabina grinned despite her churning insides. The Emperor never said anything exactly disparaging of his wife, and certainly in public they were the picture of serenity. In private . . . well, they didn't seem to *have* any "in private," did they?

"To calm your fears," Trajan was saying, "I wasn't planning on making Hadrian my heir. Or anyone else, for that matter. Not yet, anyway."

"You've made me very relieved." Sabina paused under a cypress tree, looking out at the sculpted view of the river. It glinted serpent-silver in the slanting light. "I thought that with Plotina pushing . . ."

"Well, I don't always take her advice," Trajan said testily. "You'll answer something for me now, little Sabina. You might not want to be Empress, but why don't you want Hadrian to be Emperor, eh? He wants it, and shouldn't a wife support her husband?"

"I do support him." That much was still true, she felt. Surprisingly. "I support what's best for him—and to be Emperor would be the worst thing on earth."

"Does that matter, girl? It's what's good for *Rome* that comes first."

"I know. But Hadrian . . . well, he's not made for it, whatever his pet astrologer says."

"Astrologer?" Trajan asked.

"Emperor Domitian's former astrologer, Nessus. He fed Hadrian a prophecy of how he'd be Emperor someday. Of course he believes it implicitly."

"I hate astrologers," Trajan grumbled. "I remember Nessus. He had the nerve to tell me I'd fail the first time I tried to conquer Dacia."

"He was right, wasn't he?"

"That's not the point!"

"Well, he told Hadrian he'd be Emperor, and Hadrian thinks he'll be right about that too. And Hadrian could be a good Emperor." Sabina still felt anger curling through her stomach at the thought of her husband, but she couldn't help being fair. "But it's not what's best for him, no matter what your wife thinks. It will bring out the worst in him. Is that why you won't appoint him?"

"No." Trajan tilted one burly shoulder. "I just don't like cold fish."

"Then who do you like? For an heir, I mean."

"I'd have picked your older brother, if he'd lived." Trajan looked momentarily sad. "The best man I ever knew."

"Me too." *If my big brother were still alive,* Sabina thought, *he'd pound Hadrian's bearded face through a wall for trying to whore me out to his enemies.* "So if it can't be Paulinus and it won't be Hadrian . . ."

"Jove knows who it will be, girl. Perhaps I'll die like Alexander, and leave my Empire to the strongest."

"Look what happened to Alexander's empire. Broken up to pieces in no time."

"Let me straighten out Parthia first, and then we'll see."

They walked on under the cypress trees.

CHAPTER 20

VIX

"You were looking at that girl," Mirah said as I pushed a path through the tired and chattering circus crowd.

"What girl?"

"The one in the Imperial box with the Emperor. The brown-haired one—she had a flame-colored dress." My wife's voice held a swift undercurrent of amusement, rather than jealousy. She did love to tease me.

"I never notice other girls when I'm with you," I vowed, playing along. "I was looking at the Emperor. Isn't he splendid?"

"Don't change the subject. She must be one of the Imperial family. Doesn't the Emperor have a great-niece?"

"Don't know." I'd seen Sabina up in the Imperial box at once, cheering at the Emperor's side all through the afternoon. No sign of Hadrian or that stuffy bitch Plotina; Sabina and the Emperor had been cheering away by themselves and talking between the heats. I wondered if Sabina was telling Trajan, "The Blues are utterly fucking evil," in that polite voice of hers, as she'd once told me years ago.

I wished she'd been able to look down into the vast crowd and pick me out. Me and my wife of two months.

"I wish I had a flame-colored dress," Mirah was saying. "With fire opals like the Emperor's great-niece was wearing . . ."

"Maybe I can't afford the opals, but I'll buy you a flame-colored dress."

"With this hair?" Mirah ran a hand over her chestnut head, rueful. "I'll look like a gourd."

"You'll look beautiful." I kissed the tip of her nose.

"I'll be round as a gourd too, soon enough. Round and fat with *your* baby, and here you're already looking at other girls!" She smiled, pinching my arm gently, and I smiled back.

Never let it be said I don't learn from the past. When I came home from a day of aimless waiting at the palace (orders still hadn't been passed down from the Emperor for me to take back to the Tenth) and Mirah took me out for a walk and told me she might be pregnant, I ignored the leap in my stomach, gulped a little, and said what I should have said to Demetra: "Wonderful." Then I said I'd take her to the races in celebration. Mirah preferred the theatre, especially if the play was one of those turgid weepers, but she could cheer lustily at the Circus Maximus too, and I felt the need for a little action and speed to get my mind off the flutter of nerves in my stomach. Me, a father.

"I suppose your family already knows about the baby?" I asked as we came out from the marble arches behind a cluster of dejected Greens fans and left the Circus Maximus behind us.

Mirah laughed. "My mother knew before I did. There are no secrets in my family."

Something else I was rapidly learning. When I'd married Mirah, I'd anticipated only a few weeks before I'd be collecting my new wife and the Emperor's dispatches and taking them both north back to Mog. Too short a time to bother finding rooms for us in Rome, so the two of us had stayed on at her family's house, just moving to a room with a bigger bed. But summer had gone on to fall, and I was still kicking my heels aimlessly in Rome as the Emperor's plans for Parthia's invasion inched forward. So I knew all about Mirah's family now: her aunt's bunions and her brother-in-law's nightmares, her uncle's third wife's inability to have babies and her cousin's inability to spit them out in anything but twos and threes. I knew that her niece Tirza broke out in bumps when she ate strawberries and her brother Benjamin saw ghosts under his bed; I knew that Simon wanted to marry his olive-skinned girl from a neighboring family but her father was putting up a fight about the dowry. Her family knew all about me now too: Mirah's mother always smeared my bread with clover honey, the servants knew exactly how much water to mix into my wine, and the firebrand nephews and cousins who talked about liberating Jerusalem knew not to do too much bashing of the Roman legions when I was in the room. Everybody knew everything about everybody else in this new family of mine, and I loved them for it, but I was starting to wish that I could take Mirah north so we could finally have a home all to ourselves.

"My mother's hoping you'll be delayed in Rome till the baby's born," Mirah said. "She wants to hold the naming feast."

"It won't be long before we're going north." I steered Mirah around an oozing gutter as we came through the south end of the Forum Romanum. "It's a month before the Emperor takes his army to Parthia. He'll get to my dispatches before then, and after that we're off." Not that my legate back in Mog would be missing me—an aquilifer didn't have much to do when the eagle was stuck in the chapel, and there wasn't any century yet for me to take over. And of course when I did get my century I'd be losing the eagle to a new aquilifer.

I frowned at the thought. I loved that eagle. I'd carried her for four years, after all—not through any more campaigns, but whenever we did a route march she was always there on my shoulder, and she and I had marched behind Trajan at the triumph he'd held in honor of his Dacian victories. Before heading south to Rome with my dispatches I'd spent a long time in the chapel stroking her metal wings and promising to be back soon—but I'd been gone from her side more than five months now, and I felt guilty. It would hurt to give her up to another aquilifer.

Well, she'd still be my eagle, even if I didn't carry her anymore. She belonged to all the men of the Tenth, both high and low. She'd watch proudly when I got my centurion's helmet, if I ever did get it. I wished one of the Tenth's centurions would hurry up and die, or retire, or anything as long as I got my century soon . . .

"—Maybe we can have the naming feast in advance."

"Mmm?" I shook out of my thoughts back to the present.

"For the baby." Mirah wrapped her own arms about her waist, which didn't look any different to me yet. "I want my sister there, so I can see the look on her face. No more condescending smirks about her little Isaac! I'll have one of my own."

"Do we have to name him Isaac?" I asked dubiously.

"Benjamin, maybe. Emmanuel. Something pious."

"Hannibal," I said. "Caratacus. Something warlike."

"Hannibal Emmanuel?" Mirah smirked, and doubled over laughing. She might be pious, my new wife, but God did she know how to laugh.

"Might be a girl," I pointed out.

"It's a boy," Mirah said firmly.

"You can already tell?" I grabbed her round the waist, poking her stomach.

"Yes, I can tell. Might even be twins—twins run in my family."

"Good. Then one can be Hannibal and the other can be Emmanuel."

Mirah looked around the forum with a critical eye. A shopkeeper with a stall full of brass pans was trying to catch her eye, as was a ragged thief hawking stolen beads. The butcher's shop wafted smells of blood and dung, and a pack of street dogs were fighting in the gutter over the corpse of a rat. A cluster of dirty children raced past shrieking, and hordes of harried housewives scurried with their baskets. "The city's no place for a baby," Mirah decided.

"Mog's different." A drunk reeled out of a wine shop and careened off Mirah's shoulder; I sent him hard into the nearest wall and snugged her close against my side with one arm.

"We'll need at least two rooms," Mirah was saying. "Not too far from the market. Not too far from the fort. And *not* next to any wine shops." Wrinkling her nose at the drunk.

"Two rooms? On my pay?"

"Well, if you really want to sleep in the same room with a crying baby . . ."

"Two rooms," I agreed. Secretly, though, I was hoping those two rooms wouldn't be in Mog. I was tired of Mog. I didn't want to go back to the German mud, the gray skies, the crude streets, the cold winds that would keep Mirah's bright face wrapped in a hood. I'd spent ten years of my life in Germania, and ten years was enough. I wanted sun, I wanted heat, I wanted—well, I wanted Parthia, but how likely was that? The Emperor had already chosen the legions who would be accompanying him on campaign. It was too much to hope for that the Tenth would be called halfway across the Empire.

We reached the house on the Quirinal Hill with the potted orange trees, and we'd hardly mounted the step before Mirah's mother popped out her head and demanded, "Did you tell him?"

Mirah laughed. "Yes, I told him."

"Good! Now, we'll just hope your business keeps you here in Rome until little Emmanuel is born. My Mirah shouldn't have to give birth on the road."

"Hannibal," I said, "Hannibal Emmanuel," but we had already been swept into the hall and three more aunts had descended on Mirah with cries of congratulation and a variety of Hebrew blessings, and after two months of living with my new family, I knew when to concede defeat. "There's a friend of yours here to see you," Mirah's mother said with a distracted kiss to each of my cheeks, and I took my exit while I could, escaping into the atrium as Mirah got borne upstairs.

"I understand congratulations are in order?" Titus smiled from his seat under the potted orange trees, swirling a cup of wine in one hand.

"You arse," I complained. "How did you know before I did?"

"Your mother-in-law told me while I waited, of course."

"Mirah says it's a boy." I flopped down on the bench beside him. "You think she's right?"

"Either way, I don't dare argue." A servant girl came with another wine cup for me, beaming congratulations, and Titus and I drank a toast. "What brings you here, Titus? Looking very official too." I eyed his snowy toga.

"I've been waiting on the Emperor—"

"And you call *me* the Emperor's pet! You're the one dogging his heels now—"

"He has been most kind to me, but that's not the point. He has made a few minor decisions regarding the Parthian campaign, and one or two of them might interest you."

I lowered my cup. "Like what?"

"Oh, perhaps the news can wait. I can hardly improve on your lovely wife's surprise, after all. Tell me, have you thought about names yet?"

"Tell me, you bastard!"

"Foul language," Titus reproved me, eyes dancing. "You'll have to curb your tongue, with a child around."

"Bugger the child, and bugger you. What have you learned?"

"Nothing of interest. Emperor Trajan has decided to reinforce his army in Parthia with three cohorts from another legion—namely, the Tenth Fidelis."

"Blast and bugger," I snarled. "The aquilifer won't march with just three cohorts. I'll be stuck in Mog—"

"Yes," Titus agreed. "The aquilifer will be stuck in Moguntiacum. But not the Tenth's newest centurion."

I stared at him.

"The Emperor has done some rearranging of the legion's officers," Titus continued airily. "Accordingly, there is a century with a gap . . ."

"Which one?" I gripped him by the shoulders.

"First cohort, last century." Titus lifted his cup. "Congratulations, Centurion."

First cohort. First cohort was the best men, the seasoned men, and the centurions were even better. Men on their way up the ladder. Thirty years old, bare minimum age for promotion, and I'd made *first cohort*.

I let out a whoop and flung my wine cup across the atrium against the wall of the house, where it shattered into a dozen joyous pieces. Centurion at last.

"—you'll likely have to return to Moguntiacum first, make preparations with the rest of the cohort for the march to Parthia—"

The march, I thought, heart thumping in my chest. How long would the journey to Parthia take? Where *was* Parthia? Likely we'd have to take ships, at least part of the journey. Hell's gates, I hated boats. But there'd be marching too, and eighty men looking to me for their orders. Many of them likely older than I was, and resentful about it. My stomach fluttered, and I couldn't help a nervous swallow.

"Never mind," Titus said at last, looking amused. "You're not hearing a word."

Mirah's mother got teary when we shared the news, and Simon along with a few of the firebrand nephews grumbled about the Parthian invasion, but I didn't hear them over the golden roar in my head. Titus and I drank a toast to Parthia, to Trajan, to the goddess of good fortune who had just kissed me on the cheek. Mirah drank a toast with me too, then retreated early to bed as soon as I began toasting the Parthians for being obliging enough to have a war just for me.

"I'll get Boil and Julius and Philip into my century," I decided, escorting Titus down the darkness of the hall after he'd been persuaded to stay for supper. "Centurions can do that, can't they? It'll be like the old times in Dacia."

"Not quite," Titus said, dry. "For one thing, I have no intention of being dragged along with you. The Emperor offered me a post, but I refused as fast as possible. You can fight the wars this time while I finish my bathhouse. And for another thing, Slight, in those days back in Dacia it would have been a very different girl leaning on your arm. I do hope you didn't tell your wife about her?"

"I may be a barbarian, but I'm not an idiot." It had been strange, seeing Sabina at the circus that afternoon, even from a distance. She had looked very cool and elegant on the Emperor's arm . . . but not nearly as pretty as my Mirah.

I bid good night to Titus, making my way back through the dark atrium. Most of the rest of the household had gone to bed; just a few servants hurried about, dousing the lamps. I hadn't even noticed darkness falling, not with my Parthian dreams glowing so bright.

I made my way up the stairs to the room I shared with Mirah, feeling a touch of apprehension uncoil in my stomach. She had thought we would both be returning to Mog, and now . . . legion wives could get along well enough with their men based at a fort, but a campaign was a different thing. I looked a little nervously through the shadows at the hump of blankets in the middle of the bed. Would she weep and wail like Demetra? I touched the amulet at my neck, the one my father had given me. It had seen me clear of any fight life had thrown at me yet, but who knew how well it worked on fights with wives.

"Get in here," came Mirah's voice out of the dark. "The bed's cold."

I stripped off my tunic and climbed in. She burrowed into my shoulder, shivering a little and kneading her toes against my shins, and I pulled my worn lion skin over us both. "Parthia?" she said.

"I have to go where they send me," I began, but she shushed me with a finger against my mouth.

"I could have married Eleazer, Vix. He has a string of butcher shops and a villa in Ostia, and he certainly wouldn't go galloping off to the east at a moment's notice. But I married you." She nestled her head a little deeper into my chest. "How long will you be gone?"

"Come with me," I said impulsively.

"What?"

"Why not?" Suddenly I wanted her with me. I'd gotten used to having her in bed beside me, I liked her tart conversation and the oasis of cheerful bustle that spread around her wherever she went, and I didn't want to give any of it up.

Besides, if I took her with me I wouldn't need to rely on whores like most of the legion's men did when separated from their women for the long months and even years of a campaign. Nice if I didn't have to be unfaithful to my new wife just yet.

"I can't come," Mirah was arguing. "Wives don't march to war with the legion!"

"Legates bring their wives sometimes. They go on ahead of the men, set up somewhere civilized. You could do the same."

"Your legate wouldn't allow it," Mirah pointed out.

"It won't be up to him. The detachment will answer to the Emperor. And the Emperor likes me."

"Does he?"

I smiled into the dark. "The day I met you, I delivered a load of dispatches to him at the palace. He said he wanted to take Parthia, and I said he should take me and the Tenth with him to get it." I felt foolishly happy that he had remembered. That he had taken a moment, in the middle of planning an invasion, to arrange my future along with the legion's.

"Hmm." Mirah moved against my shoulder. "Why does he want Parthia, anyway?"

"Something to do with their new king." I stroked her hair where it lay across the pillow.

"What about him?"

"Who cares? The Emperor's spent the last few years building roads and arches and columns in Rome. He's bored."

"No one," Mirah declared, "should go to war because they're bored."

It seemed a good enough reason for me, but I had the sense not to say so.

"What did the Parthians do to deserve getting invaded?" she persisted. "Especially the ones whose crops will get trampled over by *your* big feet?"

"They aren't so big." Hoping to deflect her.

"They're like boats," she said, undeflected. "Why do you follow Emperor Trajan, Vix?"

That was easier to answer. "Because he's splendid."

"He's just another Roman emperor who invades a helpless country for fun."

"He isn't!"

"Why not?" she persisted.

"You haven't met him. When you do, you'll see."

"I don't understand you Romans," she said tartly. "You'll forgive a man anything for a little charm. I'm sure the Emperor who ordered the siege of Masada was charming too."

"Now you sound like Simon." He'd gotten very fiery and indignant over the state of poor wronged Judaea the past few months. He certainly didn't like being reminded of his days in the Tenth anymore.

"Well, doesn't Uncle Simon have a point? Romans see something they want, and they take it. Whether it's a cup of wine or a new province. And your charming Trajan is just the same."

"Why all this raking over past sins?" I demanded. "Trajan didn't siege Masada, so what does it matter?"

"But—"

I wrapped my arms around her, kissing the back of her neck. I kissed my way around to her ear, and she turned her face toward me in the dark.

"You really want me to come with you?" she whispered, lips brushing mine.

My fingers brushed her stomach, and I felt suddenly guilty. "I shouldn't have asked. The baby—"

"I am *not* one of these wilting women who sit indoors for nine months and won't lift so much as a cup," Mirah said sternly. "I can ride in a wagon without any harm to little Hannibal Emmanuel. If you want me."

"Oh, I want you all right . . ."

Two days later I had my orders from the Emperor, a case full of dispatches for the Tenth's legate, and a new side-to-side centurion's crest for my helmet. The day after that I loaded Mirah and her budding belly into a traveling train, promised I'd meet her in Antioch, bid farewell to my eighty new relatives, and started north.

"Good luck," Simon said a little sourly. He'd never really approved of Mirah marrying me. I suppose it's difficult to watch your favorite niece wed a man you used to go whoring with.

"Syrus says that no man by fearing ever reaches the top," Titus said more cheerfully. "Good thing you're not afraid of anything, isn't it, Slight?"

I hardly heard either of them; just ruffled a hand over my new centurion's crest and set my eyes forward.

PLOTINA

"I don't understand, Lady."

"I think you do, Gnaeus Avidius." Plotina pushed a slate across her desk at the lean praetor who managed Trajan's newest building project. "My secretaries brought the discrepancy to my attention, and I checked the numbers myself. You have been skimming money from the building funds for the Emperor's new forum."

"Lady, I assure you—"

"Spare me the protestations of innocence." Serenely, Plotina flicked a speck of dust from the surface of her desk. "New supplies ordered here, never delivered; an order of stone there, never quarried. Quite a few sesterces you've managed to pocket, Gnaeus Avidius."

"Then someone in my pay is skimming. I assure you it isn't me, and I will provide my own accounts to prove it if necessary." The praetor picked up her slate, frowning. "Thank you for bringing this to my attention, Lady. I will apprehend the thief and have him removed at once."

"Did I ask you to take such steps?" Plotina looked up at the ceiling, ruminative. The molding in the corner was cracked—why hadn't her steward repaired it? Honestly, did the Empress of Rome have to attend to *everything* herself? "The funds set aside for the forum are lavish. Some . . . leakage . . . is to be expected. I would be willing to let the matter slide, for a small consideration. Shall we say half?"

The praetor paused a moment, then rose and bowed. "I shall pretend

I didn't hear that, Lady," he said. "And I shall deal with the thief as I see fit. I do not permit thievery from any projects under my control."

"Oh dear," Plotina said as he stamped out. So many corrupt men in Rome; usually they were quite amiable to any suggestions from their Empress. But one did hit the occasional bump in the road. She drew a neat line through the name of Gnaeus Avidius on her slate. Perhaps he would serve better in a different post. A provincial post, say. Somewhere hot and diseased. His successor might prove easier to deal with.

"I always thought my task would be done once Dear Publius was consul," she told her reflection in the mirror. "But it's really just the beginning, isn't it?" It was going to cost a great deal to ensure the post she had in mind for the Parthian invasion.

She kept that in mind, when she had the praetor banished to Africa on a convenient pretext. Difficult, really—one never liked to think of exiles, dying alone, diseased, and destitute. *Duty*, Plotina reminded herself. No matter what *some* people liked to hint about meddling and kingmaking—people like former Empress Marcella—it was all for Rome.

The next banishment was much easier. And the third hardly troubled her at all.

SABINA

Plotina's voice was deep, Hadrian's even deeper, and both were smug. The smugness wafted out of the triclinium in waves Sabina could almost see as she came down the stairs from her bedchamber. She paused a moment in the atrium, adjusting a lock of hair that had slipped its pins and listening to the conversation drifting through the half-opened doors.

"Chief of the Emperor's personal staff!" Inside the triclinium, Hadrian rolled the words with relish. "I'd hoped for a legion, but this is better."

"My dear Publius, I told you I would persuade the Emperor to give you something suitable." Plotina's low loud tones were accompanied by the *chink* of metal on metal as wine was poured. Emperor Trajan had dashed down to Ostia to review some promising troops, but the Empress had arrived for a private dinner to celebrate her protégé's recent appointment. Private by Plotina's standards, anyway: herself, Dear Publius, Sabina, Hadrian's pallid sister whom he disliked and her boring husband Servianus whom he disliked even more, and twenty-two important men of Rome who would be required merely to look envious or promise Dear Publius their support.

"Congratulations on your appointment," a quieter voice asserted. Titus—Sabina was glad she'd been able to squeeze him into Plotina's ironclad guest list. Considering what she was about to do, it would be good to have one friend in the crowd. "May I ask what your plans are for the supply lines?"

But Plotina rode over Titus's question. "My husband was stubborn, but several of his legates quite changed their minds and they persuaded him. Just as I told you they would. You must learn to trust me, dear boy."

"I will never doubt you again." Hadrian's tone was gallant. "Cakes?"

"Not until Sabina arrives. *Vibia Sabina!*"

"A moment," Sabina called back, blotting her damp palms against her skirt.

A brief inaudible grumble from Plotina, and then Sabina heard Hadrian's voice again.

"I hadn't dared hope for a staff position." Her husband sounded lazy, satisfied, doubtless leaning back on one elbow on the cushions of the dining couch.

"Nonsense, my dear. Your organizational skills, your skill at managing subordinates—so wasted on just one legion. The Emperor may have the leadership of the army, but you will have the management." Plotina sounded even smugger, if possible. Sabina wondered if the guests were rolling their eyes yet, or just resigning themselves to staying silent and getting drunk. "It would be no exaggeration, Dear Publius, to call you the second man in the Empire just now."

A maid hastening through the atrium with a tray of honeyed cakes caught sight of Sabina and stumbled. She rescued her balance and the platter, casting one astonished look over her shoulder at her mistress. Sabina laid a cautionary, conspiritorial finger to her lips and the maid gave a shake of her head and marched on into the triclinium.

"We will leave for Antioch well in advance of the Emperor," Hadrian continued from the other side of the door. "He will count on me to assemble the eastern legions for him."

"You should maintain a basis in Antioch for the duration of the invasion," Plotina agreed. "Most convenient."

"Yes, and I've always wanted to see Antioch." Hadrian's voice turned musing. Once, Sabina thought, he might have launched into an excited diatribe about Antioch's famous temples and colonnades, wondering how they compared to Rome's. Now his voice was pompous as he said, "I'm sure we have much to bring the Antiochenes. One hears they have none of the Roman virtues, and serious discipline is nonexistent—"

Sabina bent to fiddle needlessly with the lace on her sandal. *Stop stalling*, she told herself. A page boy paused with a decanter of barley water and gazed at his mistress for a wide-eyed moment before remembering himself.

"One hears the Antiochenes are disagreeable company." The Empress's nose wrinkled almost audibly on the other side of the door. "Slippery characters. It's the eastern influence, of course. The men are depraved, and the women are worse. You must take good care to safeguard Sabina's reputation; you know how she relishes adventure in such places."

Oh, for gods' sake. Sabina rose, lifted her chin, and strode toward the door.

"I'm sure Sabina will be very useful to me," Hadrian's voice returned calmly. "We will have to maintain good relations with the Antiochenes, so I'm sure her particular brand of charm will not be wasted."

"I'll do my best!" Sabina put on her most dazzling smile as she floated into the triclinium. "Plotina, Titus, everyone—how lovely to see you all."

Plotina froze in the act of reaching for a cake, as if she had been turned to stone inside her dark-blue *stola*. Titus's eyebrows climbed slowly up his forehead. The other guests looked stunned. Hadrian, reclining on his own couch, had just lifted his cup to his lips when he glanced at Sabina to see what his guests were staring at. His mouthful of wine, Sabina was pleased to see, arced clear out across at least three feet of mosaic.

"What," he said when he had stopped coughing, "is *that?*"

"You said we'll need to maintain good relations with the Antiochenes." Sabina blinked, innocent. "Don't you like it? It's the very latest fashion in Antioch. I always think it makes such a good impression to follow the local customs. Don't you agree, Plotina?"

The thunderstruck eyes of Hadrian, Plotina, Titus, and a score of Rome's most important senators, legates, officers, and officials traveled in unison from the kohl Sabina had painted in winged lines about her eyes to the heavy gold earrings that brushed her bare shoulders, to the copper snake armband coiled about one elbow, to the gown so tightly cut that her maid had had to stitch it around her body. The dress left one breast completely bare, and Sabina had painted the nipple with henna to match the designs stenciled on her hands and feet. Plotina averted her eyes with a little gasp. Titus quickly lifted his cup and took a gulp—hiding, Sabina was certain, a grin.

Hadrian's voice was low. "What is the meaning of this?"

"We can't have the Antiochenes thinking we Romans don't know their ways, can we?" Sabina explained sweetly, turning a circle so they could see from all angles. The view from the left was particularly jaw-dropping. "They're going to *love* me, Hadrian. And isn't that why you married me? Because I'm so good at charming people of all places and stations?"

Hadrian opened his mouth. He closed it again. Plotina had flushed the color of a plum. "*Vibia Sabina—*" she began thunderously.

Sabina moved toward them with the rippling little steps that were all her tight dress would allow, and saw Hadrian's hovering secretary, the page boy with the wine, twelve servitors, and all twenty-four guests trying not to stare at her bare breast. She ignored them, reaching out to give Hadrian's cheek a fond, wifely pat.

"Darling, you're going to be so proud of me!"

"I'm sorry." Sabina shook her head ruefully at Titus. "I invite you to a dinner party, and instead of a good meal all you get is a few stilted words and a lot of agonized silence."

"One of the more memorable dinner parties of my career, Sabina— long on scandal, if short on conversation."

She smiled. Hadrian stood rigid in the atrium, ushering out the last of his gleeful guests as Plotina murmured tortured courtesies at his side—but Sabina had seized Titus by the hand as he made motions toward leaving and dragged him out to the garden. "Let's at least say a proper good-bye. I know *you're* not in a rush to head out and tell everyone in Rome about my degenerate morals."

"Isn't that what you had in mind?" He eyed the dress, which she'd draped modestly with a shawl as soon as the dinner party limped to its conclusion and the rest of the guests were out of sight. "What are you up to, Vibia Sabina?"

She shrugged, turning to lean her elbows on the balustrade overlooking the moon-silvered garden. The marble was cold through the shawl on her bare breast, and she longed to get out of the tight Antiochene dress. Did being degenerate have to be so uncomfortable? "This is good-bye, isn't it?" she asked Titus. "I'm off to Antioch so soon, and you're staying here in Rome."

"I've got a bathhouse to finish," he said lightly. "And my quaestor duties, of course."

"You could have come on the invasion. Trajan wanted you for a post on his staff. Plotina and her pet legates pushed him into taking Hadrian, but the Emperor had his eye on you all along. Said he wanted to drag you along on campaign, give you a bit more taste for warfare. Why didn't you take him up on it?"

"Sand," Titus said. "Bugs. Tribesmen trying to kill me. No, thank you. I'll stick to my city payrolls and my architectural oversight."

"You're wasted as a quaestor. Trajan told me that too, you know. You didn't take the staff post, but he's still got plans for you."

"I can't think why. I was the least enthusiastic tribune on his staff in Dacia, and now I'm the most plodding quaestor in the city."

"He says you have a good head on your shoulders. He also says you're one of the few men in Rome outside the legions who gives him a straight answer when he wants one." Sabina looked over her shoulder at Titus. "Maybe you'll end up consul someday."

"Gods forbid." Titus leaned on the railing at her side, looking across the banks of night-furled flowers. "What a muck I'd make of it."

Sabina wasn't so sure. Titus had a quiet authority now, a gentle unflinching presence to go with his alert bearing and attentive gaze. Trajan thought a good deal of the rising young Titus Aurelius, and so did other notable men in Rome. Like her father.

"I'll miss you when I go to Antioch." Sabina felt a pang as she realized just how much. Titus had been such a constant friend since the day he'd walked into her life with a bunch of violets and a stammered marriage proposal. In Rome, in Dacia, in his letters during her time in Pannonia; he'd always been there. "I'll write you, of course—I hope you won't be too busy to dash out a line to me now and then? With all your new building expertise, I was hoping to get your advice on some cheap ways to shore up tenement buildings—the slums in Antioch are supposed to be even worse than the Subura in Rome, and if I'm going to be wintering there I might as well take a look about and see what I can do to help."

"Write me as soon as you get your facts and figures, and we'll put our heads together."

They straightened, trading rueful looks, and Titus cast another glance over her. "I must say, you look stunning."

"It's not really an Antiochene dress," she confessed. "I just had the dressmaker stitch up the most shocking thing I could think of." She pulled her shawl closer about herself, feeling a self-consciousness that hadn't touched her before Hadrian and Plotina.

"No, no." Titus caught the edge of her shawl, tugging it back until it slipped off her shoulders to the floor. "Put yourself on display like that, and people have a right to look."

"Do they?"

"Well, I intend to look my fill. Did you know that I love you?"

She cocked her head. "What?"

He leaned down and kissed her, his mouth gentle, parting her lips with unhurried care. His hand cupped the back of her neck, and he took his time.

"Oh, no," Sabina said when he lifted his head.

"Not the response I was hoping for," Titus murmured.

"Not the kiss. That was lovely. The other part."

"The part where I said I loved you?" For all the weight behind them, his words came lightly. "Since the day we met, if you want to know. You were everything a sixteen-year-old boy could ever dream of, and he has seen nothing better yet."

"I never guessed." Sabina remembered all the nights in Dacia that she'd spent curled up in Vix's lap and talking to Titus, and cringed inside. "Why me? I'm not really very lovable."

"Vix loved you."

"Hated me too, quite a lot of the time. I'm not very easy on the people who love me."

"Oh, I'm not eating my heart out." Titus's voice in the shadows was airy. "'If you would marry suitably, marry your equal,' as Ovid would say. And we've never really been equals, have we? I'd have bored you senseless if we'd married."

Maybe. But Sabina felt a pang of loss at the thought. Married to Titus? *I wouldn't be standing in a cold house in an uncomfortable dress with a husband who hates me, that's for certain.* "I'm sorry," Sabina said again, but hardly knew what for.

Titus bent and kissed her again, once on the lips and once, briefly, on the slope of her bare breast. "Good night, Vibia Sabina."

"Good night."

She stood on the balustrade, watching as Titus sauntered off whistling through the darkened garden. He didn't look back once, but Sabina watched until the darkness had swallowed him up.

When she turned, she saw Empress Plotina standing in the archway behind her, a look of cold loathing on her handsome marble face. "I saw you—" she began furiously.

"Oh, go get stuffed," said Sabina, and stalked off.

CHAPTER 21

VIX

"It's like this, Centurion." The grocer I'd been paying for the past few years to keep Demetra's son shuffled from foot to foot, clearing his throat. "I can't keep the boy no more. My wife's gone, my own boys are going to live with their aunt, and she don't have room for another, and—"

"You're trying to drop this on me now?" I scowled. "I'm marching to Parthia in a fortnight!"

"I know." The grocer cleared his throat. "I like the lad well enough, but I can't keep him no more."

I looked down at my charge. Seven years old now—I'd hardly recognized him when I stooped through the low door of the grocer's shop in Mog. A handsome boy, tall for his age, with fair curly hair and an open, eager little face. He looked pale and shuttered now, standing between me and the grocer, head turning between us as our voices batted back and forth.

I folded my arms across my breastplate, looking down at him. "Can you fight?"

"No," he whispered.

"Shoot a bow?"

"No."

"Use a knife?"

"No."

"Hell's gates." With all that curly hair and those eyelashes, he looked like a girl. I looked back at the grocer. "Keep him another fort-night. I'll find someone else to take him on before I march."

I heard the boy's breath catch when I turned away. But I was busy—very busy. I had a century to ready for war, and just a fortnight to do it.

"Vix, no," Boil protested when I slung the belt and insignia of an *optio* at him across the little folding table where I now handled my century's papers. "Bugger you, I don't want to be *optio*! Everyone hates those weedy toads. Why do you have to pick on me?"

"Because you're too stupid to cheat me, too cheerful to hate me, and too big to be pushed around," I said briskly. "Just what I need. And it's 'Centurion' now, you clod-pole. Get out of here and start checking the men's weapons. I want a full report by morning of what's missing."

"All the luck," Boil muttered, his broad Gallic face red as his cloak, and tramped out. None of my *contubernium* was particularly happy about my promotion, not after I made sure they all ended up in my new century. But I didn't care if they were happy. I'd dreamed for years of having my own command, and I knew just what kind of men I wanted. I begged, I borrowed, I traded, I bribed the other centurions to get the best men out of their centuries and into mine before we had to march. "I'll give you a week's pay if I can have that big African of yours—what's his name?"

"Africanus, and I'm not giving him to you. He's worth three legion-aries all on his own in a fight!"

"Is he worth three weeks' pay? Think about it."

"Aren't you the go-getter," the other centurions said sourly. They didn't like me—I'd been passed straight up to the first cohort, when they'd had to claw their way up. Hard men, career men, most of them ten and twenty years my senior. I was the most junior of the lot, and I got every unpleasant duty they could shove on me, but I didn't care. From the moment the three cohorts of men from the Tenth Fidelis started the long march from Mog to join the growing band of legions in the east, I felt a joyous, insistent little pulse inside, as if every beat that pumped blood through my body was thumping to the rhythm of *now, now, now.*

I don't remember much of that initial march. We set out of Mog at double speed, eager to join the fight, and we tumbled down every night too tired to spit. Centurions could pass their marches on horseback, but the last thing I needed was to get dumped on my head in front of the men who were supposed to obey me, respect me, but above all be in awe of me. I loaded myself up with pack and weapons, just like the rest of them, and set a killing pace. I heard them grumbling behind me the first day, but I just roared, "*Marching song!* I'll have it loud, or I'll have you all flogged!" and soon they were bawling out cadences about Parthians buggering sheep, and giving me sour looks. I ignored the looks, stifled the flutter of nervousness in my throat, whipped them into setting up camp that night, and had them take it all down when three of the tents looked sloppy. "Call that a camp?" I stood back, watching with benign ferocity as they began redoing everything to my satisfaction. "Do it again!"

"Picky bugger," I heard a low voice grumble behind me as the men began erecting their tents for the third time. "Last month he was just one of us. He gets a pat on the back from the Emperor and he thinks that makes him a real centurion?"

It wasn't much to go on, but I wanted everything settled right off. "You—front, now," I snapped. The other legionaries had formed a rough circle around me before the man reluctantly stepped forward, and my heart sank. The grumbler was Julius, and my old friend's eyes over his beaked Caesar nose were resentful and unfriendly.

So much the better, I told myself brutally. *After today, the whole century will know you don't make pets out of your former comrades.*

"Let's cut this short," I said, pitching my voice loud and stamping down the dread in my stomach. Boil grimaced from the ring around us, knowing what was coming, but the rest just looked wary.

"What?" Julius's voice was sullen, but there was an insolent edge to it. Of all the tentmates in my former *contubernium*, he'd been the most resentful about my promotion—but I hadn't thought him as resentful as this.

"That's 'What, Centurion,'" I barked. "We're going to skip the part where you spend the next three days grumbling just loud enough for me to hear, Julius, and I pretend I'm deaf until you say something too rude to ignore, and then I have you beaten for insubordination. I'm just going to beat you tonight, and we'll save everyone the time. Hit me back if you want; we used to share a tent and we've saved each other's lives a few times, and I haven't got the crest and the medals on now."

I had to hit Julius twice before he started swinging. He took me around the middle in a boar's rush—he was strong, shorter than I was but much burlier, and that was good: The other legionaries would like it better if I had to fight hard. I let my friend give me a bloody nose and waited till I saw the satisfaction spread across his face before I applied the arm lock my father had once used to teach me my place. Julius's face went down into the mud, and hard.

"There," I panted, getting up. "I don't care we used to share a tent; I don't care we used to fight side by side. I'm not going to hear one more word of complaint out of you for as long as you march in my century." I picked up my lion skin and slung it around my shoulders. "And you, all of you—you know who I am? I'm the man who brought the Dacian king's head to the Emperor. I'm the man who carried your eagle. And now I'm your centurion, you ragtag rat-bait turds, so step sharp and shut up."

"What's a turd?" Demetra's son asked me when I retreated to my tent and bedroll.

"Something you should learn to say if you want people to stop thinking you're a girl. Get me a rag?"

He fumbled in my pack, coming up with a bundle of old cloth I kept for bandages. "Did you plan that?"

I looked down at him, still wondering why he was here. Why I'd turned around in the grocer's shop instead of leaving like I should have, and looked down at that pretty little face and said, "Get your things; you're coming with me to Parthia."

I shouldn't have offered. I should have at least asked Mirah first, if she'd mind taking in another woman's child with one of her own already on the way. I didn't know much about wives yet, but that was probably the sort of thing women liked being consulted about. I probably should have told her Demetra's son existed to begin with . . . But I'd been on my best behavior, courting Mirah and marrying her and learning to live with her, and the time had never seemed quite right to tell her I was paying to raise another woman's son.

I should have planned in advance; done it better. But Mirah had already gone ahead to Antioch, and I couldn't exactly wait for a reply. And that pretty little boy had been staring up at me with those huge brown eyes, and all I could think was that the world was going to munch him up and spit out his bones if someone didn't toughen him up.

So here he was, cross-legged and bright-eyed on a bedroll of his own in my tent.

"Well?" he was pressing me eagerly. "You planned it! The fight an' the speech an'—"

"Down to the last insult." I pressed the wad of rags against my nose, mopping the blood and wondering if Julius would ever be my friend again.

Never mind. He wasn't supposed to be my friend anymore—just one of my men.

"Why'd you do it?" Antinous was asking, curious. "They're all angry and grumbly now."

"But they won't grumble tomorrow."

"They don't like you."

"They don't have to like me. They just have to respect me."

"Don't they?"

"Not yet. They won't respect me till we win a fight or two, but that's all right. I wouldn't either, in their place."

Demetra's son blinked those curly lashes of his. God, he looked soft. "I'm going to teach you how to fight," I told him. "Starting tomorrow before the march. Get some sleep."

"C'n I ride the horse tomorrow on the march?" He burrowed into his bedroll like a squirrel. "The wagon's boring. 'Sides, you don't ride the horse."

"Feel free. Don't say I didn't warn you when he bucks you off too."

His voice came in the dark as I was on the edge of sleep. "What do I call you?"

I yawned, considering. He'd never had occasion to call me much of anything before. He had just stared wide-eyed on my periodic visits, mumbling a shy *yes* or *no* to my few questions.

"Address me as *Centurion* in front of the men," I said through the dark. "But for private, *Vix* will do well enough."

"Vix?" He said it shyly, as if I'd hit him for taking liberties.

"You'd call me that if I were a brother."

"But you're not my brother."

"I'm not your father either." He'd rather have called me that, I could sense, but I wasn't having it. "You had a father, not that you knew him, and it wasn't me. But if I were a brother you'd call me *Vix*, and I've got a brother and sisters in Britannia not much older than you. So *Vix* will do."

"Vix," he said dubiously through the dark.

"Go to sleep, Antinous." Now that he was mine, I'd have to start remembering his name.

TITUS

"Any advice?" Titus asked the bust of his father. It stared back: kindly, marble, silent, and Titus gave a long exhale. It had been a long time since he'd felt the need to consult his father's stone face, but old habits were comforting. "I've never given a speech at the Rostra before," he said. "I wish you could help me."

Silence.

"No one can help me now, can they?" Titus said it softly, looking from the bust of his father to the empty niche right beside it—the niche where the funerary bust of his grandfather would be placed, after the funeral procession today. His grandfather was dead, and Titus Aurelius Fulvus Boionius Arrius Antoninus was now head of the family. People would now be looking to him for advice, not the other way around.

"Talking to statues again?" Ennia stood in the doorway, hands on skinny hips. "People will think you're moon mad, and you the paterfamilias now."

He groaned. "Don't say it."

"Not saying it don't make it less true." She came forward, adjusting the pleats of his black mourning toga. "They're all waiting for you out there."

"Then wish me luck," Titus said to both his mistress and his father, and drew a fold of black wool up over his head.

The sky was steel gray and cold overhead, but a great many worthy citizens had still come to pay their respects to a former consul and distinguished statesman of Rome. Titus paced on foot with the masked mourners, matching his steps to the solemn blare of the bronze horns, looking straight ahead with impassive eyes because too great a show of grief would be improper. Behind him he could hear his half-sisters weeping, but that was fitting for women. A paterfamilias must be stone. He felt tears prick his eyes just once, when he met the gaze of Senator Marcus Norbanus limping sturdily along to join the procession, flanked by his wife and daughter in black gowns, and the old man gave him the nod of an equal. *I'm not your equal,* Titus thought, *I'm not anyone's equal, I'm twenty-eight years old and an undistinguished public servant, and would you all stop looking at me like I'm important?* But he was important now; he was head of the family with all attendant duties and responsibilities, and Titus answered Marcus's nod with a grave one of his own and kept marching.

If it had been his own choice, the funeral procession would have ended matters. He'd have installed his grandfather's ashes in the crypt and gone thankfully home for the nine days of mourning, which he'd have spent installing his grandfather's funeral bust in its niche and perhaps chatting to it now and then while he got used to his new role. But first there was the eulogy to be given, and for a man of his grandfather's stature the eulogy must be given publicly, at the Rostra in the Forum Romanum where all Rome could hear.

Get hold of yourself, Titus told himself. *You've given speeches before.* But never a speech at the Rostra, where plebs would listen idly to critique his delivery and comment on his choice of phrase and wonder if he'd ever amount to anything in politics. Never a speech before so many of his colleagues and superiors, all of them actually listening for once instead of dozing in their seats or reading petitions during his payroll reports. Never a speech in front of a crowd like *this*. Titus swallowed as the funeral procession wound ceremonially into the forum, and he saw that every place was packed by attentive Roman citizens. The horns fell silent as he mounted the steps of the Rostra's platform and turned to face his audience. Their upturned faces were just pink blurs. He blinked, hoping to bring his sight back into clarity, but then he saw frowns, saw anticipation, saw yawns and envy and outright sneers, and wished he could have the blurs back.

Friendly faces too, though—a fellow quaestor or two, the architect who had designed Trajan's baths, Senator Norbanus smiling encouragingly between his wife and daughter. Faustina, not Sabina; Sabina had already departed for Antioch, and doubtless hadn't even heard yet of his grandfather's death. *You'll get a letter from her within the month,* Titus told himself, but he'd have traded the letter and both his hands to have her here now, standing in the crowd this morning looking up at him. She'd smile, she'd give a little nod of encouragement and melt the block of ice plugging his throat . . . he had a sudden flash of her soft mouth under his own, her even softer breast, and blinked it away hard. Dear gods, those were not thoughts to be having while he was supposed to be giving his grandfather's funeral oration.

The blurry pink faces were beginning to look impatient now. Titus cleared his throat, tucked one hand along the folds of his toga, lifted his head. What was the opening sentence again? He'd worked so hard on his speech, something grave and well composed to do his grandfather honor, and now he couldn't remember a single word.

His eyes, raking the crowd desperately, fell on Sabina's little sister. Faustina stood taller than her mother and father, fair hair covered by a black veil, and she leaned forward a little with her brows raised as if she could drag the words out of his mouth. She gave a tiny encouraging nod.

Titus cleared his throat.

"Honored citizens of Rome." His voice came out strong, unwavering. "Martial tells us 'He mourns honestly who mourns without witnesses.' But for a loss of a man such as my honored grandfather Gnaeus Arrius Antoninus, all Rome must mourn together . . ."

Not a stumble from start to finish.

VIX

People liked to say Antioch was the Rome in the east, but I couldn't see the resemblance. There might be colonnades and aqueducts and arenas all in marble, but it wasn't anything like Rome. The men wore their hair long and colored their nails like women; Hebrew and Latin and more languages I didn't even know made a spicy verbal mix in the streets, and I counted more whores in one forum than I ever saw in an entire Roman slum, or maybe that was just how all the women dressed.

"My former aquilifer!" Trajan greeted me on his first inspection of the Tenth's detachment, though he did less inspecting than making promises to all the cheering men of treasure and triumphs in the year to come. "The sea journey didn't kill you?"

"Nearly, Caesar." I saluted.

"Still wearing that lion skin you took off Decebalus, I see. Didn't feel like handing it over to the next aquilifer?"

"Over my dead body, Caesar." The pelt was a little patchy now, but

I still wore it over my red cloak, and when the First Spear centurion saw it he always frowned. "That's nonapproved for a centurion's wear," he'd said many times. "Take it off."

"Yes, sir," I always said, never obeying. I'd gotten that lion skin from Trajan's own hand, the same hand now giving me a friendly clap on my shoulder as he congratulated me on my new rank, and after that the First Spear dropped the subject of my lion skin. He already loathed me, but I didn't hate him at all—on the contrary, I was looking forward to many pleasurable months of needling him on my way to getting his job. Technically his rank meant "First File," since he led the first century of the first cohort and came first of all the legion's centurions—but I liked the sound of "First Spear" better. I planned on doing the job a lot more efficiently than the prick who currently held the title.

Antioch was stuffed, crowded, bursting with Romans. I'd thought Mog was full in the weeks before the Dacian campaign, but the Dacian campaign had only been three and a half legions, and this was a full seven, plus a *vexillatio* or two reinforcing from the legions in the west, like ours from the Tenth. There wasn't a spare room to be rented anywhere in Antioch by the time the year ended, and I was glad I'd sent Mirah ahead of me to secure us living quarters. Once I stopped kissing her hello, Mirah put her hands over my eyes and walked me blindfolded and stumbling into a cozy little set of rooms that stayed our home for the rest of the winter. My century settled into their barracks for the winter business of dicing, drinking, keeping weapons sharp, and waiting for the mountain passes to open up, and I settled in with Mirah.

"Vix!" Her voice floated in from the kitchen. "Come get your helmet out of the wash basin!"

"What's it doing in the wash basin to begin with?" I ventured into the tiny snug kitchen, where Mirah had lifted a leg of lamb from the brick oven and stood muttering over it. "Why is my helmet full of water?"

"It stank, so I washed it," she said absently. Her belly was rounded now beneath her apron. "I don't even want to think about all the times you boiled soup in it over a campfire. What exactly does helmet soup *taste* like?"

"You don't want to know." I emptied my helmet out, drying it off on the hem of my tunic. "This needs a polish." I looked over at Antinous, where he sat playing with a carved wooden horse. "How about it, sprat? You can put a better shine on metal by now than most of my men."

He zoomed off after the polishing rags. Mirah thumped the top of his head gently as he flew past. "Be sure to get it done before sundown! Polishing armor counts as work, Antinous. You know we don't do any work on Shabbat."

"You're supposed to eat a proper meal on Shabbat too." I looked over her shoulder at the lamb, which was a little black in places. "That doesn't look like a meal. Are you still learning how to manage that Antiochene oven?"

"Right now it's managing me," she muttered.

"Maybe we should get your mother out here—"

Mirah hit me with a spoon, chestnut hair gleaming in the orange light from the brick oven. "Out!"

I kissed her wide mouth. "Yes, Lady."

I could hear her singing as I thumped out of the kitchen, a sort of cheery tuneless chant punctuated by the banging of pans and the occasional burst of swearing. Mirah always pretended to cover her ears whenever I swore in her presence, but she had grown quick to mumble legionary curses whenever she dropped a pot on her foot in the kitchen. Antinous was picking it up too. "*Why* can't I say 'rat-bitten bastard'? Mirah said it to the baker yesterday when he tried to cheat us on bread!"

"I don't care if you *say* it. If you're going to swear, swear like a man. Just don't swear around my wife."

"I heard that," Mirah had said without turning. She'd looked at first questioning and then dismayed when I first arrived in Antioch and presented her with a seven-year-old child. "Who's this pretty little girl?" she'd asked, and Antinous scowled and ruffled his curls with one paw and said, "I'm a boy."

"I probably should have told you about him earlier," I'd begun with a deep breath, and by the end of it Mirah was just a little cross with me. Cross enough that she would have rearranged my face with the nearest blunt object, if I hadn't danced nimbly behind a chair and done some fast talking. Most wives, it seems, would rather be asked first if they mind raising a child not their own—and they'd rather be asked before the child in question is being led through the door. But Antinous followed Mirah about so anxiously, so desperately eager to please, smiling so radiantly whenever she praised him, that she soon thawed. "He'll be a good big brother to little Emmanuel," she said, rubbing the bulge of her stomach. "I wonder if they'll look like each other?"

"When are you going to believe me when I tell you he isn't my son? Like I said before, Antinous's mother birthed him before she even met me. His father was some Bithynian clerk; died before I even got to Mog in the first place."

"So you say, but no man pays to raise a son who isn't his own. Besides, he looks like you." Mirah eyed Antinous, prowling about his new home in the long-strided swagger he'd started copying from me.

"He doesn't look a thing like me," I scoffed. "Far too pretty. He takes after his mother."

"So his mother was pretty?" Mirah said, ominous. "Prettier than me?"

"I'd better check on the men," I said hastily, and ducked out. I didn't have to be married long to know *that* was an argument I wasn't ever going to win.

But things had smoothed over since that rocky introduction, and now Antinous was humming over my helmet with a polishing cloth as Mirah sang in the kitchen and I went rummaging for a needle to mend the torn liner in my helmet. "Where's the thread?" I called.

"Sewing things are in the basket by the chair," Mirah said without looking up. "You know that."

"Doesn't mean I'm used to it." My sandals now lived beneath the bed, just as my whetstones and polishing cloths lived beside the pile of sewing and my dirty tunics went to a woven basket at the bedside rather than to the floor. "I can't find anything anymore," I'd complained the first week of living together in Antioch.

"You'll learn," said Mirah briskly. "Now, that frieze around the wall has to go."

"What's wrong with it?"

"It's got dancing girls in it."

"They aren't naked or anything."

"They're people. You don't have pictures or carvings of people in a house," she explained, "only things, like vines and flowers and urns."

"Why not people?"

"God doesn't like images graven in his own likeness. One step from that," she said darkly, "to worshipping idols, Vercingetorix of Masada."

"Don't call me that!" I winced.

"It's true," she insisted. "You're Masada's last son."

"And does the last son of Masada have to paint out the frieze?"

"He does if he wants any peace. Not to mention dinner."

I painted over the images the next day. Philip, who had a talent for sketching when he wasn't playing dice, drew some rather nice grapevines with urns and draped ribbons, and Mirah kissed him on both cheeks and stuffed him with roast goose. "You're an ugly lout, Vix," complained Philip, who had accepted my promotion far more gracefully than Julius. "So why do you always get such good women?"

"I'm lucky," I said, and meant it. Half the other centurions had wives, but most of them were either stout or pockmarked, and all of them nagged in voices like the trumpets that called us to formation. Mirah with her light step and lively glances and the neat blue scarf over her hair put them all to shame. She liked Antioch; she liked the legion; she'd liked the journey from Rome, and what hardships there were— spiders, tedious hours of travel, strange Antiochene customs—she attacked with a torrent of muttered curses and a cheerful rolling up of sleeves. "Take that, spiders," she'd say with relish, wielding her broom till the dust flew. "Take that, sand!"

"She's looking *forward* to the march in spring?" Boil said unbelievingly.

"So she says." I couldn't help sounding smug.

"But centurions' wives aren't supposed to come along."

"This campaign isn't like Dacia, stripped down to an army and a supply train. The Emperor's got an entourage with him this time, for receiving all those Armenian kings. Laundresses, clerks, cooks, barbers, musicians—I got Mirah a place with the seamstresses. She and the boy will travel with the rest of the Imperial servants."

"Lucky bastard," Philip grumbled again, but Boil nudged him. "Sorry, sir."

I waved it off, but felt wistful. Things were so different now for my old friends. Philip and Boil and a few others still occasionally came to visit during off-hours, to be stuffed with Mirah's rich stews and trade jokes with me—Julius even started to come after a few months, making no reference to the beating I'd given him before the other men. But when we were all in armor on legion business they had to salute and call me by rank. And even around my table in the off-hours, they weren't nearly so loose with their dirty jokes and their complaints about the other officers as they used to be.

Why should they be? Titus wrote me in one of his long letters from Rome. *For all they know, you entertain the other centurions with stories about your days in the ranks. No one entirely trusts a man who works his way up the ladder, Slight.* Titus was a big man in Rome now—his grandfather had died at the end of the year, and even out in Antioch I'd heard rumors about the size of the fortune my friend had inherited. I'd have hit him up for a loan—my men's pay came irregularly, and what was the use of having a rich friend if you couldn't make use of him to tide you over the lean times?—but I'd heard from one of the Imperial secretaries that Trajan was planning on asking for a loan too, and I couldn't go following in an emperor's footsteps.

Antinous bounced up and down before me, presenting my helmet proudly. "Good?"

"Like a mirror." I threw a jab at him and he slipped inside it, thumping my ribs with a little clenched fist just as I'd taught him. "Good." I cuffed the side of his head with my other hand. "Keep your guard up, though."

"Like this?"

"Chin down, or it'll get clipped. And fold your fingers tighter, like this—"

"No, no, like this." Mirah demonstrated a clenched fist. "Thumb on the outside, Antinous. And don't underestimate the impact of a good scratch with the fingernails either—it doesn't all have to be punching."

"When did you learn how to fight?" I asked my wife, amused.

"Eight boy cousins who all liked to tease, that's how. And six girl cousins who liked to scratch."

"Let's see if they taught you anything about grappling." I lunged and took my wife around the waist. She shrieked and pummeled at my shoulders, and Antinous came in on her side and started in on my ribs with his little fists. "Two against one?" I yelped. "No fair!"

Mirah giggled as I dropped her. "All right, all right, enough roughhousing. Go wash up, both of you, you're all over dust!"

"Better listen to her," I told Antinous, man to man.

"Women," he agreed sagely, and dashed for the water basin.

Scrubbed and clean, I took my place at the small table with Antinous on my other side as Mirah covered her head and began the first of the Shabbat prayers. The candles cast friendly yellow circles of light over the table, softening the rough wattle of the wall behind, giving a soft brilliance to Mirah's eyes as she intoned the old, old words. I was learning to follow the Hebrew now, and so was Antinous. A Briton, a Greek, and a Jew, all saying Shabbat prayers around the table . . . I forked slabs of roast lamb onto the various plates when prayers were done, and Mirah ate heartily. No patrician nibbling for her. From time to time I saw her touch her rounding belly, saw her look at a gobbling Antinous and imagine how our boy would look at seven years old. I hooked my arm over the back of my chair and sipped at my mug of beer, looking around and liking what I saw. My table. My food. My wife. A boy who had somehow become my son. All in my home, earned by my sword.

I liked that.

Though even through that busy peaceful winter, I still heard the thrum in my blood: *now, now, now.*

We marched on Armenia in the spring, and then we took it. *We* took it? Trajan took it. Mountainous country, the peaks steeper and stonier than the ones I'd seen in Dacia, falling to flat green lowlands. No tangy pines like I remembered around Old Sarm; just rushing rivers and narrow mountain passes hedged by rocky cliffs. Trajan swept through those passes with eighty thousand men, and at Elegeia I watched him hold court as one Armenian prince after another came to bend the knee and offer him fealty. One of the princes handed his diadem over with one of those complacent smirks you just itch to slap off with an open palm, fully expecting Trajan to put the crown back on his head with a nice little speech, but Trajan didn't. He kicked the prince out, and I heard him protesting all the way down the hall outside, wanting to know what he'd done wrong. I could have told him: Trajan hated smirkers. He tossed the diadem to a steward and told him to melt it down for the jewels.

The satrap afterward did better by making Trajan a gift, a horse that had been trained to kneel down as if it were bowing. Trajan applauded noisily, and then yelled, "Let the poor beast up; I'm not making the horses swear fealty too!" But Hadrian had the horse kneel over and over, contemplating the long nose placed meekly at his feet. He left Elegeia after that and returned to Antioch to better manage the long supply lines already stringing out behind us. I hated that arrogant jolt-head, but I have to admit he did his job; I've never seen a campaign since where the food and supplies arrived so swiftly, so speedily, and so free of bugs.

Sabina didn't stay in Antioch, or so I heard. I hadn't once laid eyes on her before she was gone again, flitting off to Egypt to see the spring floods from a Nile barge. "You should have seen Legate Hadrian's face," my First Spear whistled to the other centurions, the news overcoming his usual loftiness. "I was waiting in the anteroom with the supply figures when a maid comes in with the message—that wife of his didn't send it till she was a day's journey away, and she had the girl announce it out loud so he wouldn't be able to yell. He didn't say a word, just went back to dictating a letter. But the next day he took off hunting for a week and he must have slaughtered half the deer in the woods." A shake of the head. "He's a funny sort. Not one I'd want to cross."

"I've crossed him," I said. "He hasn't killed me yet."

"If you're so invincible, I'll recommend you and your century to join Lusius Quietus's thrust up north," First Spear shot back. "That'll take the stuffing out of you."

"Yes, sir." But my blood was singing. Armenia had fallen speedily, but there were still little fires of resistance, and Trajan had sent his fierce Berber horsemen to stamp out the flames. I wasn't much for riding and neither were my eighty men, but I'd trained them for hard fast marches, and dear God, the time was now. *My* time was now. Trajan took Armenia that year, but I helped.

"Quietus speaks highly of you," the Emperor said during another inspection. "He usually hates us lowly foot soldiers, but he condescends to tell me that your men aren't completely useless."

"I train them specially, Caesar."

"How?" Trajan's eyes brightened; he waved off the pair of secretaries trying to get his attention with an armload of dispatches.

"I take them out of formation, Caesar. I want them able to move through rough ground, fight independently, but still snap into a turtle or a wedge at a word." I tried to find the words for what I tried so hard to get from my men. They didn't like it, they complained about being asked to leave the safety of their formations—all legionaries hate change—but I had drilled them and drilled them this winter in Antioch, and now I was honing them among the rocks and rivers of Armenia. "I want them able to fight anything. Anywhere. Any *way*."

"Still bent on using that gladiator training of yours, eh?" My Emperor forgot nothing.

"In its place, Caesar."

"I've still got that scar you gave me. Ten years ago?" He rolled up his sleeve to look at the faded pucker of purple, shaking his head at the graying hairs on his still-strong arm. "Gods' bones, we're getting old. I'll send you out with Quietus again."

Out we went, on scouting missions, on foraging expeditions, on deadly strikes across rivers at night. My century and I were flicked out into the twisting mountain roads, sent scrambling across rocky hillocks, inching on our bellies through short summer grass, plunging through the rivers leaning on our shields to keep from being swept off our feet. I killed Armenians with narrow faces and fierce beards, I collected three more campaign tokens, and my men stopped grumbling when I told them to split out of formation into a dozen smaller darts that could thread an enemy block and hack it to pieces in seconds. They called me a hard bastard, but they jingled more campaign tokens than any other century in the Tenth detachment, and I moved up two ranks. The centurion above me got killed in a raid, and the one above him died of camp fever, and the Emperor jumped me over their empty places.

"No more junior centurion!" Mirah crowed when I came to her that night. Her nimble needle had earned her a place among the Imperial servants, where she rode in a wagon with a clutch of other women, gossiping and mending endless piles of linen for the vast entourage Trajan managed to maintain on campaign. "How much do the other centurions hate you for jumping up the ladder so fast? I know your First Spear must have been *delighted*."

"Thrilled." I put a pearl ring on her finger, holding her hand up to the light. "You like it? I took it off a fat captive prince."

"Very grand," Mirah teased, admiring the ring. We had a tent now instead of the snug little apartment in Antioch, but Mirah just swept out the sand at night and shook the spiders out of the bedrolls and kept everything so neat I had no idea where anything was. "Where are the children?" I nuzzled Mirah's neck.

"Miriam's keeping them for the night. Antinous carried the baby over himself—I will say, he's a doting big brother. I didn't think boys ever liked babies."

"He likes ours." Our daughter, born a month early on our spring-time march between Antioch and Elegeia, as if she couldn't wait to join the world. Mirah had been disappointed she wasn't a boy, but I was just relieved the baby had arrived without fuss. Besides, as soon as Mirah and I started having boys, there were going to be fights about some ghastly ceremony called a *brit* or a *bris*. However it was pronounced, no son of mine was going through it. "I'm not letting anyone strip the skin off my son's cock!" I'd said in utter horror when Mirah explained the ritual to me. "Absolutely not!"

"I don't have to do that, do I?" Antinous asked uneasily.

"Over my dead body," I'd replied. "And that goes for the new baby too."

Mirah had pressed her lips together in a way I knew meant trouble. But Dinah had come along instead a few months ago, little Dinah with her swatch of dark hair and pink hands that were always screwed up in fists like infant copies of mine, and for now the argument about the *brit* was postponed.

"If Dinah's with Miriam for the night, let's take advantage of it." I bore my wife back down into the bedroll. "*Now.*"

"We'll have Miriam's boy tomorrow," Mirah warned me between kisses. "I promised, in return for her giving us tonight—"

"Perfect. I'm out on a sweep tomorrow. Give us a kiss."

My men and I bagged a satrap on that sweep, traveling in a train of rich baggage down just the wrong sweep of road—and that was just the first big catch of my summer. By fall, Mirah owned a sapphire bracelet and a gold chain set with amethysts, Antinous had a short Syrian bow and a pair of ivory-hilted daggers, and little Dinah had a silver bracelet of her very own to teethe on.

PLOTINA

"My lady—" Plotina found her hand seized and repeatedly kissed. "I cannot thank you enough for your intervention. A goddess from the skies, traveling among mankind to spread her blessings—"

"Senator, you flatter me." Plotina extracted her fingers with difficulty. She hadn't received so many kisses in her whole marriage.

"A goddess," the man went on, flushed to the top of his bald head. "I shall have my personal statue of Juno recarved with your own Imperial face. Juno stands before me now, in all her glory!"

He shielded his face, as if radiance dazzled him. Plotina inclined her head graciously but did not wave him up from his knees. It was rather pleasant to be worshipped. "You will not forget that little favor I asked of you, Senator?"

"Of course not! I shall tend to the matter myself, I assure you."

"Very good. And *promptly*, if you please." Plotina drew a line through another name on her wax tablet. Trajan's letters from the east still had distressingly little to say in praise of Dear Publius, but there were other men he praised to the skies. A certain Aulus Cornelius Palma was always being mentioned, held in high favor because of some past conquest he'd made among the Nabataean Arabs. Lucius Publilius Celsus's name too had begun cropping up with great Imperial approval. It would hardly do for their stars to shine brighter than that of Dear Publius, would it?

And when Plotina had learned of a certain renowned senator's recent batch of failed investments, it had been all too easy. The offer of a dowry for his daughter and the rescue of his family home before it went under the hammer—he had not even blinked at the price Plotina named in return.

"A little whispered slander," she murmured. "Nothing too overt, mind. Just a word or two dropped to your colleagues over the next dinner party. Perhaps you'll remember that young Palma seduced a

Roman girl of good family, who killed herself when he refused to marry her. Or that former consul Celsus lined his purse out of his last appointment." Just enough gossip to taint a man's reputation among his peers. A man whispered as a lecher or a thief among his colleagues could never be presented as Imperial heir. "You know the kind of thing I mean? It's for the good of Rome, you understand."

"Of course, Lady!"

"You might add a word or two about former consul Servianus as well," she added, musing. Dear Publius's brother-in-law, and another name that cropped up regularly in Trajan's letters. "Perhaps you'll remember to murmur to one or two people that he's a drunkard or a lecher in his private life?"

"No one will believe it, Lady—Servianus, he's the most virtuous man in Rome."

"Well, just the other two, then." Good enough for a day's work.

The senator bowed out backward, still spilling compliments. Plotina put her wax tablet aside, giving a little pat to her hair, which now had the most dignified and flattering streaks of gray along the temples. "My face on a statue of Juno," she said aloud. "I do hope you won't be offended, dear sister?"

Plotina didn't have to go to the temple now to speak with Juno. Her sister goddess, she knew, attended her every word.

CHAPTER 22

Winter A.D. 114

TITUS

"Ennia?" Titus wandered into the atrium where Ennia was giving two slave girls a brisk tongue-lashing for dawdling over the laundry. "Have a look at this, and tell me I'm reading it right."

"You know I can't read, Dominus." She dismissed the girls with a flap, coming to squint at the scroll in his hand. "Is that the Imperial seal?"

"It is." Titus read the message again—brief and brisk, in a soldier's scrawl. "By the Emperor's own hand, if I'm not mistaken."

"All the way from Armenia?" Ennia looked impressed despite herself. "What's he got to say?"

"I'm being asked for a report on the baths. Also, my opinion is requested on various other official matters—why does he want my opinion, anyway? I haven't got any ideas. Oh, and I'm being asked for a loan."

Ennia gave her raucous laugh. "Didn't take long for the news to get out, did it, Dominus?"

"I suppose not." There had been more than one surprise to hit Titus after his grandfather's death, but by far the greatest had been the terms of the will. His grandfather had left all his assets to Titus, and that had been expected; what had not been expected was just how extensive those assets were. "Who ever knew the old gentleman was so smart with his coppers, simple as he lived here at home?" Ennia had marveled. Titus had suddenly found himself the owner of a great many coppers, not to mention less tangible but no less profitable things such as silver mines, timber yards, properties in Ostia and Ravenna and Brundisium, villas in Baiae and Tivoli and Capri, a fleet of grain ships, a gladiator school, a block of tenement flats on the Esquiline Hill . . .

It had not taken long, apparently, for news of Titus's increased fortune to reach the other side of the Empire. *Campaigning's an expensive business,* Trajan had written frankly in his big open scrawl. *A loan from you would help see my men paid on time this winter, and I'd not forget the favor.*

"I suppose even emperors find themselves in debt," Titus said, wandering back into his study. "Especially when running large armies. I'll see to the loan right away."

"You'll never get it back," Ennia warned. "Emperors, they're notorious. When they say loan, they mean *give.*"

"'All men cheerfully obey when worthy men rule,'" Titus quoted, scrawling himself a reminder to consult the steward in the morning. "Trajan can have my life if he likes; who am I to deny him my money?"

"That's a quick way to end up poor."

"Perhaps I shall. But loved."

"Better get a rich wife, the way you're splashing it about," Ennia muttered. "Speaking of which, the locusts arrive in half an hour, and two of them said they're bringing their daughters."

"I believe they would prefer to be called guests rather than locusts, Ennia." But Titus couldn't help a sigh. "Daughters?"

"*And* a niece." Ominously.

"Well, see if you can squeeze them in. Preferably not next to me." Ever since the terms of his grandfather's will had become common knowledge in Rome, there had been a sharp increase in Titus's female guests. Colleagues who'd barely bothered attending his dinners were now not only begging to attend but bringing along hordes of unmarried women with them. Titus's winter had been one long parade of sisters, daughters, granddaughters, nieces . . .

"Should have married before the old gentleman died," Ennia said, whisking a spare cloak off Titus's chair and brushing it off vigorously.

"Now you're the biggest catch in Rome, and begging your pardon, Dominus, but I haven't seen one girl yet who isn't just a pretty little shark smelling blood in the water."

"There's bound to be one or two who aren't just out for the, er, blood."

"Keeping my eyes open, Dominus, believe me. I want to retire someday, you know. Running this big house all by myself—"

"Quit your grumbling," Titus chided. Ennia, he knew, had been ridiculously pleased when he asked her to stay on as his housekeeper.

"Me?" she'd said, astounded. "I'd thought I'd help you move out of your apartments back to the family house, and that would be that. You'll be needing a proper steward now."

"Like you couldn't keep that big pile of marble in order," he teased. After the mourning period was done, he'd moved back into his family home as was expected—but paterfamilias or not, it had felt strange to move through his grandfather's halls as master. "I wouldn't have anyone else to manage my household, Ennia."

"Thought you'd be getting rid of me." She'd looked up at him shrewdly. "You've got coin now for the best fancy ladies in Rome, Dominus. No need for some housekeeper with a slum lord's mouth. I know what I am."

"I know what you are too. And I know what you're worth." Titus had lifted her skinny wrist and slipped over it a heavy gold bracelet inlaid with garnet and carnelian flowers. The first really costly thing he'd ever bought, and he had to take a deep breath at the thought that such a purchase no longer cost a month's worth of his yearly allowance. "I want to keep you, Ennia. Anyone makes you a better offer to join their household, I'll double it."

"Hmm." She eyed him, speculative.

"Of course," Titus added, "I'll have to *confirm* the offer first."

She snorted, holding her arm up to admire the bracelet. "Perhaps I'd better stay on after all, Dominus. Else some snake of a girl will snap you up and make your life miserable."

"No chance of that with you on watch." And Ennia kept his house, his slaves, and his guests in better order than he'd ever hoped. Not a girl passed through the hall who didn't go through the gauntlet of her appraising up-and-down glance.

"Half an hour," Ennia reminded him again, and whisked out, yelling for the page boys to get the wine warmed before she warmed their backsides for them. Titus tipped back in his chair and read through the Emperor's letter again. *How are my baths progressing?* Trajan had written after the request for a loan. *I've a mind to put you in charge of my* alimenta *program as well; there's been skimming there and I need someone honest to put a stop to it. Tell me what you think . . .*

Titus looked up from the letter at the bust of his grandfather. The formal death mask had been placed with ceremony in the entry hall, but here he had a less formal bust of the old man, carved with the familiar kindly glint in his eye. "Emperors asking me for advice," he said. "Strange days, eh, Grandfather?" He still felt self-conscious giving the orders in his family's house, sitting in judgment when his family's clients brought their problems to him, signing his name with the authority of his family's seal ring. He was no longer just "that fellow who quotes." He was now the fellow who got personal letters from emperors. His sisters looked at him with respect now, instead of scolding him for his untidy hair and his absentmindedness. His opinions were no longer brushed aside in discussion but weighed with all seriousness. People bowed when he passed in the street.

"Fancy that," Titus told his grandfather, and went to greet his guests.

VIX

One year, just one year, and Armenia was gone.

"All Rome will rejoice at such a victory," one of the Tenth's tribunes said pompously—a useless highborn twit whose voice was still breaking. "The day is ours!"

"Easy there, sonny," I admonished him, but the little squirt was right. All Rome *was* rejoicing when word went out that we had a new province, and with hardly a pause for breath or to celebrate the new year, we marched on Mesopotamia. Our first official foray into the Parthian Empire, and how we cheered when we saw those flat fertile lands stretched out between the vast fork of the Tigris and the Euphrates.

A land in two colors: the flat sand of desert blushing into green beside the rivers; rocks and dunes turning to grassy pastures where goats grazed and nomad shepherds hastily collapsed their tents at the sight of the Roman eagles. A thousand tributaries threaded the land between the rivers, and our feet squelched from dawn to dusk as we crossed one ford after another. Trajan crossed every ford and bridge on foot beside us, bawling out bawdy marching songs, and I cuffed tears from my eyes to see him, so strong and sturdy at more than sixty years of age, making us younger men speed our steps, his iron-gray head bare under the sun. A good portion of the army was cuffing their eyes right along with me. There is no more sentimental creature in the world than the average Roman foot soldier.

We trapped Mesopotamia in a vast fork that year, Lusius Quietus moving east and the Emperor west. I was on permanent loan to Quietus now; he liked my fast-marching men who could be counted on to keep up with his cavalry and could buttress an attack with one hard smash of a charge or lie in wait in the thick of night to jump out of the dark with screams and steel. Hard fights and heady days—this war was wine, it was song, it was a woman but with none of the complications.

We lost Julius that summer in a night attack. I'd swept up a score of men to chase after what was left of a Mesopotamian cohort after we'd shattered their camp in the dead of night, and when I returned I found Julius lying on his back with a broken spear in his side and his eyes reflecting the moon. I wept, and Boil howled as he wrenched the spear from Julius's side, and I held my *optio* as he beat his big fists against my shoulders in helpless rage. The two of us dug a grave for Julius with our own hands, ordering the other men back when they tried to help. We laid Julius in the fertile black earth on the bank of the Euphrates, and I buried him with two more campaign tokens that I stripped off my own breastplate in mark of the two enemies he'd taken down before the spear took his life. One of my best scouts was a stone-mason's son, and I had him carve a stone with Julius's name. "Carve in that he was a descendant of the noble Julius Caesar."

"Was he?" My scout looked skeptical.

"He was."

The whole century stood attention around Julius's grave and one by one poured wine from their skins into the earth. Good men. They might not like me, but they liked my reputation, they liked bragging up their latest feats to the other soldiers, and they boasted there wasn't a century in the whole Tenth who could do what we did. Whether they were lumped turtle formation in one vast shielded square or whipping through a phalanx of Mesopotamian soldiers in forty separate scream-ing pairs, there didn't seem to be a fight my men could lose that year. They were the tip of the spear; they were hardness; they were death. Mesopotamia fell. I jumped up another rank.

Now, now, now.

We wintered in Antioch again at the end of that year. "Thank God," Mirah said, having somehow managed to find us a tiny room of our own on the ground floor of a tall tenement building in the western quarter of the city. "Not that I don't like a little adventure, and it is lovely seeing all this beautiful countryside before you and your locust band of soldiers move through and destroy it, but I'll be happy to give birth to this baby in a bed and not a wagon."

"You're bigger this time around, aren't you? Well, not you," I said hastily as my wife's eyes shot daggers. "You're slim as ever—look at those ankles! Just the baby, I mean. It's bigger." Mirah had quickened again when Dinah turned a year old, but I didn't mind. Our daughter wasn't much trouble: a placid baby who slept soundly at night and was even now cooing to herself and crawling around the hard-packed dirt floor with a crude little wooden horse Antinous had carved for her. At least I thought it was a horse. I'd been teaching him how to handle a knife and he might know how to stab someone with it, but he couldn't whittle worth a damn. He sat frowning in the corner now, hacking bits of wood off a crude block. "What's that going to be?" I asked him, sinking down on the edge of the bed. I'd spent so many months in bedrolls on hard ground, a mattress felt too soft for sleeping.

"Don't know." He turned the block over, optimistic. "I could make blocks, for the new baby?"

"You're a gem, Antinous." Mirah massaged the bulk under her apron. "Ooof, he's kicking like a mule."

"Sounds like it hurts." I winced.

"Not a bit; it's thrilling. Just means the baby will be big and strong." She patted her stomach again, proudly. "Hannibal might be a good name for this one."

"I thought I'd name him after Trajan," I suggested. "Or one of his names, anyway. Marcus Ulpius Trajan—"

"No son of mine is being named Ulpius!" Mirah reached around her own bulk to unlace her shoes. Her belly might be up under her chin, but she carried it with all her usual quick energy. No graceless waddling for my wife: Heat, sand, spiders, and hardship hadn't managed to slow her down, and neither did carrying a child.

"What about Marcus, then?" I pulled her feet into my lap. "That's not a bad name for a boy. And I knew another Marcus besides Trajan, a senator who gave me my start in the legions in the first place. That's a good pair of men for any boy to be named after."

"I don't know if I want to name a child of mine after a Roman emperor." Mirah winced pleasurably as my fingers began to massage her little arched feet. "I know you adore Trajan, Vix, but have you even heard what's happening outside Parthia?"

"Of course I have. I get all Titus's letters, don't I, and he always knows everything going on." Titus had some new public office back in

Rome and was apparently much relied upon. The bugger had gone and
gotten important on me, but his letters read just the same as ever. He
still quoted philosophers I hadn't read and told me I was a savage for
drinking unwatered wine.

"All this unrest with the Jews he talked about in his last letter,"
Mirah was saying. "In Cyrenaica, Cyprus, Alexandria. Grumbling
everywhere, and according to Titus, all Trajan does is send troops in
to squash things."

"Stops the grumbling, doesn't it?"

"For now." Mirah groaned as my thumbs pressed her heels. "All
your precious Emperor wants is the rest of the world to stand still and
not bother him so he can go conquering on till the end of time. That's
who you want our son to be?"

"A man like Trajan? Yes."

"Trajan has his head in the sand, and so do you," Mirah said. "You're
both living in a dream, out here on the edge of the world. People have
their own troubles all over Rome. And even Trajan can't squash trouble
just by sending troops down to step on it."

"It's worked so far."

Mirah gave me the one-sided flick of a smile that meant she thought
I was a fool but would let me get away with it. I liked provoking that
smile sometimes, just for fun.

"We don't have to name the baby after Trajan," I conceded. "You're
the one pushing him out, so I reckon you can be the one to name him."
Maybe that would soften her up for the inevitable fight about the *brit*
ceremony. I was all for tradition; Mirah and I kept Shabbat at the end
of every week when I wasn't away fighting, and I said the prayers with
her for a half a dozen more religious festivals throughout the year. But
ancient ceremony or no, nobody was getting anywhere near my son's
groin with a knife when he was only eight days old.

Little Dinah abandoned her wooden horse and came crawling over,
latching onto my sandal. I leaned down and lifted her up with one hand,

balancing her on Mirah's stomach. "Feel that, little girl? That's your brother kicking."

"He's trying to kick his way out," Mirah complained happily. "Thank God this baby will be born in a bed."

As things turned out, it wasn't.

After the Saturnalia celebrations, I hauled my men up for drills. I bellowed at Boil for a while for letting the century get rusty just because we were wintered up, and then I let everyone pair off and go through their paces while I tossed Antinous my *gladius*. "Let's see if you're as rusty as the men," I said. "Drill number five."

"Been practicing," he assured me, and I stood back with folded arms and watched him swing through the patterns. His wide brown eyes were narrowed in concentration as he swung the sword. Too heavy a weapon for a boy his age, but he'd grow into it. I'd been even younger when my father started training me. Antinous was nine now, still pretty-faced, but he fought his good looks as hard as he could. He nurtured his scrapes devotedly, hoping they'd turn into scars, and he'd stolen my dagger so he could shear his curly hair down to a half inch. "Let's see them call me a girl now," he'd said, showing me his ragged scalp.

"I must say, he's gotten tougher," Mirah approved. "He used to wilt like a plucked flower when the other children teased him for looking so pretty. Now he just starts swinging."

"You don't mind mopping up his bloody noses and scraped knees?"

"Of course not. It's a hard world; every boy should know how to defend himself. Especially one who looks like that."

But Antinous didn't really look much like a girl anymore. He was a skinny, scrappy, scabby-kneed little soldier who swung my sword like a veteran. "Again, twice as slow," I called out. "You're already fast, now we build your stamina—"

That was when the ground started to swing under my feet. For a moment I wondered if I was drunk, but the other men were reeling too, and I heard shouts of alarm. The earth bucked and I dropped to my knees, hearing the splinter of glass somewhere. I clutched at the ground with both fists, trying to hang on to the cobbles, and my men were all doing the same. I heard the crash of masonry, of stones falling. It was an age before the ground stilled.

"What," I breathed, looking up, "was that?" At my side, Antinous was looking up cautiously. He'd dropped to the ground in a ball but kept a firm grip on my sword.

"Just an earthquake," one of my scouts volunteered. He was on his feet already, dusting his hands off. The rest of us stayed huddled where we were, staring warily at the ground. "The earth trembles. Quite common where I come from, near Pompeii. No one pays attention to them back home, unless it's a big one."

"Not too comforting," I shot back. "Considering that Pompeii's just a heap of ash and rubble!" Warily I stood up. I wanted to stay down and possibly mutter a prayer or two, as little Antinous and half my men were doing, but a centurion had to set an example.

Another roar of falling stone sounded. "Now the buildings start falling down," the Pompeiian added cheerfully. "My father was a builder—he said earthquakes were always good for the building trade, since half the houses fall down and have to be rebuilt. Centurion, where are you going?"

I was sprinting for a horse, and Antinous was right on my heels.

The Emperor, I heard later, narrowly escaped dying. A roof caved in on him, but he managed to jump out of a window, though one of his visiting consuls was crushed by a falling beam. A great many others were killed too in the collapsed wreckage: dignitaries from Rome, Antiochene officials, visiting embassies. I heard screams from people trapped in their fallen houses, but I never stopped.

Until I rounded a corner and saw that nothing was left of the tenement where I'd left Mirah and our daughter but a heap of rubble.

SABINA

Sabina's reed sandals made no sound on the path, but Hadrian spoke without turning to face her. "How did you like Egypt?"

"Beautiful." She halted beside him where he stood in the shade of a laurel tree, hands clasped behind his back as he stared at the glassy surface of the little spring. "I took a barge down the Nile like Queen Cleopatra. And I stayed in Alexandria, Bubastis, Karnak—"

"Yes, Plotina sent me word of your . . . exploits."

"For such a virtuous woman, Plotina has a fevered imagination."

Hadrian's eyes lifted from the pool at his feet and traveled deliberately over Sabina from top to toe. "Aren't you cold?" He eyed the thin linen shift stopping well short of her ankles, the ankh pendant looped about her throat, the golden tan she'd picked up riding a camel to see the great pyramids where the old pharaohs had been buried.

"The cold feels lovely after Egypt."

"You should still cover yourself like a decent woman. And what's *that?*"

"This is Neferu." Sabina scratched the slim neck of the cat in her arms. Hadrian's ever-present pair of hunting hounds whined, and the cat stretched her elongated body and hissed at them. She had sleek dark fur, a haughty triangular face, and huge ears pierced with gold hoop earrings.

Hadrian ran a hand down Neferu's long back; she purred and arched into his fingers. Horses and dogs adored Hadrian, Sabina had noticed often enough—she wasn't surprised that cats did too. "I'll never understand why the Egyptians put earrings on their cats," he observed.

"Neferu's a sacred cat. A gift from the priest at the Temple of Bastet when I stayed for the rites in Bubastis."

Hadrian's brows contracted. "More orgies and strange rituals?"

"Actually, I was trapped for two weeks when the Nile flooded unexpectedly, and I pitched in to help gather the harvest before it could

spoil. The priests invited me to their rites afterward, in thanks." Sabina
lifted scornful brows. "And since when is any god *you* haven't heard of
automatically worshipped with an orgy? You didn't use to be so provincial, Hadrian."

He gave her a cold glance but returned his eyes to the spring. Sabina
tickled Neferu's chin, gazing about. The Gardens of Daphne were
famous: a walled gorge a few miles from Antioch, studded with laurel
and cypress groves even in the winter, artful cascades of water spilling
between the sculpted banks. Sabina could hear soft voices and patter-
ing footsteps as Antiochene couples idled the winding paths. But
Hadrian stood alone, staring into the spring.

"The steward says you spend a great deal of time here," she said.
"The few hours you're not working."

He ignored her. "*Will I go to Egypt someday?*" he whispered, not to
Sabina, and tossed a small coin into the spring. He crouched down,
watching intently as the water's calm surface rippled.

"So what is the all-seeing Castallian Fount telling you this time?"
Sabina put just a touch of mockery into her voice.

"The ripples tell me I will visit Egypt." Hadrian's eyes never blinked
as he watched the pool smooth to glass again. "But not for some years,
which is a pity. I would like to see the Nile in flood. And I've long
thought the style of their buildings interesting. The hypostyle hall I've
heard about, in the Temple of Amun at Karnak—I may add such a hall
to my villa, when I finally build it."

He had not spoken so civilly to Sabina in more than a year. *Then
again, I've hardly spent more than two weeks of that year in his company.*
If her husband would rather sit hunched over his ambitions than travel
the world, Sabina had no intention of following suit. She rather thought
she might go to Epidaurus next. The Asclepeion was famous; people
came from all over the world to be healed there of their ills. *I could work
in the dream hall with the sacred snakes; see if the priests are really bilking
the pilgrims out of their money for false cures. If they are, I'll write Trajan
in a heartbeat and put a stop to it . . .*

"I haven't heard you talk about your villa in a long time," Sabina said finally. If Hadrian could be civil, she was more than happy to follow suit. "Are you finally going to begin building?"

"When I have the funds. When I am Emperor."

Sabina nudged away the hounds who were now sniffing at Neferu's dangling tail. "Still nursing impossible hopes, I see."

"Impossible?" Hadrian looked over his shoulder with that superior expression that always made her fingers itch. "The Castallian Fount assures me it is inevitable."

"It's a pool of water." Sabina's voice was blunt. "You are dreaming if you think Trajan will make you his heir."

"What do you know about it? My efforts have been invaluable to his campaign; without me his legions would have no supplies—"

"Yes, and I'm sure he'll give you a clap on the back and another consulship when he's done. But not the Empire."

"Plotina assures me—"

"Plotina isn't here to whisper in Trajan's ear. I am, though. Even off in Egypt, I wrote Trajan letters every month, and I'll bet he reads mine with more pleasure than Plotina's. Unlike her, I make him laugh. What do you think we laugh about? Or rather, who?"

Hadrian whipped about with his hunter's speed, raising one hand. Neferu lifted her pointed face from Sabina's arm and hissed.

"Hit me if you like," Sabina said. "I'll show Trajan the bruise. I'm to dine with him this evening. He invited me. Did he invite you?"

Hadrian lowered his hand. His face was expressionless. "You will regret this, Vibia Sabina."

"When you're Emperor?" Sabina turned, skirting the dogs, and glided away. "You talk to your puddle about that, and I'll talk to the Emperor. Let's see which of us has better luck."

CHAPTER 23

VIX

It was two days before I found them.

I tore at the heap of stones with my bare hands. Boil pitched in silently beside me, his voice subdued as he organized my men into teams. They worked at my side, joining forces to shift some chunk of rock too big to move alone. Antinous mutely moved whatever stones were small enough for him to lift. I ignored them all, digging frantically through the heap of stone and wood and brick that had been a tenement building. Four stories had all come crashing down, and dear God, my Mirah had been on the bottom. I found the still and battered body of a woman, and my heart hammered, but it was an old woman; her hair only looked red because it was bloody. The woman's daughters wailed, and I realized there were more people digging through the wreckage, neighbors of mine who had lived in the rooms above or beside me, looking for their buried families. All through the city, people were digging and calling for husbands, sisters, children. There were looters all through the city too, men combing the wreckage for valuables. I saw a young man eagerly searching the pockets of a woman with a crushed leg lying in the street—sifting through her clothes, ignoring her whimpers of agony. I came up silently behind the young man and snapped his neck between my hands. Antinous stared at me, but I couldn't find a word to say.

Boil made me sleep sometimes. I tumbled down on the ground in my cloak and slept till I could rise and start digging again. My hands were two bloody slabs of meat. "We won't find her, Centurion," a big African who was one of my best fighters told me, and I ignored him.

On the morning of the third day, Boil found a foot.

A small high-arched foot and a trim ankle, peeking out from a heap of stones and fallen beams.

A lean Spaniard I'd had to flog last month for insubordination put a hand on my shoulder. I shook it off and fell on the pile of ruins, clawing the stones away. Two splinters ran under my thumbnail clear up to the knuckle, but the pain was distant.

Boil and the massive African grunted to shift a fallen beam, while I uncovered my wife's little foot, then a shin gray with dust, a leg with a tattered woolen hem lying limp over the knee . . .

A voice sounded somewhere from the heap of fallen beams, weak but still waspish. "Took you long enough, husband."

The wall had fallen, but the brick oven hadn't. Mirah had grabbed up little Dinah and huddled against the oven, and then the roof had come down. The falling beams should have crushed them both, but two had fallen at an angle over the stove. A rain of stones had trapped Mirah's ankle, but the beams and the oven had given her a tiny pocket of protected space. My men were cursing, yelling, straining to shift one of the beams, while I peered down through the gap I'd made in the stones. I could just see a strip of my wife's hair, a section of bruised forehead.

"You're hurt." My heart knocked like a drum in my chest as I saw the blood. She had a broad smear of it across her cheek, dried dark brown.

"No," she said, her voice hoarse. "That's birth blood."

"*What?*"

"I had a good knock from those beams. The baby started coming before the stones even settled." Her head moved, and I saw my wife's eye glaring up at me through the gap. "You swore this one would be born in a house. I didn't think I had to mention that the house should still be *standing*."

"*Move faster!*" I screamed at my men.

"We're fine, all three of us." Mirah's voice was tremulous, but it was also, God help me, cheerful. "I helped the midwife when my cousins had babies, so I knew how to tie off the cord . . ."

"*Move! Move!*"

A creaking squeal of timber, and the beam slid to one side. I jumped down where its end had rested, reached into the gap in a tumble of sliding shale, and lifted out my wife: filthy, bloody, tired, and smiling.

"Water," she rasped, and then I crushed her against me. My heart was still hammering, and I still heard the screams in my head that had begun when I found her foot in the rubble. Then I realized the screams were real, and coming in angry wails from the pair of bundles in Mirah's arms. One was Dinah, her swatch of black hair just visible over the shawl Mirah had wrapped her in. The other—

"We have another daughter." Mirah gave me a screaming little bundle of limbs still covered in dried birth blood and inadequately swaddled in her mother's blue shawl. "Thank God she came easy."

I could hear my men whispering. "That's a good omen, that is," the Spaniard was nodding. "Born in blood and ruins, but still kicking. Just like us." Boil shouted for someone to bring food, water, and bandages for the ankle Mirah held gingerly off the ground, and Antinous was off running before any of the men could jump to it. All I could do was hold her and tremble.

"I promised you'd have a midwife," I told Mirah numbly. "I promised you'd have a bed—and proper food—"

"Well, there was food of a sort." Mirah looked down at her round breasts. "My milk came in as soon as she was born, and then I could nurse them both." She lowered her voice. "I even squeezed some out to drink myself. Two days without water, well, you do what you can. I thought we could name her Chaya? It just means *alive*." Mirah's chin quivered for just an instant. "She could have died."

"You all could have died," I said, and felt tears sliding down my face. My wife, who had just been dug out of her own grave with a crying baby in each arm, ended up being the one to comfort me.

TITUS

Titus was just passing the long pool in the gardens of Senator Norbanus's house when a wave rose up from the surface out of nowhere and splashed his sandals. He stopped, looking back at the water, but the surface sparkled innocently. He turned toward the house again, and another wave came up and wetted the hem of his toga. This time he heard a giggle.

"I thought I'd offended the fountain's water nymph," he said aloud. "But I'm fairly certain nymphs don't giggle."

"I think they do." Faustina's sleek blond head rose over the pool's marble edge at his feet, and she grinned up at him. "Nymphs are very silly. All they ever do in myths is run around drinking with satyrs and periodically get turned into trees."

"A fair point. Isn't it a little cold for swimming?" Spring had arrived, but the sunlight was still thin on the new grass. "Nymphs can't catch cold, but I believe senators' daughters can."

"I like it. The cold water's like getting hit by lightning—afterward I get warm and sleepy and doze all afternoon." Faustina cocked her head up at him. "You look very serious and official."

"I'm afraid I'm in a very serious, official mood right now. Is your father inside?"

"Yes, but my mother will murder you if you disturb him. He isn't feeling well, and she's trying to get him to rest."

Titus bit back a curse. Several days of pondering and wondering before he'd decided to consult Senator Norbanus, and now he'd have to come back later.

"Is it important?" Faustina folded her wet arms along the pool's marble edge.

"I don't know. I was hoping he could tell me." Titus shifted the armload of scrolls and tablets he'd toted along in one arm. Almost too much to carry alone, but he hadn't wanted to trust them to a slave. "Something about the finances for the public baths."

"What?"

"Nothing worth disturbing your swim for—"

"Financial irregularity?" Faustina said briskly.

"Well, yes."

"Maybe I can help." She climbed the marble steps of the pool, water shedding off her shoulders and dripping from the edge of her linen tunic: Venus rising from the waves. Of course Venus was usually naked, but Faustina's tunic had been soaked into such clinging transparency that it didn't really hide . . . anything. Titus coughed, keeping his eyes firmly on the ground as she strode unselfconsciously before him into the house. The little girl he'd carried home from Sabina's wedding at age five had done quite a lot of growing up. He felt more comfortable when she picked up her discarded *palla* and swathed herself in it.

"So what have you got there?" Faustina sank into a chair in the atrium, indicating his armload of scrolls. "Let's have a look."

"I wouldn't dream of boring a lovely girl with dull financial matters."

"If not dull financial matters, it'll be suitors with dull poetry," Faustina warned. "I know which of the two I'd rather have."

"I thought most girls liked being courted."

"You'd think so." Faustina sent a slave into the house for drinks. "I thought I'd love it. I remember all the men hanging around after Sabina, and I couldn't wait till it was my turn. Now it is, and I find it's boring. The old men drone politics at me, the young men drone war stories at me, and they all try to look down my dress."

"You could try not to look quite so lovely," Titus suggested. "Though that would take rather a lot of effort. Cut off your hair? Wear hemp tunics and soot? Black out a tooth?" He shook his head. "No, I'm afraid it's useless."

"That's why I like you, Titus." Faustina tilted her head, delighted. "Any man can tell a woman she's beautiful, but you're clever enough to do it when her hair looks like a wet mop. Here, have some *mulsum*"— she tugged the nearest scroll out of his hand and replaced it with a cup of hot honeyed wine from the slave—"and I'll have a look at your papers."

Titus gave up and sat beside her. He didn't have any other duties today, after all. And besides, Sabina's last letter from Antioch had asked him to keep an eye on her little sister. *According to my father she's got more suitors now than Helen of Troy, and I'd hate to see her follow in my footsteps and lose her head over someone impossible.* No danger there, from the look of things.

Faustina pulled her chair up beside Titus's, pointing to a line of the scroll in her hand. "I assume there are receipts to match all these entries."

"Yes, right here." Titus pointed in turn, taking a sip of the warm honeyed wine. "Where did you get so good at numbers?"

"My mother taught Sabina and me to do the household accounts," Faustina said absently. "Sabina didn't apply herself much, but I did. What's that tablet there?"

"Copies of orders made from a quarry. If you look here . . ."

Half an hour later, Faustina blew out a speculative breath and looked up. "Well," she said, "you're being cheated."

Titus looked over the spread of scrolls, tablets, slates, and scribbled scraps now occupying the entire table. "I know."

"I suppose *you're* not being cheated, really," Faustina amended. "But Trajan's public baths are. Someone's skimming off the building funds, and they're skimming a *lot*."

"I came to that conclusion myself last week," Titus said, glum. "The question is, who's the thief, and what can I do about it. Because this isn't some freedman lining his purse with a bit skimmed off the top."

"It comes down to a question of access," Faustina said. "Who has the reach for this kind of skimming?"

"I've looked into that matter all week, and I can tell you that not one of my underlings could be responsible for anything on this level. They simply don't have the influence—I don't have it myself." Titus looked at Faustina in surprise. "Did your mother instruct you in the finer points of financial fraud as well as household accounts?"

"Of course. Slaves and freedmen are always trying to skim." Faustina twisted her wet hair into a rope, pulling it over one shoulder. "Flour stolen from the storeroom or marble stolen from the quarry delivery; it's all just money. And it seems to me that if you want to find your thief, you have two choices. Start looking up the ladder . . ."

"Or?"

"Or don't. Because whoever's stealing this much won't want to stop, and if they're higher up than you, it's not someone you want angry."

Titus thought of the bathhouse, its walls rising from the foundations now as gracefully as Faustina had risen from the pool. "I shall take it under advisement."

They sat in silence for a while. Titus tapped a stylus slowly against the table. Faustina piled her wet hair on top of her head, the curved ends still sending drops of water sliding down her neck.

"You're going to try to stop this anyway, aren't you?" she said at last.

"Well, yes." The Imperial household . . . Empress Plotina had hundreds of stewards and secretaries with oversight into official projects; any one of them might be using the Imperial name to help themselves. He said as much to Faustina.

"It's a start." Faustina took the stylus out of Titus's hand, jabbing it through the knot of her wet hair to keep it in place. "Be careful, Titus."

"The Empress will support me, I'm sure." Only someone as relentlessly virtuous as Empress Plotina would understand Titus's indignation in the first place, really. *Everyone steals from public works*, most officials in Rome would be far more likely to scoff. *Everyone skims, everyone steals, everyone helps themselves. It's the way of the world.*

Maybe it is, Titus thought. *But not on* my *project.*

VIX

By the end of that year, Parthia was ours. Adenystrae, Babylon, Seleucia, Ctesiphon—one impossibly named city after another fell.

It's getting very difficult to keep up with all these victories, Titus wrote me in one of his letters. *I gather you've marched over Gaugamela, much like Alexander, and with much the same result. The Senate spends half its time these days just trying to figure out who all the players and heroes in this drama are. One of them, I've heard, is you. Congratulations on making First Spear.*

I'd done it. First centurion in the Tenth Fidelis, and one of the youngest ever to achieve that rank. Maybe *the* youngest; I didn't know. There were plenty who hated me for it, plenty who muttered that I'd never have risen so high and so fast if Trajan didn't favor me, or if the camp fevers and the Parthians weren't making so many vacancies among the ranks of the centurions. No fever or Parthian had managed to kill me yet, though, and so Trajan himself bypassed tradition and quite a few other candidates and made me First Spear of the Tenth Fidelis. The former First Spear had been transferred back to Rome, and he looked very sour as he handed his insignia to me. I'd be prefect of the camp next, and after that—well, maybe my impossible dream of commanding a legion wasn't so out of reach after all.

"I'll get it," I told Mirah as she put the girls to bed in their little cot in the next room. "Two more years of this war, and I'll get it."

"God forbid the war end, then," she said dryly, kissing both our daughters as she tucked the blanket around them. Both our girls were pink-skinned and dark-haired, having somehow missed the reddish hair of both their parents, and they looked like identical little rosebuds squeezed together in sleep. "Pretty as pictures," Mirah said, admiring our girls. "Goodness, I hope they don't grow up as pretty as Antinous."

"Why?" Antinous was almost ten now, growing like a young sapling, and what he was growing into was something arresting. The youthful pudginess was dropping away from his face and revealing starkly beautiful bones: a firmly modeled jaw, a carved nose like a god on a temple, cheekbones sharp enough to cut marble. I hadn't been able to remember Demetra's face for years, but it came back to me now every time I looked at her son.

"Because looks like his just mean trouble. You know at least three men have come up to me on the street and offered to *buy* him?" Mirah wrinkled her nose. "You wouldn't believe what they offered. Or how hard they were slavering. I wanted to take a bath afterward."

"Antiochenes and pretty boys," I muttered. "I'd better take him with me on campaign this year."

"Won't that just make things worse? Roman soldiers are even worse than Antiochenes!" My wife's mouth firmed. "Vix, I know what goes on between men in your camps, and I know you take an easy view of it. But that doesn't make it right."

"Not when it involves my nine-year-old son, it's not right." I dropped a kiss on the part in her hair. "Don't worry, we'll keep him safe."

"You'll have to do it yourself, I'm afraid, because I'm staying in Antioch this year. Hard enough following the legion with one baby, let alone two. We'll stay cozy in the city, thank you."

"Just not in a ground-floor apartment," I made her promise. I missed having Mirah beside me on campaign that year, but there was enough army business in Antioch that I could manage visits often enough. I'd come through the door calling Mirah's name, Antinous at my heels; Dinah would toddle over to cling to my boot and I'd set my helmet down on her head and laugh when she took it off and began chewing on the feathered crest. And Antinous would pry Dinah off my boot and toss her in the air, and Mirah would come in with Chaya on her hip, wiping her hands on her apron and scolding me for not letting her know we were coming; she would have bought a goose if she'd known she'd be feeding five, or more like seven considering how much it took to fill my bottomless hole of a stomach . . .

"This war has been good to us," I said, and held out my arm as Mirah closed the door of our bedchamber. Her hair gleamed red in the last flare of light as she blew out the lamp, and I could hear the uneven pad of her feet as she came to bed and slid in beside me. She limped a little now at the end of the day, when she was tired. The ankle she'd broken in the earthquake had healed well but stiff.

"I know the war's been good to us." Mirah plaited her fingers together with mine under the blankets. "But surely that's a sin of some kind, rejoicing in the benefits of war? It doesn't feel right."

"It isn't a sin to be among the winners."

"Even when the winners rape and loot their way across the world?"

"My men don't." I didn't allow it, and Trajan discouraged it too. "I want a province capable of paying decent taxes at the end of all this," was the way he put it when he told his legates to keep their soldiers under control.

"I got a letter from Uncle Simon today," Mirah was saying, drawing a circle on my bare chest with her finger. "He got his grant of land in Judaea—he says he's moving his family there by the end of the year."

"Bad time for it," I said. There had been a Jewish revolt in Cyrene, or maybe it was Cyrenaica. Trajan had dispatched my old commander Quietus and his cavalry back to Mesopotamia to keep order there, before the revolt spread.

"Judaea outlasts everything." Her head twisted on my shoulder as she looked at me through the dark. "Maybe we should settle there."

"What?" I laughed.

"You're not a common soldier anymore, tied to the Tenth. Centurions are always being transferred between legions. Maybe when your term as First Spear is done, and the invasion is over"—I could almost hear her little nose wrinkling—"you could angle for a posting in Judaea. Settle among our own people."

"My people are in Britannia," I pointed out. "About as far from Judaea as it's possible to get."

"Judaea is the real home of every Jew." Firmly. "Us too. I'd like the girls to see it. It's all very well to haul them around in reed baskets behind an army when they're babies, but they should grow up somewhere proper and settled."

"Later." I closed my eyes, yawning. "When we finish with Parthia. I go back to Ctesiphon tomorrow . . ."

Did I really want to finish with Parthia, though? Did my Emperor? I remember something Trajan said to me one fine summer evening on the deck of a boat, shortly after the capture of Ctesiphon. I'd made a report to him on the rumored Jewish unrest in Cyprus, standing in my armor before his desk. It was supposed to be a simple pleasure cruise down the Tigris, a few days of sunlit leisure for the man who had conquered three new provinces, but Trajan was already bored with leisure. He'd dragged his desk out onto the deck and sat surrounded by scrolls and jotting notes on a slate. "We'll need to raise the ferry charges across the Tigris for camels and horses," he said absently when I paused. "Do you have a report from Quietus about the Jews in Cyprus?"

"Rumors of a revolt, Caesar. Roman citizens murdered, the usual whispers."

"What whispers?"

"That the Jews eat their victims, make belts out of their guts, and tan their skins to wear for cloaks."

"What do you make of it?" Trajan squinted at a slate, then held it up closer. "Gods' bones, my eyes are going—"

"My wife's a Jew, Caesar." I fingered a corner of the faded blue scarf I now wore wrapped around my arm under the greave, ever since the earthquake when I'd pulled Mirah out of the rubble. "She's yet to make a belt out of my entrails, even when I track mud on her floors instead of wiping my feet."

"Good man. I'm sending you to Cyprus; if you have a Jewish wife you may have a lighter touch feeling them out. Take that fast-moving century of yours with you."

"I'm having all the centuries trained for speed now, Caesar." Now that I was First Spear, I could make the other centurions do it my way. They didn't like it, but they still had to obey. Hell's gates, but I loved being in charge.

"Take a few cohorts, then," Trajan decided, "and go make me a report from Cyprus."

"Yes, Caesar."

He flung down his stylus and rose from the desk, stumping past me toward the railing of the boat. It was near sunset; the river was gold in the light and the banks purple. I looked overhead to the sail snapping in the breeze; it was embroidered with Trajan's name and titles, all in gold. In the setting sun the name looked like it had been written in fire.

"Look at that boat there." Trajan pointed, and I came to join him at the railing. His guards stood nearby, and couriers with message cases and secretaries waiting to take dictation and a few lounging members of the Imperial retinue, but he spoke only to me, the two of us leaning on the rail of a boat like any pair of soldiers enjoying an idle chat. "That barge with the red sail. She'll be heading to Charax, and then to India. Imagine that. India!"

I couldn't imagine it. Did the world extend so far? Surely if we went any farther east, we'd fall right off the edge of the horizon. "What's India like, Caesar?"

"I don't know." He sounded wistful. "I'd like to find out—keep marching, keep conquering. That's a life worth living. You want to go to India, Vercingetorix?"

"Not if we have to sail there," I said. "I hate boats."

He laughed. "March overland then. I'll give you half my legions to march from the north; the other half will come with me and aim for the coast. We'll meet in the middle. How does that sound?"

"Like a good plan, Caesar."

"Maybe it is. Gods, I wish I were twenty-two instead of sixty-two."

"Sixty-two or no, Caesar, I'm there behind you. Even if you make me go by boat."

Trajan lifted an arm and waved at the red-sailed boat gliding past on her eastern journey. "Oh, get on with you. Go to Cyprus. Find out why in the name of all the gods the Jews are rebelling again."

I saluted, took my leave, assembled my men, did a fast march back toward Antioch, and took ship for Cyprus.

When I landed—

That's a day I don't like to remember.

The dreams are bad enough.

PLOTINA

"My dear, what a vision you are." Plotina kissed the tall blond column of a girl on both cheeks. "Senator Norbanus, I hear your Faustina is the toast of Rome. You've not arranged a marriage for her yet?"

"She'll make her own choice, as long as the Emperor approves it." Senator Norbanus had to tilt his head back to smile at his much-taller daughter. "I admit I'm quite selfishly glad she hasn't chosen yet."

"I've met none who measure up to my father." Faustina kissed his cheek. "Oh, gods, here comes that tedious old prat Servianus. Father, do you mind if I hide?"

"I'd hide myself if I could." Marcus waved her away, tolerant, and Faustina curtsied swiftly to Plotina and disappeared into the atrium full of guests to reappear at her mother's side. *Nineteen years old*, Plotina thought, *and what a picture*. Beautiful but demure in her floating yards of pale yellow silk; vivacious but dignified with her greetings for each guest. A royal pedigree and a royal dowry to match; hips made for babies and manners made for a palace. Why, *why* hadn't little Faustina been born the elder daughter? She'd have made a far better wife for Dear Publius than her globe-trotting harlot of a sister. Plotina closed her eyes, thinking of the dinner party when That Dress had shocked so many of Dear Publius's associates. Thank goodness the slut was off disporting herself in Ephesus or Syria or someplace—far enough away, at any rate, for her escapades to be filtered and muted by distance. Irritatingly, there was far more discussion in Rome about the hospital Sabina had founded in some Pannonian sinkhole, or the dowries she donated to poor freeborn girls in Campania, than there was gossip about her lovers! Plotina had to give the little whore credit; she was certainly clever enough to cover her misdoings with a cloak of good works.

The guests were taking their places now in the triclinium, where the dining couches had been banished for long rows of chairs. A public reading of Senator Norbanus's latest treatise—he might have retired from the Senate this year, but his pen flowed on unchecked. Plotina frowned, taking her own place of honor at the head of the guests. Really, what a relief it would be when the good senator was finally taken to the afterlife, or at least stopped meddling in politics. His opinion still carried far too much weight for her taste, and he had never been more than politely supportive of Dear Publius. Still, the occasion offered certain opportunities.

"Legate Urbicus! Might I have a word? Former consul Hadrian wrote to me so glowingly of your exploits in Germania . . . you are acquainted with him, of course? He is seeking support on one or two small matters I might draw to your attention . . . I understand you are looking for a wife. Perhaps I might draw your eye to Senator Norbanus's daughter Faustina? Such a beauty, and the dowry . . . yes, I have some influence with the girl's family. I could ensure her choice; perhaps you should speak with Hadrian soon. He would welcome your support . . ."

The speaker rose to begin the reading, and Legate Urbicus hastened off to his seat, quite puffed up with promises. Plotina smoothed the folds of her dark-green gown over her lap, pleased. It wasn't just funds that kept Dear Publius climbing the ladder, oh no. Supporters, allies,

friends in high places—far more important, and such men would rear
back like offended snakes to be offered *money*. Other things, though,
proved more welcome.

"Magistrate, perhaps you will sit by me? We might have a word or
two for one another." Plotina dropped her voice to a murmur, inaudible
below the orator's. Senator Norbanus had declared himself too old for
public oration and had invited young Titus Aurelius to perform the
reading for him. The senator had never invited Dear Publius to read
one of his treatises, and Dear Publius was his own son-in-law! No doubt
the good senator, just like everyone else in Rome, was falling all over
Titus Aurelius simply because his grandfather had left him such a
fortune. Plotina frowned as the young man took his place, rolling off
the first words of the treatise in a confident measured baritone, and
turned back to the magistrate still waiting at her side. "I heard about
the death of your wife, magistrate—so sad. I understand you are looking to marry again soon . . . a mother for your children, yes, very sensible. Might I suggest Senator Norbanus's daughter Faustina? That's
her in the front row, in the yellow. A beauty, isn't she? I assure you I
have some standing with her family and can easily influence her choice.
Perhaps I might talk to you about one or two judicial matters that have
arisen recently? Matters very dear to the heart of former consul
Hadrian . . ."

Plotina sat back, fanning herself. Young Titus made a joke to end
the first portion of the reading, and she laughed along with the rest of
the audience, not listening. Young Faustina jumped up to congratulate
him during the brief interval, and Plotina watched her benignly. She'd
make a fine wife—to the legate or the magistrate, whoever proved more
useful. *I'll invite the girl to the palace to assist with the weaving*, Plotina
decided. *She'll be honored, and I can give her a hint what choice to make.*

Though it really was a pity the girl couldn't just marry Dear Publius.

CHAPTER 24

VIX

"... Vix?"

"What?" I bashed the stopper off a new jug of wine, sloshed a cup brim-full, and drank it off without water. It burned all the way down.

"You've hardly said a word since you came back." Mirah eyed me cautiously, Chaya balanced on her hip and Dinah clinging to her skirts. "Aren't you going to tell me what happened?"

I grunted, refilling my cup. Two days since the ship had brought my men and me back from Cyprus. Mirah and the children had run to the door to greet me, beaming, but I'd brushed right past my wife in her new red dress and the girls in their rose smocks, straight to the wine, and started drinking. Two days later, and I still wasn't nearly as drunk as I wanted to be.

"*Vix*." Mirah was starting to sound exasperated now. "Won't you talk to me?"

"No," I said, and drank off another cup. Little Dinah retreated behind her mother, hearing the harshness in my voice, and Antinous gave me a long troubled look from the corner where he sat practicing his letters. He hadn't been with me in Cyprus, thank God, but he'd tagged along on enough campaigns by now to know the look on my face after a bad fight. He'd taken one glance at me when I returned from Cyprus, and retreated to the very back of the house.

"How long are you going to sit there getting soused and staring at the wall?" Mirah's voice rose. "You go back to the legion in two more days, Vix, and you're not in any condition to ride."

I held a swallow of wine in my mouth until my teeth burned. Didn't help. I swallowed.

"What *happened* in Cyprus?" I heard the rustle of my wife's skirts as she came closer. "You were gone more than a month; I thought it was only going to be—"

"Takes time, digging graves."

Little Dinah peeked out from behind Mirah's skirts, staring at me through a fringe of dark hair that had escaped its ribbon. I'd buried a little girl just her age. Her hair had been stiff with dried blood. No need for a ribbon.

Mirah looked at me another long moment, then took Dinah by the hand and disappeared into the bedroom, Antinous trotting behind like a young deer. I looked around our lodgings: the usual scrubbed and cheerful domesticity that Mirah managed to impart to all our varied homes. A little frieze of leaves and vines about the door; a pot in the courtyard just outside the door where she grew a few herbs to flavor the soup; a clutter of the children's toys on the floor. So ordinary. So *wholesome.* The whole scene was blurred from all the wine I'd drunk. Or maybe from tears.

Mirah came back alone. She dropped to her knees before me, putting her eyes on a level with mine. "What happened?"

"The Jews in Cyprus revolted." My hand tightened around the cup. "By the time I arrived, it was already all over. Just the bodies to clean up."

She put a hand to her mouth. "Oh. Oh, God."

"No, I didn't see much of Him over in Cyprus."

Mirah jumped to her feet and began to pace, arms folded tight about her neat sashed waist. "It's everywhere." Her voice was taut. "As soon as we came back to Antioch, I started to hear the rumors. In Alexandria they're saying a hundred thousand Jews were slaughtered. And now in *Cyprus*—"

"It wasn't the Jews who were slaughtered in Cyprus." I tossed off the last of the wine in my cup. "They did the slaughtering."

"Good," said my wife.

I stared at her. "Children," I said finally. "Mothers, old women, old men—innocents. Slaughtered."

"The Romans are doing it to the innocents in Alexandria!" Mirah's voice rose. "And in Mesopotamia—dear God, do you know who the Emperor sent to clean out the Jews there? That commander of yours, Lusius Quietus!"

"Mirah—"

"And do you know *how* he cleaned out the province? By killing every Jew he could get his hands on." She gave a little blind shake of her head. "If what you say about Cyprus is true—well, at least they killed a few in return."

"They killed thousands, actually." I rose from my chair. "You know how many I helped bury? There was one woman who looked like you. A little thing with reddish hair. She must have been pretty. Not that I could tell, after she'd been stripped, raped, and stabbed a few dozen times. Roman legionaries aren't the only ones in the world who ravage and murder."

"And what will happen now, because of a few Roman citizens killed in Cyprus?" Her voice was shrill. "How many Jews get to die in return for one Roman woman?"

"Oh, it was more than one," I snarled. "And they couldn't even tell me *why* they went on a killing frenzy. Why they woke up one morning and decided to kill off every neighbor they had who didn't celebrate Shabbat at week's end."

Mirah still stood hugging herself as if she were cold. "You don't understand."

"No, I don't." I turned away from her. "I never will."

"Hundreds of years—" She spoke jerkily. "Being blamed every time a plague comes or a drought hits—being murdered or exiled or robbed of what we own every time a new emperor has a whim—"

"None of that has ever happened to you," I snapped, whirling around again. "You and your family, perfectly peaceful and prosperous and living in the thick of Rome for three generations—"

"When it happens to one, it happens to all. Why do you think we remember Masada, Vix? Because they were our *brothers*. You should know that better than anyone!"

"All I know is that I spent weeks and weeks digging graves." I hurled my cup against the wall and it shattered. "And now I've got orders to go join Quietus in Mesopotamia and probably dig a few more."

"Graves for Jews this time. If there are any left in Mesopotamia." Mirah bit her lip.

"See for yourself. You'll come with me this time, you and the children."

"No. I won't go."

"I'm not leaving you in Antioch if Jews are being killed! With me you'll be safe."

"You think I'll trail after that butcher Quietus?" she shouted. "Have your supper ready every night after you come home from a day of rounding up Jewish rebels? I'm not going. I'm staying here, and so are my daughters."

"*Your* daughters? They're mine too, and you're my wife, and you'll go where I tell you—"

"I wouldn't go with you on this campaign if you held a sword to my throat."

I nearly hit her. She saw it and she put her chin up, daring me. I stalked back to the wine and didn't bother with a cup this time, just lifted the jug in both hands and swigged directly. From behind me I heard a stifled sob and Mirah's light footsteps retreating into the bedroom. I didn't turn, just took another long draught. I drank all the wine in the house that night, but it wasn't enough. I still saw the graves in that sunny little island. Such a pretty place to hold such horrors.

I woke the next day in bright afternoon, still huddled on the floor. My tongue had grown a coat of fur and a blacksmith was pounding sheet iron inside my skull, but someone had unlaced my sandals and dropped a blanket over me. I unpeeled one eye and saw my wife looking at me, perched neat and tidy on my chair, her arms wrapped around her knees. Her eyes were red-rimmed, and her wide mouth had no smiles.

"Urgh." I closed the eye again.

A pause, and I felt her narrow little fingers tangling with mine. She said nothing. I said nothing.

I went back to my legion alone.

Nothing went right after that.

No sooner did I get back to the Tenth than the bad news started to hit. More revolts—Armenia, Mesopotamia, Babylonia, all going up in flames. Every new-conquered territory that had seemed so quiet.

"We're overextended," Boil told me bluntly. I'd made him a centurion in his own right as soon as I made First Spear; he ran his big fingers back and forth through the scarlet crest on his helmet as he gave me his report. "There's a king making trouble in Armenia, and a legate got killed in Mesopotamia last week on a bad scrap of a fight. Too much territory to cover with seven legions."

"Well, we don't have to cover all of it," I said wearily. "Where's the Tenth been dispatched?"

Within twelve hours we were marching. Quietus, that fierce old Berber, greeted me with a hand clasp and a nod. "That your boy?" he demanded, nodding at Antinous, who had once again come along as my page. "Looks less like a girl than he used to."

Antinous beamed. He had a *gladius* of his own now, and a curved Syrian knife he used to hack his hair short whenever it got long enough to even think about curling. Last time he'd decided to shave Dinah and Chaya's heads along with his own. "They wanted haircuts too," Antinous explained, and Mirah shook a rueful head at the sight of our bald daughters and told me maybe I should take Antinous with me on campaign again. I took him, but I kept a close eye on him. Mirah was right; there were plenty in the legions who liked pretty boys, and even with the chopped hair and sunburned face, Antinous was disturbingly hand-some. That was when I got him a *gladius* of his own and told him not to be shy about using it if he had to.

"Can you swing that sword, boy?" Quietus growled at him, also noting the *gladius*. "Or is it just for show?"

"Been swinging it since I was eight," Antinous said proudly. "And Vix is teaching me how to hunt! I can already shoot a rabbit at fifty paces, and—"

I cuffed him to keep still. Quietus just chuckled, and I wondered if Mirah had spoken the truth. If he'd really massacred every Jew in the province he could find.

I didn't ask. Couldn't ask.

We took back Osrhoene, thanks to several nasty little fights and a nice bit of trickery I'd thought up (never mind what). Took a few other cities back too, but it was just a random spot of order in all the chaos. We rode along the Euphrates, and this time I felt eyes assessing us flatly from the reeds, eyes that wanted nothing better than to decorate the spot between my shoulder blades with a dagger hilt. I didn't tumble into sleep half giddy on triumph, as I had when I first marched through this land.

There was a battle late that year, a proper one outside Ctesiphon. The kind of battle I'd dreamed of when I was a boy, rank upon rank of soldiers lined up behind their shields, unbending, unbreaking, the wicked javelin points glistening in the sun. Trajan led us himself, and I saw his mag-nificent gray head from a distance and heard his Praetorians begging him to wear his helmet. I saw my men taut and eager and primed, and touched the amulet around my neck to mutter a quick prayer to the god of war, who in my mind's eye still looked like my father. I muttered another prayer to Mirah's god—the more divine protection before a fight, the better—and then I kicked off my horse and joined the line to fight on foot. I killed six or seven men that day, and those Parthians might part their hair with scented oils and paint kohl around their eyes, but they were savage fighters. I got pressed badly between three men who'd seen me shouting orders and figured that they would crumple my men by taking out their leader. *Idiots,* I thought irritably, *my men would carry this fight straight on over my corpse.* But the Parthians didn't know that, and they pressed around me and I spitted one and thumped my shield boss into a second, but the third would have buried his curved sword in my neck if Philip on my right arm hadn't whipped his javelin through the man's throat. I saw the man look down at the bloody spearhead that had cored his Adam's apple as he crumpled to the trampled ground, and I gave Philip one of those wordless panting battlefield nods that have more thanks in them than an hour of flowery speeches. He nodded back, and then he screamed because another curved Parthian sword had found the gap between his breastplate and backplate, and Philip was dead before the scream choked off in his throat. I screamed back, and everything slipped sideways at that point and later Boil had to tell me three times that the enemy fled—that we won. We won, or so I was told. My hands were gloved in blood up to the elbow after that battle, from hacking apart the Parthian who'd killed Philip, and that was when the men in the Tenth started calling me Vercingetorix the Red.

Another series of lightning-fast marches once the year turned—how many miles of the Empire had I marched? More night marches, more scrappy little fights in squelching marshlands or arid desert sands. Not nearly enough nights in Antioch with Mirah. I came home after a few months' absence, and little Chaya had no idea who I was. She cried and hid her face in her mother's neck at the sight of me in my tall helmet.

"She'll get to know you again," Mirah told me.

"When? I leave tomorrow. The Emperor wants me in Hatra, and after that—"

"Oh," said my wife, her face blank.

"It won't be for long." I tried to sound encouraging. "As soon as we take Hatra, I'll be back here to Antioch."

"You said that after Seleucia."

"Well, you're the one who insisted on staying here," I said shortly.

"They spit on me when I go to the market." Her voice was expressionless. "They ask me if I eat dead babies, like the Jews who rebelled

in Alexandria. I tell them there aren't any Jews left alive in Alexandria
to eat anything, much less babies. That's usually when they spit on me."

"Mirah—"

"I don't take the girls out much. Who spits on little girls?" Her hand
caressed Chaya's cap of fine dark hair, finally grown out from Antinous's
ragged haircut. "Romans."

"Antiochenes," I shot back.

"They're all Romans," Mirah said wearily. "When can we go
home, Vix?"

"I don't know," I said, and kissed her. She kissed me back, and the
dimple by her mouth flickered, but later that night when she thought
I'd gone to sleep I heard her crying. Long shuddering sobs racking the
body she'd curled into a ball as far away on the bed as possible. God
help me, I was glad to get away.

TITUS

"A girl to see you, Dominus."

"It's not Lady Julia Statilia, is it?" A certain notorious young widow,
a friend to Titus's sisters, who had lately decided Titus would make
her a splendid fourth husband. Titus wasn't quite so keen on the idea.
"Tell her I'm out. In fact, tell her I've gone to Africa, or maybe India.
Which one's farther away?"

"It's not that Gorgon at the door, Dominus." Ennia's voice sounded
approving. "It's Senator Norbanus's daughter."

"Faustina?" Titus rose from his desk. "Show her in."

Sabina's little sister swept in, trailing a freedman and a brace of
maids, flushed pink as her gown from the summer heat of the street
outside and looking very pleased with herself. "Tell me I'm wonderful."

"You're wonderful," Titus agreed.

"Tell me I'm clever too. And brave."

"All those things, to be sure." He bowed from behind his desk. "But why?"

Faustina looked smug. "Because I've found your bathhouse thief for you!"

"'To accept a favor is to sell freedom,'" Titus murmured.

"Syrus," Faustina said, triumphant.

"Syrus or Cyrus?"

Her face fell. "There's more than one?"

"Never mind. Either way, I will take your favor and become your slave. Who's my bathhouse thief?"

Faustina turned to Ennia with a dazzling smile. "Ennia, isn't it? Can you take my maids to the kitchens and see they get a cold drink? They've been very patient tramping after me all afternoon, and they deserve to sit down."

"Yes, Lady." Titus's housekeeper gave Faustina a speculative glance from piled blond hair to rose-pink hem. "Come along, girls."

Faustina turned back to Titus as the door of the study closed. "I promised Bassus we'd have privacy for this."

"Bassus?" Titus scrutinized the freedman who had edged into the room behind Faustina's maids and now stood looking nervous and cornered. "Is this our thief?"

The man looked indignant. "See here, Lady Faustina never said anything about being accused—"

"No one's accusing you of anything." Faustina gave his shoulder a cajoling pat, leading him to a chair. "Just sit a moment, will you, while I talk to Titus Aurelius?"

"I knew this would happen," the man muttered. An Imperial freedman, Titus judged from the neat toga and ink-stained hands. A young secretary from Greece, perhaps, making a living off tidy handwriting and a knowledge of languages. "Open my mouth, and soon I'm the one with my hands nailed on a board for being a thief—why did I ever listen to you, Lady?" the man wailed.

"No one's nailing anyone's hands anywhere," Faustina soothed, and dragged Titus off to the opposite corner. "Try not to make him nervous," she whispered. "I had a demon of a time getting him here at all."

"If he's not our thief, then who is he?" Titus lowered his own voice.

"Well." Faustina cleared her throat as if preparing an oration. "We thought your thief might be a steward or official in the Imperial household, someone with access and oversight, but I knew you hadn't had any luck finding out who."

"No, not much." Every trail Titus had followed over the past months seemed to lead to a tablet that had just gone missing from the public archives, or a surveyor who had just been transferred to Africa. Or an official who went red-faced and tight-lipped and refused to say a word even after Titus offered gold. "I feel like keeping my head on my shoulders, thank you," one fat little praetor had told Titus shortly, and left without waiting to be excused. The trail had gone inexplicably cold.

"So," Faustina said, off-hand, "I thought, why not go to the source?"

Titus eyed her in growing trepidation. He looked at Bassus, then back to Faustina. "What did you do?"

Ennia reappeared with a knock, making the freedman jump nervously in his chair. "Cold mulberry infusions," she announced, handing Faustina three chilled goblets. "Make sure Dominus drinks his, Lady. Healthful on a hot day like this. Dominus, I've canceled your afternoon session with the Aurelii clients."

"You didn't have to—"

"Take all the time you need," Ennia interrupted, and thumped out emphatically.

"I like her." Faustina looked after Titus's housekeeper, speculative. "Is she your mistress?"

Titus spluttered. "Now, really—"

"What? I'm not shocked at all. Mother always said she wished my father had had the good sense to keep an in-house freedwoman for a mistress when he was in between wives. If he had, his house and his laundry might have been in a little better order when Mother moved in." Faustina patted the immaculate folds of toga at Titus's shoulder. "I can see Ennia keeps you *and* your house turned out in immaculate fashion."

"This is *not* a matter for discussion!"

"Nothing interesting ever is." Faustina handed a goblet to the nervous freedman with another reassuring pat, then brought the other back to Titus. "Here, drink your mulberries. Now, I go to the palace quite often—Empress Plotina invites me to the palace to help with the weaving, you see. Mostly to tell me which of my suitors I should choose, and hint how much she wishes I'd been the one to marry Hadrian instead of Sabina. Ugh, perish the thought. But last time she got called away for a moment, and I was alone in her rooms, and I just happened to see where she keeps her private accounts. Well," Faustina amended, "I rummaged through her things until I found where she keeps her private accounts."

Titus choked on his drink. "You spied on the *Empress of Rome?*"

"*Spy* is such an ugly word." Faustina's voice was airy. "Let's just say that thanks to good fortune, an empty room, and some concerted snooping, I stumbled upon some interesting information in her files. You know she keeps records on everyone who works in the Imperial household?"

Why? Titus couldn't help wondering. Public matters like judicial cases and lists of public appointments were hardly within Plotina's purview. Why would the Empress of Rome need to keep her own record? "What did you find?"

"Nothing." Faustina shoved aside a stack of scrolls so she could lean against his desk. "That was the odd part. The Empress doesn't buy a yard of linen without recording the cost from her personal accounts—and suddenly huge sums are coming in, but there isn't one word to say where they come from. I couldn't take anything away with me, but I copied down these entries—"

"Hardly indicative," Titus pointed out as she produced a handful of jotted scraps.

"I know. Which is why I spent another week poking among the Empress's freedmen, and finally I found Bassus. One of Plotina's undersecretaries, and when I asked him about these entries he went white as the moon. He refused to say a word about it to me, but I finally persuaded him to come have a talk with you."

"How did you pull that off?"

"Because no one can say no to me," Faustina said candidly. "And because I may have pointed out that you're one of the richest men in Rome and can pay a lot for the information."

"So you've promised gods know how much money out of my purse for gods know what kind of testimony?"

"That's about the long and short of it." Faustina dimpled up at him: fresh and rosy in her airy pink silks, looking as innocent as a newborn lamb. Her dark eyes danced.

Titus closed his own eyes. "Tempted into crime by a slip of a girl," he murmured. "Well, I'm in deep now. Let's hear what your freedman has to say."

Bassus was sweating openly when Faustina led him over. "I don't want trouble, sir," he mumbled. "I just want out. Back to Athens where I can get a post copying lectures. I tell you what I know, and I have to be gone afterward. You understand, sir?"

"A ship to Athens and a purse to keep you there a full year," Titus said. It still astounded him that he could snap his fingers and dispense such sums without even blinking—that he could simply throw money at a problem until it was solved. "What do you have to tell me, Bassus?"

The freedman's eyes slid sideways. Faustina squeezed his arm, giving the kind of smile that had probably served Helen of Troy well when persuading a decade's worth of Trojans to march to their death on her behalf. Bassus gulped.

"The things I've seen," he blurted. "It's not just your bathhouse fund, though that's certainly been milked for all it's worth. Money comes in from a hundred different places, sir, and it goes right back out. Bribes, gifts, loans under the table. Posts being promised or traded or outright sold. People being blackmailed, and there's more than one been banished outright. Lady Faustina's notes; I can show you—"

"Who?" Titus cut in. "*Who* is doing this? The stealing, the bribing, the blackmailing?"

"Haven't you figured that out, sir?" Bassus looked blank. "Empress Plotina."

VIX

Hatra was a hellhole. I cursed the minute I laid eyes on it. A dusty citadel squatting on the eastern road toward Babylon; nothing but sand and buffeting winds stretching around for miles. The men were bitching about the flies before they even had their tents unfolded, a hot and furious summer rain poured down amid cracks of thunder just long enough to get all the kindling wet, and the legionaries I saw in their camps looked like desiccated mummies with their parched lips and the scarves they'd wrapped around their noses to keep out the blowing sand.

"The legate'll be glad for the extra men," the First Spear told me when I made my report. "But I hope they brought their own water. Hardly a drop to drink anywhere in this pile of sand." He squinted at me—one of Trajan's brand of officers, I could tell. The kind who still looked fit in a breastplate, and spoke Latin no more refined than mine. "You're Vercingetorix the Red, aren't you?"

"Yes, sir."

"Heard that name. Lusius Quietus says you aren't completely useless in a fight."

"He mention I saved his life a few times?"

"Berbers, they need saving. They're all crazy. Go make your report to the Emperor; he'll want the updates about Seleucia directly. He's out watching the latest cavalry attack fail miserably." The First Spear let out a short bark of laughter. "Welcome to Hades. I'll wager you didn't think it would be *this* hot."

I hadn't seen my Emperor in some months, and I had to control my expression when he turned on his horse in his cluster of Praetorians and staff officers and greeted me. Trajan had deep new lines about his mouth, his eyes seemed sunken, and one corner of his mouth dragged downward in a permanent small frown. I remembered hearing a rumor that the Emperor had suffered a collapse a few months before and had been kept to his bed for a week, fuming all the while. I'd brushed it off as idle gossip. Trajan, ill? The man who could still walk a full day's route march and then drink an entire legion under the table? Impossible. *He looks ill now*, I couldn't help thinking as I got off my horse and saluted him. But his grin as he waved me up was as warm as ever.

"Vercingetorix! Just the man to join us on our little siege. What do you think—easier than Old Sarm?"

I squinted at the walls, which seemed to be rising out of a haze of dust. Roman cavalry were making a halfhearted attack on the gates, and I heard the distant thrum of arrows. "I'd say harder, Caesar."

"Me too," the Emperor said. "No pipes to break this time. *That* was easy."

"That was my idea, Caesar," I volunteered. "Breaking the pipes? I had Titus present it for me."

"Did you, by Jove? Good fellow, young Titus Aurelius. One of the few honest men in Rome, if I'm not mistaken. Doesn't hurt that he's now one of the richest either."

"He's a good sort," I agreed. "I didn't mind he got the credit for my pipes."

"Hadrian tried to claim it," Trajan snorted. "Now, tell me about Seleucia."

"Shouldn't we retire, Caesar?" I heard another thump of an arrow. "We're within range, one lucky shot—" And the Imperial idiot wasn't wearing his helmet. His bare head gleamed under the harsh sun like a burnished silver coin.

"Don't be ridiculous." The Emperor waved my fears away. "Seleucia! Tell me."

Trajan wore armor like a common soldier on campaign, but someone else on the walls of Hatra must have recognized that magnificent gray head. Halfway through my report on the sacked city of Seleucia, I heard the thrum of an arrow much closer. A hoarse gurgle sounded, and the cavalry officer on the horse beside Trajan's, who had been fanning himself with one sweaty hand and complaining about the flies, was trying to talk around the shaft in his throat. He pitched over, and I saw blood drip down on the sand.

No time to yell. I lunged forward, grabbed Trajan's arm, and in one ferocious yank tugged the Emperor of Rome out of his saddle. A streak of fire shot through my shoulder, but I paid it no heed as Trajan came tumbling down on the ground. I hurled him flat and flung myself over him, and then I could hear shouts and stamping hooves as Praetorians rallied around us. Someone pulled me up, three guards surrounded their Emperor with protectively drawn swords and hastened him back toward the lines, and in the middle of it all, Trajan was laughing. I took a step after him and felt a bolt of pain in my right shoulder. Looking down, I saw that I had an arrow in my shoulder just at the edge of my breastplate. "Wonderful," I snarled. Three and a half years in Parthia, in and out of the hottest fighting in the region with never a wound, and now I'd been winged on my first day in Hatra. I gritted my teeth and yanked the arrow out. Blood began to spurt down my arm. Shield practice was going to be great fun tomorrow.

"Vercingetorix!" I heard someone call, and looked up to see my Emperor. No more deep lines around his mouth; he was grinning like a boy. "That was a well-timed tackle of yours, I must thank you—"

"Sir!" I cut him off in my harshest centurion's growl. I took a deep breath, trying to control myself as the Emperor blinked and his officers stared at me in surprise. *Do not shout at the Emperor of Rome*, I told myself, and then I bellowed, "HOW MANY TIMES DO WE HAVE TO TELL YOU TO WEAR YOUR BLOODY HELMET?"

The Emperor opened his mouth, but I wasn't having any of his excuses. Jaws dropped further in the circle of guards and officers behind him (and hands hovered over sword hilts) as I jabbed a finger into Trajan's chest and told him at the top of my lungs that he was an idiot. An idiot to get that close to the enemy, and an even greater idiot for getting that close to the enemy during an active attack. When I ran out of things to tell him I just cursed. When I ran out of curses, I just glared. The Emperor of Rome gazed at me in silent amusement, and when I finally trailed off, he patted my wounded shoulder.

"There, there, boy. Don't excite yourself."

"EXCITE MYSELF?" I shouted, and that probably would have started me off again, but even that gentle pat had sent a bolt of pain through my arm, and I clutched at the wound with a stifled oath.

"Go get that patched up," the Emperor told me.

"Yes, Caesar," I muttered, still scowling.

"Then come see me in my tent. I want you and your men here with me until I take Hatra, but after that I'm dispatching you back to Germania."

"*Germania?*" Rage faded abruptly. I started after him as he turned at his usual brisk pace and strode off. I loped to keep up, still holding my shoulder.

"Those Dacians are stirring up trouble again," Trajan said, not slowing. "Probably think I can't keep my eye on them from all the way out here, the bastards. And I have been borrowing a bit heavily from the legions back in Germania; they're stretched thin. You know Dacia, you were there the first time around, so you'll take your men and the rest of the detachment back, take command of the legion, march on Dacia, and restore order. Congratulations, Vercingetorix." He thumped me on the unwounded shoulder. "The Tenth Fidelis is yours."

Mine?

"For—" I heard myself floundering like a boy and saw the other officers exchange glances, looking just as startled as I felt. "Giving me a legion—just for pulling you out of that archer's way? I didn't—I mean, I didn't plan—"

"No, I'd already planned to give you a legion. A bellow like that is wasted on a centurion. Your term as First Spear is up, isn't it?"

"Yes, Caesar."

"Good, then you'll be eligible to join the *equites*. All the plunder we've taken, you should be able to afford the fees. Now, I can't make you legate of the Tenth; I'll have to find some senatorial prat for that."

Trajan's eyelid dropped in a wink. "But I can drag a bit on appointing one, eh? And I'll give you some pliant fellow who knows how to manage the payroll and sign his name where you tell him. It's going to get dangerous up in Dacia again, and I want a *soldier* in command. Not a sprig in a toga who just wants to be consul someday."

"Caesar," I choked.

"Don't thank me yet. I'll probably work you to death up there. But for saving my life just now, I hope you will take this"—my Emperor pulled a ring from his finger and put it in my hand—"and this." He kissed me heartily on the cheek. "Now get that shoulder bandaged up and come see me for your orders."

I opened my mouth, but nothing came out. I had tears in my throat, blood on my arm, a kiss on my cheek, and joy in my heart. The other officers all looked at me as they filed past after Trajan, some with amusement, some with disdain, most with outright envy. If I was young to be a First Spear, how young was I to command a legion? *You made a slew of enemies the minute he raised you up*, I thought, but I didn't care. I didn't care at all. I just looked down at the ring in my hand as my Emperor moved away. A plain thing of heavy gold, carved with the word *Parthicus*. The title Trajan had been awarded by the Senate: "Conqueror of Parthia." I slipped it over my middle finger, and it fit as though it had been made for me. "Parthicus," I said, and my voice was thick.

"Glad you shouted at him," one of Trajan's Praetorians grumped in passing. "How many times have we told him he has to wear his helmet, but does he listen to us? He'll get himself killed someday, the royal fool."

"Not while I've got breath," I said, and I felt no pain at all when the surgeon stitched up my torn shoulder. When he was done I had it tattooed with an X. An X for *Tenth*.

My Tenth.

CHAPTER 25

PLOTINA

"Apologies, Domina, but someone is requesting an audience."

"I am far too busy." Plotina made a careful note on one wax tablet and reached for another. Four slave girls hurried behind her, busying themselves with a pile of silk gowns ready for pressing; two more slaves sat with the mending, and a pair of pages hovered ready to run errands, but the Empress of Rome at her desk in the middle of the bustle was busier than any of them. A statue of Trajan to be raised in his new forum . . . her winter gowns and cloaks to be unfolded from storage and checked for moths . . . a certain gentleman among the provincial governors who had recently gotten into debt, and who might be most amenable to throwing his support behind Dear Publius if a tidy loan came with it . . . spiders getting into the wine stores again . . . Dear Juno, how much there was to do. The Empress of the Roman Empire was the biggest slave in it!

"He is most insistent, Domina," her steward persisted. "It's—"

"I don't care who it is. I have no time to see anyone this morning." Plotina scanned the latest letter from her husband—short and courteous, as always, looking like it had been carved out with a sword between battles. Trajan really had no gift for elegant correspondence. Plotina supposed she would have to plan a state visit to see him if this campaign dragged on much longer. She'd made the trek to Antioch two years ago to spend a very official month or two at his side, as a dutiful wife should, but the journey had hardly been pleasant. Eastern fleas, eastern wine, and eastern whores who called themselves Roman ladies and actually expected to *dine* with her. *Perhaps I can put the visit off another year.*

"It's Titus Aurelius Fulvus Boionius Arrius Antoninus, Lady." Her steward still hovered. "He said it was most important."

"Is he deaf, or are you? I am not to be disturbed." Certainly not for the likes of that jumped-up boy whom everyone seemed to regard as quite the coming man. Trajan's rare letters hardly went a page without praising some action of Titus's to the skies—the progress on the public baths, the tact with which he had smoothed over some fracas in the Senate. As if Dear Publius hadn't done far more impressive things, and to far less applause! Plotina had spread a few rumors about this new favorite of Trajan's—that he was a drunkard, that he worshipped obscene foreign cults like Isis and Ancasta and Taranis rather than good Roman gods—but nothing seemed to stick. The boy was dully, distressingly virtuous.

"I fear it can't wait, Lady." A firm voice interrupted the steward, and Plotina looked up to see the boy himself planted solidly before her desk. "I must speak with you, and I would prefer to do so in private."

"You have no right to barge into my private quarters—"

"You have no right to help yourself illegally to public funds," he returned. "But if you wish to discuss it before your slaves, I will do so."

Plotina stared. Behind Titus, the steward stood pop-eyed. Two slave girls folding Plotina's silks looked up, startled, and a third girl whispered behind her hand to the page boy holding Plotina's cup of barley water.

"Leave us," said the Empress.

Titus waited until the last slave had filed out, and the door swung shut. "Thank you," he said, and sat uninvited. He wore a tunic and sandals—not even the dignity of a toga!—and he was unshaven as though he'd risen straight from bed without a stop at the bathhouse.

"Is this how you call upon your Empress?" Plotina said icily. "With a stubbled chin and a mouthful of wild accusations?"

He produced a handful of scrolls, arraying them across her desk. "Hardly wild."

Plotina glanced at the first scroll. "What, are you pretending these come from my private accounts? I assure you, I review my accounts daily and nothing is missing."

"I made sure of that. My informant put copies into your study after bringing me the originals."

Informant? Plotina snatched across the desk to tear open the first scroll. Just a line or two was enough to chill her to the bone. "How did you lay hands on my private papers?" One of the slaves? *I'll have the wretch crucified, I'll—*

"Never mind who brought them to me. They're long gone, and you won't find them."

"How dare you—"

"I'm very tired, Lady. I spent most of a week untangling your cheap little financial schemes, and most of another week wondering what to do about it all. So I'll be plain." Titus brushed the hair out of his eyes, looking at her squarely. "You have been stealing funds, Empress Plotina, and I can prove it. From the building monies set aside for the Emperor's public baths, from the *alimenta* program, and from other projects as well."

"I do not have to explain myself to the likes of you." Plotina summoned all the crispness she could manage. Crisp but impersonal, yes, as if she were dealing with an impertinent slave. "An empress has reasons of which a common little man like you knows nothing."

"I'm not interested in your reasons, Lady."

Ah. Plotina sat back a little in her chair, feeling the ground begin to solidify beneath her. "What are you interested in, then?"

He looked at her silently.

"You can hardly want a rich wife, considering the fortune left to you by your grandfather. But perhaps you would like to add something a bit more illustrious to your title than *quaestor*." She lifted an inviting hand. "Would *consul* suit you better? I can see your name on the list for next year."

Perhaps this was no bad thing. Young Titus Aurelius, one of the richest men in Rome, in her debt. A rich young consul who could easily be led about by the nose; oh, yes, that would be quite an ally for Dear Publius.

"And after a year as consul your name would be eligible for a governorship," she went on. "Shall we say Germania? Or Hispania, if you prefer something warmer. Or perhaps—"

"My dear lady," Titus sighed, "are you really trying to bribe me?"

Plotina's teeth snapped shut on an offer to see him Prefect of Egypt within five years if he made a few timely loans and some public support to Dear Publius. She could feel the familiar twin pinpoints of pain begin to hammer faintly at her temples. She had not felt those steely drilling pains in so long; it had been so many years since anyone had thwarted her—since anyone had looked at her and not simply *obeyed*—

"Let me make myself plain." Titus looked at her, weary and implacable. "I want nothing from you. Nothing but the immediate halt of your petty pilfering from the Imperium."

"You dare—"

"I'm not the thief in this room, Lady, so yes, I do dare. No more skimming from the building funds for the baths—that should be easy enough; the baths are nearly complete. But the Emperor has just informed me that I am to oversee the *alimenta* project next, in support of Roman children orphaned in the provinces, and you've helped yourself from that quite generously over the years. It stops now. And really," he added, exasperated, "your famous moral scruples should have stopped you from stooping that low. Skimming off a building fund is one thing, but stealing from *orphans?*"

Plotina surged to her feet, the twin pains hammering now against her skull. "You think you can threaten the Empress of Rome?"

"Of course I can threaten you. I have enough definitive proof to expose you to the Emperor. I doubt he'd be pleased with me, and I doubt you'd suffer much punishment. But everyone in Rome would know, and I doubt you'd like that at all. 'Empress Plotina, so virtuous and high-minded. Empress Plotina, the common thief.'"

"You dare—"

"Skip the threats, Lady. And if you're thinking of going on to blackmail, I'd advise you to skip that too. There is nothing in my life you can use to buy my silence. One advantage, I suppose, of being a dull little plodder. Dull little plodders have nothing to hide."

"Oh?" Plotina gave a vicious smile. "Your affair with Vibia Sabina is nothing you wish to hide? I saw you with her, before she left for Antioch. Usually she is more discreet, but when she wore that whore's dress I suppose you couldn't keep your hands off her."

"No, I couldn't," Titus agreed, unruffled. "And that was the only intimacy I have ever enjoyed with Vibia Sabina, not that you'll believe me."

"Never mind what I believe—will her husband believe you? Will anyone in Rome?"

"I don't particularly care if they do or not. By all means, spread the news that I managed to steal your protégé's fascinating wife out from under his nose. My reputation could use a little spice."

"You wretched, interfering little stork!"

"I promised myself I could leave as soon as insults started to fly." Titus rose. Plotina could hardly see him through a red mist. *I will see you in the arena for this*, she thought. *Disemboweled by lions—strung up for the vultures to eat your eyes out*—if she'd had a blade in her hand she would have plunged it through his throat.

"One more thing." Titus looked back at her over his shoulder. "You'll soon find some other way to skim money for your schemes, and I know I probably won't be able to stop you. I'll be satisfied if you just don't try it with any project of mine. Not ever. Agree to that, and I'll keep what I know from the Emperor. Do we have a bargain?"

"I will not bargain with you! I am the Empress of Rome!"

"And you're trying to buy the next Emperor."

The words sent a jolt up Plotina's spine, and she stared at the weary young man looking back at her over the desk. Such an unassuming boy; so trifling; so unimportant. "What do you mean?" she said through stiff lips.

"Give me some credit, Lady. You live modestly here, you have few expenses, you barely spend your household allowance. What would *you* need with more than two million sesterces?" Titus's gaze traveled around her neat apartments, comfortable but hardly sumptuous with their dark marble walls, their unadorned couches and low tables, the woolen hangings Plotina had woven with her own hands. "No, you don't need to steal money on your own account. But I imagine it cost quite a lot to maintain your protégé Hadrian in suitable style as consul. Not to mention his new post as governor of Syria. Two million sesterces—that's a good start, buying him the kind of support he'd need to become Imperial heir."

Titus shook his head. "The thing is, if you'd simply *asked* me to support Hadrian . . . well, I'd have done it. He'd make a good emperor. I don't imagine he even knows about all this, does he? He may be a cold fish, but he'd rather die than become a thief."

Plotina's voice came out in a guttural rasp. "I will see you dead for this."

"No, you won't," Titus said. "Because if you do—if some sudden accident should befall me—the information about your misdoings will be made public anyway. You think I would come to see you today without making certain I could walk out alive afterward?"

He left quietly, closing the door with a faint click. Plotina opened her mouth in a silent shriek, her head clamped in a huge vise of agony. *No.* She strode back and forth, blundering into the furniture. *No, no, no.* A box of linens tripped her and she kicked it away, showering neatly folded tunics over the floor. *He will not, he will NOT—*

Plotina took herself to Juno. She ordered the worshippers of the temple out in a whisper that had them fleeing for the doors, and unburdened herself to her sister. Juno listened, stone-carved and sympathetic as Plotina wept and raged and tore at her hair.

"He'll pay," she said at last, in a voice hoarse from screaming. "No one speaks to a goddess that way."

Juno agreed.

"If he thinks he's stopped me, he's a naïve little bumbler. My Publius will be Emperor. He'll be Emperor, and then I'll see that interfering little wretch's corpse on the *floor*."

Juno understood.

"I'll go to Trajan. Make that journey to Antioch after all, and right away. He'll hear how I was slandered. He'll believe *me*, not that interfering boy. I am his *wife*."

Juno sympathized.

"You'll help me, won't you?" Plotina leaned her aching head against Juno's marble skirts, spent and drained. "You'll help me dispose of him?"

Juno would.

SABINA

"I thought your physicians told you to rest, Caesar."

Trajan leaned back on his elbows against the couch cushions, and a slave refilled his goblet. "I am resting."

"This is hardly what I would call peaceful," Sabina said, amused. Trajan's return from Hatra to Antioch had been marked by an immense banquet: visiting dignitaries in striped eastern robes, senators and governors in snowy togas, legates and tribunes in their armor. Trajan's usual crush of wine, noise, cheer, and above all informality. No one was keeping to their couches, the dancers barely had a chance to finish their performance before being dragged off to join the party, and a pair of drunken legates had volunteered to carve up the roast ox with their swords. Trajan had laughed until Sabina had to pound him on the back.

"Gods' bones, don't you nag me now," the Emperor warned as a team of lithe Parthian acrobats began their drumbeat-backed tumbling. "I'll get enough of that when Plotina arrives."

Sabina groaned. "She's coming soon?"

"Took ship from Rome not long ago, and I hear there's been fair winds." Trajan waved a hand over the hilarity in the hall. "I'll have to tone all of this down a bit while she's here."

"Else be scolded till your ears bleed," Sabina agreed. "How long is she staying?"

"Not long, I wager. She doesn't like the east—too dirty and exotic for my Plotina. She'll stay long enough to make a few public appearances and give me two years' worth of good advice, then take her leave. And in the time she's here, little Sabina, you can refrain from needling her! I've got enough to fill my time without adding a houseful of quarreling women on top."

"Yes, Caesar." Sabina gave a meek little salute. "I suppose I can take two years of advice right along with you."

"Not just the advice." Trajan sounded gloomy. "Just you wait and see, she'll want me to go back to Rome with her."

"Why don't you?" Sabina said it lightly.

"I've still got Hatra to crack, girl. A tough nut, that is. After that, I've a mind to head back into Mesopotamia and put out a few fires . . ."

Trajan arranged a plate of cheese and grapes into Hatra's defenses, eating the enemy troops that had been killed in the siege, marching a chunk of bread through the city gates for the attack he was planning when he returned. Sabina watched him thoughtfully. She had not seen Trajan for more than a year, with her own journeys to Egypt and Greece and his dashing all over Parthia. He had lost weight; his arms were still powerful but the skin over them seemed loose and papery; and she thought she saw a tremor in his hands when he reached for another chunk of bread.

"Are you well, Caesar?" she asked quietly. "I heard you collapsed outside Hatra."

"A man gets a little dizzy from the sun and everyone starts having the vapors," Trajan complained. "I'm well enough." He applauded the acrobats as they leaped down from their pyramid, and immediately called the handsomest of the tumblers over to his couch. Sabina slid discreetly away. Hadrian stood bearded and benign in a circle of senators beside a frieze of lascivious satyrs, a half-dozen hangers-on vying for his attention: He had been made governor of Syria recently (though he would have to pretend he hadn't heard already when Plotina arrived to gloat with the news), and next year he would take another consulship. "Will you deign to accompany me to Syria?" he'd asked Sabina coldly this evening as they readied themselves for the banquet. "Or do you prefer to travel with your lovers?"

Do you really think I spend all my time bedding other men? Sabina thought in exasperation. She'd gone back to Vindobona in Pannonia to check on the hospital she'd gotten funded there while Hadrian was governor; she'd spent a month tramping about the work site arguing about the need for more physicians—and did anyone believe her? No; all they wanted to hear about was her lovers. But she just said lightly, "I think I've had my fill of orgies for a while. Perversion is so dull, don't you think?"

They had entered the hall together, Sabina's fingertips barely brushing her husband's arm and dropping away the minute they were through the carved double doors. *Syria,* she reminded herself, swirling the wine in her cup as she watched Hadrian disappear into a cloud of well-wishers. She'd never been to Syria before; surely it would be a fascinating journey . . . but somehow, Sabina found her thoughts turning more and more toward home lately. Her sister Faustina would be getting married soon: *"Hopefully I can bring the man I want up to scratch before I turn a hundred. Gods, he's thick!"* Faustina's choice of suitors wasn't the only drama in the family; their brother Linus was begging to join the legions as a tribune, though he wasn't even seventeen. And of course Father was getting frail these days—Calpurnia had finally persuaded him to retire from the Senate, and his latest letter had told of the treatise he had just completed on the financial reorganization of Rome's temples. Titus's letters spoke of the splendid new baths, his supervision of the *alimenta* scheme and how it had pleased the Emperor . . .

"I believe I'm homesick," Sabina mused aloud. After years of wandering too—how strange. Somehow, the thought of Syria held no charm at all.

"Talking to yourself?" A voice sounded behind her, so familiar it went straight to the pit of her stomach and resonated there warmly before she even thought of its owner's name. "I always knew you were crazy, Lady Sabina."

"You're not the one to make accusations, Vercingetorix." Sabina turned, smiling. "I heard about that night attack you made on Osrhoene. Eighty men taking on two hundred in the guard tower, in the pitch dark. Now *that* would be the act of a madman."

"Worked, didn't it?" The row of campaign tokens strung across his belt jingled, and his eyes flicked to her head. "Where'd your hair go?"

"I razored it all off in Egypt." Sabina ruffled the short velvety brush of her hair, lopped from the middle of her back to within an inch of her scalp. "It's so hot there, everyone shaves their heads and just wears wigs for formal occasions. After a while I decided I'd forgo the wigs too."

"I like it."

"Hadrian despises it."

"Then I really like it." Vix's gray eyes flicked over Sabina briefly, from her deep-green silk dress to the band of jade around one ankle to the powdered malachite she'd used to line and wing her eyes. "You look well, Lady."

If I'd known you were going to be here, I'd have worn that one-breast dress I used to give Plotina fits. "You look well too," Sabina said. "Wearing armor at a party, though . . ."

"I've got duties to attend to after this. No point changing into a synthesis, not when the Emperor doesn't care what his soldiers wear to dinner."

"It suits you." To say the least. From that brash boy with the inarticulate glower to this: Vix's russet head loomed a hand-span taller than any other man in the room; his feet were planted over an aggressive measure of space that dared anyone to encroach on it; his eyes moved keen and restless over the crowd, missing nothing. In his tattered lion skin and his spotless battered armor he looked broad and powerful, sunburned and deadly. *They should carve you in granite and put you on display in front of every legion recruiter in Rome,* Sabina thought. *They'll fill the ranks in a heartbeat, just by telling envious boys that someday, maybe, they could be you.*

"It's just as well armor suits him." The woman at Vix's side broke the little silence. "I hardly ever see him in anything else."

"I do apologize." Sabina shifted her eyes to the woman. "I should have introduced myself. I am Vibia Sabina."

"Mirah," Vix said abruptly. "My wife."

The hand that pressed Sabina's looked small and capable. The woman had reddish hair, a good match for Vix's. Taller than Sabina, with a smoke-blue gown and pearls swinging in her ears. "You have a fine husband, Mirah." *Does he still snore like a saw going through a tree?*

"I do have a fine husband." A dimple flashed unexpectedly in Mirah's chin. "Lady Vibia Sabina—the Emperor's great-niece? Vix, you're always talking about the Emperor but you never said you'd met the Imperial family too."

"Long time ago," Vix said at once. "Very long."

Eight years, since they had last spoken face to face? At a party very much like this one, in fact. "Vix was a guard in my father's house," Sabina explained to Mirah, who was looking puzzled. "Long before he joined the Tenth."

"I can't imagine Vix without the Tenth." Mirah's smile turned a little stiff.

"Well, he was very young. Big feet, like a puppy. And always starting fights in the street."

"I need to speak with you, Lady Sabina." Vix spoke even more abruptly. "Now."

"If you like."

"No, alone." He turned to his wife. "I won't be long. Be on your guard—that flabby bastard in the toga over there has been eyeing you all night, and once you're alone he'll probably ask you to be his bedwarmer."

"Be on *your* guard," Mirah whispered back, almost inaudibly, but Sabina's ear caught it. "Someone's eyeing you for the same reason." Sabina didn't smile until Vix had stalked through the crowded banqueting hall to the atrium, moving people out of the way with a quirk of his lowered brows. As they reached the moonlit shadows outside, Sabina released the laugh she'd been holding in. "I like your Mirah. Ginger in the soul as well as the hair—and she'll need it, if she married you. Do you have children?"

"Two. Girls." Vix ran a hand through his hair, a gesture she'd forgotten but now it came back vividly. "I don't want to talk about Mirah."

"All right." Sabina drifted past him toward the pool sunk in the floor, a glossy black square reflecting the half moon through the open roof above. It looked like the moon was trapped in the pool. A couple wandered out the other end of the atrium, giggling softly on their way to the gardens, but otherwise they were alone. "Last time we talked, it was in an atrium like this," Sabina said. "Don't toss me in the water this time, will you?"

Grudging amusement laced his voice. "You deserved it."

"Maybe I did." She turned, leaning against a slender carved pillar. "What is it, Vercingetorix?"

"The Emperor." Vix folded his arms across his chest. "He listens to you?"

"He won't let me divorce Hadrian." Sabina traced one idle finger along the pillar. "But otherwise, yes. He listens to me."

"You tried to divorce Hadrian?"

"It's not important. The Emperor?"

"Yes. Well. I want you to talk to him."

"You already have your legion, don't you? Congratulations, by the way."

"No—this isn't about me. You don't have to talk to him about me. I'm making my own way." Vix's face was mostly in shadow, but Sabina could see the worry that brought his brows together and tightened his jaw. More than worry—fear. "Persuade Trajan to go back to Rome."

"What?"

"He collapsed during the siege at Hatra." Vix spoke jerkily. "Six hours on a horse under the burning sun, the idiot—he fainted right out of his saddle. He was up again in a day, but he's not the same, I see him getting tired and his hands shake—"

"I noticed that."

"He's ill. He won't admit it; we barely persuaded him to abandon Hatra, and now he's talking about leading the legions back down the Tigris. Another month of marching in the heat might kill him. He's *sixty-three*." Vix's eyes pleaded with her. "The physician nags him, his guards nag him, I'm sure the Empress will nag him till his ears bleed once she gets here. Maybe you'll have better luck. Make him go back to Rome, Sabina. Get him to sit in a cool garden and put his feet up. Get him to *rest*."

Sabina tilted her head up at her old lover. "You love him, don't you?"

"More than—" Vix raked a hand through his hair again. "Anything. More than Mirah. Even more than my girls, God help me."

"Then I'll talk to him." Sabina touched the back of Vix's hand, very lightly. "I love him too."

TITUS

"Faustina?" Titus blinked at the familiar figure in pale blue, framed by the columns of the long hall of Trajan's baths. "What are you doing here?"

"I called on you, and Ennia sent me here. She's worried." Faustina came forward, gesturing her maids to wait. "So am I, to be frank."

Titus gestured at the walls of the baths rising around them. "You know it's almost done? The glazing isn't finished, and the mosaics will need to be laid. One or two other things. But it's near to completed."

"What happened with the Empress?" Faustina demanded. "I know you went to the palace before she left for Antioch."

"I did."

"She left very suddenly too."

"She did. Walk with me?"

Faustina tucked her hand into his arm, falling in at his side. Their footsteps echoed in the silence; Titus had let most of the workmen go early so he could wander the complex alone. The baths were at their best in the afternoon, the sunlight streaming in long bars through the high windows, making warm puddles on the marble and turning the water in the pools to shimmering liquid glass. Or rather it would, when the pools were filled.

"*And?*" Faustina pressed, impatient. "Don't torture me! You confronted her, didn't you?"

Titus felt a smile breaking out. Faustina gave a shriek, flinging her arms around him, and he hugged her back. One of the few girls he didn't have to bend in half at the waist to embrace.

"You idiot!" She pulled back, shaking him a little. "Bearding the Empress of Rome in her den, just to call her a thief—"

"I didn't just call her a thief. I told her I'd keep her secret as long as she stopped."

"As if that will work." Faustina blew out a breath. "*Why* couldn't you just let it go? It was just a building fund!"

"Today, maybe. And perhaps she didn't do much harm. As you can see, the baths still got built." Titus gestured at the graceful vaulted walls rising around them. "But she had her hands in other things too, like the *alimenta* funds, and that's a dowry for some poor girl who just got orphaned in Ostia. That's money that means a girl either gets married and raises a family, or has to turn to whoring. Money that puts a boy into a respectable trade, instead of thieving on the streets." Titus wrinkled his nose. "And after stealing from orphans, who knows what would come next?"

"But plenty of other people have to have known the Empress was skimming. Why not let one of them call her to account?"

"Because none of them did."

Faustina tilted her head. "You're still an idiot," she decided. "But I'm proud of you. I'm sure your father and grandfather would be too."

"You know, I rather think you're right."

"Were you terrified?" Faustina lowered her voice. "Empress Plotina turns me into absolute jelly when she's in a *good* mood."

"I was petrified," Titus confessed. "My knees were knocking the whole time."

"She'll be your enemy now." Faustina looked suddenly grave. "We both know why she took sail for Antioch so suddenly, and it's not because she's desperately missing Trajan. She's paying him a visit so she can tell him everything, and put you in the bad. He'll get her version of the truth—"

"Which is why he already has mine," Titus said. "I consulted with your father, and we agreed that it would be prudent if I sent a letter with all my findings to Antioch before I ever paid Plotina a visit. Trajan knows everything by now. And he might not believe me alone, but he'll believe me if I'm endorsed by Senator Marcus Norbanus."

"But you promised Plotina you'd keep her secret if she stopped."

"I lied," Titus confessed.

Faustina gave him an approving sweep of her lashes. "Perhaps you aren't such an idiot after all."

"No, only an idiot would have faced the Empress down in the first place. But at least I'm a careful idiot."

It had been all Titus could do to turn his unprotected back and walk away from the Empress of Rome. She had looked so white and strange at the end, rage sending odd ripples across her still face like a sea monster turning languid circles under the surface of a calm ocean.

I will see you dead for this. Her voice had sent splinters of ice down his spine. Even now, safe in the sunlit hall with Plotina half an Empire away and sailing for Antioch, Titus shuddered.

Empty threats, he reminded himself. *The Emperor knows the truth now; he won't listen to any of her poison.* And once Trajan was gone, well, Plotina wouldn't be Empress anymore. She'd have no more influence in Imperial matters.

I will see you dead for this.

Well, it was a risk.

Titus realized he still had his arm about Faustina's waist, and she was gazing anxiously up at him. "You're worrying," she accused. "I can always tell when you're worrying. You get this little crease between your eyebrows, and the corner of your mouth puckers on the left side."

"I'm not worrying too much." He stepped back, offered her his arm. "May I show you something?"

He led her to the *frigidarium*, placed on the far side of the bathhouse complex away from the sunlight so it would keep its coolness even in the middle of summer. A pair of builders fussed about making measurements, and Titus dismissed them, going to the lamps and lighting them one by one. Faustina stood admiring the swirling blue-and-green tiles of the high ceiling, the floor waiting for its mosaic, the blue-veined marble of the sunken pool. "Why is this pool filled up?" she asked. "All the others are empty."

"The builder was worried there might be a crack in the lining, so he had it filled. Nothing leaking so far." Titus took a scroll from his belt and unrolled it. "All finished in here, you see, except the mosaic for the floor. That's being commissioned now. My builder suggested naked mermaids, but I had another idea."

Faustina bent over the scroll. A sea monster, all coiling scales in rippling shades of green and black, rearing from the blue waves toward a girl chained to a rock. "Andromeda and the sea monster?"

"Take a look at her face. Andromeda, not the monster."

Faustina peered closer at the tall blond girl in her shackles and wind-whipped blue draperies. "It's me!"

"Not the most appropriate myth," Titus confessed. "Andromeda has to get rescued by Perseus, and you're the one who rescued me with your timely corruption of the Empress's undersecretary. At the very least, I thought I could immortalize you in a floor."

Faustina regarded him thoughtfully. "There are other ways of saying thank you, you know."

Titus tilted his head. "Like what?"

"Oh, dear gods," Faustina said, and pushed him into the pool.

The cold water shocked him all over like a strike of lightning. Titus yelled in surprise, coughed as water rushed into his mouth, and thrashed to find the slippery tiles underfoot. The pool was full, just up to his shoulders, and he broke the surface spluttering. "What did you do that for?"

"To wake you up." Faustina stood at the lip of the pool, hands on hips as she glowered down at him. "What does it take to get your attention, Titus? Most men need a hint now and then, but you need to be bashed over the head with a *brick*!"

"Um." The heavy sodden folds of his toga weighed him down in the water; he began working himself loose of the soaked wool. "I'm afraid I don't follow you."

A pair of curious slaves passing by with baskets of gravel paused to peer in, drawn by the voices and the splashing. "*Out!*" Faustina yelled, and they disappeared hastily. She turned back to Titus with another withering look.

"You think I go around bribing Imperial freedmen for all my suitors?" Faustina continued. "You think I put on my best dress on the hottest afternoon of the year to casually drop in on all the unmarried men in Rome? You think I spy on the Empress for every admirer I have?"

Titus wondered if she expected answers to these questions. *Oh, maybe not.* He yanked half a ton of sodden toga over his head and tossed it into the other end of the pool with a splash. The wet tunic he wore underneath wouldn't weigh him down too much if he had to get out of the pool and make a run for it . . .

"I was prepared to be patient—Father didn't want me marrying too young anyway, so I thought that would give you time. But this is getting ridiculous." Faustina folded her arms across her breasts. "I know you've been mooning after my sister for years, but—"

Titus spluttered again, not from the water this time. "*What?*"

"You told me yourself. When I was five years old, and you carried me home from her wedding."

"Um. You were so young, you couldn't possibly remember—"

"I've seen it for myself every time you *look* at Sabina. Everyone in Rome knows! Your Ennia even gave me a warning—she said I'd have a rare problem with you and your ridiculous romantic obsession with the first fascinating girl who ever took an interest in you. When, I might add, you were younger than I am now!"

Titus wondered again if flight was an option. But Faustina was blocking the only steps up out of the pool, and she didn't look like she was moving anytime soon. He hoped the cold water was hiding the blush he could feel spreading to the tips of his ears.

"I don't mind that you've been in love with my sister," Faustina continued. "She *is* fascinating, and she's much cleverer than me. But she'd make you miserable with all her trotting around the world, and here I am. Much prettier than Sabina, *and* better suited to you. You think Sabina ever taught herself how to make your favorite lamb stew?"

Faustina looked serious now rather than exasperated. Serious and beautiful, cheeks flushed pink and eyes sparkling and breasts heaving. *The man I hire to put her in the mosaic as Andromeda won't want to cover her up in blue draperies,* Titus found himself thinking. *He'll say it's a crime to hide those breasts, and I must say he'll be right.*

"I know you've known me since I was a child, but I've grown up." Faustina gestured down at herself. "You had to have noticed *that* when I climbed out of the pool in a dress wet enough to see through!"

Yes, he'd noticed. Faustina rising out of the water all but naked—that image had returned to his mind this year with embarrassing frequency.

"I really think you might have taken the hint, Titus," Faustina scolded. "If I'd minded you seeing me half naked, I'd have grabbed my cloak a lot faster and I certainly wouldn't have walked in *front* of you into the house. Really, what does it take? I've been laying a trail for you ever since I was eleven and you told me I'd grow up to be a beauty someday. You liked me before I was beautiful, and I liked you before you inherited your grandfather's fortune. Doesn't that put me ahead of all those other girls who just want to get their hands on your money?"

She scuffed one sandal along the plain stone underfoot. "So really, I'm very flattered that you want to put me in a floor. But it's not the best way you could have repaid me, if you were really feeling thankful."

"I'm not putting you in a floor," Titus said, and made a lunge. He got hold of Faustina's wrist and gave one tremendous yank. She fell into the pool with a shriek and a huge splash, pale-blue silks darkening to turquoise. She surfaced much more gracefully than Titus had, slicking her hair back from her face with both hands. Her lashes made silky spikes about her huge dark eyes, her wet hair gleamed like a gold coin at the bottom of a river, and she looked nothing like Sabina. She looked like herself, like Annia Galeria Faustina, and she was beautiful. He could smell the faintest trace of hyacinth perfume rinsing away with the water. Hyacinth—she must have known it was his favorite flower.

"You should know a few things, if you don't already," he told her. "I'm not witty, I'm not brilliant, and I'm certainly not handsome—"

"What are you—"

"I once proposed marriage to your sister by telling her all the reasons I'd make her an unsatisfactory husband. She turned me down, and you should have a fair chance to do the same." Titus smoothed a tendril of wet hair back behind Faustina's ear. "Now. You already know about my complete lack of originality; I've been spouting Horace and Cato quotes for years. People used to just yawn in my face; now they tell me I'm terribly clever. I suspect the change came somewhere around the time I inherited my grandfather's assets."

Dimples were starting to quiver in Faustina's chin. Titus continued on in his sternest from-the-Rostra-to-the-back-of-the-Forum baritone.

"I live simply, and I hate pomp. I expect I'll be a praetor someday, but nothing much grander than that. I'm a thoroughgoing plodder, I'll add no luster to your name, and since my grandfather and father both went bald it's a safe assumption I will too."

"That's a shame," Faustina said gravely. "I prefer men who go gray."

"So, Annia Galeria Faustina—" Titus lifted her wet hair, coiling it into a rope around his hand. "I've decided not to put you in blue draperies in the floor. I'd rather put you in a red veil, and in my bed. If you have no objection to having the dullest, most ordinary husband in Rome?"

She tasted like water when she leaned forward and kissed him: bottomless, calm, and sweet. Her wet silks floated around him like blue smoke as he gathered her close, and her hands pressed urgently against his chest, gathering handfuls of his tunic and pulling him closer. He reached around her neck for the clasp of the gold heart amulet that Roman girls wore until the day they married and unfastened it, letting the heart spin away into the water.

"Oh, good," Faustina murmured between kisses. "Ennia will be so pleased."

CHAPTER 26

PLOTINA

"My dear." Plotina couldn't help a note of reproach. "Two years apart, and you didn't join me to eat?"

"A busy schedule, I'm afraid." Trajan did not look up from the dispatch he was scanning. His table was piled with scrolls, tablets, spare whetstones, a discarded scabbard missing its dagger, and a broken bust of Alexander that Trajan had used to weigh down a stack of maps. Secretaries busily took dictation, aides hovered with more stacks of dispatches, freedmen brushed past Plotina into the hall on errands and came rushing back with new messages.

"A tiresome crossing, if you must know," Plotina persisted when he did not ask. Her husband had greeted her briefly at the docks when her ship arrived, but excused himself immediately afterward and had not bothered to make an appearance at the noon meal. She'd been forced to hunt him down in his quarters afterward, like a tardy petitioner. "Dear Publius was kind enough to dine with me, did you know? So considerate of him, seeing how busy he is with all the work you've given him. And what a good job he makes of it!"

Trajan grunted. Plotina sighed. One of his moods. She'd gotten out of the habit of dealing with them, these past four years. Dear Publius had been far more pleasant company—delight, such sheer delight to see the dear boy's face again! So handsome, so distinguished. Every inch a young god.

"It looks like a magpie's nest in here." Plotina looked about her at the cramped little study. The quarters here in Antioch were entirely unsuitable for an emperor, much less his empress, but her husband had never paid any attention to his surroundings. "I hope you do not expect me to live in this mess?"

"It won't be for long." Trajan rolled up a scroll with a snap. "We depart soon for Rome."

"Rome?" Plotina blinked. "Rather sudden, isn't it? I've just arrived—"

"If you had written before your departure, I'd have had time to write you back. Tell you to spare yourself the journey."

"Impulsive of me, I know," Plotina confessed. "Can a wife not be allowed to miss her husband? Even an Imperial wife."

"Some wives might miss their husbands." Trajan looked up at her, and she noted again the signs of aging he'd acquired in the past two years since her last visit. The iron-colored hair, the sun-pitted skin, the deep lines. "Not you, Plotina. Not you."

Plotina forced herself to smile, crossing the room to squeeze his arm. She had dressed as regally as she could in this hot, depraved sink-hole of a city—deep-purple *stola*, pearls, a diadem crowning her hair. Trajan's Empress in all her finest, but more than that. His eternal, loyal, capable, *trustworthy* wife. "Well, at least I'll be able to tend you myself on the journey back to Rome," she said brightly. "I've been wanting you home so long, I'd quite given up nagging you. Four years away— why now?"

And what a dent that would put in her tidy palace arrange-ments. Really, it had all been so convenient with Trajan gone in the east. Her palace floors unmarred by muddy boots, her quiet halls unbroken by loud male laughter, her parties hushed and tidy affairs without crude military jokes or goose bones being made into fort dia-grams. No one to mess up *her* tables with discarded quills and slates and scabbards. No one to interfere with her management of Imperial funds, her oversight of Imperial projects. No one to interfere with any-thing, really.

"Why now?" Trajan echoed her. "One or two things have come to my attention. Seems it's time to come home and put my house in order."

"I couldn't agree more." Plotina sank down on a chair beside him, waving the secretaries and freedmen back out of earshot with a flick of her fingers. "There was a matter I wished to bring up, in fact. That young Titus Aurelius everyone seems to be making so much of these days." She lowered her voice to a cozy regret. "I know you've thought highly of him, but I believe you've been mistaken."

"Have I?"

"Yes. I found out—"

"I think you mean, you *were* found out." And Trajan tossed a creased, much-folded, much-read letter into Plotina's lap.

A long letter. There were pages of figures, calculations, receipts, and account book entries, all meticulously noted. But Plotina only had to read the first paragraph, and a blue wave of bile swamped her throat. *He said he wouldn't tell*, she thought disjointedly. *He said he wouldn't tell the Emperor—Juno, you* heard *him say it!*

That sly treacherous poisonous little weasel.

"Goodness, what an impressive packet of lies." Plotina looked up from the letter with careless contempt. "Surely you can't believe that ambitious toad. He'd say anything, he—"

"No, Plotina."

"But I—"

"No."

The harsh bark of his battlefield voice cut her voice off in her throat like a sword.

"I return to Rome," Trajan continued crisply, as if briefing an aide. "You will return with me, but not your Publius. He can stay here, as governor of Syria—he'll make a good job of it, I'll say that much for him. What he does afterward is none of my business, since he'll no longer be a member of the Imperial family. I've a mind to grant little Sabina that divorce she's been wanting."

Plotina felt the words scrape out of her throat like stones. "You can't."

Trajan continued as if he hadn't heard her. "You've been nagging me about the succession for a while now, and perhaps you're right. Time to give the matter my full attention. I thought I'd take young Titus under my wing once I got back to Rome; see what I can make of him. Any man with enough nerve to tell me my wife is a thief has got balls of brass, and I like that in a man."

The stones in her throat had become boulders, tearing their way out in a shriek. "*You. CAN'T.*"

"Don't bother unpacking." Trajan had already gone back to his dispatches, gesturing for his secretaries, who had clustered whispering at the other end of the study. "We leave within the fortnight."

VIX

Three days on a ship, and I spent all three of them puking. I hate boats.

"How can you possibly have anything left to throw up by now?" Sabina asked, coming up on the rail beside me as I was bent over it heaving.

"I suppose you've got a cast-iron stomach?" I reeled upright, wiping my mouth on the back of my hand. "Bitch."

She made a mischievous face at me, stroking the cat who curled purring in her arms. It felt odd, talking with Sabina again. She looked different, small and neat in a narrow Egyptian sheath that left her arms and ankles bare, a charm of some kind knotted around one wrist, her face tanned and freckled under the short cap of hair. But she sounded exactly the same as she ever did. I didn't get the old lurch in my stomach when I looked at her anymore . . . but I didn't mind laughing with her. She'd gotten Trajan on a boat back to Rome, and for that I would have forgiven her anything.

"He looks better." I nodded to the stern, where the Emperor sat playing *latrunculi* under a purple canopy rigged to keep the sun off his head. Plotina fanned herself woodenly at his side, strangely silent for once instead of droning at everyone in earshot. A dozen more hangers-on lounged about the deck as the sailors padded about knotting ropes and twitching at sails, and the water sparkled behind the rails of the boat, impossibly blue. "Doesn't he look better?"

"Mmm. I'll be glad when he gets back to Rome. I intend to keep him in a chair with his feet propped up for the rest of the summer."

"I thought you were going to Syria with Hadrian?"

Sabina shook her cropped head, tickling under the cat's chin. "I want to stay with my family for a while. Aren't you going to miss yours?"

I ducked that question. Mirah knew she wouldn't be joining me in Germania until I was established; that had long been settled—but she'd wanted me to take Antinous with me, and I'd refused, and the subject had become sore. "Another active campaign," I'd said just before I left, gathering my scattered tunics from the bed and stuffing them into my pack. "He's had enough of that for the time being."

"He's almost eleven," she'd argued, bringing my spare sandals and whetstones to pack. "Boys that age need their fathers."

"I've told you and told you, he's not my son!"

"But you want one. Men want sons—I thought you'd want to keep him with you, since I haven't . . . well, two girls . . ."

"Two good girls." I dropped my load of tunics, leaning down to pick up Dinah and toss her in the air until she shrieked. Chaya regarded me from the floor with big dark eyes, edging back when I reached over to stroke the soft down of her little head. She was still wary of me, the way I blew in and out of her life every few months with my clattering sword and jingling armor.

"They are good girls," Mirah said a little more brightly, but then she hesitated. "Vix, if the Emperor, doesn't recover—"

"He'll recover." Any alternative was unthinkable.

"If he doesn't. You'll still go to Dacia?"

"Why wouldn't I? My own legion, I've waited all my life for that."

"Serving Rome," she pointed out. "You'll be serving Rome, not Trajan."

"Trajan *is* Rome." I kissed her out-thrust chin.

"Not forever," she'd said, but I bent myself back to bundling my belongings for the sea voyage. There was room in the Emperor's trireme for me on the journey back to Rome; I'd disembark somewhere along the way, hire horses, and proceed on north to Germania. The rest of the detachment from the Tenth would follow on a later ship out of Parthia and meet me there. Once I had my legion reunited and in order, I'd send for Mirah and the girls and plan my campaign into Dacia. "Back and forth along the Empire like a message case," she said wearily, but she'd waved me good-bye with a brave face when I took ship from Antioch three days ago. I'd watched her neat little figure diminish as the watery gap widened. When she was just a speck, with the upright young spear that was Antinous standing at her side, and the little girls in her arms no longer visible at all, I kissed a corner of her blue scarf still wrapped around my arm under the greave.

On the other end of the deck, I saw Trajan toss his dice aside and rise with a mild curse. He put his hands to his back, stretching, and that sour-faced Plotina asked some question that he ignored. "How *did* you get him to go back to Rome?" I asked Sabina.

"I hate to admit it, but I cried." Sabina made a face. "I can't abide women who cry to get their way, but Trajan always was a soft touch for a woman's tears. I scolded him a while about how he had to be sensible and preserve his own health if he had any hope of preserving this Empire he's built, and then just as he was getting angry I let my chin quiver. In truth, I think he wants to go back home for a little while. He's tired."

"You'll look after him?" I said anxiously. "Properly, I mean? Old Stoneface Plotina hasn't got a nurturing bone in her body." I'd heard she hadn't been pleased to arrive in Antioch and be told that her husband was taking ship for home within the fortnight. "You'd think she'd be glad to have him home again after four years of absence, but I suppose a cow like that likes running everything her own way."

"She won't have everything her own way this time. I'll make sure to give her plenty of headaches." Sabina's voice was full of relish. "And I might just stay in Rome for a while."

"Hadrian doesn't mind going without you?"

"Not at all."

"Time was you two never went traveling without the other."

"Times change." Her voice was coolly neutral, and I took a glance at her. Her face was as blank as a new slate. Well, it was none of my business anymore what went on in her odd marriage and her even odder mind. She glanced over at me over the cat's head, her face oblique and pointed, and for a moment she and the enigmatic earringed cat looked just alike. Then she gave a smile, changing the subject, and the resemblance vanished. "Your shoulder—why the bandage?"

"I took an arrow at Hatra, pulling the Emperor out of the way. Better my shoulder than his neck."

"No wonder he gave you a legion."

"He'd already planned on that, he said. You know how many of his officers hate me now, for getting jumped over their heads? Last week a group of them tried to waylay me in the bathhouse—"

I heard a cry and whirled. As if from the end of a long tunnel of darkness I saw Trajan stagger, clutching at his suddenly dangling arm. He went to his knees, overturning the game board in a shower of carved pieces, and I saw the lips skin back from his teeth as he tried to stand. *Get up*, I thought, *oh please, get up!* But he fell. He fell.

Oh God, he fell.

SABINA

"You cannot see him, Vibia Sabina. He is resting."

"He asked for me." Sabina moved around Plotina. "So I'm going to him."

"He would be better off resting." Plotina drew herself up, more a granite pillar than ever in a charcoal-gray gown. The gray in her hair matched it, winging along her temples. "I do not permit it."

Sabina smiled sweetly at the Empress of Rome. "Go fuck a horse," she said with great precision, and shoved past Plotina into Trajan's sickroom.

The window had no shutters, so the physicians had pinned a blanket over the sill to give darkness. The bed had had to be brought from the trireme and assembled. The floor was packed clay, and spiderwebs grew in the corners. *No room for an emperor to die*, Sabina thought.

"Don't bustle around me, damn it." The voice from the bed was hoarse, slurred. Trajan lay on his back, heaped with blankets despite the heat, and he batted a hand weakly at the physician trying to measure his pulse. "Is that little Sabina? Come here. The rest of you, out."

The physician fell back obediently. His face as he passed Sabina was taut and sad, and the slaves who filed out behind him all looked as if they had been weeping. The Praetorian at the door kept repeatedly cuffing at his eyes.

"Take that blanket down. I want some light."

"Of course." Sabina dragged the blanket off the window. The harbor sparkled outside, impossibly blue under an even bluer sky. An abandoned harbor, though. The emperor's ship had put into the nearest available port: empty, ruined Selinus, sacked in a long-ago war and never rebuilt. A few squatters nested in derelict buildings along with the crows, but there had been no one to greet the frantic Imperial entourage when Trajan had been carried off the ship to one of the few houses that still boasted an intact roof. Sabina could see the ruins of an old temple cresting the hills above, but for once she felt no urge to go exploring.

"Come here, girl," Trajan rasped, and she came and knelt by the bed. He seemed to have shrunk in just two days, his cheeks hollowed, the skin of his hands loose and wattled, the corner of his mouth dragged down now in a permanent snarl. He could not move the right side of his body; every breath wheezed in his throat. Sabina took his hand between hers and felt no answering squeeze.

"I'll be on my feet in a few days," Trajan said, and coughed. Sabina slid an arm under his shoulders and helped raise him to breathe easier. "A week at most."

"Of course you will, Caesar," Sabina lied.

"So this is strictly a precaution, mind. I want to write a letter—the succession. Leave instructions who's to follow me."

"But—" Sabina blinked. "Not that I don't approve, but why talk to *me* about it?"

"Because if I talk to any of my officers they'll all be putting their own names forward, and I've already heard everything I want to hear on the subject from Plotina." Another cough. "You won't try to influence my choice, Vibia Sabina. You'll listen and keep your mouth shut, like a good soldier."

"True." Sabina felt her heart fluttering in her chest like a moth. "So who *will* follow you?"

"That's the question, eh? Thought I'd draw up a list and let the Senate choose. The buggers have a need to feel consulted, so I thought I'd give them five names."

"I see . . . and is Hadrian one of them?"

"Gods' bones, no."

Sabina let out a long breath. She felt oddly giddy. The matter had been hanging over her head for so long, living in every silence between her and Hadrian—and now it was gone.

Publius Aelius Hadrian would not be emperor.

"Five names," Trajan was saying. "First, former consuls Palma and Celsus."

"Are you sure, Caesar?" Sabina said doubtfully, dragging her mind back to the matter at hand. "They're both—well, I remember you saying Palma was a hothead and Celsus was an honest man but a fool."

Trajan paid no attention. "Lusius Quietus for the third name—"

"The Senate will never choose a Berber, Caesar." Sabina blinked. "Um . . . have you really thought about these names?"

"Of course I have, girl." Trajan sounded waspish, if slurred. "Give

me a little credit! The Senate won't choose any of them. Fools and
hotheads and Berbers don't get to be Emperor of Rome! The Senate
will flick past all three with a shudder, and settle on the name I really
want."

"Ah." Sabina raised her eyebrows. "Very cunning, Caesar. I always
knew that simple soldier act of yours was a sham."

Trajan tried to wink at her, but his eyelid just twitched. "They'll
pick Gaius Avidius Nigrinus. Solid fellow, honest. A safe pair of hands.
Not much flair, but he'll do."

Sabina pondered. "But that's only four names. Three impossible
choices, and your real candidate. Who's the fifth—former consul Servianus, maybe?"

"That old tortoise? Are you mad?"

"You've mentioned his name before. At a dinner party, you said he
would make a fine candidate for—"

"I was drunk. No, my fifth name has to be my backup in case the
Senate doesn't choose Nigrinus. And that name is Titus Aurelius Fulvus Boionius Arrius Antoninus."

She nearly felt her jaw drop. "*Titus?*"

"Why not? I've had my eye on him for a while. Quiet, conscientious,
a hard worker. A fine old family; pots of money; and he did a fine job
as quaestor. Not much liking for military matters, but he's got
courage—brought a nasty little matter to my attention recently, and
I owe him for it. Rome owes him for it, truth be told."

Sabina tried to collect her thoughts. Titus, forever claiming he'd
never be anything more than a plodder, now a candidate for Emperor
of Rome? "He's very young, Caesar," she ventured at last. "Surely the
Senate wouldn't approve a man under thirty-five to be Emperor?"

"They might," Trajan rasped. "The idiots fell all over young Nero
and young Caligula, didn't they? They just might pick Titus if Nigrinus
has too many rivals blocking his path. Or they might give Nigrinus the
purple, but have him adopt Titus as his heir. Either way, he's my backup
plan. Not that I need a backup plan. I'll be on my feet in a day or two,

and when I get back to Rome I'll take the boy under my wing and see how he does with a little grooming. Give me five years to season him, and I'd pick him over Nigrinus any day." Trajan's chest heaved. "Gods, just five years. That's all I ask."

"Titus." The more Sabina thought of the idea, the more she liked it. "He hasn't an enemy in the world, I'll say that. How many men can make that claim?" She thought inconsequentially of Vix, even now sitting somewhere outside with his head bowed and his fists clenched together. Vix, who bashed through life making one enemy after another . . . oh, gods, the cry that had torn out of him when Trajan fell!

"Plenty of spineless jellyfish don't have enemies," Trajan slurred. "Not many brave honest men, though. And I can think of at least one enemy young Titus has made, but it was on my behalf so I can't complain. He's my fifth name, anyway. Get Phaedimus for me to make it official. He's my secretary of grants and promotions; he'll know how to write it up." Trajan's chest heaved in another bout of coughing. "Damn me. I left this too long, didn't I? Should have done it years ago."

"You were too busy conquering the world," Sabina said gently, and withdrew to thread her way through the crowds of restless idlers outside, all trying their best to peer into the Imperial sickroom. "The Emperor wishes to be alone," Sabina said over and over, finally squeezing back inside and pushing the door shut. Phaedimus proved to be one of the Imperial freedmen—a handsome one, and from the way he fell to his knees by the bed and pressed his lips to Trajan's hand, he'd been more to the Emperor than a secretary of grants and promotions. "Caesar—"

"Get out your pens, young man." Trajan's wasted fingers tweaked the lean cheek. "No more weeping. Take down a letter for me. 'To the honorable senators of Rome' or maybe 'Most noble senators of Rome'— just do it up properly for me; you know how to flatter that pack of proud buggers by now . . ."

Phaedimus wrote neatly and rapidly, pen never pausing while the tears dripped down his face. Sabina helped Trajan sit up partway in bed, supporting his deadened shoulder while he crookedly signed at the bottom.

"There." He fell back, the pen dropping from his fingers. "You keep that for the time being, Phaedimus. Till I've broken the news to Plotina and the others. Tomorrow, maybe." His voice trailed off. "Can't face her hissing at me today . . . she's already likely trying to poison me, angry as I made her in Antioch . . ."

Sabina couldn't make out the rest of the mumbled words, but she leaned down to kiss Trajan's forehead. "Rest now." The skin under her lips was as dry as parchment, and cold to the touch.

Phaedimus looked at her with miserable swollen eyes as they passed out of the sickroom. "He's going to die, isn't he?"

Sabina eased the door closed. "Yes."

VIX

I stood watching an emperor die, but somehow I couldn't see him. My eyes couldn't focus on that shrunken figure in the bed. I kept seeing him the way he'd looked during his triumph in Rome, after the Dacian campaign. Tall, godlike, standing like a colossus in his own chariot at the center of the parade, his face daubed with celebratory red paint and a wreath of laurel leaves crowning his head—I could see him so clearly, as if the triumph had happened last week instead of nearly a decade ago. The little room where an emperor lay dying was full of people, but I couldn't see any of them. I was too busy remembering.

I remembered marching along with my lion skin hot in the sun and the eagle screaming silently over my head. I remembered shouting rude insults at Trajan along with the rest of the legionaries—an old tradition for the troops at a victorious general's triumph. He'd seemed to know the insults were fond; his grin split the paint on his face, and he made encouraging waves to inspire us to new heights of vulgarity. The crowds pressing in on each side screamed so loud when they finally caught sight of him that I was deaf for the next three hours. A slave stood behind the Emperor murmuring in his ear: "*You are only a man . . . you are only a man . . .*" Another Roman custom for a triumphant general, and a custom I didn't entirely understand; something about keeping a man humble even in his moment of victory. But I doubted the Emperor had heard one word that slave was muttering. He was too happy, too radiantly happy with his laurel wreath cocked back on his head at a boyish angle and his people shouting his name.

Romans are strange. Why on earth would anyone ever tell such a god that he was only a man?

The little room was stifling. Trajan's officers stood crammed along the walls, spaced here and there by Praetorians who stood looking helpless because it was their job to keep the Emperor alive, but what could they do here to save him? His freedmen stood in frightened little clusters, and senators flocked together like whispering old hens. I was crammed somewhere at the back, the Emperor's newest and most junior commander, but I could see over all the heads before me. The Empress sat on one side of the bed, rigid as ever in a wooden chair, one hand resting on her husband's. Sabina had slipped from her chair to her knees on the bed's other side; her cropped head leaned against Trajan's deadened arm, her fingers ceaselessly stroking his motionless hand. Her eyes were closed, but when the Imperial physician tried to pin a blanket up over the window to block the fading light, her head whipped up and she snapped, "Leave it! He wants light."

"The air is unhealthful—"

"*I said leave it!*"

Plotina drew a breath as if to remonstrate. Sabina's furious eyes bored into her. Silence fell again. Just the shuffle of feet, an occasional cough—and above all, the terrible rasp of Trajan's breathing. Coming slower now.

Slower.

"Clear the room," Plotina ordered. "It's unfitting for him to go to the gods in such a crowd." Sabina began to argue with her, but the freedmen were already streaming out, and I trailed after them. I couldn't watch—couldn't look at that waxen figure on the bed, couldn't bear to hear that slow rasp of breath, couldn't bear to see my Emperor die. My Emperor, the man I'd followed to Dacia and Parthia and hell too if he'd asked it of me . . .

Half the soldiers were already weeping, unashamed. A handsome secretary stood outside the now-closed bedchamber door, bent nearly double, shoulders heaving. I just stumbled away, out of that nameless little house. Such a small place, too small and ordinary to contain the last breath of a man like Trajan. Why couldn't he die on a battlefield? The last arrow of the last battle, while subduing the last enemy on the last unconquered province in the world? Why this dead and dusty little town full of ghosts?

I stumbled past a series of ruined shacks, over a road missing half its paving stones but still leading up a mild slope toward a temple now roofless and godless. A beautiful day, the sea sparkling distantly, the sun shining. Shouldn't it be raining? Shouldn't the skies weep when an emperor dies?

I lurched up the cracked mossy steps of the temple. A temple of Jupiter, maybe, or some unknown god. Now it was just a few crumbling columns on a mossy foundation. One of the columns seemed to come at me, hitting me in my wounded shoulder, and I leaned against it. Clutched it, my hands shaking against the stone. My shoulder burned. My eyes burned. Shouldn't a soldier weep when his general dies?

I don't know how long I stood there, trembling against the column. But I picked my head up, looking around me aimlessly, and I saw Sabina. Standing across the temple in the crumpled shift she'd worn day and night as she tended Trajan, dwarfed by the columns. Her eyes were bright with unshed tears. I took a step toward her, another step, lurching like a drunk.

She opened her arms and I dropped into them, crashing to my knees. "He's dying," I said against her waist.

"Ssshh," she said, her fingers running through my hair.

The first sob tore out of my throat. "He's dying. He's *dying*—"

"Hush, my love," she whispered, just as she'd whispered to me in Dacia after I killed a king on a solar disc. I'd gripped her then, drowning, and she held me now as I drowned again, howling into her linen shift. Mirah would have tried to comfort me, told me not to weep, told me Trajan would go to the next world and be happy there. Sabina just held me. She sank down where she stood, sitting on a fallen column, and she gripped me tight as I sobbed into her lap like a heartbroken child.

My tears went eventually, but I stayed where I was, huddled numbly in the arms of a woman I used to love and used to hate. The sun set, the moon rose; warmth was gone and chill had replaced it. How could the world just go on as though nothing had changed? Everything was changing.

"Stand up, Vix. It's getting cold." Sabina tugged me to my feet with gentle hands. I stood there dumbly, an ox waiting for the sacrificial knife. I was a soldier of Rome; we didn't go anywhere without orders. Who would give me my orders, once my general was dead?

"Come with me," said Sabina, and I took her outstretched hand and followed her obediently. Those orders would do for now.

The house where Trajan—*that house* was still deathly quiet, a ring of Praetorians keeping the hovering onlookers at bay. Soldiers paced outside, some weeping, some white-faced, some blank with shock. *They should be inside*, I thought. Trajan belonged with his men in his last hour—not with his sour bitch of a wife, crouched like a vulture on her death watch.

Sabina skirted the crowds, leading me to another house that wasn't much more than four crumbling stone walls and a roof. She got a bedroll from somewhere, laying it out with the expert neatness she still remembered from her days with the Tenth. She eased me into it, covered me up, took my hand in hers, and curled herself against the wall. She was still there when I woke in the morning.

Which was when we found out we had been locked inside.

PLOTINA

"Well done." Plotina extended a gracious hand to the stocky Praetorian guard in his red-and-gold armor. "You were most convincing. You certainly fooled them all."

"I don't like fooling people, Lady." The guard shifted from foot to foot, uneasy. "You're sure it was necessary?"

"Essential." Plotina gave her most reassuring smile. "Rome owes you a great debt, and so do I."

"If you say so, Lady."

"I do. And so would the Emperor." Plotina picked up her husband's cold hand and stroked it. "The former Emperor, that is. The new Emperor will thank you himself upon his arrival."

"Yes, Lady."

"You may go. Not a word, now."

"No, Lady." But the guard still looked uneasy as he tramped out; Plotina could see that. "I think I shall have to take care of him, don't you?" she told her husband. "Perhaps a convenient fall from one of these rocky cliffs. What do you think?"

Trajan's corpse lay silent. His flesh had a marble chill and his limbs had gone stiff, but the heaped blankets had concealed that quite artfully.

"Now, I hope you aren't angry with me," Plotina chided, sinking back onto the stool at her husband's bedside. She didn't bother lowering her voice—a few slaves lined the walls, waiting to be called upon, but they all knew she'd have them crucified if they ever spoke of what they'd seen in this room. "It's just a *tiny* deception, husband. We'll announce your death as soon as Dear Publius arrives from Antioch.

For now, everyone can go on thinking you're alive. It will make the transition much smoother, and you know how I always like to smooth things out for you."

The Praetorian had done a good job indeed. He had a gruff voice not unlike his Emperor's; he had stood concealed in the shadows of the bed's curtains and read the lines Plotina had given him. Plotina's only task had been to chafe Trajan's dead hand and shed a tear or two. The clerk who recorded the last wishes of Marcus Ulpius Trajan had been sitting well back, far too occupied with the importance of the moment, and the crowd of witnesses stood at a respectful distance in the dimly lit room. Plotina had only ushered them back into the bedchamber once she'd had everything made ready, and most had been weeping too hard to notice that the Emperor's chest had not been rising and falling under the heap of carefully arranged blankets. Sabina would have noticed, but Sabina had been confined and kept out of the way.

"I didn't hurt her, if that's what you're wondering," Plotina told Trajan. "Just shut her away for a few days, until I could settle everything satisfactorily. I know you were fond of the girl, but you must admit she has a tendency to interfere. I couldn't have that, now could I?"

Plotina paused a moment, frowning. That Girl with her indecent dresses and her tart tongue and her odd ideas of charity had Plotina's own position now. First lady of Rome. Somehow it was the first time Plotina had considered the reality of it. *That foul-mouthed little slut, taking my place?*

Well, hardly. Little Sabina would have other duties, after all. And perhaps, somewhere, along the line, she could be quietly divorced. Her connection to Trajan had served its purpose, after all. Another girl could be found if necessary, someone more biddable. Her sister was a likely prospect, if the laws could be sufficiently bent . . .

Sabina had been kept safely away from the matter at hand. That was the important thing.

"It was quite funny, really," Plotina assured her husband. "My little deception about your will, I mean. Like a mummer's farce—you'd have laughed. And I did carry out your wishes, you know. You *would* have chosen Dear Publius as heir in the end. I know you were annoyed with me about my little efforts in that direction, but I knew what I was doing. If you'd simply let me explain, I'd have made you understand."

Trajan's drying lips were beginning to peel back from his teeth, as if he were snarling at her. Plotina reached out a hand to smooth his face. "Don't growl, dear. I'm not angry with you anymore, in spite of the things you said to me in Antioch. It's all worked out for the best."

Really, it had. Juno's hand, no doubt, reaching down to save her sister. Plotina had felt more frozen with every narrowing mile of water between the trireme and Rome. Disgrace, scandal, ostracism—would Trajan go so far as to divorce her, after all her hard work and initiative? On the word of that little snake Titus Aurelius, whose reward would apparently be Dear Publius's birthright? *What can I do, what can I do?* Frozen panic had been giving way to pure terror when Juno acted. "You should be proud," Plotina told her husband. "Only the queen of the heavens could strike down a god like you."

A knock sounded at the door. Plotina started, then rose hastily and pulled the bed curtains to mask Trajan's still body. "The Emperor is not to be disturbed."

"I'm sorry, Lady." A young secretary entered hesitantly, twisting a scroll between diffident hands. "I didn't mean . . . how is he?"

"Resting now." Plotina gave a brave, distant smile. "He pushed himself so hard, giving us his last wishes. I think it will not be long now."

She had fed him an extra mix of sleeping draught at the end, just to make sure. A dicey business, really: giving him just enough to keep him unconscious but *not* kill him, and in the end—his real end, which had come in private just after she shooed everyone out—perhaps she'd given him a bit too much. *Really, how tiring. One moment you're trying to give a man a peaceful death, and the next you have to pretend he's alive again!*

"See, that's where I'm confused, Lady," the secretary was hedging.

"It surprised me that the Emperor changed his mind. He dictated a letter to me—"

Plotina took the scroll from his hand before he could proffer it. "Did he, now."

"Yes, his list of heirs for the Senate . . . as I said, it seemed odd he'd changed his mind."

"A dying man often wanders in his last hours." Swiftly she scanned the list of names. Celsus, Palma, Quietus, Nigrinus . . . oh, dear, something *would* be have to be done about all of them. Then she read the last name, and a bubble of pure joy rose in her chest.

Titus Aurelius Fulvus Boionius Arrius Antoninus.

This time the name gave a thrill of satisfaction instead of hammering pains to her temples. Titus. Yes, something could definitely be done about him.

"Thank you for bringing this to my attention." Plotina turned her attention back to the secretary, barely remembering to hide her beam of happiness. "Phaedimus, isn't it?"

"Yes, Lady." His eyes were red-rimmed as he stared at the bed with its silent mound of blankets. A handsome young fellow. One of Trajan's whores, no doubt.

Plotina smiled at him. "Guard!"

The stocky Praetorian entered again.

"Take this man outside and dispense with him." Plotina rolled up the scroll again tightly, speaking very low so her words only reached the guard. "A cliff should do nicely. There's a purse in it for you if it looks like suicide."

The guard never blinked. "As you wish, Lady."

Yes, she'd chosen well when she selected him. Loyal men, so rare these days. Pity he'd have to go over the cliff too, in a day or so.

"Lady?" The secretary looked more puzzled than alarmed as the Praetorian seized his arm. "What—"

Plotina dropped Trajan's ridiculous letter and its ridiculous list of names into the brazier. It caught at once, flaring up in a bright arrow of flame.

"Lady, wait!"

"No one else is to enter," she called after the guard as he dragged Phaedimus out. "I do not wish the Emperor's last hours disturbed."

The door thumped shut. Plotina dusted off her fingertips as the letter flared into ash, and turned back to her husband. "Titus Aurelius?" she chided. "Really, Trajan. Whatever were you thinking?"

His snarl had returned. Maybe he was trying to say he was sorry?

"Perhaps I should announce your death in the morning," she told him, coming back to the bed. "Before you begin to—well, smell. We'll have the funeral pyre here when Dear Publius arrives, and take your ashes back to Rome. I'll see them interred under your triumphal column, my dear. The one recording all your Dacian victories."

She sat beside his still body, leaning forward to brush a strand of iron-gray hair off his forehead. "Thirty years of marriage, and I've never seen you look happier than you did at that triumph. You were a wonder of a man, you know. You should have let me have children. We'd have birthed a race of gods."

A yawn struck her. Goodness, could it be dark already? So exhausting, this whole business. When she returned to Rome, she would sleep for a week.

"You don't mind if I rest now, do you?" Plotina asked her husband, curling up beside him on the nest of blankets. "We never did share a bed together, not even on the night of our wedding. So cold. You're cold now, but I suppose one can't have everything."

Empress Pompeia Plotina put her head on her husband's stiff shoulder and fell happily asleep.

CHAPTER 27

SABINA

Sabina stormed into the room Plotina had transformed into a study, and the former Empress bowed very low indeed at the sight of her. "My dear," Trajan's widow smiled. "I fear I have been neglecting you. So very busy, but of course that is no excuse, is it? You, after all, are the Empress of Rome now."

Sabina did not stop to reflect on her new title, though it was the first time she had heard it. She just hit Plotina fast and hard across the face, not a dainty slap but a close-fisted hammer of a blow that she'd seen centurions deal out to disobedient soldiers. The impact sent a jolt of furious pleasure through her like a spear shaft. "You bitch," she said, and had to fight to keep her voice even. "You know Trajan would have rather died than have your precious Publius take the purple."

As one, the slaves bolted out of the room without waiting to be dismissed.

"But Trajan *is* dead." Plotina's face remained serene, though one sallow cheek now glowed red. "And I am pleased to say he had a change of heart shortly before he went to the gods. He was able to dictate a letter to the Senate announcing his true choice."

"Yes, the letter *you* signed. When did he ever have you sign anything for him before?"

"My dear, he was too weak to hold the pen."

"Too *weak?* He was already dead! He died, and you dictated that letter for him!"

"An empress really shouldn't put stock in such wild rumors."

Sabina flung herself down into the nearest chair, crossing one leg over the other in the way that she knew irritated Plotina. "And this letter is your only proof?"

"Hardly." Plotina seated herself behind the folding desk—Trajan's desk, Trajan's lamps and rugs and couches, transported from the trireme to this damp stony little room to give the Empress—the former Empress—all the comfort she required. "My husband verbally announced his intention to adopt Hadrian as his son and heir. There are witnesses."

"I heard about them too. Standing well back in a darkened room while you wept over a corpse's hand. If you really wanted witnesses, why wasn't I allowed to be present?"

"I was told you were in bed with your latest lover. A legionary, I believe?"

Sabina laughed. "Is that the best you have? Me locked into a confined room, probably on your orders, where I spent the hours drying the tears of one of Trajan's officers? Someone, by the way, who mourned his Emperor much more passionately than you seem to be doing."

"I will leave matters of *passion* up to you, Vibia Sabina. You know so much more than I about the sordid business."

Plotina leaned back to a scroll spread over the desk, writing rapidly. Sabina considered her for a moment, feeling rage seep away inside like bathwater, leaving cold calculation behind. "You will never get away with it," she said at last.

"With what?" Plotina did not bother to look up from her parchment. "Dear Publius has probably already received the letter announcing his adoption—I sent it before Trajan even died, on the fastest ship here. Hadrian will take that same ship back here to take charge of my husband's funeral cortege, and then return to Rome. Word has been sent to the Senate as well, on a fast ship, and their approval will be a matter of a mere week or so. The legates and officials here have been instructed to inform their legions—"

"And what about Trajan's real letter?" Sabina snapped. "The list of candidates he wished to send the Senate, so that *they* might choose? I assure you, Hadrian was not on that list." *Titus . . .*

"What letter would that be?" Plotina blinked. "We searched my husband's papers thoroughly, of course. Everything is a sad tangle. Phaedimus, that freedman who wrote letters for grants and promotions, has committed suicide. He leaped off a cliff . . . a noble gesture, wishing to follow his Emperor into the grave, but one wishes he had left the Imperial documentation in better order."

Sabina felt a ribbon of ice crawling down her spine. "I was there when Trajan dictated that letter," she managed to say. "I know what names were listed, and I will tell anyone who wishes to know that Hadrian was not one of them. Can you have me killed as easily as an inconsequential little freedman?"

"No. But who will believe you, my dear? A woman who keeps such questionable company. Closeted with a lover when her Imperial great-uncle lay dying . . . not your first lover either. I saw you carrying on with that young Titus Aurelius before you left for Antioch. I wonder how many people know about your affair with him. Not to mention all the other men."

Sabina chuckled lightly, as if this were all nothing more than idle gossip over a good meal. "You want to soil the reputation of Dear Publius's wife just when he wants to look impeccable? By all means, Plotina. Tell everyone I'm the great whore of Rome and I've been making a fool of my husband for years with half the men in the legions. Dear Publius will *love* you for that."

"Dear Publius loves me anyway. I have made him Emperor of Rome." Plotina's voice oiled out, deep and unctuous and satisfied. "Perhaps we might strike a different bargain, Vibia Sabina. We may have had our differences in the past, but it doesn't prevent us from striking a new alliance, does it? I will refrain from darkening your reputation any further, and you will greet your husband properly when he arrives, wearing something more dignified than that shift."

"Die slowly, Plotina." Sabina rose, speaking slowly and distinctly. "Dear gods, was there ever a woman better named than you? You sallow plotting scheming treacherous bitch."

She turned for the door.

"You really will have to improve your language, Vibia Sabina," Plotina called after her. Sabina could hear the smile. "There can be no swearing for the Empress of Rome."

TITUS

The Norbanus house seemed strangely silent when Titus entered the atrium. The slave who ushered him inside was white-faced and distracted, vanishing without taking Titus's cloak or asking whom he had come to see. When Titus had come to this atrium hand in hand with Faustina, soaking wet and asking her father's permission for a betrothal, the house had rung top to bottom with congratulations: Calpurnia showering them both with kisses, Marcus beaming pleasure, Faustina's brothers making sly jokes about why their big sister was drenched head to toe, the slaves trading smug whispers of "Told you so!" Now the house was silent as a crypt.

They already know, he thought. Good. It would make things easier.

"Faustina!" He found her sitting in the gardens, a splash of peach-colored linen and fair hair, staring at the splashing fountain. "You heard, I take it." He kissed the top of his betrothed's smooth blond head. *Betrothed. Future wife. Wife-to-be.* Words he'd reveled in these past weeks, because they were all just so many delicious synonyms for *mine.*

Faustina looked up at him, but he didn't see the familiar leap of happiness in her face. Her dark eyes were larger than ever, and blank as stones. "He's dead."

Titus swallowed. "I know."

He'd had the news from Ennia, of all people. A freedwoman house-keeper, better informed than one of the richest men in Rome . . . she had a brother who worked the Tiber docks, and she'd been visiting him when the black-sailed ship came gliding home. She'd come running direct into Titus's chamber, where he sat ostensibly looking at *alimenta* reports and in reality making happy plans for his wedding. How many guests to invite to the banquet; whether Faustina would prefer an old-fashioned iron ring or the new kind with gold set in iron . . . he'd been doodling her profile in the margin of a wax tablet when Ennia came running in, sickly pale under her olive tan, to tell him the news that had just barely come to Rome.

Emperor Trajan was dead.

"I don't think many people know yet," Titus said to Faustina. "There will be a formal announcement for the Senate, but—"

"Of course no one knows yet," Faustina interrupted, puzzled. "It only happened an hour ago."

"What?"

"My father."

For a moment he couldn't speak, couldn't collect his reeling thoughts. "Your *father?*"

"Mother found him at his desk." Faustina's voice was thin. "He looked so peaceful, she thought he must be sleeping. He must have drifted off over his books—he never called out."

Titus sank down on the bench and took her in his arms. Trajan dead. Marcus Norbanus, dead. *Oh, no. Oh, no no no.*

That changed everything.

"What were you talking about?" Faustina's eyes were full of tears, but she was trying valiantly to hold them back. "Is someone else dead?"

He hesitated. *She's lost her father; don't burden her.* But Faustina was no fragile blossom who couldn't bear a breath of bad news—if there was anything she shared with Sabina, it was toughness. "Trajan."

The tears spilled over then. Titus held her, not ashamed to find his own eyes leaking. They clung together on the bench, Faustina burrowing into his shoulder like a child, Titus turning his face against her smooth fragrant hair.

"I'm glad Father didn't know." Faustina finally sat up, dashing the last tears off her cheeks with the back of her hand. "He worshipped Trajan. Who's to be Emperor now?"

Titus forced the words out. "Your brother-in-law. Hadrian."

Faustina's tear-drowned eyes sprang wide. "*Hadrian?* We can't know that yet, the Senate hasn't—"

"He was acclaimed on Trajan's deathbed. It's already all over the city." News like that shouldn't have leaked out, not before the Senate had been informed first, but somehow it had. Titus wondered if the Empress had had a hand in that. Far harder for the Senate to reject Publius Aelius Hadrian as Emperor of Rome when the rumor had already spread through the city that Trajan had adopted him as son and heir on his deathbed.

Faustina gave a small dazed shake of her head. "Hadrian," she repeated, blank. "Trajan would never have chosen him!"

Surely not, after he got my letter. And Trajan *had* received Titus's letter—he'd sent a brusque note of thanks, and mentioned something about a longer talk once he was back in Rome. *I've got plans for you, boy,* he'd written in his soldier's scrawl.

Not anymore. But Empress Plotina would have plans of her own. Oh, yes. Titus remembered the strange ripple of her face when he'd confronted her, the dread he had of turning away, as if she might spring onto his unprotected back in one mad leap like a spider. *You're safe,* he'd told himself. *The Emperor knows the truth now; he won't listen to any of her poison. And once Trajan is gone, she won't be Empress anymore. She'll have no influence in Imperial matters.*

He hadn't counted on Trajan dying. Hadn't counted on Plotina *succeeding*, actually being able to buy her protégé the purple.

However she'd pulled it off, it was done. Plotina had made her Dear Publius emperor, and doubtless he'd be grateful for the favor. Titus heard her snarl again in his ear, clear as if she stood an inch behind him. *I will see you dead for this.*

"Titus?" Faustina's voice brought him back—that low, sweet-toned voice that could vibrate through his chest like the plucked string of a lyre. "You're a thousand miles away."

"Just wondering how Sabina will take it." He forced a smile after the lie. "Being Empress. Somehow I don't think it will suit her."

"It would suit me!" Faustina tried to smile, but her eyes began to fill again. "Gods, I don't care if Hadrian's emperor, or my sister's empress. I don't care about any of it. Father, Trajan—the two best men in Rome are dead."

And so am I, Titus thought.

He took a deep breath and said it. The thing he'd come here to say, the thing that had squatted painfully in his throat like a ball of thorns all the way to the Norbanus house. "I can't marry you, Faustina. Not now. Not ever."

Her head jerked up and she stared at him.

"You'd be marrying a dead man." The words came out very flat. "Plotina's wanted me dead since I exposed her for a thief, and now that Hadrian's taken the purple she'll get her wish."

"That's absurd!" Color flooded Faustina's cheeks. "Hadrian doesn't have any reason to—"

"He's disliked me since the campaign in Dacia where I showed him up for a fool in front of Trajan." And for another reason he had no intention of telling Faustina: Plotina had seen Titus that night when he kissed Sabina. She'd have told Hadrian about that by now, certainly, and he wasn't a man to overlook such a slight. No, the new Emperor had no reason to extend any mercy to Titus.

"Sabina wouldn't allow it! If she's the Empress of Rome—"

"She won't be the real Empress. Not the one with the power." Titus thought of the coltish senator's daughter who had sprawled on the floor with a map, planning to see the world. *My poor girl, you won't be seeing much of it now.*

"My father," Faustina began automatically, and stopped.

Marcus Norbanus's support might have given Titus some protection—he was a patron even an emperor might hesitate to cross. Titus had come here today to consult with him, see if there might be protection from Plotina's vengeance. But Marcus Norbanus was dead.

"You see why I can't marry you." Titus released her hands, putting them gently away from him. "You deserve a husband who will last out the year, and—"

"Shut up!" Faustina jumped to her feet. "You think you're getting rid of me that easily, Titus?"

He looked up at her, standing there before him. Lovely, lissome, steady, and sweet—and safe. Safe as long as he didn't marry her, anyway. Because any wife he took would be a widow within the year . . . or would be dragged down with him.

The pain kicked him then, square in the chest. *I can't do it*, he thought numbly. The hurt clawed at his innards like a live thing. *Dear gods, I can't give her up. I just found her!*

Be quiet, he told himself harshly. *She's not for you. She never was.*

"I'll be leaving now." He rose from the marble bench. "Give my sympathies to your mother, and explain why I won't be attending your father's funeral procession. It will be easier that way for both of us."

Tears had flooded into her eyes again, but she refused to let them spill over. "You don't mean it," she whispered. "You can't."

He averted his eyes. "I'd better go. The madness about Trajan's death will be hitting soon, I imagine."

He hoped desperately that she wouldn't cry, wouldn't cling to his hand and beg him to stay . . . but she just lifted her head bravely, reaching out to straighten the folds of his toga over his shoulder. Somehow that was worse.

She stepped against him, taking his face between her hands, and pressed her lips to his. His arms rose to circle her, and her mouth opened under his like a bud. *Stop*, Titus thought, but he drank her desperately and it was a mistake.

His hands gripped her long waist, skimmed her round breasts, buried themselves in her hair. She pressed herself against him hungrily, and the strap of her dress fell down her arm and the warm silk of her bare shoulder was under his mouth. She murmured wordlessly, tugging him backward without ever moving away, until they fetched up hard against the wall of the house, out of sight from the garden or the atrium. Faustina pulled his head down again, and the other strap of her dress slid down, and Titus could have drowned in her hyacinth scent.

A shutter slammed open on the other side of the house, and Titus heard the sound of a woman's stifled sob. A slave, perhaps, grieving for a kind master as she went about her duties. The sound brought Titus out of himself; sent a wash of confused shame through him. *Not one hour ago I heard the Emperor of Rome was dead—and I'm undressing his great-niece against a wall?* Marcus's daughter . . .

Faustina had stilled in his arms, as if the world had suddenly come rushing back to her too, and as if she found it a frightening place. "My father is dead," she said in a thin voice, and just leaned her head against Titus's chest.

He held her quietly. On the other side of the house there was another slam as the shutters banged closed, and another muffled sniff of suppressed tears. Definitely a slave woman. Soon, Titus supposed, another slave would be sent to look for the daughter of the house.

He stepped away from the gentle weight of Faustina's head against his shoulder, and somehow that was harder than stepping away from her kisses. "I suppose you thought you'd seduce me, and then I'd be honor-bound to marry you?" His voice came out reasonably steady, and his hand too as he eased the shoulders of her dress back up. "I'm afraid that's not going to work."

"I didn't really think it would, but it was worth a try." Faustina met his eyes square, her blond hair uncoiling down her back from its neat pins, her mouth swollen from kissing and her eyes swollen from tears. Her voice, though, was pure steel. "I am *not* giving you up, Titus."

"I'm going to *die*, don't you understand?" He said it brutally. "Once Plotina sees her precious protégé crowned, she'll start settling old scores. She'll probably send a squad of butchers for me in the middle of the night. So for once in your life, Faustina, won't you do as you're told and stay away from me?"

"I don't think you really like women who do as they're told, Titus. Sabina always does exactly as she pleases and gets exactly what she wants, and so do I. We may not be much alike in other respects, but we have that one thing very much in common."

Titus turned away from his betrothed. His hand clenched and unclenched about a crushed fold of his toga, and his eyes burned. He could still taste the sweet smooth skin of her bare shoulder.

"Maybe you're right." Faustina's arms slid about his waist from behind, and he felt her warm cheek lean against his back. "Maybe Hadrian won't let you live. But the worst thing that will happen to me, Titus, is that I'll be a very, *very* wealthy widow."

He gave a short laugh, and for one wild moment thought of fleeing. Taking Faustina and running with her to Britannia, to Hispania, to anywhere.

But where did you go when your enemy was master of the world?

He turned, folding her back into his arms. "I love you, Annia Galeria Faustina."

They clung together silently in the dusk. *Walk away*, Titus told himself. *Walk away now.* But he couldn't move, not with Faustina's arms knotted around his waist like a circle of rope.

"Do you want an old-fashioned iron ring?" he asked her. "Or one of the new ones with gold set in iron?"

"Just iron." Faustina tilted her head up at him, giving a watery smile. "Iron lasts, and we're going to last too. We'll be *old* together, Titus. Hadrian won't kill you, you'll see. You won't be dooming me when we get married—you'll be saving yourself. Hadrian won't be able to touch you once you're his brother-in-law."

He let her think it. She scolded him a little as she scrubbed at her eyes—"You'll have to buy me something very expensive to make up for this, you know!"—and he just feasted his eyes on her, wondering how long he would have to enjoy his wife.

And who they would finally send to kill him.

VIX

The day after he arrived in Selinus, my new Emperor sent for me.

No. Not *my* Emperor. Just *the* Emperor. That supercilious prat Hadrian would never be my Emperor, not if he ruled a thousand years.

I saluted as I came into the little study with its makeshift luxuries. Hadrian leaned back in the most comfortable of the cushioned chairs, bearded and busy in a black toga, reading a letter and at the same time dictating another to a hovering secretary. Freedmen scurried to and fro with armloads of correspondence, slates and scrolls, gifts from officials eager to show the new Emperor their loyalty. Hadrian managed to direct the stream with flicks of his free hand, never missing a beat in either his reading or his dictating, gently rubbing one foot along the back of the dog sleeping at his feet—and he still had an eye to spare for me as I entered.

"Sir." I came to parade rest.

"—about the gardens outside Antioch. I want the Castallian Fount blocked up with a stone. It predicted I would become Emperor, and I won't have it predicting the same for anyone else. Sign it, *Hadrian, son of Trajan Caesar.*" He gestured the secretary to carry on, and raised his eyebrows at me pointedly. "'Sir?'"

"... Caesar," I managed to choke out, saluting again.

"Better," he said, and held out his hand for the secretary's scroll. "I'll sign that now, thank you. Bring me the packet for Vercingetorix, please."

I fixed my gaze somewhere over Hadrian's shoulder as he signed a series of documents. I couldn't look at him without the gorge rising in my throat. He had arrived yesterday on what was undoubtedly the fastest ship that could leave from Antioch. He had disembarked from his black-sailed trireme, head covered in mourning, and bowed before the rise of cheers started off by Empress Plotina—former Empress Plotina—and her ring of toadies. I had not clapped once, from my spot in the back of the crowd of officers. All I wanted was to get out of this barren ghostly little town and back to my men. Back to route marches and battles and the clash of javelins and the swearing of my legionaries. Back to the things I understood.

I hadn't expected to be summoned. Surely a new Emperor had better things to do than demote old enemies? And my record spoke for itself. Hadrian might be a cold bastard, but cold bastards are practical men. Surely he would let me continue the work I'd done so well for Trajan?

But I remembered the cool murderous gaze Hadrian had leveled on me in a feasting hall in Germania, a gaze I'd given back in full furious measure, and I couldn't help a shiver.

Hadrian didn't seem very interested in me now, though. He wrote something else on a fresh scroll and made a gesture to one of the dashing secretaries, who presented me with a thick packet of sealed letters and passes. "Your new orders, Vercingetorix."

"Orders, Caesar?" To have my head sliced off? To strip me of my rank? To toss me out on some barren rock in the middle of the ocean to die?

"You are to take leave of Selinus at once."

I breathed easier at that. If I could just take my men to Germania—well, Germania was a long way from Rome. How much would I have to think about Hadrian, from all the way up north? I'd be fighting Dacian warriors again and running my legion as I saw fit. It wouldn't matter who wore the purple all the way down in Rome.

If Trajan doesn't recover, I heard Mirah's voice whisper in my ear, *you'll be serving* Rome. *Not Trajan.*

Trajan is Rome, I'd said, brash and stupid.

Not forever.

I shivered again, but I thrust her words out of my head and took the packet of letters. "Take leave to Germania? Caesar?" Belatedly.

"No." Hadrian didn't look up from his slate. "To Rome."

". . . Rome?"

"Yes, you are receiving a promotion. I am making you part of my Praetorian Guard."

For a moment I couldn't speak. The secretaries still bustled with their letters, the freedmen still dashed with their baskets, the slaves still hovered with their pen cases—apparently unaware that I'd been turned to stone in the midst of all the activity. "But I have a legion," I said hoarsely. "The Tenth Fidelis." *My* Tenth, mine at last.

"Not anymore." Hadrian lifted his slate, scanning it as he held out a hand for a new pen. "We will not be needing so many new commanders, as there will not be nearly so many campaigns planned along the borders. Dacia has proven an untenable drain of resources; therefore it will be surrendered back to the rebels and no longer requires the presence of an active legion. Also," Hadrian added disinterestedly, "the Parthian campaign is to be halted at once. Armenia, Mesopotamia, Assyria, and all other territories acquired are to be abandoned."

If I'd already turned to stone, I now turned to ice.

Dacia, where I'd killed a king who had the strength of ten and first earned the pride of carrying my eagle. Armenia, where I'd made my mark on my first command. Mesopotamia, where I'd buried Julius by the Euphrates. Assyria, where I'd watched Philip die before my eyes and taken an arrow for Trajan and earned the name Vercingetorix the Red. All gone. All for nothing. Trajan's ring burned on my finger with its carved title. *Parthicus.* Conqueror of Parthia.

"Why?" I croaked.

Hadrian looked up at me for the first time, and I saw that his dark eyes were amused. "You think I will debate Imperial policy with a guard?"

That was when I felt the rage start to bank in my stomach.

"Never fear," the new Emperor said. "I have taken note of your various talents, and they will be used. You will be a fine addition to my Praetorians. I even have a small matter you can take care of on your way back to Rome." He tilted his head at his bustling entourage. "Leave us."

The secretaries, the freedmen, the slaves filed out. I still stood like a pillar, clutching the bundle of orders that had just eaten my future and invalidated my past.

Hadrian's smile vanished as the doors thudded shut. "You will not find these orders in the packet you hold. They come direct from me. There are five men who must be eliminated. Rivals of mine. I will give you the names later. Take whatever men you require to get the job done, but I want those five men dealt with. Then you may return to Rome and take up your new duties as a Praetorian."

In answer, I whipped the packet of orders across the room at his head.

The bastard was quick, I'll say that for him. One heavy hand lashed out and sent them spinning into the wall before they could touch him.

I folded my arms across my chest and spat on the floor. "I'm no man's assassin." Not bothering with *Caesar* this time. "Find a common thug for your dirty work."

"You *are* a common thug," Hadrian said calmly. "But a talented one. I want you at my side, and under my rule you will rise high. You buy that place with five dead men."

"If you think I'm going to kill off your rivals for you—"

"Oh, but you will. You have a wife, I believe, and two daughters, and a boy you keep for a ward? Surely you wish to keep them safe."

"I *can* keep them safe." I'd take Mirah and the children, disappear so fast into the wilds outside Rome that even Hadrian's eyes and ears couldn't find me.

"What about your men?" The new Emperor's big hunting hound had risen, eyeing me as my voice rose, and Hadrian scratched it fondly behind the ear. "A Gallic centurion of yours who was part of your *contubernium* when you first joined the Tenth. An African you just promoted to *optio* for saving your life outside Osrhoene. The rest of them. The entire Tenth, as a matter of fact—I can order them decimated, on some offense or other. And I will make sure that every tenth man chosen happens to be one you care for. And after that, I'll disband the Tenth Fidelis altogether, fold the surviving men into other legions. So much for those tattoos I can see on your arms, the X and the eagle. The Tenth Fidelis and anything it ever accomplished will be forgotten."

My hand dropped to the place where my sword hilt should have been. But of course it wasn't. No one was allowed armed into the Emperor's presence.

"That's the spirit." Hadrian gave an unexpected grin, teeth gleaming white in the darkness of his beard. "Hate me if you wish—think of me when you slit those five throats. And focus on the good rather than the bad. You'll find me grateful, when I return to Rome. I might even make you Praetorian Prefect. The Senate can be counted on to raise a fuss about the deaths of those five men I've named. I'll make sure blame for this overhasty batch of executions is shifted to the current Prefect. He'll be eased out and allowed to commit suicide, and if you prove yourself, I'll allow you to take his place. A sizable increase in pay, prestige, and position. Not a bad reward for a thug like you."

Praetorians. The elite, supposedly, but those of us in more active duty knew better. Praetorians were palace guards in breastplates who never saw blood or dust or a sword-dent. Tramping dutifully after the Emperor wherever he went, getting fat and lazy on guard duty. And as for the Prefects? The Emperor's watchdogs, spending their nights filtering out conspiracy theories and setting informers to spy on the Emperor's friends. Powerful. Feared. And bored to death.

"Caesar," I grated out, "I would rather sink a knife in your back than guard it."

"I'm counting on it." Hadrian tilted his chair back, still aiming that maddening smile at me. "I would rather have an enemy guard my back than a friend any day. Friends expect favors; friends are soured when they don't get the rewards they want; friends turn on you. Enemies can be counted on to turn on you, so there are no surprises. And I know you, Vercingetorix. I know your record; the things you've done in the field. You'll guard my back against other enemies because you want to keep me safe for your own vengeance." Hadrian's smile deepened at my expression. "Trajan liked to be loved by those who served him. I am not Trajan."

"You're not fit to wipe Trajan's boots!"

"True," said Hadrian.

In an hour full of shocks, that somehow shocked me most of all.

"Trajan was a good man," Hadrian went on, rubbing a hand thoughtfully down the dog's long back. "It's necessary for an emperor to be a good man, if he wishes to last. Augustus knew that—a ruthless despot, really, but he calculated a very nice pose as a likable fellow. Intelligent of him, because ruthless despots get themselves murdered— Caligula, Nero, Domitian. The good men rule long years—Vespasian, Trajan. My name will be listed with theirs. But they were good men by nature, and I am not. I know how to be cruel. I also know how to put on a good show, so few people know it. Hunting helps keep it in check; allowable bloodshed, as it were . . ."

I remembered Hadrian killing that stag in Dacia, smiling down at the spray of blood across his foot.

He shook himself a little, returning to the present. "Make no mistake, Vercingetorix—kindness, for me, is all sham. I tend to revert to form if crossed. Don't cross me."

He rose from the chair then in his immaculate pleated black linens, crossing to pick up the packet of orders I'd flung at him. "You may go." Offering the little bundle. "I think we will work well together."

"And I think you're a dank spotty little coward," I said evenly. "You always were. Now you're just a dank spotty little coward in a purple cloak."

Hadrian's face rippled, like a lake with something powerful and chitinous moving under the surface. His hand lashed up to strike me, but he wasn't the only one who was fast. I caught his wrist with one hand, throwing it away with such force that he stumbled. The dog growled.

"You struck me once in Dacia," I said. "I'll work for you, *Caesar*, since you haven't left me much choice. I'll work for you, and I'll kill your enemies, and I'll even guard your fucking back. But as I told you years ago—you will *never* strike me again."

He straightened slowly, and I should have been afraid. That still, bearded face, those stony eyes, they would have terrified a god. But I'm not a god, just a stupid barbarian who never knows when to back down, so I looked him right in the eye.

"Go," Hadrian said at last, in a voice as even as mine. "You have new duties to perform, and I have a funeral cortege to plan. Trajan must be properly mourned. A great man," he said, and what floored me most was that I could see the bastard meant it. "Will you tell my wife she may enter? She should be waiting outside."

I turned to go.

"That reminds me." He waited until I turned. "Empress Vibia Sabina. I am told by Dowager Empress Plotina that you and Sabina were much in each other's company the day Trajan died. And previously." Hadrian looked up from his wax tablet. "Have you slept with my wife?"

I remembered Sabina telling me I couldn't lie to save my life.

I thought of my men, of Mirah and the children.

"No," I said.

"Then you may go, Vercingetorix." Hadrian returned to his tablet, the dog curling up at his feet again. "That will be all."

A day later and the new Emperor was ready to take sail. He'd ordered the pyre for Trajan's body built on the beach before the assembled throng, and had already prepared an urn to take the Imperial ashes back to Rome. The abandoned harbor throbbed with activity as the trireme was draped in black, officials jostled for place, slaves ran about frantically loading last-minute items into the ship, and soldiers pressed into position to give their Emperor—their *real* Emperor—his final salute. A good many were weeping, but even more were gabbling on about Hadrian. Such a fine man, they said. So learned. So experienced. A worthy successor for Trajan.

I couldn't stomach it, and fortunately I didn't have to. I wasn't to go on the trireme back to Rome, after all. So I wandered up into the hills behind Selinus, up the path overgrown with weeds to the ruined temple where I'd wept for Trajan with no idea what fresh hell was coming for me.

Sabina was there. She sat slumped on a fallen pillar, already dressed in black for the leave-taking ceremony. A stiff mourning *stola*, obviously Plotina's choice, with a gold veil and a wig of false blond plaits very properly covering her cropped hair.

"Go away." Her back was stiff too, and she didn't turn as she heard my footfall. "I'll come down when it's time to leave, not before."

"It's me," I said.

She turned, and I saw her eyes were red. "I thought I'd given my Praetorians the slip," she said, eyeing my new armor.

"Not quite." I looked down at the whole loathsome outfit: the useless muscled cuirass, the ridiculous red kilt, the absurd fine-woven cloak too flimsy to keep out the rain. "I feel like a damned rooster. Probably about as useful. Can't lay eggs, can't go kill Dacians."

"No worse than me." Sabina swept the blond wig off her head and flung it into the weeds beside the column. "We've both been promoted. I never saw that happening, did you?"

When we'd been locked up together on Plotina's orders for nearly two and a half days, we'd spent a good deal of time speculating what was going to happen to us both. We knew how coups started; it had looked like a likely prospect. Sabina had spent most of our hours either pacing back and forth like her cat or trying to pry answers from the

Praetorians outside and being told to keep silent. I'd spent most of our hours calculating just how many of those pretty palace guards I could kill once they finally came in to dispose of me. How wrong we'd both been, because here we were—no longer simply Vix and Sabina, scarred soldier and world traveler, but Empress Vibia Sabina and Praetorian Guard Vercingetorix.

"I've gotten my orders," I said, and briefly outlined her husband's dreadful terms. My promotion and demotion, my reward and punishment.

"All neatly tied up in one tidy little package," Sabina winced. "How very Hadrian."

"You hear he's pulling back too? Giving it all away, the new provinces we fought for. Armenia, Mesopotamia, Assyria, even Dacia."

"We might not have kept them anyway." Sabina's voice was gentle. "Could you really have kept all that territory without Trajan?"

"We had four years of victories!"

"'You made a desert,'" Sabina quoted, "'and called it peace.'"

"Did Titus say that?"

"Tacitus first. Then Titus, in one of his letters. Both of them are right, you know. All this"—she looked out over the rocky cliffs, the jewel-blue horizon where all those conquered deserts lay—"we couldn't have held it. Even Trajan knew he was getting overextended."

"So we just give up?" I chafed my sore shoulder, feeling the phantom shaft of the arrow I'd taken at Hatra. "After all that effort? All those lives?" Julius. Philip. The countless other men I'd buried by the Euphrates.

"I guess we do," said Sabina.

"Then what do we have to show for it?" I cried out. "What do I have to show for it?"

Sabina had no answer for that. Why would she? Aside from a few scars, all I had to show for a life of wandering and fighting were the odds and ends that had collected at the bottom of my pack. A father's amulet. An emperor's ring. A wife's scarf. A lion's pelt. A string of campaign tokens. A lover's earring.

Not very much, when you came down to it.

I sat down on the other end of the ruined column, swinging my ridiculous new crested helmet by its ridiculous chin strap. Sabina wrapped her arms about her own knees, and we sat in silence for a while. Birds hopped among the abandoned columns, twittering impudently now that there were no indignant priests to chase them out. A bright blue morning, so beautiful.

"'Empress of Rome,'" I said at last, tasting her new title. "Who'd have thought?"

She gave me a wan little half smile. "At the very least, it will be interesting."

"That's the spirit."

"Interesting or not, I'd trade it for another chance to go back to being eighteen and stay in my father's house forever. Never get married at all."

I should have stayed in her father's house too. Stayed a bodyguard, never joined the legions. If I had, I'd still be living my uneventful life walking Senator Norbanus back and forth from the Capitoline Library, not sitting in a weed-choked temple at the arse-end of nowhere.

"Maybe my father can help." Sabina's voice was bleak, and her hands twined each other around her knees. "Perhaps he can challenge this mad charade Plotina put on to get Hadrian adopted . . ." She shook her head, as if arguing with herself. "Gods, I can't go to my father. He's so frail now."

I thought of my own father. He'd be Trajan's age by now, if he was even still alive. The last letter I'd managed to get from my mother had been more than two years ago; all had been well, but a great deal could happen in two years. Was he still rooting ineptly in his garden, with hair as gray as Trajan's? Or had he too died gasping for breath in bed, before I'd ever had a chance to see him again? Suddenly I wanted to go home.

Brigantia. Was it even my home? Or did I have a home at all anymore?

What does it matter? I thought. Wherever home was, Hadrian would never give me leave to go there. My father and mother would die, and I'd never see them again. Not since I was eighteen and I left with so many dreams of glory.

"All my life—" Sabina's voice was ragged, and I realized she was weeping. I'd never seen her weep before, not once in all the years I'd known her. The tears slid down her still face and dripped off her little chin. "All my life I thought I could go adventuring, just because I wanted to. I could do my duty, do some good in the world, but I could have the life I wanted doing it. But that wasn't true, was it? I got to go adventuring because my father let me, and then Hadrian let me, and then Trajan. Any of them could have stopped me anytime they liked, and now Hadrian *is* stopping me. No adventures for the Empress of Rome."

I could think of endless times over the years when I'd ached to see that serene shell of hers cracked in half. See her weep, see her break. Now I was seeing it, and the only thing breaking was me.

She looked at me, her face white and wet and ravaged. "I never had any freedom at all, did I?"

"Most of us don't," I said.

"'Vibia Sabina, Empress of the seven hills.'" She gave her new title a bitter twist. "When you come right down to it, an empress is just another wife. Nothing but that."

I wondered if I'd ever see *my* wife again. Mirah's reddish hair, her neat sashed waist, the way she gestured with her chin when her hands were full. My thumb found a tiny corner of the blue scarf tied under my greave, caressed the worn cloth. Why hadn't I begged a transfer to a legion in Judaea, given Mirah the life of honor and respect she wanted as the wife of Masada's last living heir?

I banished Mirah from my mind. I couldn't think of her, not when I already hurt inside like I'd been gutted with a spear. "Maybe *Empress* only means *wife*," I said to Sabina. "But *Praetorian* means *assassin*. That's what I am now. I'm to stop off on my way back to Rome and kill all your husband's enemies for him."

"*All* his enemies?" Sabina's voice was bitter. "That's too long a list for one man. Even you."

"His top five enemies, anyway." I hadn't gotten the list until this morning. Celsus and Palma, two former consuls. A former governor of Dacia. Lusius Quietus, my former cavalry commander . . . my heart had lurched when I read that, and then died entirely in my chest when I saw the final name.

Titus.

I remembered one of his absurd quotations, Ovid or maybe Juvenal; something Titus had trotted out to me once when I was gloomy over some failure. *Be patient, and tough,* he'd said with his gentle expression. *Someday this pain will be useful to you.*

But how could *this* pain ever be useful? The pain of knowing I had to put a sword through the heart of the best man I'd ever known?

"Maybe I'll just put a sword through my own heart instead," I said aloud. "What I should have done when Trajan died."

"The Empire would be poorer for it," said Sabina. She rested her cheek on her folded arms, and we sat in silence again. I fingered my row of campaign tokens—the only item I'd officially been allowed to carry over to my new Praetorian armor. Campaign tokens won for territories that would now go back to the weeds and the wild men. I wasn't supposed to wear my lion skin with the new armor, or any of the precious good-luck tokens from my wife or my father or Sabina. "Praetorians do not drape themselves in superstitious trash," or so I'd already been told by the Praetorian whom Hadrian had assigned to brief me on my new duties. I'd hit him short and hard in the nose, and he'd howled. I suppose I was out of practice at being told what to do.

"I'll need to go soon." Sabina looked down the rocky path toward the abandoned harbor. Even from here, I could see the swarm of activity. "They'll need me for my new duties. Namely standing like a statue and smiling. There's a lot of that when you're an empress. Though of course I'll have many more important responsibilities once I reach Rome and am installed in the palace. Weaving the household cloth, for example. Overseeing the slaves. Hosting Imperial dinner parties. Those are my duties now, Plotina says. Gods, did I underestimate her."

"I'm sure you'll find a way to keep making the bitch miserable."

"She also wants me to start whelping babies, but thank the gods, Hadrian isn't so interested in that. He doesn't seem to care about heirs, at least not from me." A grimace. "Can you imagine a child of Hadrian's inheriting the Empire? It would destroy the human race."

"A child of yours too. Surely it wouldn't be so bad as that." Oh, Hell's gates, my daughters—both of them so young, Dinah just three and Chaya barely out of babyhood, but they'd be Hadrian's hold on me forever. Hostages to my good behavior, not that they knew it. Did they even know *me*? If I were to die now, would they remember their father at all?

"Maybe I should get myself pregnant," Sabina was musing. "Hadrian would know it wasn't his—he'd have to divorce me . . ."

"Don't be stupid. He'd kill you rather than divorce you."

"Yes, he hates being made a fool of."

"Make a fool of him anyway." My voice was savage. "Keep your head shaved, keep your pleb friends, keep hiring street urchins for your maids and wading barefoot in the Tiber and taking lovers who snicker at him over the pillow. Don't turn into the wife he wants, some perfect marble-carved empress. Keep Rome laughing. Make him sorry he ever married you."

"Excellent idea," said Sabina. "Let's start now."

I looked at her. Her face was hard, mocking, a gleam of anger turning her eyes to blue ice.

"Want to help me?" she asked. "Help me make a fool out of him?"

Have you slept with my wife? Hadrian whispered in my ear, and behind the whisper I heard the deadly hiss of steel. I gazed at the new Empress of Rome, and she gazed back.

I didn't want her. God help me, I didn't want her, I wanted my Mirah. But my hand was already stretching out, jerking Sabina up from the column, and my mouth was biting down on hers. She jumped up into my arms, her legs clinging about my waist, kissing me ferociously as I yanked the clasps out of her stiff formal dress and ran my fingers through her short hair.

"Promise me you won't grow your hair," I murmured as I pressed her down into the weeds. "He hates the hair."

"I promise." She laced her fingers behind my neck, pulling me down into her. "Now shut up and take me." No finesse, no tenderness—just rage.

And maybe friendship. Maybe all the lust and the love and my occasional bouts of hatred over the years had given us that.

Afterward I gave her a hand up, and she straightened her dress and put the blond wig back into place, and we stood for a moment looking down the slope of the hill to the beach. The trireme waited there, and a hundred Imperial retainers laying wood for an emperor's funeral pyre, but I don't think either of us saw it. I think we saw Rome—but not the Rome we knew. The new and dangerous Rome that awaited us.

I put my hand on Sabina's shoulder. She reached up, lacing her fingers briefly with mine, and her mouth flicked wryly. Then she pulled the gold veil up over her hair and descended the path alone, going down to stand like a polite statue as the new Emperor was hailed on his way back to Rome. I stood with the other soldiers, and I still had tears left to weep after all as Trajan's funeral pyre was lit. My Emperor. The new Emperor presided, his head ostentatiously bowed.

Have you slept with my wife?

Yes, Caesar, I thought straight at him. *The day after you took my legion away and put a kill list in its place, I slept with your wife. And someday, I will watch you die.*

Maybe I should have gone into astrology instead of soldiering, because that was another prophecy that ended up coming true. I didn't get all the details right—I didn't know yet that I'd gotten Sabina pregnant up on that hilltop full of ruins. But I would someday watch Hadrian die.

Never mind how.

I'll tell you later.

HISTORICAL NOTE

Except for Vix and a few minor players, every character in *Empress of the Seven Hills* is a real person. Emperors Trajan and Hadrian, their wives Plotina and Sabina, Vix's friends Titus and Simon, even Vix's adopted son Antinous all existed in real life. Vix's life and career are based on those of several notable soldiers of the day, especially a cavalry officer named Tiberius Claudius Maximus, who captured the dying Dacian king Decebalus and brought his head and right hand back to the Emperor, and one Marcius Turbo, who was promoted through the ranks on grit and bravery to end up Hadrian's Praetorian Prefect. Vix is therefore guilty of stealing the credit for other men's deeds, which I doubt would bother him at all. Not many common legionaries pulled off the kind of meteoric rise through the ranks that Vix does, but it was possible: Trajan's many active years of campaigning meant heavy casualties among his officers and swift promotion for those who managed to stay alive. Battlefield promotions were frequently handed out for acts of bravery, and patronage was all: With the backing of the Emperor or some other powerful Roman, even a common legionary like Vix could dream of command.

Sabina's adventures are not recorded by history, but what is recorded is a deep hostility between her and her husband. Hadrian, openly homosexual, married her for political ends but found her "moody and difficult." In return, Sabina remarked publicly that she would never bear him children because they would harm the human race. The historical Sabina managed to travel a great deal, inviting herself along on most of her husband's wanderings, so she must have had some taste for adventure. Her level of freedom might be unusual, but it was not unheard of: Roman women had as much liberty as their husbands or fathers allowed them to have, and despite the traditional image of an iron-handed *paterfamilias*, ancient Rome had plenty of doting fathers (Cicero was notoriously indulgent to his daughter) and lenient husbands. Many Roman women traveled extensively in the provinces, bringing up their children in the Empire's wild places while their husbands ruled as provincial governors or served in provincial military outposts, and the occasional adventurous woman got to see a military campaign firsthand. Emperor Augustus's granddaughter Agrippina the Elder famously accompanied her husband's army throughout all his wars, and I decided Sabina (and Mirah) might easily do the same. Sabina's interest in good works would have been a traditional occupation for a well-connected woman; record exists of the huge contribution she made to Trajan's *alimenta* scheme supporting Roman orphans. It's not known if Sabina had affairs outside her barren marriage, but Hadrian later notoriously reprimanded and dismissed several men for being "too informal" with his wife—including one career soldier in the Praetorian Guard. We have no way of knowing if such a charge means Sabina took lovers or simply had a gift for informality in her friendships.

Empress Pompeia Plotina is another matter. I have probably been very unfair to Trajan's wife, whom history records as a perfectly pleasant and conventional woman who did not meddle much in Imperial politics. But Trajan's deathbed adoption of Hadrian was definitely a fishy affair, and a persistent rumor circulated at the time that Plotina had masterminded the whole thing. She had always made a pet out of Trajan's ward Hadrian; she pushed his marriage to Sabina to tie him to the Imperial family, and she made no secret of her hopes that he would succeed her husband. Trajan awarded Hadrian considerable honors, but their relations were never very warm, and we don't know if Trajan ever planned for Hadrian to succeed him. He did propose sending the Senate a short list of candidates (though Titus, as a rising but young politician, would probably not have been on it) and he may have had his freedman Phaedimus write one up. But Plotina wrote a decree of adoption for Hadrian instead and signed it for her husband while he lay dying. Plotina's elaborate pretense that Trajan was still alive so she could fake a deathbed adoption of Hadrian may sound like bad farce, but it's another persistent rumor that comes down to us through the ages from Plotina's contemporaries. I may have wronged Plotina by implying that she was either a madwoman or a thief—but ancient sources record that Trajan on his deathbed believed he might have been poisoned by someone in his inner circle, and that his secretary freedman Phaedimus died suddenly on the same day of Hadrian's acclamation, as if someone wanted to silence him.

I have taken some liberties with small historical details, compressing events, places, and timelines in order to serve the story. The Dacian Wars and the Cyprus rebellion have been moved up a bit in time to suit Vix's convenience, and Hadrian's year in Athens as magistrate moved back. Annia Galeria Faustina was in reality Sabina's half-niece instead of her half-sister (their family tree is a Rubik's cube of connections and counterconnections that desperately needed simplification) and although the date of Faustina's betrothal to Titus is not known, it probably happened a few years earlier than I made it happen here, as did Sabina's own marriage. It's not known whether Titus ever served as tribune in a legion, though it was a traditional starting point for many young politicians, and he was notoriously averse to the military for the rest of his life. To suit Titus's career I have also fudged a few building dates on projects such as Trajan's Column and his massive public baths, which both still stand today as splendid ruins in the middle of Rome. Vix's legion, the Tenth Fidelis, is fictional, but its exploits are based on those of real legions that took part in the Dacian and Parthian wars. Hadrian was present at the siege of Sarmizegetusa, though as the legate of a different legion, and the Dacian and Parthian wars unfolded much as I have described them.

Conversely, many of the book's more outlandish details are entirely true. The idea of secret astrological prophecies sounds ridiculous, but historians record that Hadrian recieved such a prophecy at a young age foretelling his rise to the purple (of course, many other emperors supposedly did too). Trajan's various near-death experiences are also fact— he narrowly missed dying at Hatra when an enemy archer spotted him without his helmet, and he also escaped being crushed to death by the devastating earthquake in Antioch. Mention is made, during that earthquake, of a woman trapped in the rubble who managed to keep both herself and her newborn baby alive on her own breast milk until they could be rescued.

A modern audience might find it surprising that two of Rome's most famous and effective emperors were openly homosexual, or at least bisexual with a strong preference for men. Ancient Romans held a very relaxed view of sexual preferences: Bisexuality was the norm rather than the exception among upper-class Roman men. Both Trajan and Hadrian made political marriages, but their relationships with their wives are assumed to have remained platonic since both men openly preferred male lovers. Neither emperor was ever reviled as less of a man or a soldier.

Trajan's easy nature and rampant popularity are well documented, but Hadrian is a much more elusive figure. He appears to have been a very difficult man to understand: The *Historia Augusta* chronicle wrote of him in frustration: "He was, in the same person, austere and genial, dignified and playful, dilatory and quick to act, niggardly and generous, deceitful and straightforward, cruel and merciful, and always in all things changeable." Thanks to historians like Gibbon, he is now considered one of Rome's Five Good Emperors (a term originally coined by Machiavelli), and certainly Hadrian was well-spoken and well-read, with a gift for organization, a formidable intellect, myriad artistic interests, a famous love of animals, and a powerful ability to charm. But despite his gifts he was one of the most unpopular emperors Rome ever had—at least during his lifetime. That unpopularity kicked off at the beginning of his reign when he first relinquished Trajan's hard-won new provinces and then went on to purge a number of his political enemies in a series of murders. Hadrian denied all involvement in the bloodbath, but Rome remained convinced he masterminded the executions, and his reputation never recovered. The most famous fictional portrait of Hadrian is Marguerite Yourcenar's *Memoirs of Hadrian*, which takes a positive slant on most of his actions and portrays him as thoughtful and saintly—but I had fun exploring another possible side of his character: the man seen by his fellow Romans as a brilliant schemer smart enough to hide his innate cruelty behind an affable mask. Vix, Sabina, and Titus are all in for plenty of adventures now that their mortal enemy has become Emperor of Rome.

Special thanks to my friend Helen Shankman, who not only answered many of my questions on early Judaism, but put me in touch with Professor Steven Fine, who took time from New York's Yeshiva University to answer the questions Helen could not. Thanks as well to Ben Kane for recommending me to RomanArmy.com, a wonderful online forum full of helpful experts on Rome's complex military system. I was lucky enough to make the acquaintance there of Nathan Ross, Paul Elliott, Max Conzemius, and Quinton Johansen, who were kind enough to answer my questions about Vix's legionary career and tactfully point out my mistakes.

And a final fervent thank-you to Anthony Everitt, whose splendid biography *Hadrian and the Triumph of Rome* has been my bible and security blanket during the entire writing process of *Empress of the Seven Hills*.

CHARACTERS

IMPERIAL FAMILY

*Marcus Ulpius TRAJAN, Emperor of Rome

*Empress Pompeia PLOTINA, his wife

*Publius Aelius HADRIAN, his ward

*Domitia Longina, called MARCELLA, widow of Emperor Domitian and former Empress of Rome

ROMAN SENATORS AND THEIR FAMILIES

Senator MARCUS Vibius Augustus Norbanus

CALPURNIA, his third wife

*Vibia SABINA, his daughter from his second wife

*Annia Galeria FAUSTINA, his daughter by Calpurnia

Linus and his three brothers, Marcus and Calpurnia's sons

Gaia, a slave girl in the Norbanus house

Quintus, steward of the Norbanus house

*TITUS Aurelius Fulvus Boionius Arrius Antoninus, patrician

Ennia, his housekeeper

*Celsus, a consul

*Palma, a consul

*Gaius Avidius Nigrinus, a governor of Dacia

ROMAN SOLDIERS AND THEIR FAMILIES

Vercingetorix, called VIX, bodyguard, legionary, and former gladiator

*SIMON ben Cosiba, legionary

MIRAH, his niece

Dinah and Chaya, her daughters

Boil, legionary

Julius, legionary

Philip, legionary

*Lusius Quietus, Berber cavalry commander

ROMAN CITIZENS AND SUBJECTS

DEMETRA, a bakehouse cook in Moguntiacum

*ANTINOUS, her son

*Decebalus, King of Dacia, rebel against Rome

Bassus, under-secretary to Empress Plotina

*Phaedimus, Imperial freedman

denotes real historical figure

Turn the page for an excerpt from

MISTRESS OF ROME

Available in paperback
from Berkley

THEA

Rome, September A.D. 81

I opened my wrist with one firm stroke of the knife, watching with interest as the blood leaped out of the vein. My wrists were latticed with knife scars, but I still found the sight of my own blood fascinating. There was always the element of danger: After so many years, would I finally get careless and cut too deep? Would this be the day I watched my young life stream away into the blue pottery bowl with the nice frieze of nymphs on the side? The thought much brightened a life of minimum excitement.

But this time it was not to be. The first leap of blood slowed to a trickle, and I settled back against the mosaic pillar in the atrium, blue bowl in my lap. Soon a pleasant haze would descend over my eyes and the world would take on an agreeably distant hue. I needed that haze today. I would be accompanying my new mistress to the Colosseum, to see the gladiatorial games for the accession of the new Emperor. And from what I'd heard about the games . . .

"Thea!"

My mistress's voice. I muttered something rude in a combination of Greek, Hebrew, and gutter Latin, none of which she understood.

The blue bowl held a shallow cup of my blood. I wrapped my wrist in a strip of linen, tying off the knot with my teeth, then emptied the bowl into the atrium fountain. I took care not to drip on my brown wool tunic. My mistress's eagle eyes would spot a bloodstain in half a second, and I would not care to explain to her exactly why, once or twice a month, I took a blue bowl with a nice frieze of nymphs on the side and filled it with my own blood. However, fairly speaking, there was very little that I would care to tell my mistress at all. She hadn't owned me long, but I already knew *that*.

"Thea!"

I turned too quickly and had to lean against the pillars of the atrium. Maybe I'd overdone it. Drain too much blood, and nausea set in. Surely not good on a day when I would have to watch thousands of animals and men get slaughtered.

"Thea, quit dawdling." My mistress poked her pretty head out the bedroom door, her annoyed features agreeably hazy to my eyes. "Father's waiting, and you still have to dress me."

I drifted obediently after her, my feet seeming to float several inches above the floor. A tasteless floor with a mosaic scene of gladiators fighting it out with tridents, blood splashing copiously in square red tiles. Tasteless but appropriate: My mistress's father, Quintus Pollio, was one of several organizers of the Imperial gladiatorial games.

"The blue gown, Thea. With the pearl pins at the shoulders."

"Yes, my lady."

Lady Lepida Pollia. I had been purchased for her several months ago when she turned fourteen: a maid of her own age to do her hair and carry her fan now that she was so nearly a woman. As a gift I didn't rank as high as the pearl necklace and the silver bangles and the half-dozen silk gowns she'd also received from her doting father, but she certainly liked having her own personal shadow.

"Cut yourself at dinner again, Thea?" She caught sight of my bandaged wrist at once. "You really are a fumble-fingers. Just don't drop my jewel box, or I'll be very cross. Now, I want the gold bands in my hair, in the Greek style. I'll be a Greek for the day . . . just like you, Thea."

She knew I was no Greek, despite the name bestowed on me by the Athenian merchant who was my first owner. "Yes, my lady," I murmured in my purest Greek. A frown flickered between her fine black brows. I was better educated than my mistress, and it annoyed her no end. I tried to remind her at least once a week.

"Don't go giving yourself airs, Thea. You're just another little Jew slave. Remember that."

"Yes, my lady." Meekly I coiled and pinned her curls. She was already chattering on.

". . . Father says that Belleraphon will fight this afternoon. Really, I know he's our best gladiator, but that flat face! He may dress like a dandy, but all the perfume in the world won't turn him into an Apollo. Of course he is wonderfully graceful, even when he's sticking someone right through the throat—ouch! You pricked me!"

"Sorry, my lady."

"You certainly look green. There's no reason to get sick over the games, you know. Gladiators and slaves and prisoners—they'd all die anyway. At least this way we get some fun out of it."

"Maybe it's my Jewish blood," I suggested. "We don't usually find death amusing."

"Maybe that's it." Lepida examined her varnished nails. "At least the games are bound to be thrilling today. What with the Emperor getting sick and dying in the middle of the season, we haven't had a good show for months."

"Inconsiderate of him," I agreed.

"At least the new Emperor is supposed to love the games. Emperor Domitian. Titus Flavius Domitianus . . . I wonder what he'll be like? Father went to no end of trouble arranging the best bouts for him. Pearl earrings, Thea."

"Yes, my lady."

"And the musk perfume. There." Lepida surveyed herself in the polished steel mirror. She was very young—fourteen, same as me—and too young, really, for the rich silk gown, the pearls, the rouge. But she had no mother and Quintus Pollio, so shrewd in dealing with slave merchants and *lanistae*, was clay in the hands of his only child. Besides, there was no doubt that she cut a dash. Her beauty was not in the peacock-blue eyes or even the yard of silky black hair that was her pride and joy. It was in her Olympian poise. On the basis of that poise, Lady

Lepida Pollia aimed to catch a distinguished husband, a patrician who would raise the family Pollii at last into the highest ranks of Roman society.

She beckoned me closer, peacock fan languidly stirring her sculpted curls. In the mirror behind her I was a dark-brown shadow: lanky where she was luscious, sunburned where she was white-skinned, drab where she was brilliant. Very flattering, at least for her.

"Most effective," she announced, mirroring my thoughts. "But you really do need a new dress, Thea. You look like a tall dead tree. Come along, Father's waiting."

Father was indeed waiting. But his impatience softened as Lepida dimpled at him and pirouetted girlishly. "Yes, you look very pretty. Be sure to smile at Aemilius Graccus today; that's a very important family, and he's got an eye for pretty girls."

I could have told him that it wasn't pretty *girls* Aemilius Graccus had an eye for, but he didn't ask me. Maybe he should have. Slaves heard everything.

Most Romans had to get up at daybreak to get a good seat in the Colosseum. But the Pollio seats were reserved, so we tripped out just fashionably late enough to nod at all the great families. Lepida sparkled at Aemilius Graccus, at a party of patrician officers lounging on the street corner, at anyone with a purple-bordered toga and an old name. Her father importantly exchanged gossip with any patrician who favored him with an obligatory smile.

". . . I heard Emperor Domitian's planning a campaign in Germania next season! Wants to pick up where his brother left off, eh? No doubting Emperor Titus cut those barbarians down to size, we'll see if Domitian can do any better . . ."

"Quintus Pollio," I overheard a patrician voice drawl. "Really, his perfume alone—!"

"But he does his job so well. What's a smile now and then if it keeps him working hard?"

So Quintus Pollio went on bowing and smirking. He would have sold thirty years of his life for the honor of carrying the family name of the Julii, the Gracchi, or the Sulpicii. So would my mistress, for that matter.

I amused myself by peering into the vendors' stalls that crowded the streets. Souvenirs of dead gladiators, the blood of this or that great fighter preserved in sand, little wooden medallions painted with the face of the famous Belleraphon. These last weren't selling very well, since not even the artists could give Belleraphon a pretty face. Portraits of a handsome Thracian trident fighter did much better.

"He's so beautiful!" Out of the corner of my eye I saw a cluster of girls mooning over a medallion. "I sleep with his picture under my pillow every night—"

I smiled. We Jewish girls, we liked our men to be fighters too—but we liked them real and we liked them long-lived. The kind who take the head off a legionnaire in the morning and come home at night to preside over the Sabbath table. Only Roman girls mooned over crude garish portraits of men they'd never met, men who would probably be dead before the year was out. On the other hand, perhaps a short-lived man was better for daydreaming about. He'd never be old, he'd never lose his looks, and if you tired of him he'd soon be gone.

The crowds grew thicker around the Colosseum. I'd walked often enough in its vast marble shadow as I ran errands for my mistress, but this was my first time inside and I struggled not to gape. So huge, so many marble arches, so many statues staring arrogantly from their plinths, so many seats. Fifty thousand eager spectators could cram inside, so they said. An arena fit for the gods, begun by the late Emperor Vespasian, finished by his son the late Emperor Titus, opened today in celebration for Titus's younger brother who had just donned the Imperial purple as Emperor Domitian.

So much marble for a charnel house. I'd have preferred a theatre, but then I would rather hear music than watch men die. I imagined singing for a crowd as large as this one, a real audience, instead of the frogs in the conservatorium when I scrubbed the tiles . . .

"Keep that fan moving, Thea." Lepida settled into her velvet cushions, waving like an Empress at the crowds who had a small cheer for her father. Men and women usually sat separately to watch the games, but Quintus Pollio as organizer of the games could sit with his daughter if he liked. "Faster than that, Thea. It's going to be gruesomely hot. Really, why won't it cool down? It's supposed to be *fall*."

Obediently I waved the fan back and forth. The games would last all day, which meant that I had a good six hours of feather-waving in front of me. Oh, my arms were going to ache.

Trumpets blared brassily. Even my heart skipped a beat at that thrilling fanfare. The new Emperor stepped out into the Imperial box, raising his hand to the crowd, and I stretched on my toes for a look at him. Domitian, third Emperor of the Flavian dynasty: tall, ruddy-cheeked, dazzling the eye in his purple cloak and golden circlet.

"Father." Lepida tugged on her father's sleeve. "Is the Emperor *really* a man of secret vices? At the bathhouse yesterday, I heard—"

I could have told her that all Emperors were rumored to be men of secret vices. Emperor Tiberius and his little slave boys, Emperor Caligula who slept with his sisters, Emperor Titus and his mistresses— what was the point of having an Emperor if you couldn't cook up spicy rumors about him?

Domitian's Empress, now, was less gossipworthy. Tall, statuesque, lovely as she stepped forward beside her Imperial husband to wave at the roaring crowds—but disappointed reports had it that the Empress was an impeccable wife. Still, her green silk *stola* and emeralds caused a certain buzz of feminine admiration. Green, no doubt, would become *the* color of the season.

"Father." Lepida tugged at her father's arm again. "You know I'm always so admired in green. An emerald necklace like the Empress's—"

Various other Imperial cousins filed after the Emperor—there was a niece, Emperor Titus's younger daughter Lady Julia, who had supposedly petitioned to join the Vestal Virgins but had been refused.

Otherwise, a dull lot. I was disappointed. My first sight of the Imperial family, and they looked like any other clutch of languid patricians.

The Emperor came forward, raising his arm, and shouted the introduction of the games. Secret vices or not, he had a fine reverberating voice.

The other slaves had explained the games to me many times, incredulous at my ignorance. Duels between wild beasts always opened the morning festivities; first on the list today was a battle between an elephant and a rhinoceros. The rhinoceros put out the elephant's eye with its tusk. I could have happily lived my entire life without knowing what an elephant's scream sounded like.

"Marvelous!" Pollio threw a few coins into the arena. Lepida picked through a plate of honeyed dates. I concentrated on the peacock fan. *Swish, swish, swish.*

A bull and a bear battled next, then a lion and a leopard. Tidbits to whet the appetite, as it were. The bear was sullen, and three handlers with sharp rods had to goad its flanks bloody before it attacked the bull, but the lion and the leopard screamed and flew at each other the moment the chains were released. The crowd cheered and chattered, sighed and settled back. Pomp and spectacle came next, dazzling the eye after the crowd's attention was honed: tame cheetahs in silver harnesses padding round the arena, white bulls with little golden boys capering on their backs, jeweled and tasseled elephants lumbering in stately dance steps accompanied by Nubian flute players . . .

"Father, can't I have a Nubian slave?" Lepida plucked at her father's arm. "Two, even. A matched pair to carry my packages when I go shopping—"

Comic acts next. A tame tiger was released into the arena after a dozen sprinting hares, bounding in a flash of stripes to collect them one by one in his jaws and return them unharmed to the trainer. Rather nice, really. I enjoyed it, but there were scattered boos through the stands. Fans of the Colosseum didn't come for games; they came for blood.

"The Emperor," Quintus Pollio was droning, "is especially fond of the goddess Minerva. He has built a new shrine to her in his palace. Perhaps we should make a few large public offerings—"

The tame tiger and his handler padded out, replaced by a hundred white deer and a hundred long-necked ostriches who were released galloping into the arena and shot down one by one by archers on high. Lepida saw some acquaintance in a neighboring box and cooed greetings through most of the blood.

More animal fights. Spearmen against lions, against buffaloes, against bulls. The buffaloes went down bewildered and mooing, the bulls ran maddened onto the spears that gouged their chests open, but the lions snarled and stalked and took a spearman with them before they were chased down and gutted. Such wonderful fun. *Swish, swish, swish.*

"Oh, the gladiators." Lepida cast the plate of dates aside and sat up. "Fine specimens, Father."

"Nothing but the best for the Emperor." He chucked his daughter's chin. "And for my little one who loves the games! The Emperor wanted a battle today, not just the usual duels. Something big and special before the midday executions—"

In purple cloaks the gladiators filed out of the gates, making a slow circle of the arena as the fans cheered. Some strutted proudly; some stalked ahead without looking right or left. The handsome Thracian trident fighter blew kisses to the crowd and was showered with roses by adoring women. Fifty gladiators, paired off to fight to the death. Twenty-five would exit in triumph through the arena's Gate of Life. Twenty-five would be dragged out through the Gate of Death on iron hooks.

"*Hail, Emperor!*" As one they roared out toward the Imperial box. "*We salute you from death's shadow!*"

The clank of sharpened weapons. The scrape of plated armor. The crunch of many feet on sand as they spread out in their pairs. A few mock combats first with wooden weapons, and then the Emperor dropped his hand.

The blades crashed. The audience surged forward, straining against the marble barriers, shouting encouragement to the favorites, cursing the clumsy. Waving, wagering, shrieking.

Don't look. Swish, swish, went the fan. *Don't look.*

"Thea," Lepida said sweetly. "What do you think of that German?"

I looked. "Unlucky," I said as the man died howling on his opponent's trident. In the next box, a senator threw down a handful of coins in disgust.

The arena was a raging sea of fighters. Already the sand was patched with blood.

"The Gaul over there wants mercy." Pollio peered out, sipping at his wine cup. "Poor show, he dropped his shield. *Iugula!*"

Iugula—"Kill him." There was also *Mitte*—"spare him"—but you didn't hear that nearly so often. As I was to find out, it took an extraordinary show of courage to move the Colosseum to mercy. They wanted heroism, they wanted blood, they wanted death. Not scared men. Not mercy.

It was over quite quickly. The victors strutted before the Imperial box, where the Emperor tossed coins to those who had fought well. The losers lay crumpled and silent on the sand, waiting to be raked away by the arena attendants. One or two men still writhed in their death throes, shrieking as they tried to stuff the guts back into their own bellies. Laughing tribunes and giggling girls laid bets on how long it would take them to die.

Swish, swish, swish. My arms ached.

"Fruit, Dominus?" A slave came to Pollio's elbow with a tray of grapes and figs. Lepida gestured for more wine, and all through the patrician boxes I saw people sitting back to chatter. In the tiers above, plebs fanned themselves and looked for the hawkers who darted with bread and beer for sale. In his Imperial box the Emperor leaned back on one elbow, rolling dice with his guards. The morning had flown. For some, dragged.

For the midday break, business was attended to inside the arena. The dead gladiators had all been carted away, the patches of blood raked over, and now the arena guards led out a shuffling line of shackled figures. Slaves, criminals, prisoners; all sentenced for execution.

"Father, can't I have more wine? It's a special occasion!"

Down in the arena, the man at the head of the shackled line blinked as a blunt sword was shoved into his hands. He stared at it, dull-eyed and bent-backed, and the arena guard prodded him. He turned wearily and hacked at the chained man behind him. A dull blade, because it took a great deal of hacking. I could hardly hear the man's screams over the chatter in the stands. No one seemed to be paying attention to the arena at all.

The arena guards disarmed the first slave roughly, passing the sword to the next in line. A woman. She killed the man, roughly cutting his throat; was disarmed, killed in turn by the next who tried vainly to stab her through the heart. It took a dozen strokes of the dull sword.

I looked down the chained line. Perhaps twenty prisoners. Old and young, men and women, identical in their bent shoulders and shuffling feet. Only one stood straight, a big man gazing around him with blank eyes. Even from the stands I could see the whip marks latticing his bare back.

"Father, when does Belleraphon's bout come up? I'm dying to see what he can do against that Thracian—"

The guards gave the blunt sword to the man with the scars. He hefted it a moment in his shackled hands, gave it a swing. No hacking for him; he killed the man who had gone before him in one efficient thrust. I winced.

The arena guard reached for the sword and the big scarred man fell a step back, holding the blade up between them. The guard gestured, holding out an impatient hand, and then it all went to hell.

* * *

"Hand it over," the guard said.

He stood spraddle-legged on the hot sand, heaving air into his parched lungs. The sun scorched down on his naked shoulders and he could feel every separate grain beneath his bare, hardened feet. Sweat stung his wrists and ankles under the rusty cuffs of his chains. His hands had welded around the sword hilt.

"Hand over that sword," the guard ordered. "You're holding up the show."

He stared back glassy-eyed.

"Hand—over—that—sword." Extending an imperious hand.

He cut it off.

The guard screamed. The slick of blood gleamed bright in the midday sun. The other guards rushed.

He had not held a sword in over ten years. Much too long, he would have said, to remember anything. But it came back. Fueled by rage it came back fast—the sweet weight of the hilt in his hand, the bite of blade into bone, the black demon's fury that filmed the eyes and whispered in the ear.

Kill them, it said. *Kill them all.*

He met the first guard in a savage joyful rush, swords meeting with a dull screech. He bore down with every muscle, feeling his body arch like a good bow, and saw the sudden leap of fear in the guard's eyes as he felt the strength on the other end of the blade. These Romans with their plumes and pride and shiny breastplates, they didn't think a slave could be strong. In two more thrusts he reduced the guard to a heap of twitching meat on the sand.

More Romans, bright blurs in their feathered crests. A guard fell writhing as dull iron chewed through his hamstrings. A liquid scream.

He savored it. Lunged for another bronze breastplate. The blade slid neatly through the armhole. Another shield falling, another scream.

Not enough, the demon voice whispered. *Not enough.*

He felt distant pain along his back as a blade cut deep, and smiled, turning to chop down savagely. A slave's toughest flesh was on his back, but they didn't know that—these men whose vineyards were tended by captive warriors from Gaul and their beds warmed by sullen Thracian slave girls. They didn't know anything. He cut the guard down, tasting blood in his rough beard.

Not enough.

The sky whirled and turned white as something struck the back of his head. He staggered, turned, raised his blade, felt his entire arm go numb as a guard smashed an iron shield boss against his elbow. Distantly he watched the sword drop from his fingers, falling to hands and knees as a sword hilt crashed against his skull. Sweat trickled into his eyes. Acid, bitter. He sighed as the armored boots buffeted his sides, as the black demon in his head turned back in on itself like a snake devouring its own tail. A familiar road. One he had trodden all his years under whips and chains. With a sword in his hand, everything had been so simple.

Not enough. Never enough.

Over the sound of his own cracking bones, he heard a roar. A vast, impersonal roar like the crashing of the sea. For the first time he turned his eyes outward and saw them: spectators, packed tier upon tier in their thousands. Senators in purple-bordered togas. Matrons in bright silk *stolas*. Priests in white robes. So many . . . did the world hold so many people? He saw a boy's face leap out at him from the front tier, crazily distinct, a boy in a fine toga shouting through a mouthful of figs—and clapping.

They were all clapping. The great arena resounded with applause.

Through dimming eyes, he made out the Imperial balcony. He was close enough to see a fair-haired girl with a white appalled face, one of the Imperial nieces . . . close enough to see the Emperor, his ruddy cheeks, his purple cloak, his amused gaze . . . close enough to see the Imperial hand rise carelessly.

Holding out a hand in the sign of mercy.

Why? he thought. *Why?*

Then the world disappeared.

Lepida chattered on as I undressed her for bed that night—not about the games, of course; all that death and blood was old news. Her father had mentioned a certain senator, a man who might be a possible husband for her, and that was all she could talk about. "Senator Marcus Norbanus, his name is, and he's *terribly* old—" I hardly heard a word.

The slave with the scarred back. A Briton, a Gaul? He had fought so savagely, swinging his sword like Goliath, ignoring his own wounds. He'd been snarling even when they brought him down, not caring if he lived or died as long as he took a few with him.

"Thea, be careful with those pearls. They're worth three of you."

I'd seen a hundred slaves like him, served beside them and avoided them. They drank too much, they scowled at their masters and were flogged for troublemakers and did as little work as they could get away with. Men to avoid in quiet corners of the house, if no one was near enough to hear you struggling. Thugs.

So why did I weep suddenly when they brought him down in the arena? I hadn't wept when I was sold to Lepida. I hadn't even wept when I watched the gladiators and the poor bewildered animals slaughtered before my eyes. Why had I wept for a thug?

I didn't even know his name.

"Well, I don't think Emperor Domitian is terribly handsome, but it's hard to tell from a distance, isn't it?" Lepida frowned at a chipped nail. "I do wish we could have some handsome dashing Emperor instead of these stolid middle-aged men."

The Emperor. Why had he bothered to save a half-dead slave? The crowd had clapped for his death as much as for the show he put on. Why save him?

"Go away, Thea. I don't want you anymore. You're quite stupid tonight."

"As you wish," I said in Greek, blowing out her lamp. "You cheap, snide little shrew."

I weaved my way down the hall, leaning against the shadowed pillars for balance, trying not to think of my blue bowl. Not good to bleed myself twice in one day, but oh, I wanted to.

"Ah, Thea. Just what I need."

I stared blurrily at the two Quintus Pollios who beckoned me into the bedchamber and onto the silver sleeping couch. I closed my eyes, stifling a yawn and hoping I wouldn't fall asleep in the middle of his huffing and puffing. Slave girls aren't expected to be enthusiastic, but they are expected to be cheerful. I patted his shoulder as he labored over me. His lips peeled back from his teeth like a mule's during the act of . . . well, whatever you want to call it.

"What a good girl you are, Thea." Sleepily patting my flank. "Run along, now."

I shook down my tunic and slipped out the door. Likely tomorrow he'd slip me a copper.

PART I

JULIA

In the Temple of Vesta

Yesterday, Titus Flavius Domitianus was just my brusque and rather strange uncle. Today he is Lord and God, Pontifex Maximus, Emperor of Rome. Like my father and grandfather before him, he is master of the world. And I am afraid.

But he has been kind to me. He says I will marry my cousin Gaius soon, and he promised me splendid games for the celebration. I couldn't tell him that I hate the games. He means to be kind. He says his Empress will fit me for my wedding gown. She is very beautiful in her green silk and emeralds, and they whisper that he's mad with love for her. They also whisper that she hates him—but people like to whisper.

I stare at the flame until there are two flames.

I'm afraid. I'm always afraid. Shadows under the bed, shapes in the dark, voices in the air.

My uncle watched a thousand men die in the arena today—and he saved just one. He hates the rest of the family—but is kind to me.

What does my uncle want? Does anyone know?

Vesta, goddess of hearth and home, watch over me. I need you, now.